THE WORLD PERIL OF 1910

Books by George Griffith

The Angel of the Revolution
A Honeymoon in Space
An Island Love Story
A Mayfair Magician
The Mummy and Miss Nitocris
The Romance of Golden Star
The Rose of Judah
Valdar the Oft-Born
The Virgin of the Sun
A Conquest of Fortune
His Better Half
The World Peril of 1910

THE WORLD PERIL OF 1910

George Griffith

ÆGYPAN PRESS

1907

George Griffith sometimes used the bylines George Chetwynd Griffith, George Chetwynd Griffith-Jones, and may well have used others pseudonyms as well.

Special thanks to Bruce Albrecht, Martin Pettit, and the Online Distributed Proofreading Team (which can be found at http://www.pgdp.net).

The World Peril of 1910
A publication of
ÆGYPAN PRESS

www.aegypan.com

Prologue

A RACE FOR A WOMAN

In Clifden, the chief coast town of Connemara, there is a house at the end of a triangle which the two streets of the town form, the front windows of which look straight down the beautiful harbor and bay, whose waters stretch out beyond the islands which are scattered along the coast and, with the many submerged reefs, make the entrance so difficult.

In the first-floor double-windowed room of this house, furnished as a bed-sitting room, there was a man sitting at a writing-table – not an ordinary writing-table, but one the dimensions of which were more suited to the needs of an architect or an engineer than to those of a writer. In the middle of the table was a large drawing-desk, and on it was pinned a sheet of cartridge paper, which was almost covered with portions of designs.

In one corner there was what might be the conception of an engine designed for a destroyer or a submarine. In another corner there was a sketch of something that looked like a lighthouse, and over against this the design of what might have been a lantern. The top left-hand corner of the sheet was merely a blur of curved lines and shadings and cross-lines, running at a hundred different angles which no one, save the man who had drawn them, could understand the meaning of.

In the middle of the sheet there was a very carefully-outlined drawing in hard pencil of a craft which was different from anything that had ever sailed upon the waters or below them, or, for the matter of that, above them.

To the right hand there was a rough, but absolutely accurate, copy of this same craft leaving the water and flying into the air, and just underneath this a tiny sketch of a flying fish doing the same thing.

The man sitting before the drawing-board was an Irishman. He was one of those men with the strong, crisp hair, black brows and deep brown eyes, straight, strong nose almost in a line with his forehead, thin, nervous lips and pointed jaw, strong at the angles but weak at the point, which come only from one descent.

Nearly four hundred years before, one of the ships of the great Armada had been wrecked on Achill Island, about twenty miles from where he sat. Half a dozen or so of the crew had been saved, and one of these was a Spanish gentleman, captain of Arquebusiers who, drenched and bedraggled as he was when the half-wild Irish fishermen got him out of the water, still looked what he was, a Hidalgo of Spain. He had been nursed back to health and strength in a miserable mud and turf-walled cottage, and, broken in fortune – for he was one of the many gentlemen of Spain who had risked their all on the fortunes of King Philip and the Great Armada, and lost – he refused to go back to his own country a beaten man.

And meanwhile he had fallen in love with the daughter of his nurse, the wife of the fisherman who had taken him more than half dead out of the raging Atlantic surf.

No man ever knew who he was, save that he was a gentleman, a Spaniard, and a Catholic. But when he returned to the perfection of physical and mental health, and had married the grey-eyed, dark-browed girl, who had seemed to him during his long hours of sickness the guardian angel who had brought him back across the line which marks the frontier between life and death, he developed an extraordinary talent in boat-building, which was the real origin of the wonderful sea-worthiness of small craft which to this day brave, almost with impunity, the terrible seas which, after an unbroken run of almost two thousand miles, burst upon the rock-bound, island-fenced coast of Connemara.

The man at the table was the descendant in the sixth generation of the unknown Spanish Hidalgo, who nearly four hundred years before had said in reply to a question as to what his name was:

"Juan de Castillano."

As the generations had passed, the name, as usual, had got modified, and this man's name was John Castellan.

"I think that will about do for the present," he said, getting up from the table and throwing his pencil down. "I've got it almost perfect now;" and then as he bent down again over the table, and looked over every line of his drawings, "Yes, it's about all there. I wonder what my Lords of the British Admiralty would give to know what that means. Well, God save Ireland, they shall some day!"

He unpinned the paper from the board, rolled it up, and put it into the top drawer of an old oak cabinet, which one would hardly have expected to find in such a room as that, and locked the drawer with a key on his keychain. Then he took his cap from a peg on the door, and his gun from the corner beside it, and went out.

There are three ways out of Clifden to the west, one to the southward takes you over the old bridge, which arches the narrow rock-walled gorge, which gathers up the waters of the river after they have had their frolic over the rocks above. The other is a continuation of the main street, and this, as it approaches the harbor, where you may now see boats built on the pattern which John Castellan's ancestor had designed, divides into two roads, one leading along the shore of the bay, and the other, rough, stony, and ill-kept, takes you above the coast-guard station, and leads to nowhere but the Atlantic Ocean.

Between these two roads lies in what was once a park, but which is now a wilderness, Clifden Castle. Castle in Irish means country house, and all over the south and west of Ireland you may find such houses as this with doors screwed up, windows covered with planks, roofs and eaves stripped of the lead and slates which once protected them from the storms which rise up from the Atlantic, and burst in wind and rain, snow and sleet over Connemara, long ago taken away to sell by the bankrupt heirs of those who ruined themselves, mortgaged and sold every acre of ground and every stick and stone they owned to maintain what they called the dignity of their families at the Vice-Regal Court in Dublin.

John Castellan took the lower road, looking for duck. The old house had been the home of his grandfather, but he had never lived in it. The ruin had come in his father's time, before he had learned to walk. He looked at it as he passed, and his teeth clenched and his brows came together in a straight line.

Almost at the same moment that he left his house an Englishman came out of the Railway Hotel. He also had a gun over his shoulder, and he took the upper road. These two men, who were to meet for the first time that day, were destined to decide the fate of the world between them.

As John Castellan walked past the ruined distillery, which overlooks the beach on which the fishing boats are drawn up, he saw a couple of duck flying seaward. He quickened his pace, and walked on until he turned the bend of the road, at which on the right-hand side a path leads up to a gate in the old wall, which still guards the ragged domains of Clifden Castle. A few hundred yards away there is a little peninsula, on which stands a house built somewhat in bungalow fashion. The curve of the peninsula turns to the eastward, and makes a tiny bay of almost crescent shape. In this the pair of duck settled.

John Castellan picked up a stone from the road, and threw it into the water. As the birds rose his gun went up. His right barrel banged and the duck fell. The drake flew landward: he fired his left barrel and missed. Then came a bang from the upper road, and the drake dropped. The Englishman had killed it with a wire cartridge in his choked left barrel.

"I wonder who the devil did that!" said Castellan, as he saw the bird fall. "It was eighty yards if it was an inch, and that's a good gun with a good man behind it."

The Englishman left the road to pick up the bird and then went down the steep, stony hillside towards the shore of the silver-mouthed bay in the hope of getting another shot farther on, for the birds were now beginning to come over; and so it came about that he and the Irishman met within a few yards of each other, one on either side of a low spit of sand and shingle.

"That was a fine shot you killed the drake with," said the Irishman, looking at the bird he was carrying by the legs in his left hand.

"A good gun, and a wire cartridge, I fancy, were mainly responsible for his death," laughed the Englishman. "See you've got the other."

"Yes, and missed yours," said the Irishman.

The other recognized the tone as that of a man to whom failure, even in the most insignificant matter, was hateful, and he saw a quick gleam in his eyes which he remembered afterwards under very different circumstances.

But it so happened that the rivalry between them which was hereafter to have such momentous consequences was to be manifested there and then in a fashion much more serious than the hitting or missing of a brace of wild fowl.

Out on the smooth waters of the bay, about a quarter of a mile from the spit on which they stood, there were two boats. One was a light skiff, in which a girl, clad in white jersey and white flannel skirt, with a white Tam o' Shanter pinned on her head, was sculling leisurely towards the town. From the swing of her body, the poise of her head and shoulders, and the smoothness with which her sculls dropped in the water and left it, it was plain that she was a perfect mistress of the art; wherefore the two men looked at her, and admired.

The other craft was an ordinary rowing boat, manned by three lads out for a spree. There was no one steering and the oars were going in and out of the water with a total disregard of time. The result was that her course was anything but a straight line. The girl's sculls made no noise, and the youths were talking and laughing loudly.

Suddenly the boat veered sharply towards the skiff. The Englishman put his hands to his mouth, and yelled with all the strength of his lungs.

"Look out, you idiots, keep off shore!"

But it was too late. The long, steady strokes were sending the skiff pretty fast through the smooth water. The boat swerved again, hit the skiff about midway between the stem and the rowlocks, and the next moment the sculler was in the water. In the same moment two guns and two ducks were flung to the ground, two jackets were torn off, two pairs of shoes kicked away, and two men splashed into the water. Meanwhile the sculler had dropped quietly out of the sinking skiff, and after a glance at the two heads, one fair and the other dark, plowing towards her, turned on her side and began to swim slowly in their direction so as to lessen the distance as much as possible.

The boys, horrified at what they had done, made such a frantic effort to go to the rescue, that one of them caught a very bad crab; so bad, indeed that the consequent roll of the boat sent him headlong into the water; and so the two others, one of whom was his elder brother, perhaps naturally left the girl to her fate, and devoted their energies to saving their companion.

Both John Castellan and the Englishman were good swimmers, and the race was a very close thing. Still, four hundred yards with most of your clothes on is a task calculated to try the strongest swimmer, and, although the student had swum almost since he could walk, his muscles were not quite in such good form as those of the ex-athlete of Cambridge who, six months before, had won the Thames Swimming Club Half-mile Handicap from scratch.

Using side stroke and breast-stroke alternately they went at it almost stroke for stroke about half a dozen yards apart, and until they were within thirty yards or so of the third swimmer, they were practically neck and neck, though Castellan had the advantage of what might be called the inside track. In other words he was a little nearer to the girl than the Englishman.

When circumstances permitted they looked at each other, but, of course, neither of them was fool enough to waste his breath in speech. Still, each clearly understood that the other was going to get the girl first if he could.

So the tenth yard from the prize was reached, and then the Englishman shook his head up an inch, filled his lungs, rolled on to his side, and made a spurt with the reserve of strength which he had kept for the purpose. Inch by inch he drew ahead obliquely across Castellan's course and, less than a yard in front of him, he put his right hand under the girl's right side.

A lovely face, beautiful even though it was splashed all over with wet strands of dark chestnut hair, turned towards him; a pair of big blue eyes which shone in spite of the salt water which made them blink, looked at him; and, after a cough, a very sweet voice with just a suspicion of Boston accent in it, said:

"Thank you so much! It was real good of you! I can swim, but I don't think I could have got there with all these things on, and so I reckon I owe you two gentlemen my life."

Castellan had swum round, and they took her under the arms to give her a rest. The two boys left in the boat had managed to get an oar out to their comrade just in time, and then haul him into the boat, which was now about fifty yards away; so as soon as the girl had got her breath they swam with her to the boat, and lifted her hands on to the gunwale.

"If you wouldn't mind, sir, picking up those oars," said the Englishman, "I will get the young lady into the boat, and then we can row back."

Castellan gave him another look which said as plainly as words: "Well, I suppose she's your prize for the present," and swam off for the oars. With the eager help of the boys, who were now very frightened and very penitent, the Englishman soon had the girl in the boat; and so it came about that an adventure which might well have deprived America of one of her most beautiful and brilliant heiresses, resulted in nothing more than a ducking for two men and one girl, a wet, but somehow not altogether unpleasant walk, and a slight chill from which she had quite recovered the next morning.

The after consequences of that race for the rescue were of course, quite another matter.

Chapter I

A MOMENTOUS EXPERIMENT

On the first day of July, 1908, a scene which was destined to become historic took place in the great Lecture Theater in the Imperial College at Potsdam. It was just a year and a few days after the swimming race between John Castellan and the Englishman in Clifden Bay.

There were four people present. The doors were locked and guarded by two sentries outside. The German Emperor, Count Herold von Steinitz, Chancellor of the Empire, Field-Marshal Count Friedrich von Moltke, grandson of the great Organizer of Victory, and John Castellan, were standing round a great glass tank, twenty-five feet long, and fifteen broad, supported on a series of trestles. The tank was filled with water up to within about six inches of the upper edge. The depth was ten feet. A dozen models of battleships, cruisers and torpedo craft were floating on the surface of the water. Five feet under the surface, a grey, fish-shaped craft with tail and fins, almost exactly resembling those of a flying fish, was darting about, now jumping forward like a cat pouncing on a bird, now drawing back, and then suddenly coming to a standstill. Another moment, it sank to the bottom, and lay there as if it had been a wreck. The next it darted up to the surface, cruised about in swift curves, turning in and out about the models, but touching none.

Every now and then John Castellan went to a little table in the corner of the room, on which there was a machine something like a typewriter, and touched two or three of the keys. There was no visible connection between them – the machine and the tank – but the little grey shape in the water responded instantly to the touch of every key.

"That, I hope, will be enough to prove to your Majesty that as submarine the *Flying Fish* is quite under control. Of course the real *Flying Fish* will be controlled inside, not from outside."

"There is no doubt about the control," said the Kaiser. "It is marvelous, and I think the Chancellor and the Field Marshal will agree with me in that."

"Wonderful," said the Chancellor.

"A miracle," said the Field Marshal, "if it can only be realized."

"There is no doubt about that, gentlemen," said Castellan, going back to the machine. "Which of the models would your Majesty like to see destroyed first?"

The Kaiser pointed to the model of a battleship which was a very good imitation of one of the most up-to-date British battleships.

"We will take that one first," he said.

Castellan smiled, and began to play the keys. The grey shape of the *Flying Fish* dropped to the bottom of the tank, rose, and seemed all at once to become endowed with human reason, or a likeness of it, which was so horrible that even the Kaiser and his two chiefs could hardly repress a shudder. It rose very slowly, circled among the floating models about two feet under the surface and then, like an animal smelling out its prey, it made a dart at the ship which the Kaiser had indicated, and struck it from underneath. They saw a green flash stream through the water, and the next moment the model had crumbled to pieces and sank.

"Donner-Wetter!" exclaimed the Chancellor, forgetting in his wonder that he was in the presence of His Majesty, "that is wonderful, horrible!"

"Can there be anything too horrible for the enemies of the Fatherland, Herr Kanztler," said the Kaiser, looking across the tank at him, with a glint in his eyes, which no man in Germany cares to see.

"I must ask pardon, your Majesty," replied the Chancellor. "I was astonished, indeed, almost frightened – frightened, if your Majesty will allow me to say so, for the sake of Humanity, if such an awful invention as that becomes realized."

"And what is your opinion, Field Marshal?" asked the Kaiser with a laugh.

"A most excellent invention, your Majesty, provided always that it belongs to the Fatherland."

"Exactly," said the Kaiser. "As that very intelligent American officer, Admiral Mahan, has told us, the sea-power is world-power, and there you have sea-power; but that is not the limit of the capabilities of Mr. Castellan's invention, according to the specifications which I have read, and on the strength of which I have asked him to give us this demonstration of its powers. He calls it, as you know, the *Flying Fish.* So far you have seen it as a fish. Now, Mr. Castellan, perhaps you will be kind enough to let us see it fly."

"With pleasure, your Majesty," replied the Irishman, "but, in case of accident, I must ask you and the Chancellor and the Field Marshal to stand against the wall by the door there. With your Majesty's permission, I am now going to destroy the rest of the fleet."

"The rest of the fleet!" exclaimed the Field Marshal. "It is impossible."

"We shall see, Feldherr!" laughed the Kaiser. "Meanwhile, suppose we come out of the danger zone."

The three greatest men in Germany, and perhaps on the Continent of Europe, lined up with their backs to the wall at the farther end of the room from the tank, and the Irishman sat down to his machine. The keys began to click rapidly, and they began to feel a tenseness in the air of the room. After a few seconds they would not have been surprised if they had seen a flash of lightning pass over their heads. The *Flying Fish* had sunk to the bottom of the tank, and backed into one of the corners. The keys of the machine clicked louder and faster. Her nose tilted upwards to an angle of about sixty degrees. The six-bladed propeller at her stem whirled round in the water like the flurry of a whale's fluke in its death agony. Her side-fins inclined upwards, and, like a flash, she leapt from the water, and began to circle round the room.

The Kaiser shut his teeth hard and watched. The Chancellor opened his mouth as if he was going to say something, and shut it again. The Field Marshal stroked his moustache slowly, and followed the strange shape fluttering about the room. It circled twice round the tank, and then crossed it. A sharp click came from the machine, something fell from the body of the *Flying Fish* into the tank. There was a dull sound of a smothered explosion. For a moment the very water itself seemed aflame, then it boiled up into a mass of seething foam. Every one of the models was overwhelmed and engulfed at the same moment. Castellan got up from the machine, caught the *Flying Fish* in his hand, as it dropped towards the water, took it to the Kaiser, and said:

"Is your Majesty convinced? It is quite harmless now."

"God's thunder, yes!" said the War Lord of Germany, taking hold of the model. "It is almost superhuman."

"Yes," said the Chancellor, "it is damnable!"

"I," said the Field Marshal, dryly, "think it's admirable, always supposing that Mr. Castellan is prepared to place this mysterious invention at the disposal of his Majesty."

"Yes," said the Kaiser, leaning with his back against the door, "that is, of course, the first proposition to be considered. What are your terms, Mr. Castellan?"

Castellan looked at the three men all armed. The Chancellor and the Field Marshal wore their swords, and the Kaiser had a revolver in his hip pocket. The Chancellor and the Field Marshal straightened up as the Kaiser spoke, and their hands moved instinctively towards their sword hilts. The Kaiser looked at the model of the *Flying Fish* in his hand. His face was, as usual, like a mask. He saw nothing, thought of nothing. For the moment he was not a man: he was just the incarnation of an idea.

"Field Marshal, you are a soldier," said Castellan, "and I see that your hand has gone to your sword-hilt. Swords, of course, are the emblems of military rank, but there is no use for them now."

"What do you mean, sir?" exclaimed the Count, clapping his right hand on the hilt. After what he had seen he honestly believed that this Irishman was a wizard of science who ought not to be trusted in the same room with the Kaiser. Castellan went back to his machine and said:

"Draw your sword, sir, and see."

And then the keys began to click.

The Field Marshal's sword flashed out of the sheath. A second later the Chancellor's did the same, and the Kaiser's right hand went back towards his hip pocket.

Castellan got up and said:

"Your Majesty has a revolver. Be good enough, as you value your own safety, to unload it, and throw the cartridges out of the window."

"But why?" exclaimed the Kaiser, pulling a Mauser repeating pistol out of his hip-pocket. "Who are you, that you should give orders to me?"

"Only a man, your Majesty," replied Castellan, with a bow and a smile; "a man who could explode every cartridge in that pistol of yours at once before you had time to fire a shot. You have seen what has happened already."

William the Second had seen enough. He walked to one of the windows opening on the enclosed gardens, threw it open, dropped the pistol out, and said:

"Now, let us have the proof of what you say."

"In a moment, your Majesty," replied Castellan, going back to his machine, and beginning to work the keys rapidly. "I am here, an unarmed man; let their Excellencies, the Chancellor and the Field Marshal, attack me with their swords if they can. I am not joking. I am staking my life on the success or failure of this experiment."

"Does your Majesty consent?" said the Field Marshal, raising his sword.

"There could be no better test," replied the Kaiser. "Mr. Castellan makes an experiment on which he stakes his life; we are making an experiment on which we stake the welfare of the German Empire, and, perhaps, the fate of the world. If he is willing, I am."

"And I am ready," replied Castellan, working the keys faster and faster as he spoke, and looking at the two swords as carelessly as if they had been a couple of walking sticks.

The sword points advanced towards him; the keys of the machine clicked faster and faster. The atmosphere of the room became tenser and tenser; the Kaiser leaned back against the door with his arms folded. When the points were within three feet of Castellan's head, the steel began to gleam with a bluish green light. The Chancellor and the Field Marshal stopped; they saw sparkles of blue flame running along the sword blades. Then came paralysis! the swords dropped from their hands, and they staggered back.

"Great God, this is too much," gasped the Chancellor. "The man is impregnable. It is too much, your Majesty. I fought through the war of '70 and '71, but I surrender to this; this is not human."

"I beg your pardon, Excellency," said Castellan, getting up from the machine, and picking the two swords from the floor, "it is quite human, only a little science that the majority of humanity does not happen to know. Your swords, gentlemen," and he presented the hilts to them.

"Bravo!" exclaimed the Kaiser, "well done! You have beaten the two best soldiers in the German Empire, and you have done it like a gentleman. But you are not altogether an Irishman, are you, Mr. Castellan?"

"No, sir, I am a Spaniard as well. The earliest ancestor that I know commanded the *Santiago,* wrecked on Achill Island, when the Armada came south from the Pentland Firth. The rest of me is Irish. I need hardly say more. That is why I am here now."

The Kaiser looked at the Chancellor and the Field Marshal, and they looked back at him, and in a moment the situation – the crisis upon which the fate of the world might depend – was decided. It was not a time when men who are men talk. A few moments of silence passed; the four men looking at each other with eyes that had the destinies of nations in the brains behind them. Then the Kaiser took three swift strides towards Castellan, held out his hand, and said in a voice which had an unwonted note of respect in it:

"Sir, you have convinced me. Henceforth you are Director of the Naval and Military operations of the German Empire, subject, of course, to the conditions which will be arranged by myself and those who are entrusted with the tactical and strategical developments of such plan of campaign as I may decide to carry out on sea and land. And now, to put it rudely – brutally, if you like, your price?"

Castellan took the Kaiser's hand in a strong, nervous grip, and said:

"I shall not state my price in money, your Majesty. I am not working for money, but you will understand that I cannot convert what I have shown you today into the fighting reality. Only a nation can do that. It will cost ten millions of marks, at least, to – well, to so far develop this experiment that no fleet save your Majesty's shall sail the seas, and that no armies save yours shall without your consent march over the battlefields of the world's Armageddon."

"Make it twenty millions, fifty millions," laughed the Kaiser, "and it will be cheap at the price. What do you think, Herr Kantzler and Feldherr?"

"Under the present circumstances of the other monarchies of Europe, your Majesty," replied the Chancellor, "it would be cheap at a hundred millions, especially with reference to a certain fleet, which appears to be making the ocean its own country."

"Quite so," said the Field Marshal. "If what we have seen today can be realized it would not be necessary to pump out the North Sea in order to invade England."

"Or to get back again," laughed the Kaiser. "I think that is what your grandfather said, didn't he?"

"Yes, your Majesty. He found eight ways of getting into England, but he hadn't thought of one of getting out again."

Since the days of the Prophets no man had ever uttered more prophetic words than Friedrich Helmuth von Moltke spoke then, all unconsciously. But in the days to come they were fulfilled in such fashion that only one man in all the world had ever dreamed of, and that was the man who had beaten John Castellan by a yard in the swimming race for the rescue of that American girl from drowning.

Chapter II

NORAH'S GOOD-BYE

The scene had shifted back from the royal city of Potsdam to the little coast town in Connemara. John Castellan was sitting on a corner of his big writing-table swinging his legs to and fro, and looking a little uncomfortable. Leaning against the wall opposite the windows, with her hands folded behind her back, was a girl of about nineteen, an almost perfect incarnation of the Irish girl at her best. Tall, black-haired, black-browed, grey-eyed, perfectly-shaped, and with that indescribable charm of feature which neither the pen nor the camera can do justice to – Norah Castellan was facing him, her eyes gleaming and almost black with anger, and her whole body instinct with intense vitality.

"And so Ireland hasn't troubles enough of her own, John, that you must bring new ones upon her, and what for? To realize a dream that was never anything else but a dream, and to satisfy a revenge that is three hundred years old! If that theory of yours about re-incarnation is true, you may have been a Spaniard once, but remember that you're an Irishman now; and you're no good Irishman if you sell yourself to these foreigners to do a thing like that, and it's your sister that's telling you."

"And it's your brother, Norah," he replied, his black brows meeting almost in a straight line across his forehead, "who tells you that Ireland is going to have her independence; that the shackles of the Saxon shall be shaken off once and forever, even if all Europe blazes up with war in the doing of it. I have the power and I will use it. Spaniard or Irishman, what does it matter? I hate England and everything English."

"Hate England, John!" said the girl. "Are you quite sure that it isn't an Englishman that you hate?"

"Well, and what if I do? I hate all Englishmen, and I'm the first Irishman who has ever had the power to put his hatred into acts instead of words – and you, an Irish girl, with six generations of Irish blood in your veins, you, to talk to me like this. What are you thinking about, Norah? Is that what you call patriotism?"

"Patriotism!" she echoed, unclasping her hands, and holding her right hand out towards him. "I'm as Irish as you are, and as Spanish, too, for the matter of that, for the same blood is in the veins of both of us. You're a scholar and a genius, and all the rest of it, I grant you; but haven't you learned history enough to know that Ireland never was independent, and never could be? What brought the English here first? Four miserable provinces that called themselves kingdoms, and all fighting against each other, and the king of one of them stole the wife of the king of another of them, and that's how the English came.

"I love Ireland as well as you do, John, but Ireland is not worth setting the world swimming in blood for. You're lighting a match-box to set the world ablaze with. It isn't Ireland only, remember. There are Irish all over the world, millions of them, and remember how the Irish fought in the African War. I don't mean Lynch and his traitors, but the Dublin boys. Who were the first in and the last out – Irishmen, but they had the sense to know that they were British first and Irish afterwards. I tell you, you shall be shot for what you've done, and if I wasn't the daughter of your father and mother, I'd inform against you now."

"And if you did, Norah, you would do very little good to the Saxon cause," replied her brother, pointing with his thumb out of one of the windows. "You see that yacht in the bay there. Everything is on board of her. If you went out into the street now, gave me in charge of the constabulary, to those two men in front of the hotel there, it would make no difference. There's nothing to be proved, no, not even if my own sister tried to swear my life and liberty away. It would only be that the Germans and the Russians, and the Austrians, and the rest of them would work out my ideas instead of me working them out, and it might be that they would make a worse use of them. You've half an hour to give me up, if you like."

And then he began to collect the papers that were scattered about the big drawing-table, sorting them out and folding them up and then taking other papers and plans from the drawers and packing them into a little black dispatch box.

"But, John, John," she said, crossing the room, and putting her hand on his shoulder. "Don't tell me that you're going to plunge the world in war just for this. Think of what it means – the tens of thousands of lives that will be lost, the thousands of homes that will be made desolate, the women who will be crying for their husbands, and the children for their fathers, the dead men buried in graves that will never have a name on them, and the wounded, broken men coming back to their homes that they will never be able to keep up again, not only here and in England, but all over Europe and perhaps in America as well! Genius you may be; but what are you that you should bring calamity like this upon humanity?"

"I'm an Irishman, and I hate England, and that's enough," he replied sullenly, as he went on packing his papers.

"You hate that Englishman worse than you hate England, John."

"And I wouldn't wonder if you loved that Englishman more than you loved Ireland, Norah," he replied, with a snarl in his voice.

"And if I did," she said, with blazing eyes and flaming cheeks, "isn't England nearer to Ireland than America?"

"Geographically, perhaps, but in sentiment –"

"Sentiment! Yes, when you have finished with this bloody business of yours that you have begun on, go you through Ireland and England and Europe, and ask the widows and the fatherless, and the girls who kissed their lovers 'good-bye,' and never saw them again, what they think of that sentiment! But it's no use arguing with you now; there's your German yacht. You're no brother of mine. You've made me sorry that we had the same father and mother."

As she spoke, she went to the door, opened it and, before he could reply, slammed it behind her, and went to her room to seek and find a woman's usual relief from extreme mental tension.

John Castellan went on packing his papers, his face grey, and his features hard-set. He loved his beautiful sister, but he thought that he loved his country more. When he had finished he went and knocked at her door, and said:

"Norah, I'm going. Won't you say 'good-bye?'"

The door was swung open, and she faced him, her face wet with tears, her eyes glistening, and her lips twitching.

"Yes, good-bye, John," she said. "Go to your German friends; but, when all the horrors that you are going to bring upon this country through their help come to pass, remember you have no sister left in Ireland. You've sold yourself, and I have no brother who is a traitor. Good-bye!"

The door swung to and she locked it. John Castellan hesitated for a moment or two, and then with a slow shake of his head he went away down the stairs out into the street, and along to the little jetty where the German yacht's boat was waiting to take him on board.

Norah had thrown herself on her bed in her locked room shedding the first but not the last tear that John Castellan's decision was destined to draw from women's eyes.

About half an hour later the encircling hills of the bay echoed the shriek of a siren. She got up, looked out of the window, and saw the white shape of the German yacht moving out towards the fringe of islands which guard the outward bay.

"And there he goes!" she said in a voice that was almost choked with sobs, "there he goes, my own brother, it may be taking the fate of the world with him – yes, and on a German ship, too. He that knows every island and creek and cove and harbor from Cape Wrath to Cape Clear – he that's got all those inventions in his head, too, and the son of my own father and mother, sold his country to the foreigner, thinking those dirty Germans will keep their word with him.

"Not they, John, not they. The saints forgive me for thinking it, but for Ireland's sake I hope that ship will never reach Germany. If it does, we'll see the German Eagle floating over Dublin Castle before you'll be able to haul up the Green Flag. Well, well, there it is; it's done now, I suppose, and there's no help for it. God forgive you, John, I don't think man ever will!"

As she said this the white yacht turned the southern point of the inner bay, and disappeared to the southward. Norah bathed her face, brushed out her hair, and coiled it up again; then she put on her hat and jacket, and went out to do a little shopping.

It is perhaps a merciful provision of Providence that in this human life of ours the course of the greatest events shall be interrupted by the most trivial necessities of existence. Were it not for that the inevitable might become the unendurable.

The plain fact was that Norah Castellan had some friends and acquaintances coming to supper that evening. Her brother had left at a few hours' notice from his foreign masters, as she called them, and there would have to be some explanation of his absence, especially as a friend of his, Arthur Lismore, the owner of the finest salmon streams for twenty miles round, and a man who was quite hopelessly in love with herself, was coming to brew the punch after the fashion of his ancestors, and so, of course, it was necessary that there should be nothing wanting.

Moreover, she was beginning to feel the want of some hard physical exercise, and an hour or so in that lovely air of Connemara, which, as those who know, say, is as soft as silk and as bright as champagne. So she went out, and as she turned the corner round the head of the harbor to the left towards the waterfall, almost the first person she met was Arthur Lismore himself – a brown-faced, chestnut-haired, blue-eyed, young giant of twenty-eight or so; as goodly a man as God ever put His own seal upon.

His cap came off, his head bowed with that peculiar grace of deference which no one has ever yet been able to copy from an Irishman, and he said in the strong, and yet curiously mellow tone which you only hear in the west of Ireland:

"Good afternoon, Miss Norah. I've heard that you're to be left alone for a time, and that we won't see John tonight."

"Yes," she said, her eyes meeting his, "that is true. He went away in that German yacht that left the bay less than an hour ago."

"A German yacht!" he echoed. "Well now, how stupid of me, I've been trying to think all the afternoon what that flag was she carried when she came in."

"The German Imperial Yacht Club," she said, "that was the ensign she was flying, and John has gone to Germany in her."

"To Germany! John gone to Germany! But what for? Surely now –"

"Yes, to Germany, to help the Emperor to set the world on fire."

"You're not saying that, Miss Norah?"

"I am," she said, more gravely than he had ever heard her speak. "Mr. Lismore, it's a sick and sorry girl I am this afternoon. You were the first Irishman on the top of Wagon Hill, and you'll understand what I mean. If you have nothing better to do, perhaps you'll walk down to the Fall with me, and I'll tell you."

"I could have nothing better to do, Norah, and it's yourself that knows that as well as I do," he replied. "I only wish the road was longer. And it's yourself that's sick and sorry, is it? If it wasn't John, I'd like to get the reason out of any other man. That's Irish, but it's true."

He turned, and they walked down the steeply sloping street for several minutes in silence.

Chapter III

SEEN UNDER THE MOON

It was a few minutes after four bells on a grey morning in November 1909 that Lieutenant-Commander Francis Erskine, in command of his

Majesty's Fishery Cruiser, the *Cormorant,* got up on to the navigating bridge, and, as usual, took a general squint about him, and buttoned the top button of his oil-skin coat.

The *Cormorant* was just a few yards inside the three-mile limit on Flamborough Head, and, officially, she was looking for trespassers, who either did not fly the British flag, or flew it fraudulently. There were plenty of foreign poachers on the rich fishing grounds to the north and east away to the Dogger, and there were also plenty of floating grog shops from Bremen and Hamburg, and Rotterdam and Flushing, and a good many other places, loaded up to their decks with liquor, whose mission was not only to sell their poison at about four hundred percent profit to the British fishers on the Dogger, but also to persuade them, at a price, to smuggle more of the said poison into the British Islands to be made into Scotch and Irish whisky, brandy, Hollands, gin, rum, and even green and yellow Chartreuse, or any other alcoholic potion which simply wanted the help of the chemist to transform potato and beet spirit into anything that would taste like what it was called.

"Beast of a morning, Castellan," he said to his first officer, whom he was relieving, "dirty sea, dirty sky, and not a thing to be seen. You don't have worse weather than this even off Connemara, do you?"

"No," said Castellan, "and I've seen better; but look you, there's the sky clearing to the east; yes, and there's Venus, herald of the sun: and faith, she's bright, too, like a little moon, now isn't she? I suppose it'll be a bit too early for Norah to be looking at her, won't it?"

"Don't talk rot, man," replied the Lieutenant-Commander. "I hope your sister hasn't finished her beauty sleep by this time."

The clouds parted still wider, making a great gap of blue-grey sky to the eastward, as the westward bank drifted downward. The moon sent a sudden flood of white light over their heads, which silvered the edges of the clouds, and then turned the leaden waters into silver as it had done to the grey of the cloud.

"She'd wake fast enough if she had a nightmare or a morning mare, or something of that sort, and could see a thing like that," exclaimed Castellan, gripping the Lieutenant-Commander by the shoulder with his right hand, and pointing to the east with his left. "Look, man, look! By all the Holy Powers, what is it? See there! Thanks for the blessed moonlight that has shown it to us, for I'm thinking it doesn't mean any good to old England or Ireland."

Erskine was an Englishman, and a naval officer at that, and therefore his reply consisted of only a few words hardly fitted for publication. The last words were, "What is it?"

"What is it?" said Castellan with a stamp of his feet on the bridge, "what is it? Now wouldn't I like to know just as well as you would, and don't you think the Lords of the British Admiralty would like to know a lot better? But there's one thing I think I can tell you, it's one of those new inventions that the British Admiralty never buy, and let go to other countries, and what's more, as you've seen with your eyes, as I have with mine, it came out of the water on the edge of that moon-lit piece, it flew across it, it sighted us, I suppose, it found it had made a mistake, and it went down again. Now what do you make of that?"

"Combination of submarine and airship it looks like," said Erskine, seriously, "and if that doesn't belong to us, it's going to be fairly dangerous. Good Lord! a thing like that might do anything with a fleet, and whatever Power owns it may just as well have a hundred as one. Look here, Castellan, I'm going straight into Scarborough. This is a lot more important than the Dogger Fleet. There's the *Seagull* at Hull. She can relieve us, and Franklin can take this old coffee-grinder round. You and I are going to London as soon as we can get there. Take the latitude, longitude, and exact time, and also the evidence of the watch if anyone of them saw it."

"You think it's as serious as that?"

"Certainly. It's one of two things. Either that thing belongs to us or it belongs to a possible enemy. The Fleet, even to a humble fishery cruiser, means the eyes and ears of the British Empire. If that belongs to the Admiralty, well and good; we shall get censured for leaving the ship; that's the risk we take. If it doesn't, the Naval Board may possibly have the civility to thank us for telling them about it; but in either case we are going to do our duty. Send Franklin up to the bridge, make the course for Scarborough, get the evidence of any of the watch who saw what we have seen, and I'll go and make the report. Then you can countersign it, and the men can make theirs. I think that's the best we can do."

"I think so, sir," said the Lieutenant, saluting.

The Lieutenant-Commander walked from port to starboard and starboard to port thinking pretty hard until the navigating lieutenant came to take charge of the bridge. Of submarines he knew a good deal. He knew that the British navy possessed the very best type of this craft which navigated the under-waters. He had also, of course, read the aërial experiments which had been made by inventors of what the newspapers called airships, and which he, with his hard naval common-sense, called gas-bags with motor engines slung under them. He knew the deadly possibilities of the submarine; the flying gas-bag he looked upon as gas and not much more. The real flying machine he had considered up till a few moments ago as a dream of the future; but a combination of submarine and flying ship such as he and Castellan, if they had not both been drunk or dreaming, had seen a few moments ago, was quite another matter. The possibilities of a thing like that were absolutely limitless, limitless for good or evil, and if it did belong to a possible enemy of Britain, there was only one conclusion to be arrived at – The Isle Inviolate would be inviolate no more.

Lieutenant Franklin came on to the bridge and saluted; he returned the salute, gave the orders for changing the course, and went down to his cabin, muttering:

"Good Lord, if that's only so. Why, half a dozen things like that could fight a fleet, then go on gaily to tackle the forts. I wonder whether my Lords of the Naval Council will see me tomorrow, and believe me if they do see me."

By great good luck it happened that the Commander of the North-eastern District had come up from Hull to Scarborough for a few days' holiday. When he saw the *Cormorant* steam into the bay, he very naturally wanted to know what was the matter, and so he went down to the pier-head, and met the *Cormorant's* cutter. As Erskine came up the steps he recognized him and saluted.

"Good-morning, sir."

"Good-morning, Erskine. What's the matter? You're a little off your ground, aren't you? Of course, there must be a reason for it. Anything serious?" replied the District Commander, as he held out his hand. "Ah, good morning, Castellan. So you've both come ashore. Well, now, what is it?"

Erskine took a rapid glance round at the promenaders who were coming down to have a look at the cruiser, and said in a low tone:

"Yes, sir. I am afraid it is rather serious; but it is hardly the sort of thing one could discuss here. In fact, I was taking the responsibility of going straight to London with Castellan, to present a report which we have drawn up to the Board of Admiralty."

The District Commander's iron-grey eyebrows lifted for the fraction of a minute, and he said:

"H'm. Well, Erskine, I know you're not the sort of man to do that sort of thing without pretty good reason. Come up to the hotel, both of you, and let us go into it."

"Thank you, sir," replied Erskine. "It is really quite fortunate that we met you here, because I think when you've seen the report you will feel justified in giving us formal leave instead of French leave."

"I hope so," he replied, somewhat grimly, for a rule of the Service had been broken all to pieces, and his own sense of discipline was sorely outraged by the knowledge that two responsible officers had left their ship with the intention of going to London without leave.

But when he had locked the door of his sitting room at the hotel, and heard the amazing story which Erskine and Castellan had to tell, and had read their report, and the evidence of the men who had also seen the strange apparition which had leapt from the sea into the air, and then returned to the waters, he put in a few moments of silent thinking, and then he looked up, and said gravely:

"Well, gentlemen, I know that British naval officers and British seamen don't see things that are not there, as the Russians did a few years ago on the Dogger Bank. I am of course bound to believe you, and I think they will do the same in London. You have taken a very irregular course; but a man who is not prepared to do that at a pinch seldom does anything else. I have seen and heard enough to convince me for the present; and so I shall have great pleasure, in fact I shall only be doing my duty, in giving you both leave for a week.

"I will order the *Seagull* up from Hull, she's about ready, and I think I can put an Acting-Commander on board the *Cormorant* for the present. Now, you will just have time for an early lunch with me, and catch the 1.17, which will get you to town at 5.15, and you will probably find somebody at the Admiralty then, because I know they're working overtime. Anyhow, if you don't find Sir John Fisher there, I should go straight to his house, if I were you; and even if you don't see him, you'll be able to get an early appointment for tomorrow."

"That was a pretty good slice of luck meeting the noble Crocker, wasn't it?" said Castellan, as the train began to move out of the station, about three hours later. They had reserved a compartment in the corridor express, and were able to talk State secrets at their ease.

"We're inside the law now, at any rate."

"Law or no law, it was good enough to risk a court-martial for," said Erskine, biting off the end of a cigar. "There's no doubt about the existence of the thing, and if it doesn't belong to us, which is a fact that only my Lords of the Naval Council can know, it simply means, as you must see for yourself, that the invasion of England, which has been a naval and military impossibility for the last seven hundred years or so, will not only become possible but comparatively easy. There's nothing upon the waters or under them that could stand against a thing like that."

"Oh, you're right enough there," said Castellan, speaking with his soft West of Ireland brogue. "There's no doubt of that, and it's the very devil. A dozen of those things would play havoc with a whole fleet, and when the fleet's gone, or even badly hurt, what's to stop our good friends over yonder landing two or three million men just anywhere they choose, and doing pretty well what they like afterwards? By the Saints, that would be a horrible thing. We've nothing on land that could stand against them, though, of course, the boys would stand till they fell down; but fall they would."

"Yes," said Erskine, seriously. "It wouldn't exactly be a walk over for them, but I'm afraid there couldn't be very much doubt at the end, if the fleet once went."

"I'm afraid not," replied Castellan, "and we can only hope that our Lords of the Council will be of the same opinion, or, better still, that the infernal thing we saw belongs to us."

"I hope so," said Erskine, gravely. "If it doesn't – well, I wouldn't give half-a-crown for the biggest battleship in the British Navy."

Chapter IV

THE SHADOW OF THE TERROR

By a curious coincidence which, as events proved, was to have some serious consequences, almost at the same moment that Commander Erskine began to write his report on the strange vision which he and his Lieutenant had seen, Gilbert Lennard came out of the Observatory which Mr. Ratliffe Parmenter had built on the south of the Whernside Hills in Yorkshire.

Mr. Ratliffe Parmenter had two ambitions in life, one of which he had fulfilled. This was to pile millions upon millions by any possible means. As he used to say to his associates in his poorer days, "You've got to get there somehow, so get there" – and he had "got there." It is not necessary for the purpose of the present narrative to say how he did it. He had done it, and that is why he bought the Hill of Whernside and about a thousand acres around it and built an Observatory on the top with which, to use his own words, he meant to lick Creation by seeing further into Creation than anyone else had done, and that is just what his great reflector had enabled his astronomer to do.

When he had locked the door Lennard looked up to the eastward where the morning star hung flashing like a huge diamond in splendid solitude against the brightening background of the sky. His face was the face of a man who had seen something that he would not like to describe to any other man. His features were hard set, and there were lines in his face which time might have drawn twenty or thirty years later. His lips made a straight line, and his eyes, although he had hardly slept three hours a night for as many nights, had a look in them that was not to be accounted for by ordinary insomnia.

His work was over for the night, and, if he chose, he could go down to the house three-quarters of a mile away and sleep for the rest of the day, or, at any rate, until lunch time; and yet he looked another long look at the morning star, thrust his hands down into his trousers pockets and turned up a side path that led through the heather, and spent the rest of the morning walking and thinking – walking slowly, and thinking very quickly.

When he came in to breakfast at nine the next morning, after he had had a shave and a bath, Mr. Parmenter said to him:

"Look here, young man, I'm old enough to be your father, and so you'll excuse me putting it that way; if you're going along like this I reckon I'll have to shut that Observatory down for the time being and take you on a trip to the States to see how they're getting on with their telescopes in the Alleghenies and the Rockies, and maybe down South too in Peru, to that Harvard Observatory above Arequipa on the Misti, as a sort of holiday. I asked you to come here to work, not to wear yourself out. As I've told you before, we've got plenty of men in the States who can sign their checks for millions of dollars and can't eat a dinner, to say nothing of a breakfast, and you're too young for that.

"What's the matter? More trouble about that new comet of yours. You've been up all night looking at it, haven't you? Of course it's all right that you got hold of it before anybody else, but all the same I don't want you to be worrying yourself for nothing and get laid up before the time comes to take the glory of the discovery."

While he was speaking the door of the breakfast-room opened and Auriole came in. She looked with a just perceptible admiration at the man who, as it seemed to her, was beginning to show a slight stoop in the broad shoulders and a little falling forward of the head which she had first seen driving through the water to her rescue in the Bay of Connemara. Her eyelids lifted a shade as she looked at him, and she said with a half smile:

"Good morning, Mr. Lennard; I am afraid you've been sacrificing yourself a little bit too much to science. You don't seem to have had a sleep for the last two or three nights. You've been blinding your eyes over those tangles of figures and equations, parallaxes and cube roots and that sort of thing. I know something about them because I had some struggles with them myself at Vassar."

"That's about it, Auriole," said her father. "Just what I've been saying; and I hope our friend is not going on with this kind of business too long. Now, really, Mr. Lennard, you know you must not, and that's all there is to it."

"Oh, no, I don't think you need be frightened of anything of that sort," said Lennard, who had considerably brightened up as Auriole entered the room; "perhaps I may have been going a little too long without sleep; but, you see, a man who has the great luck to discover a new comet is something like one of the old navigators who discovered new islands and continents. Of course you remember the story of Columbus. When he thought he was going to find what is now the country which has had the honor –"

"I know you're going to say something nice, Mr. Lennard," interrupted Auriole, "but breakfast is ready; here it comes. If you take my advice you will have your coffee and something to eat and tell us the rest of it while you're getting something that will do you good. What do you think, Poppa?"

"Hard sense, Auriole, hard sense. Your mother used to talk just like that, and I reckon you've got it from her. Well now, here's the food, let's begin. I've got a hunger on me that I'd have wanted five dollars to stop at the time when I couldn't buy a breakfast."

They sat down, Miss Auriole at the head of the table and her father and Lennard facing each other, and for the next few minutes there was a semi-silence which was very well employed in the commencement of one of the most important functions of the human day.

When Mr. Parmenter had got through his first cup of coffee, his two poached eggs on toast, and was beginning on the fish, he looked across the table and said:

"Well now, Mr. Lennard, I guess you're feeling a bit better, as I do, and so, maybe, you can tell us something new about comets."

"I certainly am feeling better," said Lennard with a glance at Auriole, "but, you see, I've got into a state of mind which is not unlike the physical state of the Red Indian who starves for a few days and then takes his meals, I mean the arrears of meals, all at once. When I have had a good long sleep, as I am going to have until tonight, I might –

in fact, I hope I shall be able to tell you something definite about the question of the comet."

"What – the question?" echoed Mr. Parmenter. "About the comet? I didn't understand that there was any question. You have discovered it, haven't you?"

"I have made a certain discovery, Mr. Parmenter," said Lennard, with a gravity which made Auriole raise her eyelids quickly, "but whether I have found a comet so far unknown to astronomy or not, is quite another matter. Thanks to that splendid instrument of yours, I have found a something in a part of the heavens where no comet, not even a star, has even been seen yet, and, speaking in all seriousness, I may say that this discovery contradicts all calculations as to the orbits and velocities of any known comet. That is what I have been thinking about all night."

"What?" said Auriole, looking up again. "Really something quite unknown?"

"Unknown except to the three people sitting at this table, unless another miracle has happened – I mean such a one as happened in the case of the discovery of Neptune which, as of course you know, Adams at Cambridge and Le Verrier at Paris –"

"Yes, yes," said Auriole, "two men who didn't know each other; both looked for something that couldn't be seen, and found it. If you've done anything like that, Mr. Lennard, I reckon Poppa will have good cause to be proud of his reflector –"

"And of the man behind it," added her father. "A telescope's like a gun; no use without a good man behind it. Well, if that's so, Mr. Lennard, this discovery of yours ought to shake the world up a bit."

"From what I have seen so far," replied Lennard, "I have not the slightest doubt that it will."

"And when may I see this wonderful discovery of yours, Mr. Lennard," said Auriole, "this something which is going to be so important, this something that no one else's eyes have seen except yours. Really, you know, you've made me quite longing to get a sight of this stranger from the outer wilderness of space."

"If the night is clear enough, I may hope to be able to introduce you to the new celestial visitor about a quarter-past eleven tonight, or to be quite accurate eleven hours, sixteen minutes and thirty-nine seconds p.m."

"I think that's good enough, Auriole," said her father. "If the heavens are only kind enough, we'll go up to the observatory and, as Mr. Lennard says, see something that no one else has ever seen."

"And then," laughed Auriole, "I suppose you will have achieved the second ambition of your life. You have already piled up a bigger heap of dollars than anybody else in the world, and by midnight you will have seen farther into Creation than anybody else. But you will let me have the first look, won't you?"

"Why, certainly," he replied. "As soon as Mr. Lennard has got the telescope fixed, you go first, and I reckon that won't take very long."

"No," replied Lennard, "I've worked out the position for tonight, and it's only a matter of winding up the clockwork and setting the telescope. And now," he continued, rising, "if you will allow me, I will say – well, I was going to say good-night, but of course it's good-morning – I'm going to bed."

"Will you come down to lunch, or shall I have some sent up to you?" said Auriole.

"No, thanks. I don't think there will be any need to trouble you about that. When I once get to sleep, I hope I shall forget all things earthly, and heavenly too for the matter of that, until about six o'clock, and if you will have me called then, I will be ready for dinner."

"Certainly," replied Auriole, "and I hope you will sleep as well as you deserve to do, after all these nights of watching."

He did sleep. He slept the sleep of a man physically and mentally tired, in spite of the load of unspeakable anxiety which was weighing upon his mind. For during his last night's work, he had learnt what no other man in the world knew. He had learnt that, unless a miracle happened, or some almost superhuman feat of ingenuity and daring was accomplished, that day thirteen months hence would see the annihilation of every living thing on earth, and the planet Terra converted into a dark and lifeless orb, a wilderness drifting through space, the blackened and desolated sepulcher of the countless millions of living beings which now inhabited it.

Chapter V

A GLIMPSE OF THE DOOM

After dinner Lennard excused himself, saying that he wanted to make a few more calculations; and then he got outside and lit his pipe, and walked up the winding path towards the observatory.

"What am I to do?" he said between his teeth. "It's a ghastly position for a man to be placed in. Fancy – just a poor, ordinary, human being like myself having the power of losing or saving the world in his hands! And then, of course, there's a woman in the question – the Eternal Feminine – even in such a colossal problem as this!

"It's mean, and I know it; but, after all, I saved her life – though, if I hadn't reached her first, that other chap might have got her. I love her and he loves her; there's no doubt about that, and Papa Parmenter wants to marry her to a coronet. There's one thing certain, Castellan shall not have her, and I love her a lot too much to see her made My Lady This, or the Marchioness of So-and-so, just because she's beautiful and has millions, and the other fellow, whoever he may be, may have a coronet that probably wants re-gilding; and yet, after all, it's only the same old story in a rather more serious form – a woman against the world. I suppose Papa Parmenter would show me the door tomorrow morning if I, a poor explorer of the realm of Space, dared to tell him that I want to marry his daughter.

"And yet how miserable and trivial all these wretched distinctions of wealth and position look now; or would look if the world only knew and believed what I could tell it – and that reminds me – shall I tell her, or them? Of course, I must before long; simply because in a month or so those American fellows will be on it, and they won't have any scruples when it comes to a matter of scare head-lines. Yes, I think it may as well be tonight as any other time. Still, it's a pretty awful thing for a humble individual like myself to say, especially to a girl one happens to be very much in love with – nothing less than the death-sentence of Humanity. Ah, well, she's got to hear it some time and from someone, and why shouldn't she hear it now and from me?"

When he got back to the house, there was a carriage at the door, and Mr. Parmenter was just coming down the avenue, followed by a man with a small portmanteau in his hand.

"Sorry, Mr. Lennard," he said, holding out his hand, "I've just had a wire about a company tangle in London that I've got to go and shake out at once, so I'll have to see what you have to show me later on. Still, that needn't trouble anyone. It looks as if it were going to be a splendid night for star-gazing, and I don't want Auriole disappointed, so she can go up to the observatory with you at the proper time and see what there is to be seen. See you later, I have only just about time to get the connection for London."

Lennard was not altogether sorry that this accident had happened. Naturally, the prospect of an hour or so with Auriole alone in his temple of Science was very pleasant, and moreover, he felt that, as the momentous tidings had to be told, he would prefer to tell them to her first. And so it came about.

A little after half-past eleven that night Miss Auriole was looking wonderingly into the eye-piece of the great Reflector, watching a tiny little patch of mist, somewhat brighter towards one end than the other; like a little wisp of white smoke rising from a very faint spark that was apparently floating across an unfathomable sea of darkness.

She seemed to see this through black darkness, and behind it a swarm of stars of all sizes and colors. They appeared very much more wonderful and glorious and important than the little spray of white smoke, because she hadn't yet the faintest conception of its true import to her and every other human being on earth: but she was very soon to know now.

While she was watching it in breathless silence, in which the clicking of the mechanism which kept the great telescope moving so as to exactly counteract the motion of the machinery of the Universe, sounded like the blows of a sledge-hammer on an anvil, Gilbert Lennard stood beside her, wondering if he should begin to tell her, and what he should say.

At last she turned away from the eye-piece, and looked at him with something like a scared expression in her eyes, and said:

"It's very wonderful, isn't it, that one should be able to see all that just by looking into a little bit of a hole in a telescope? And you tell me that all those great big bright stars around your comet are so far away that if you look at them just with your own eyes you don't even see them – and there they look almost as if you could put out your hand and touch them. It's just a little bit awful, too!" she added, with a little shiver.

"Yes," he said, speaking slowly and even more gravely that she thought the subject warranted, "yes, it is both wonderful and, in a way, awful. Do you know that some of those stars you have seen in there are so far away that the light which you see them by may have left them when Solomon was king in Jerusalem? They may be quite dead and dark now, or reduced into fire-mist by collision with some other star. And then, perhaps, there are others behind them again so far away that their light has not even reached us yet, and may never do while there are human eyes on earth to see it."

"Yes, I know," she said, smiling. "You don't forget that I have been to college – and light travels about a hundred and eighty-six thousand miles a second, doesn't it? But come, Mr. Lennard, aren't you what they call stretching the probabilities a little when you say that the light of some of them will never get here, as far as we're concerned? I always thought we had a few million years of life to look forward to before this old world of ours gets worn out."

"There are other ends possible for this world besides wearing out, Miss Parmenter," he answered, this time almost solemnly. "Other worlds have, as I say, been reduced to fire-mist. Some have been shattered to tiny fragments to make asteroids and meteorites – stars and worlds, in comparison with which this bit of a planet of ours is nothing more than a speck of sand, a mere atom of matter drifting over the wilderness of immensity. In fact, such a trifle is it in the organism of the Universe, that if some celestial body collided with it – say a comet with a sufficiently solid nucleus – and the heat developed by the impact turned it into a mass of blazing gas, an astronomer on Neptune, one of our own planets, wouldn't even notice the accident, unless he happened to be watching the earth through a powerful telescope at the time."

"And is such an accident, as you call it, possible, Mr. Lennard?" she asked, jumping womanlike, by a sort of unconscious intuition, to the very point to which he was so clumsily trying to lead up.

"I thought you spoke rather queerly about this comet of yours at breakfast this morning. I hope there isn't any chance of its getting on to the same track as this terrestrial locomotive of ours. That would be just awful, wouldn't it? Why, what's the matter? You are going to be ill, I know. You had better get down to the house, and go to bed. It's want of sleep, isn't it? You'll be driving yourself mad that way."

A sudden and terrible change had come over him while she was speaking. It was only for the moment, and yet to him it was an eternity. It might, as she said, have been the want of sleep, for insomnia plays strange tricks sometimes with the strongest of intellects.

More probably, it might have been the horror of his secret working on the great love that he had for this girl who was sitting there alone with him in the silence of that dim room and in the midst of the glories and the mysteries of the Universe.

His eyes had grown fixed and staring, and looked sightlessly at her, and his face shone ghastly pale in the dim light of the solitary shaded lamp. Certainly, one of those mysterious crises which are among the unsolved secrets of psychology had come upon him like some swift access of delirium.

He no longer saw her sitting there by the telescope, calm, gracious, and beautiful. He saw her as, by his pitiless calculations, he must do that day thirteen months to come – with her soft grey eyes, starting, horror-driven from their orbits, staring blank and wide and hideous at the overwhelming hell that would be falling down from heaven upon the devoted earth. He saw her fresh young face withered and horror-lined and old, and the bright-brown hair grown grey with the years that would pass in those few final moments. He saw the sweet red lips which had tempted him so often to wild thoughts parched and black, wide open and gasping vainly for the breath of life in a hot, burned-out atmosphere.

Then he saw – no, it was only a glimpse; and with that the strange trance-vision ended. What must have come after that would in all certainty have driven him mad there and then, before his work had even begun; but at that moment, swiftly severing the darkness that was falling over his soul, there came to him an idea, bright, luminous, and lovely as an inspiration from Heaven itself, and with it came back the calm sanity of the sternly-disciplined intellect, prepared to contemplate, not only the destruction of the world he lived in, but even the loss of the woman he loved – the only human being who could make the world beautiful or even tolerable for him.

The vision was blotted out from the sight of his soul; the darkness cleared away from his eyes, and he saw her again as she still was. It had all passed in a few moments and yet in them he had been down into hell – and he had come back to earth, and into her presence.

Almost by the time she had uttered her last word, he had regained command of his voice, and he began clearly and quietly to answer the question which was still echoing through the chambers of his brain.

"It was only a little passing faintness, thank you; and something else which you will understand when I have done, if you have patience to hear me to the end," he said, looking straight at her for a moment, and then beginning to walk slowly up and down the room past her chair.

"I am going to surprise you, perhaps to frighten you, and very probably to offend you deeply," he began again in a quiet, dry sort of tone, which somehow impressed her against all her convictions that he didn't much care whether or not he did any or all of these things: but there was something else in his tone and manner which held her to her seat, silent and attentive, although she was conscious of a distinct desire to get up and run away.

"Your guess about the comet, or whatever it may prove to be, is quite correct. I don't think it is a new one. From what I have seen of it so far, I have every reason to believe that it is Gambert's comet, which was discovered in 1826, and became visible to the naked eye in the autumn of 1833. It then crossed the orbit of the earth one month after the earth had passed the point of intersection. After that, some force divided it, and in '46 and '52 it reappeared as twin comets constantly separating. Now it would seem that the two masses have come together again: and as they are both larger in bulk and greater in density it would appear that, somewhere in the distant fields of Space, they have united with some other and denser body. The result is, that what is practically a new comet, with a much denser nucleus than any so far seen, is approaching our system. Unless a miracle happens, or there is a practically impossible error in my calculations, it will cross the orbit of the earth thirteen months from today, at the moment that the earth itself arrives at the point of intersection."

So far Auriole had listened to the stiff scientific phraseology with more interest than alarm; but now she took advantage of a little pause, and said:

"And the consequences, Mr. Lennard? I mean the consequences to us as living beings. You may as well tell me everything now that you've gone so far."

"I am going to," he said, stopping for a moment in his walk, "and I am going to tell you something more than that. Granted that what I have said happens, one of two things must follow. If the nucleus of the comet is solid enough to pass through our atmosphere without being dissipated, it will strike the surface with so much force that both it and the earth will probably be transformed into fiery vapor by the conversion of the motion of the two bodies into heat. If not, its contact with the oxygen of the earth's atmosphere will produce an aërial conflagration which, if it does not roast alive every living thing on earth, will convert the oxygen, by combustion, into an irrespirable and poisonous gas, and so kill us by a slower, but no less fatal, process."

"Horrible!" she said, shivering this time. "You speak like a judge pronouncing sentence of death on the whole human race! I suppose there is no possibility of reprieve? Well, go on!"

"Yes," he said, "there is something else. Those are the scientific facts, as far as they go. I am going to tell you the chances now – and something more. There is just one chance – one possible way of averting universal ruin from the earth, and substituting for it nothing more serious than an unparalleled display of celestial fireworks. All that will be necessary is perfect calculation and illimitable expenditure of money."

"Well," she said, "can't you do the calculations, Mr. Lennard, and hasn't dad got millions enough? How could he spend them better than in saving the human race from being burned alive? There isn't anything else, is there?"

"There was something else," he said, stopping in front of her again. She had risen to her feet as she said the last words, and the two stood facing each other in the dim light, while the mechanism of the telescope kept on clicking away in its heedless, mechanical fashion.

"Yes, there was something else, and I may as well tell you after all; for, even if you never see or speak to me again, it won't stop the work being done now. I could have kept this discovery to myself till it would have been too late to do anything: for no other telescope without my help would even find the comet for four months to come, and even now there is hardly a day to be lost if the work is to be done in time. And then – well, I suppose I must have gone mad for the time being, for I thought – you will hardly believe me, I suppose – that I could make you the price of the world's safety.

"From that, you will see how much I have loved you, however mad I may have been. Losing you, I would have lost the world with you. If my love lives, I thought, the world shall live: if not, if you die, the world shall die. But just now, when you thought I was taken ill, I had a sort of vision, and I saw you, – yes, you, Auriole as, if my one chance fails, you must infallibly be this night thirteen months hence. I didn't see any of the other millions who would be choking and gasping for breath and writhing in the torture of the universal fire – I only saw you and my own baseness in thinking, even for a moment, that such a bargain would be possible.

"And then," he went on, more slowly, and with a different ring in his voice, "there are the other men."

"Which other men?" she asked, looking up at him with a flush on her cheeks and a gleam in her eyes.

"To be quite frank, and in such a situation as this, I don't see that anything but complete candor is of any use," he replied slowly. "I need hardly tell you that they are John Castellan and the Marquis of Westerham. Castellan, I know, has loved you just as I have done, from the moment we had the good luck to pick you out of the bay at Clifden.

Lord Westerham also wants you, so do I. That, put plainly, brutally, if you like, is the situation. Of your own feelings, of course, I do not pretend to have the remotest idea; but I confess that when this knowledge came to me, the first thought that crossed my mind was the thought of you as another man's wife – and then came the vision of the world in flames. At first I chose the world in flames. I see that I was wrong. That is all."

She had not interrupted even by a gesture, but as she listened, a thousand signs and trifles which alone had meant nothing to her, now seemed to come together and make one clear and definite revelation. This strong, reserved, silent man had all the time loved her so desperately that he was going mad about her – so mad that, as he had said, he had even dreamed of weighing the possession of her single, insignificant self against the safety of the whole world, with all its innumerable millions of people – mostly as good in their way as she was.

Well – it might be that the love of such a man was a thing worth to weigh even against a coronet – not in her eyes, for there was no question of that now, but in her father's. But that was a matter for future consideration. She drew herself up a little stiffly, and said, in just such a tone as she might have used if what he had just been saying had had no personal interest for her – had, in fact, been about some other girl:

"I think it's about time to be going down to the house, Mr. Lennard, isn't it? I am quite sure a night's rest won't do you any harm. No, I'm not offended, and I don't think I'm even frightened yet. It somehow seems too big and too awful a thing to be only frightened at – too much like the Day of Judgment, you know. I am glad you've told me – yes, everything – and I'm glad that what you call your madness is over. You will be able to do your work in saving the world all the better. Only don't tell dad anything except – well – just the scientific and necessary part of it. You know, saving a world is a very much greater matter than winning a woman – at least it is in one particular woman's eyes – and I've learnt somewhere in mathematics something about the greater including the less. And now, don't you think we had better be going down into the house? It's getting quite late."

Chapter VI

THE NOTE OF WAR

The *Official Gazette,* published November the 25th, 1909, contained the following announcement: –

> "Naval Promotions. Lieutenant-Commander Francis Erskine, of H.M. Fishery Cruiser *Cormorant,* to be Captain of H.M. Cruiser *Ithuriel.* Lieutenant Denis Castellan, also of the *Cormorant,* to be First Lieutenant of the *Ithuriel.*"

On the evening of the same day, Mr. Chamberlain, the Prime Minister, rose amidst the tense silence of a crowded House to make another announcement, which was not altogether unconnected with the notice in the *Gazette.*

"Sir," he said in a low, but vibrant and penetrating voice, which many years before had helped to make his fame as an orator, "it is my painful duty to inform this honorable House that a state of war exists between His Majesty and a Confederation of European countries, including Germany, Russia, France, Spain, Holland and Belgium."

He paused for a moment, and looked round at the hundreds of faces, most of them pale and fixed, that were turned toward the front Treasury Bench. Since Mr. Balfour, now Lord Whittinghame, and Leader of the Conservative Party in the House of Lords, had made his memorable speech on the 12th of October 1899, informing the House of Commons and the world that the Ultimatum of the South African Republic had been rejected, and that the struggle for the mastery of South Africa was inevitable, no such momentous announcement had been made in the House of Commons.

Mr. Chamberlain referred to that bygone crisis in the following terms:

"It will be within the memory of many Members of this House that, almost exactly ten years ago today, the British Empire was challenged to fight for the supremacy of South Africa. That challenge was accepted not because there was any desire on the part of the Government or the people of this country to destroy the self-government of what were then the South African Republic and the Orange Free State, but because the Government of her late Majesty, Queen Victoria, knew that the fate of an empire, however great, depends upon its supremacy throughout its dominions.

"To lose one of these, however small and apparently insignificant, is to take a stone out of an arch with the result of inevitable collapse of the whole structure. It is not necessary for me, sir, to make any further allusion to that struggle, save than to say that the policy of Her Majesty's Ministers has been completely justified by the consequences which have followed from it.

"The Transvaal and Orange River Colonies have taken their place among the other self-governing Colonies of the Empire. They are prosperous, contented and loyal, and they will not be the last, I think, to come to the help of the Mother Country in such a crisis as this. But, sir, I do not think that I should be fulfilling the duties of the responsible position which I have the honor to occupy if I did not remind this House, and through this House the citizens of the British Empire, that the present crisis is infinitely more serious than that with which we were faced in 1899. Then we were waging a war in another hemisphere, six thousand miles away. Our unconquered, and, as I hope it will prove, unconquerable Navy, kept the peace of the world, and policed the ocean highways along which it was necessary for our ships to travel. It is true that there were menaces and threats heard in many quarters, but they never passed beyond the region of insult and calumny.

"Our possible enemies then, our actual enemies now, were in those days willing to wound, and yet afraid to strike. Today, they have lost their fear in the confidence of combination. Today the war cloud is not six thousand miles away in the southern hemisphere; it is here, in Europe, and a strip of water, twenty-one miles broad, separates us from the enemy, which, even as I am speaking, may already be knocking at our gates. Even now, the thunder of the guns may be echoing along the shores of the English Channel.

"This, sir, is a war in which I might venture to say the most ardent member of the Peace Society would not hesitate to engage. For it involves the most sacred duty of humanity, the defense of our country, and our homes.

"We remember, sir, the words which Francis Drake wrote, and which have remained true from his day until now: 'The frontiers of an island country are the coasts of its possible enemies.' We remember also that when the great Napoleon had massed nearly half a million men on the heights above Boulogne, and more than a thousand pontoons were waiting to carry that force to the Kentish shore, there was only one old English frigate cruising up and down the Straits of Dover.

"Sir, there is on the heights of Boulogne a monument, built to commemorate the assembly of the Grand Army, and collectors of coins still cherish those productions of the Paris Mint, which bear the legend, 'Napoleon, Emperor, London, 1804.' But, sir, the statue of Napoleon which stands on the summit of that monument faces not westward but eastward. The Grand Army could have crossed that narrow strip of water. It could, no doubt, have made a landing on British soil, but Napoleon, possibly the greatest military genius the world has ever seen, anticipated Field-Marshal von Moltke, who said that he had found eight ways of getting into England, but he had not found one of getting out again, unless it were possible to pump the North Sea dry, and march the men over. In other words, sir, the British Navy was then, as now, paramount on seas; the oceans were our territories, and the coasts of Europe our frontiers.

"Again, sir, we must not forget that those were the days of sails, and that these are the days of steam. What was then a matter of days is now only a matter of hours. It is two hundred and forty-two years since the sound of hostile guns was heard in the city of London. Tomorrow morning their thunder may awaken us.

"It has been said, sir, that Great Britain plays the game of Diplomacy with her cards face upwards on the table. That, in a sense, is true, and His Majesty's Government propose to play the same game now. The demands which have been presented by the Federation of European Powers, at the head of which stands the German Emperor – demands which, it is hardly necessary for me to say, were instantly rejected – are these: That Gibraltar shall be given back to Spain; that Malta shall be dismantled, and cease to be a British naval base; that the British occupation of Egypt and the Sudan shall cease, and that the Suez Canal and the Trans-Continental Railway from Cairo to the Cape shall be handed over to the control of an International Board, upon which the British Empire will be graciously allowed one representative.

"It is further demanded that Singapore, the Gate of the East, shall be placed under the control of the same International Board, and that the fortifications of Hong Kong shall be demolished. That, sir, would amount to the surrender of the British Empire, an empire which can only exist as long as the ocean paths between its various portions are kept inviolate.

"Those proposals, sir, in plain English are threats, and His Majesty's Government has returned the only possible answer to them, and that answer is war – war, let us remember, which may within a few weeks, or even days, be brought to our own doors. Whatever our enemies may have said of us it is still true that Britain stands for peace, security, and prosperity. We have used the force of arms to conquer the forces of barbarism and semi-civilization, but the most hostile of our critics may be safely challenged to point to any country or province upon which we have imposed the Pax Britannica, which is not now the better for it. It is no idle boast, sir, to say that all the world over, the rule of His Majesty means the rule of peace and prosperity. There are only two causes in which a nation or an empire may justly go to war. One, is to make peace where strife was before, and the other is to defend that which has been won, and made secure by patient toil and endeavor, no less than by blood and suffering. It is that which the challenge of Europe calls upon us now to defend. Our answer to the leagued nations is this: What we have fought for and worked for and won is ours. Take it from us if you can.

"And, sir, I believe that I can say with perfect confidence, that what His Majesty's Government has done His Majesty's subjects will enforce to a man, and, if necessary, countersign the declaration of war in their own blood.

"Let us remember, too, those weighty words of warning which the Laureate of the Empire wrote nearly twenty years ago, of this Imperial inheritance of ours:

> "'It is not made with the mountains, it is not one with the deep, Men, not gods, devised it, men, not gods, must keep. Men not children, servants, or kinsfolk called from afar, But each man born in the island broke to the matter of war.
>
> "'So ye shall bide, sure-guarded, when the restless lightnings wake, In the boom of the blotting war-cloud, and the pallid nations quake. So, at the haggard trumpets, instant your soul shall leap, Forthright, accoutered, accepting – alert from the walls of sleep. So at the threat ye shall summon – so at the need ye shall send, Men, not children, or servants, tempered and taught to the end.'

"Sir, it has been said that poets are prophets. The hour of the fulfillment of that prophecy has now come, and I shall be much mistaken in my estimate of the temper of my countrymen and fellow-subjects of His Majesty here in Britain, and in the greater Britains over sea, if, granted the possibility of an armed invasion of the Motherland, every man, soldier or civilian, who is able to use a rifle, will not, if necessary, use it in the defense of his country and his home."

The Prime Minister sat down amid absolute silence. The tremendous possibilities which he had summed up in his brief speech seemed to have stunned his hearers for the time being. Some members said afterwards that they could hear their own watches ticking. Then Mr. John Redmond, the Leader of the Irish Nationalist Party, rose and said, in a slow, and deliberate voice, which contrasted strikingly with his usual style of oratory:

"Sir, this is not a time for what has been with a certain amount of double-meaning described as Parliamentary speeches. Still less is it a time for party or for racial differences. The silence in which this House has received the speech of the Prime Minister is the most eloquent tribute that could be paid to the solemnity of his utterances. But, sir, I have a reason for calling attention to one omission in that speech, an omission which may have been made purposely. The last time that a foeman's foot trod British soil was not eight hundred years ago. It was in December 1796 that French soldiers and sailors landed on the shores of Bantry Bay. Sir, the Ireland of those days was discontented, and, if you please to call it so, disloyal. There are those who say she is so now, but, sir, whatever our domestic difficulties and quarrels may be, and however much I and the party which I have the honor to lead may differ from the home policy of the Right Honorable gentleman who has made this momentous pronouncement, it shall not be said that any of those difficulties or differences will be taken advantage of by any man who is worth the name of Irishman.

"As the Prime Minister has told us, the thunder of the enemy's guns may even now be echoing along our southern coasts. We have, I hope, learnt a little wisdom on both sides of the Irish Sea during the last twenty years, and this time, sir, I think I can promise that, while the guns are talking, there shall be no sound of dispute on party matters in this House as far as we are concerned. From this moment, the Irish Nationalist Party, as such, ceases to exist, at any rate until the war's over.

"In 1796, the French fleet carrying the invading force was scattered over the seas by one of the worst storms that ever was known on the west coast of Ireland. As Queen Elizabeth's medal said of the Spanish Armada, 'God blew, and they were scattered.' With God's help, sir, we will scatter these new enemies who threaten us with invasion and conquest. Henceforth, there must be no more Englishmen, Irishmen, Scotchmen, or Welshmen. We are just subjects of the King, and inhabitants of the British Islands; and the man who does not believe that, and act upon his belief, should get out of these islands as soon as he can, for he isn't fit to live in them.

"I remember, sir, a car-driver in Galway, who was taking an English tourist – and he was a politician as well – around the country about that half-ruined city. The English tourist was inquiring into the troubles of Ireland, and he asked him what was the greatest affliction that Ireland suffered from, and when he answered him he described just the sort of Irishman who won't be wanted in Ireland now. He said, 'It's the absentee landlords, your honor. This unfortunate country is absolutely swarming with them.'"

It was an anti-climax such as only an Irishman could have achieved. The tension which had held every nerve of every member on the stretch while the Prime Minister was speaking was broken. The Irish members, almost to a man, jumped to their feet, as Mr. Redmond picked up his hat, waved it round his head, and said, in a tone which rang clear and true through the crowded Chamber:

"God save the King!"

And then for the first time in its history, the House of Commons rose and sang the National Anthem.

There was no division that night. The Prime Minister formally put the motion for the voting of such credit as might be necessary to meet the expenses of the war, and when the Speaker put the question, Aye or Nay, every member stood up bareheaded, and a deep-voiced, thunderous "Aye" told the leagued nations of Europe that Britain had accepted their challenge.

Chapter VII

CAUGHT!

The events of that memorable night formed a most emphatic contradiction to the prophecy in Macaulay's "Armada":

"Such night in England ne'er had been, nor e'er again shall be."

The speeches in the House of Commons and in the House of Peers were being printed even as they were spoken; hundreds of printing-presses were grinding out millions of copies of newspapers. Thousands of newsboys were running along the pavements, or with great bags of new editions slung on their shoulders tearing through the traffic on bicycles; but all the speeches in the two Houses of Parliament, all the reports and hurriedly-written leaders in the papers just represented to the popular mind one word, and that word was war.

It was true that for over a hundred years no year had passed in which the British Empire had not been engaged in a war of some kind, but they were wars waged somewhere in the outlands of the earth. To the stop-at-home man in the street they were rather more matters of latitude and longitude than battle, murder, and sudden death. The South African War, and even the terrible struggle between Russia and Japan, were already memories drifting out of sight in the rush of the headlong current of twentieth-century life.

But this was quite another matter; here was war – not war that was being waged thousands of miles away in another hemisphere or on another side of the globe – but war within twenty-one miles of English land – within two or three hours, as it were, of every Englishman's front door.

This went home to every man who had a home, or who possessed anything worth living for. It was not now a case of sending soldiers, militia and yeomanry away in transports, and cheering them as they went. Not now, as Kipling too truly had said of the fight for South Africa:

> "When your strong men cheered in their millions, while your
> striplings went to the war."

Now it was the turn of the strong men; the turn of every man who had the strength and courage to fight in defense of all that was nearest and dearest to him.

As yet there was no excitement. At every theater and every music hall in London and the great provincial cities and towns, the performances were stopped as soon as the news was received by telegraph. The managers read the news from the stage, the orchestras played the first bar of the National Anthem, the audiences rose to their feet, and all over the British Islands millions of voices sang "God save the King," and then, obeying some impulse, which seemed to have inspired the whole land, burst into the triumphant psalm of "Rule Britannia."

And when the theaters and music halls closed, men and women went on their way home quietly discussing the tremendous tidings which had been officially announced. There was no attempt at demonstration, there was very little cheering. It was too serious a matter for that. The men and women of Britain were thinking, not about what they should say, but about what they should do. There was no time for shouting, for tomorrow, perhaps even tonight, the guns would be talking – "The drumming guns which have no doubts."

The House rose at half-past eleven, and at ten minutes to twelve Lieutenant Denis Castellan, came into the smoking-room of the Keppel's Head Hotel, Portsmouth, with a copy of the last edition of the *Southern Evening News* in his hand, and said to Captain Erskine:

"It's all right, my boy. It's war, and you've got the *Ithuriel.* Your own ship, too. Designer, creator, captain; and I'm your First Luff."

"I think that's about good enough for a bottle of the best, Castellan," said Erskine, in the quiet tone in which the officer of the finest Service in the world always speaks. "Touch the button, will you?"

As Denis Castellan put his finger on the button of the electric bell, a man got up from an armchair on the opposite side of the room, and said, as he came towards the table at which Erskine was sitting:

"You will pardon me, I hope, if I introduce myself without the usual formalities. My name is Gilbert Lennard."

"Then, I take it, you're the man who swam that race with my brother John, in Clifden Bay, when Miss Parmenter was thrown out of her skiff. But he's no brother of mine now. He's sold himself to the Germans, and," he continued, suddenly lowering his voice almost to a whisper, "come up to my room, we'll have the bottle there, and Mr. Lennard will join us. Yes, waiter, you can take it up to No. 24, we can't talk here," he went on in a louder tone. "There's a German spy in the room, and by the piper that was supposed to play before Moses, if he's here when I come back, I'll throw him out."

Everyone in the smoking-room looked up. Castellan walked out, looking at a fair-haired, clean-shaven little man, sitting at a table in the right-hand corner of the room from the door. He also looked up, and glanced vacantly about the room; then as the three went out, he took a sip of the whisky and soda beside him, and looked back on to the paper that he was reading.

"Who's that chap?" asked Erskine, as they went upstairs.

"I'll tell you when we're a bit more to ourselves," replied Castellan; and when they had got into his sitting room, and the waiter had brought the wine, he locked the door, and said:

"That is Staff-Captain Count Karl von Eckstein, of the German Imperial Navy, and also of His Majesty, the Kaiser's, Secret Service. He knows a little more than we do about every dockyard and fort on the South Coast, to say nothing of the ships. That's his district, and thanks to the most obliging kindness of the British authorities he has made very good use of it."

"But, surely," exclaimed Lennard, "now that there is a state of war, such a man as that could be arrested."

"Faith," said Denis Castellan, as he filled the glasses. "Law or no law, he will be arrested tonight if he stops here long enough for me to lay hands upon him. Now then, what's the news, Mr. Lennard? I'm told that you've just come back from the United States, what's the opinion of things over there?"

Such news that Lennard had was, of course, even more terrible than the news of war and invasion, which was now thrilling through England like an electric shock, and he kept it to himself, thinking quite rightly that the people of England had quite enough to occupy their attention for the immediate present, and so he replied as he raised the glass which Denis had filled for him:

"I am afraid that I have no news except this: that from all I have heard in the States, if it does come to death-grips, the States will be with us. But you see, of course, that I have only just got back, and this thing has been sprung on us so suddenly. In fact, it was only this morning that we got an aerogram from the Lizard as we came up Channel to say that war was almost a certainty, and advising us to get into Southampton as soon as we could."

"Well," said Erskine, taking up his glass, "that's all right, as far as it goes. I've always believed that it's all rot saying that blood isn't thicker than water. It is. Of course, relations quarrel more than other people do, but it's only over domestic matters. Let an outsider start a row, and he very soon sees what happens, and that's what I believe our friends on the other side of the Channel are going to find out if it comes to extremities. Well, Mr. Lennard, I am very pleased that you have introduced yourself to us tonight. Of course, we have both known you publicly, and therefore we have all the more pleasure in knowing you privately."

"Thanks," replied Lennard, putting his hand into the inside pocket of his coat and taking out an envelope. "But to be quite candid with you, although of course I am very pleased to make your acquaintance, I did not introduce myself to you and Mr. Castellan only for personal reasons. I have devoted some attention to the higher chemistry as well as the higher mathematics and astronomy, and I have also had the pleasure of going through the designs of the cruiser which you have invented, and which you are now to command. I have been greatly interested in them, and for that reason I think that this may interest you. I brought it here in the hope of meeting you, as I knew that your ship was lying here."

Erskine opened the envelope, and took out a sheet of notepaper, on which were written just a few chemical formulæ and about forty words.

Castellan, who was watching him keenly, for the first time since they had sailed together through stress and storm under the White Ensign, saw him start. The pupils of his eyes suddenly dilated; his eyelids and eyebrows went up for an instant and came down again, and the rigid calm of the British Naval Officer came back. He put the letter into his hip pocket, buttoned it up, and said, very quietly:

"Thank you, Mr. Lennard. You have done me a very great personal service, and your country a greater one still. I shall, of course, make use of this. I am afraid if you had sent it to the Ordnance Department you wouldn't have heard anything about it for the next three months or more; perhaps not till the war was over."

"And that is just why I brought it to you," laughed Lennard. "Well, here's good luck to you and the *Ithuriel*, and all honor, and God save the King!"

"God save the King!" repeated Erskine and Castellan, with that note of seriousness in their tone which you can hear in the voice of no man who has not fought, or is not going to fight; in short, to put his words into action.

They emptied their glasses, and as they put them down on the table again there came a knock at the door, sharp, almost imperative.

"Come in," said Erskine.

The head waiter threw the door open, and a Naval messenger walked in, saluted, handed Erskine an official envelope, and said:

"Immediately, sir. The steam pinnace is down at the end of the Railway Quay."

Erskine tore open the envelope and read the brief order that it contained, and said:

"Very good. We shall be on board in ten minutes."

The messenger, who was a very useful-looking specimen of the handy man, saluted and left the room. Castellan ran out after him, and they went downstairs together. At the door of the hotel the messenger put two fingers into his mouth, and gave three soft whistles, not unlike the sounds of a boatswain's pipe. In two minutes a dozen bluejackets had appeared from nowhere, and just as a matter of formality were asked to have a drink at the bar. Meanwhile Denis Castellan had gone into the smoking-room, where he found the sandy-haired, blue-eyed man still sitting at his table in the corner, smoking his cigar, and looking over the paper. He touched him on the shoulder and whispered, in perfectly idiomatic German:

"I thought you were a cleverer man than that, Count. Didn't I give you a warning? God's thunder, man. You ought to have been miles away by this time; haven't you a motor that would take you to Southampton in an hour, and put you on the last of the German liners that's leaving? You know it will be a shooting or a hanging matter if you're caught here. Come on now. My name's Castellan, and that should be good enough for you. Come on, now, and I'll see you safe."

The name of Castellan was already well known to every German confidential agent, though it was not known that John Castellan had a brother who was a Lieutenant in the British Navy.

Captain Count Karl von Eckstein got up, and took his hat down from the pegs, pulled on his gloves, and said deliberately:

"I am very much obliged to you, Mr. Castellan, for your warning, which I ought to have taken at first, but I hope there is still time. I will go and telephone for my motor at once."

"Yes, come along and do it," said Castellan, catching him by the arm. "You haven't much time to lose, I can tell you."

They went out of the smoking-room, turned to the left, and went into the hall. Then Castellan snatched his hand away from Eckstein's arm, took him by the shoulders, and pitched him forward into the middle of the semicircle of bluejackets, who were waiting for him, saying:

"That's your man, boys. Take him down to the pinnace, and put him on board. I'll take the consequences, and I think the owners will, too, when they know the facts."

Von Eckstein tried to shout, but a hand about half the size of a shoulder of mutton came down hard over his mouth and nose. Other hands, with grips like vices, picked him off his feet, and out he went, half stifled, along the yard, and up to the Railway Pier.

"Rather summary proceedings, weren't they, Castellan?"

Denis drew himself up, formally saluted his superior officer, and said, with a curious mixture of fun and seriousness in his voice:

"That man's the most dangerous German spy in the South of England, sir, and all's fair in war and the other thing. We've got him. In half an hour he'd have been aboard a fast yacht he's got here in the harbor, and across to Dieppe, with a portmanteau full of plans and photographs of our forts that would be worth millions in men and money to the people we've got to fight. I can't say it here, but you know why I know."

Captain Erskine nodded, and did his best to conceal an unofficial smile.

"That's right, Castellan," he said. "I'll take your word for it. Get that chap on board, lads, as quick as you can. We'll follow at once."

Ship's Corporal Sandy M'Grath, the huge Scotsman, whose great fist had stifled Count von Eckstein's attempt to cry out, touched his cap and said: "Awa' wi' him, boys," and out they went at a run. Then Erskine turned to Lennard, and said:

"We can do all this that you've given me on board the *Ithuriel.* It isn't quite regular, but in consideration of this, if you like to take a cruise, and see your own work done, I'll take the responsibility of inviting you, only mind, there will probably be some fighting."

Even as he spoke two deep dull bangs shook the atmosphere and the windows of the hotel shivered in their frames.

"I'll come," said Lennard. "They seem to have begun already."

"Begorra they have," said Denis Castellan, making a dash to the door. "Come on. If that's so, there'll be blood for supper tonight, and the sooner we're aboard the better."

The next moment the three were outside, and sprinting for the end of the Railway Pier for all they were worth.

Chapter VIII

FIRST BLOOD

When they got to the end of the Railway Pier where the pinnace was lying panting and puffing, a Flag-Lieutenant touched his cap to Erskine, took him by the arm and led him aside. He took an envelope out of his pocket and said, in a low tone:

"Here are your instructions, Erskine. They've jumped on us a bit more quickly than we thought they would, but the Commander-in-Chief trusts to you and your ship to do the needful. The position is this: one division of the Russian, German and Dutch fleets is making a combined attack on Hull and Newcastle. Two other divisions are going for the mouth of the Thames, and the North Sea Squadron is going to look after them. The French North Sea Squadron is making a rush on Dover, and will get very considerably pounded in the process. Two French fleets from Cherbourg and Brest are coming up Channel, and each of them has a screen of torpedo boats and destroyers. The Southern Fleet Reserve is concentrated here and at Portland. The Channel Fleet is outside, and we hope to get it in their rear, so that we'll have them between the ships and the forts. If we do, they'll have just about as hot a time of it as anybody wants.

"As far as we've been able to learn, the French are going to try Togo's tactics at Port Arthur, and rush Portsmouth with the small craft. You'll find that it's your business to look after them. Sink, smash and generally destroy. Go for everything you see. There isn't a craft of ours within twenty miles outside. Good-bye, and good luck to you!"

"Good-bye!" said Erskine, as they shook hands, "and if we don't come back, give my love to the Lords of the Admiralty and thank them for giving me the chance with the *Ithuriel.* Bye-bye!"

Their hands gripped again and the captain of the *Ithuriel* ran down the steps like a boy going to a picnic.

The pinnace gave a little squeak from its siren and sped away down the harbor between the two forts, in which the gunners were standing by the new fourteen-inch wire-wound guns, whose long chases were prevented from drooping after continuous discharge by an ingenious application of the principle of the cantilever bridge, invented by the creator of the *Ithuriel.* In the breech-chamber of each of them was a thousand-pound shell, carrying a bursting charge of five hundred pounds of an explosive which was an improvement on blasting gelatine, and the guns were capable of throwing these to a distance of twelve miles with precision. They were the most formidable weapons either ashore or afloat.

Just outside the harbor the pinnace swung round to the westward and in a few minutes stopped alongside the *Ithuriel.*

As far as Lennard could see she was neither cruiser nor destroyer nor submarine, but a sort of compound of all three. She did not appear to be a steamer because she had no funnels. She was not exactly a submarine because she had a signal-mast forward and carried five long, ugly-looking guns, three ahead and two astern, of a type that he had never seen before. Forward of the mast there was a conning-tower of oval shape, with the lesser curves fore and aft. The breech-ends of the guns were covered by a long hood of steel, apparently of great thickness, and that was all.

As soon as they got on board Erskine said to Lennard:

"Come into the conning-tower with me. I believe we can make use of this invention of yours at once. I've got a pretty well-fitted laboratory down below and we might have a try. But you must excuse me a moment, I will just run through this."

He opened the envelope containing his instructions, put them down on the little desk in front of him and then read a note that was enclosed with them.

"By Jove," he said, "they're pretty quick up at headquarters. You'll have to excuse me a minute or two, Mr. Lennard. Just stand on that side, will you, please? Close up, we haven't too much room here. Good-bye for the present."

In front of the desk and above the little steering-wheel there was a mahogany board studded with two sets of ivory buttons, disposed in two lines of six each. He touched one of these, and Lennard saw him disappear through the floor of the conning-tower. Within a few moments the portion of the floor upon which he had stood returned to its place, and Lennard said to himself:

"If the rest of her works like that, she ought to be a lovely study in engineering."

While Captain Erskine is communicating his instructions to his second in command, and arranging the details of the coming fight, there will be time to give a brief description of the craft on board of which Lennard so unexpectedly found himself, and which an invention of his own was destined to make even more formidable than it was.

To put it as briefly as possible, the *Ithuriel* was a combination of destroyer, cruiser, submarine and ram, and she had cost Erskine three years of hard work to think out. She was three hundred feet long, fifty feet broad, and thirty feet from her upper keel to her deck. This was of course an abnormal depth for a vessel of her length, but then the *Ithuriel* was quite an abnormal warship. One-third of her depth consisted of a sinking-chamber, protected by twelve-inch armor, and this chamber could be filled in a few minutes with four thousand tons of water. This is of course the same thing as saying she had two waterlines. The normal cruising line gave her a freeboard of ten feet. Above the sinking-tanks her vitals were protected by ten-inch armor. In short, as regards armor, she was an entire reversal of the ordinary type of warship, and she had the advantage of being impervious to torpedo attack. Loaded torpedoes had been fired at her and had burst like eggs against a wall, with no more effect than to make her heel over a few degrees to the other side. Submarines had attacked her and got their noses badly bruised in the process. It was, indeed, admitted by the experts of the Admiralty that under water she was impregnable.

Her propelling power consisted of four sets of engines, all well below the waterline. Three of these drove three propellers astern: the fourth drove a suction screw which revolved just underneath the ram. This was a mass of steel weighing fifty tons and curved upwards like the inverted beak of an eagle. Erskine had taken this idea from the Russian ice-breakers which had been designed by the Russian Admiral Makaroff and built at Elswick. The screw was protected by a steel grating of which the forward protecting girder completed the curve of the stem. Aft, there was a similar ram, weighing thirty tons and a like protection to the after-screws.

The driving power was derived from a combination of petrol and pulverized smokeless coal, treated with liquid oxygen, which made combustion practically perfect. There was no boilers or furnaces, only combustion chambers, and this fact made the carrying of the great weight of armor under the waterline possible. The speed of the *Ithuriel* was forty-five knots ahead when all four screws were driving and pulling, and thirty knots astern when they were reversed. Her total capacity was five thousand two hundred tons.

Behind the three forward guns was a dome-shaped conning-tower of nine-inch steel, hardened like the rest of the armor by an improvement on the Harvey process. Above the conning-tower were two searchlight projectors, both capable of throwing a clear ray to a distance of four miles and controlled from within the conning-tower.

"Well, I am afraid I have kept you waiting, Mr. Lennard," said Erskine, as the platform brought him up again into the conning-tower, in much shorter time than was necessary to make this needful description of what was probably the most formidable craft in the British Navy. "We're off now. I've fitted up half a dozen shells with that diabolical invention of yours. If we run across a battleship or a cruiser, we'll try them. I think our friends the enemy will find them somewhat of a paralyzer, and there's nothing like beginning pretty strong."

"Nothing like hitting them hard at first, and I hope that those things of mine will be what I think they are, and unless all my theories are quite wrong, I fancy you'll find them all right."

"They would be the first theories of yours that have gone wrong, Mr. Lennard," replied Erskine, "but anyhow, we shall soon see. I have put three of your shells in the forward guns. We'll try them there first, and if they're all right we'll use the other three. I've got the after guns loaded with my own shell, so if we come across anything big, we shall be able to try them against each other. At present, my instructions are to deal with the lighter craft only: destroyers and that sort of thing, you know."

"But don't you fire on them?" said Lennard. "What would happen if they got a torpedo under you?"

"Well," said Erskine, "as a matter of fact I don't think destroyers are worth shooting at. Our guns are meant for bigger game. But it's no good trying to explain things now. You'll see, pretty soon, and you'll learn more in half an hour than I could tell you in four hours."

They were clear of the harbor by this time and running out at about ten knots between the two old North and South Spithead forts on the top of each of which one of the new fourteen-inch thousand-pounders had been mounted on disappearing carriages.

"Now," he continued, "if we're going to find them anywhere, we shall find them here, or hereabouts. My orders are to smash everything that I can get at."

"Fairly comprehensive," said Lennard.

"Yes, Lennard, and it's an order that I'm going to fill. We may as well quicken up a bit now. You understand, Castellan is looking after the guns, and his sub., Mackenzie is communicating orders to my Chief Engineer, who looks after the speed."

"And the speed?" asked Lennard.

"I'll leave you to judge that when we get to business," said Erskine, putting his forefinger on one of the buttons on the left-hand side of the board as he spoke.

The next moment Lennard felt the rubber-covered floor of the conning-tower jump under his feet. All the coast lights were extinguished but there was a half-moon and he saw the outlines of the shore slip away faster behind them. The eastern heights of the Isle of Wight loomed up like a cloud and dropped away astern.

"Pretty fast, that," he said.

"Only twenty-five knots," replied Erskine, as he gave the steering-wheel a very gentle movement and swung the *Ithuriel's* head round to the eastward. "If these chaps are going to make a rush in the way Togo did at Port Arthur, they've got to do it between Selsey Bill and Nettlestone Point. If they're mad enough to try the other way between Round Tower Point and Hurst Castle, they'll get blown out of the water in very small pieces, so we needn't worry about them there. Our business is to keep them out of this side. Ah, look now, there are two or three of them there. See, ahead of the port bow. We'll tackle these gentlemen first."

Lennard looked out through the narrow semicircular window of six-inch crystal glass running across the front of the conning-tower, which was almost as strong as steel, and saw three little dark, moving spots on the half-moonlit water, about two miles ahead, stealing up in line abreast.

"Those chaps are trying to get in between the Spithead forts," said Erskine. "They're slowed down to almost nothing, waiting for the clouds to come over the moon, and then they'll make a dash for it. At least, they think they will. I don't."

As he spoke he gave another turn to the steering-wheel and touched another button. The *Ithuriel* leapt forward again and swung about three points to the eastward. In three minutes she was off Black Point, and this movement brought her into a straight line with the three destroyers. He gave the steering-wheel another half turn and her head swung round in a short quarter circle. He put his finger on to the bottom button on the right-hand side of the signal board and said to Lennard:

"Hold tight now, she's going."

Lennard held tight, for he felt the floor jump harder under him this time.

In the dim light he saw the nearest of the destroyers, as it seemed to him, rush towards them sideways. Erskine touched another button. A shudder ran through the fabric of the *Ithuriel* and her bow rose above five feet from the water. A couple of minutes later it hit the destroyer amidships, rolled her over, broke her in two like a log of wood, amidst a roar of crackling guns and a scream of escaping steam, went over her and headed for the next one.

Lennard clenched his teeth and said nothing. He was thinking too hard to say anything just then.

The second destroyer opened fire with her twelve-and six-pounders and dropped a couple of torpedoes as the *Ithuriel* rushed at her. The *Ithuriel* was now traveling at forty knots an hour. The torpedoes at thirty. The combined speed was therefore nearly a hundred statute miles an hour. Erskine saw the two white shapes drop into the water, their courses converging towards him. A half turn of the wheel to port swung the *Ithuriel* out and just cleared them. It was a fairly narrow shave, for one of them grated along her side, but the *Ithuriel* had no angles. The actual result was that one of the torpedoes deflected from its course, hit the other one and both exploded. A mountain of foam-crowned water rose up and the commander of the French destroyer congratulated himself on the annihilation of at least one of the English warships, but the next moment the grey-blue, almost invisible shape of the *Ithuriel* leapt up out of the semi-darkness, and her long pointed ram struck amidships, cut him down to the waterline, and almost before the two halves of his vessel had sunk the same fate had befallen the third destroyer.

"Well, what do you think of that?" said Erskine, as he touched a couple more buttons and the *Ithuriel* swung round to the eastward again.

"Well," said Lennard, slowly, "of course it's war, and those fellows were coming in to do all the damage they could. But it is just a bit terrible, for all that. It's just seven minutes since you rammed the first boat: you haven't fired a shot and there are three big destroyers and I suppose three hundred and fifty men at the bottom of the sea. Pretty awful, you know."

"My dear sir," replied Erskine, without looking round, "all war is awful and entirely horrible, and naval war is of course the most horrible of all. There is no chance for the defeated: my orders do not even allow me to pick up a man from one of those vessels. On the other hand, one must remember that if one of those destroyers had got in, they could have let go half a dozen torpedoes apiece among the ships of the Fleet Reserve, and perhaps half a dozen ships and five or six thousand men might have been at the bottom of the Solent by this time, and those torpedoes wouldn't have had any sentiment in them. Hallo, there's another!"

A long, black shape surmounted by a signal-mast and four funnels slid up and out of the darkness into a patch of moonlight lying on the water. Erskine gave a quarter turn to the wheel and touched the two buttons again. The *Ithuriel* swung round and ran down on her prey. The two fifteen-and the six twelve-pounder guns ahead and astern and on the broadside of the destroyer crackled out and a hail of shells came whistling across the water. A few of them struck the *Ithuriel,* glanced off and exploded.

"There," said Erskine, "they've knocked some of our nice new paint off. Now they're going to pay for it."

"Couldn't you give them a shot back?" said Lennard.

"Not worth it, my dear sir," said Erskine. "We keep our guns for bigger game. We haven't an angle that a shell would hit. You might just as well fire boiled peas at a hippopotamus as those little things at us. Of course a big shell square amidships would hurt us, but then she's so handy that I think I could stop it hitting her straight."

While he was speaking the *Ithuriel* got up to full speed again. Lennard shut his eyes. He felt a slight shock, and then a dull grinding. A crash of guns and a roar of escaping steam, and when he looked out again, the destroyer had disappeared. The next moment a blinding glare of light streamed across the water from the direction of Selsey.

"A big cruiser, or battleship," said Erskine. "French or German. Now we'll see what those shells of yours are made of."

Chapter IX

THE "FLYING FISH" APPEARS

A huge, black shape loomed up into the moonlight. As she came nearer Lennard could see that the vessel carried a big mast forward with a fighting-top, two funnels a little aft of it, and two other funnels a few feet forward of the after mast.

Erskine put his glasses up to his eyes and said:

"That's the *Dupleix,* one of the improved *Desaix* class. Steams twenty-four knots. I suppose she's been shepherding those destroyers that we've just finished with. I hope she hasn't seen what happened. If she thinks that they've got in all right, we've got her. She has a heavy fore and aft and broadside gunfire, two 6.4 guns ahead and astern and amidships, in pairs, and as I suppose they'll be using melinite shells, we shall get fits unless we take them unawares."

"And what does that mean?" asked Lennard.

"Show you in a minute," answered Erskine, touching three or four of the buttons on the right-hand side as he spoke.

Another shudder ran through the frame of the *Ithuriel* and Lennard felt the deck sink under his feet. If he hadn't had as good a head on him as he had, he would have said something, for the *Ithuriel* sank until her decks were almost awash. She jumped forward again now almost invisible, and circled round to the southeastward. A big cloud drifted across the moon and Erskine said:

"Thank God for that! We shall get her now."

Another quarter turn of the wheel brought the *Ithuriel's* head at right angles to the French cruiser's broadside. He took the transmitter of the telephone down from the hooks and said:

"Are you there, Castellan?"

"Yes. What's that big thing ahead there?"

"It's the *Dupleix.* Ready with your forward guns. I'm going to fire first, then ram. Stand by, center first, then starboard and port, and keep your eye on them. These are Mr. Lennard's shells and we want to see what they'll do. Are you ready?"

"Yes. When you like."

"Half speed, then, and tell Mackenzie to stand by and order full speed when I give the word. We shall want it in a jump."

"Very good, sir. Is that all?"

"Yes, that's all."

Erskine put the receiver back on the hooks.

"That's it. Now we'll try your shells. If they're what I think they are, we'll smash that fellow's top works into scrap-iron, and then we'll go for him."

"I think I see," said Lennard, "that's why you've half submerged her."

"Yes. The *Ithuriel* is designed to deal with both light and heavy craft. With the light ones, as you have seen, she just walked over them. Now, we've got something bigger to tackle, and if everything goes right that ship will be at the bottom of the sea in five minutes."

"Horrible," replied Lennard, "but I suppose it's necessary."

"Absolutely," said Erskine, taking the receiver down from the hooks. "If we didn't do it with them, they'd do it with us. That's war."

Lennard made no reply. He was looking hard at the now rapidly approaching shape of the big French cruiser, and when men are thinking hard, they don't usually say much.

The *Ithuriel* completed her quarter-circle and dead head on to the *Dupleix,* Erskine said, "Center gun ready, forward – fire. Port and starboard concentrate – fire."

There was no report – only a low, hissing sound – and then Lennard saw three flashes of bluish-green blaze out over the French cruiser.

"Hit her! I think those shells of yours got home," said Erskine between his clenched teeth. And then he added through the telephone, "Well aimed, Castellan! They all got there. Load up again – three more shots and I'm going to ram – quick now, and full speed ahead when you've fired."

"All ready!" came back over the telephone, "I've told Mackenzie that you'll want it."

"Good man," replied Erskine. "When I touch the button, you do the rest. Now – are you ready?"

"Yes."

"Let her have it – then full speed. Ah," Erskine continued, turning to Lennard, "he's shooting back."

The cruiser burst into a thunderstorm of smoke and flame and shell, but there was nothing to shoot at. Only three feet of freeboard would have been visible even in broad daylight. The signal mast had been telescoped. There was nothing but the deck, the guns and the conning-tower to be seen. The shells screamed through the air a good ten feet over her and incidentally wrecked the Marine Hotel on Selsey Bill.

Erskine pressed the top button on the right-hand side three times. The smokeless, nameless guns spoke again, and again the three flashes of blue-green flame broke out on the Frenchman's decks.

"Good enough," said Erskine, taking the transmitter down from the hooks again. "Now, Mr. Lennard, just come for'ard and watch."

Lennard crept up beside him and took the glasses.

"Down guns – full speed ahead – going to ram," said Erskine, quietly, into the telephone.

To his utter astonishment, Lennard saw the three big guns sink down under the deck and the steel hoods move forward and cover the emplacements. The floor of the conning-tower jumped under his feet again and the huge shape of the French cruiser seemed to rush towards him. There was a roar of artillery, a thunder of 6.4 guns, a crash of bursting shells, a shudder and a shock, and the fifty-ton ram of the *Ithuriel* hit her forward of the conning-tower and went through the two-inch armor belt as a knife would go through a piece of paper. The big cruiser stopped as an animal on land does, struck by a bullet in its vitals, or a whale when the lance is driven home. Half her officers and men were lying about the decks asphyxiated by Lennard's shells. The after barbette swung round, and at the same moment, or perhaps half a minute before, Erskine touched two other buttons in rapid succession. The *Dupleix* lurched down on the starboard side, the two big guns went off and hit the water. Erskine touched another button, and the *Ithuriel* ran back from her victim. A minute later the French cruiser heeled over and sank.

"Good God, how did you do that?" said Lennard, looking round at him with eyes rather more wide open than usual.

"That's the effect of the suction screw," replied Erskine. "I got the idea from the Russian ice-breaker, the *Yermack.* The old idea was just main strength and stupidity, charge the ice and break through if you could. The better idea was to suck the water away from under the ice and go over it – that's what we've done. I rammed that chap, pulled the water away from under him, and, of course, he's gone down."

He gave the wheel a quarter-turn to starboard, took down the transmitter and said: "Full speed again – in two minutes, three quarters and then half."

"But surely," exclaimed Lennard, "you can do something to help those poor fellows. Are you going to leave them all to drown?"

"I have no orders, except to sink and destroy," replied Erskine between his teeth. "You must remember that this is a war of one country against a continent, and of one fleet against four. Ah, there's another! A third-class cruiser – I think I know her, she's the old *Leger* – they must have thought they had an easy job of it if they sent her here. Low free board, not worth shooting at. We'll go over her. No armor – what idiots they are to put a thing like that into the fighting line!"

He took the transmitter down and said:

"Stand by there, Castellan! Get your pumps to work, and I shall want full speed ahead – I'm going to run that old croak down – hurry up."

He put the transmitter back on the hooks and presently Lennard saw the bows of the *Ithuriel* rise quickly out of the water. The doomed vessel in front of them was a long, low-lying French torpedo-catcher, with one big funnel between two signal-masts, hopelessly out of date, and evidently intended only to go in and take her share of the spoils. Erskine switched off the searchlight, called for full speed ahead and then with clenched teeth and set eyes, he sent the *Ithuriel* flying at her victim.

Within five minutes it was all over. The fifty-ton ram rose over the *Leger's* side, crushed it down into the water, ground its way through her, cut her in half and went on.

"That ship ought to have been on the scrap-heap ten years ago," said Erskine as he signaled for half-speed and swung the *Ithuriel* round to the westward.

"She's got a scrap-heap all to herself now, I suppose," said Lennard, with a bit of a check in his voice. "I've no doubt, as you say, this sort of thing may be necessary, but my personal opinion of it is that it's damnable."

"Exactly my opinion too," said Erskine, "but it has to be done."

The next instant, Lennard heard a sound such as he had never heard before. It was a smothered rumble which seemed to come out of the depths, then there came a shock which flung him off his feet, and shot him against the opposite wall of the conning-tower. The *Ithuriel* heeled over to port, a huge volume of water rose on her starboard side and burst into a torrent over her decks, then she righted.

Erskine, holding on hard to the iron table to which the signaling board was bolted, saved himself from a fall.

"I hope you're not hurt, Mr. Lennard," said he, looking round, "that was a submarine. Let a torpedo go at us, I suppose, and didn't know they were hitting twelve-inch armor."

"It's all right," said Lennard, picking himself up. "Only a bruise or two; nothing broken. It seems to me that this new naval warfare of yours is going to get a bit exciting."

"Yes," said Erskine, "I think it is. Halloa, Great Cæsar! That must be that infernal invention of Castellan's brother's; the thing he sold to the Germans – the sweep!"

As he spoke a grey shape leapt up out of the water and began to circle over the *Ithuriel.* He snatched the transmitter from the hooks, and said, in quick, clear tones:

"Castellan – sink – quick, quick as you can."

The pumps of the *Ithuriel* worked furiously the next moment. Lennard held his breath as he saw the waves rise up over the decks.

"Full speed ahead again, and dive," said Erskine into the transmitter. "Hold tight, Lennard."

The floor of the conning-tower took an angle of about sixty degrees, and Lennard gripped the holdfasts, of which there were two on each wall of the tower. He heard a rush of overwhelming waters – then came darkness. The *Ithuriel* rushed forward at her highest speed. Then something hit the sea, and a quick succession of shocks sent a shudder through the vessel.

"I thought so," said Erskine. "That's John Castellan's combined airship and submarine right enough, and that was an aërial torpedo. If it had hit us when we were above water, we should have been where those French chaps are now. You're quite right, this sort of naval warfare is getting rather exciting."

Chapter X

FIRST BLOWS FROM THE AIR

The *Flying Fish,* the prototype of the extraordinary craft which played such a terrible part in the invasion of England, was a magnified reproduction, with improvements which suggested themselves during construction, of the model whose performances had so astonished the Kaiser at Potsdam. She was shaped exactly like her namesake of the deep, upon which, indeed, her inventor had modeled her. She was one hundred and fifty feet long and twenty feet broad by twenty-five feet deep in her widest part, which, as she was fish-shaped, was considerably forward of her center.

She was built of a newly-discovered compound, something like papier-mâché, as hard and rigid as steel, with only about one-tenth the weight. Her engines were of the simplest description in spite of the fact that they developed enormous power. They consisted merely of cylinders into which, by an automatic mechanism, two drops of liquid were brought every second. These liquids when joined produced a gas of enormously expansive power, more than a hundred times that of steam, which actuated the pistons. There were sixteen of these cylinders, and the pistons all connected with a small engine invented by Castellan, which he called an accelerator. By means of this device he could regulate the speed of the propellers which drove the vessel under water and in the air from sixty up to two thousand revolutions a minute.

The *Flying Fish* was driven by nine propellers, three of these, four-bladed and six feet diameter, revolved a little forward amidships on either side under what might be called the fins. These fins collapsed close against the sides of the vessel when under water and expanded to a spread of twenty feet when she took the air. They worked on a pivot and could be inclined either way from the horizontal to an angle of thirty degrees. Midway between the end of these and the stern was a smaller pair with one driving screw. The eighth screw was an ordinary propeller at the stern, but the outside portion of the shaft worked on a ball and socket joint so that it could be used for both steering and driving purposes. It was in fact the tail of the *Flying Fish.* Steering in the air was effected by means of a vertical fin placed right aft.

She was submerged as the *Ithuriel* was, by pumping water into the lower part of her hull. When these chambers were empty she floated like a cork. The difference between swimming and flying was merely the difference between the revolutions of the screws and the inclination of the fins. A thousand raised her from the water: twelve hundred gave her twenty-five or thirty miles an hour through the air: fifteen hundred gave her fifty, and two thousand gave her eighty to a hundred, according to the state of the atmosphere.

Her armament consisted of four torpedo tubes which swung at any angle from the horizontal to the vertical and so were capable of use both under water and in the air. They discharged a small, insignificant-looking torpedo containing twenty pounds of an explosive, discovered almost accidentally by Castellan and known only to himself, the German Emperor, the Chancellor, and the Commander-in-Chief. It was this which he had used in tiny quantities in the experiment at Potsdam. Its action was so terrific that it did not rend or crack metal or stone which it struck. It overcame the chemical forces by which the substance was held together and reduced them to gas and powder.

And now, after this somewhat formal but necessary description of the most destructive fighting-machine ever created we can proceed with the story.

There were twenty *Flying Fishes* attached to the Allied Forces, all of them under the command of German engineers, with the exception of the original *Flying Fish.* Two of these were attached to the three squadrons which were attacking Hull, Newcastle and Dover: three had been detailed for the attack on Portsmouth: two more to Plymouth, two to Bristol and Liverpool respectively, on which combined cruiser and torpedo attacks were to be made, and two supported by a small swift cruiser and torpedo flotilla for an assault on Cardiff, in order if possible to terrorize that city into submission and so obtain what may be called the life-blood of a modern navy. The rest, in case of accidents to any of these, were reserved for the final attack on London.

When the *Ithuriel* disappeared and his torpedo struck a piece of floating wreckage and exploded with a terrific shock, John Castellan, standing in the conning-tower directing the movements of the *Flying Fish,* naturally concluded that he had destroyed a British submarine scout. He knew of the existence, but nothing of the real powers of the *Ithuriel.* The only foreigner who knew that was Captain Count Karl von Eckstein, and he was locked safely in a cabin on board her.

He had been searching the under-waters between Nettlestone Point and Hayling Island for hours on the look-out for British submarines and torpedo scouts, and had found nothing, therefore he was ignorant of the destruction which the *Ithuriel* had already wrought, and as, of course, he had heard no firing under the water, he believed that the three destroyers supported by the *Dupleix* and *Leger* had succeeded in slipping through the entrance to Spithead.

He knew that a second flotilla of six destroyers with three swift second-class cruisers were following in to complete the work, which by this time should have begun, and that after them came the main French squadron, consisting of six first-class battleships with a screen of ten first and five second-class cruisers, the work of which would be to maintain a blockade against any relieving force, after the submarines and destroyers had sunk and crippled the ships of the Fleet Reserve and cut the connections of the contact mines.

He knew also that the *See Adler,* which was *Flying Fish II.,* was waiting about the Needles to attack Hurst Castle and the forts on the Isle of

Wight side, preparatory to a rush of two battleships and three cruisers through the narrows, while another was lurking under Hayling Island ready to take the air and rain destruction on the forts of Portsmouth before the fight became general.

What thoroughly surprised him, however, was the absolute silence and inaction of the British. True, two shots had been fired, but whether from fort or warship, and with what intent, he hadn't the remotest notion. The hour arranged upon for the general assault was fast approaching. The British must be aware that an attack would be made, and yet there was not so much as a second-class torpedo boat to be seen outside Spithead. This puzzled him, so he decided to go and investigate for himself. He took up a speaking-tube and said to his Lieutenant, M'Carthy – one of too many renegade Irishmen who in the terrible times that were to come joined their country's enemies as Lynch and his traitors had done in the Boer War:

"I don't quite make it out, M'Carthy. We'll go down and get under – it's about time the fun began – and I haven't heard a shot fired or seen an English ship except that submarine we smashed. My orders are for twelve o'clock, and I'm going to obey them."

There was one more device on board the *Flying Fish* which should be described in order that her wonderful maneuvering under water may be understood. Just in front of the steering-wheel in the conning-tower was a square glass box measuring a foot in the side, and in the center of this, attached to top and bottom by slender films of asbestos, was a needle ten inches long, so hung that it could turn and dip in any direction. The forward half of this needle was made of highly magnetized steel, and the other of aluminum which exactly counter-balanced it. The glass case was completely insulated and therefore the extremely sensitive needle was unaffected by any of the steel parts used in the construction of the vessel. But let any other vessel, save of course a wooden ship, come within a thousand yards, the needle began to tremble and sway, and the nearer the *Flying Fish* approached it, the steadier it became and the more directly it pointed towards the object. If the vessel was on the surface, it of course pointed upward: if it was a submarine, it pointed either level or downwards with unerring precision. This needle was, in fact, the eyes of the *Flying Fish* when she was under water.

Castellan swung her head round to the northwest and dropped gently on to the water about midway between Selsey Bill and the Isle of Wight. Then the *Flying Fish* folded her wings and sank to a depth of twenty feet. Then, at a speed of ten knots, she worked her way in a zigzag course back and forth across the narrowing waters, up the channel towards Portsmouth.

To his surprise, the needle remained steady, showing that there was neither submarine nor torpedo boat near. This meant, as far as he could see, that the main approach to the greatest naval fortress in England had been left unguarded, a fact so extraordinary as to be exceedingly suspicious. His water-ray apparatus, a recent development of the X-rays which enabled him to see under water for a distance of fifty yards, had detected no contact mines, and yet Spithead ought to be enstrewn with them, just as it ought to have been swarming with submarines and destroyers. There must be some deep meaning to such apparently incomprehensible neglect, but what was it?

If his brother Denis had not happened to recognize Captain Count Karl von Eckstein and haled him so unceremoniously on board the *Ithuriel*, and if his portmanteau full of papers had been got on board a French warship, instead of being left for the inspection of the British Admiralty, that reason would have been made very plain to him.

Completely mystified, and fearing that either he was going into some trap or that some unforeseen disaster had happened, he swung round, ran out past the forts and rose into the air again. When he had reached the height of about a thousand feet, three rockets rose into the air and burst into three showers of stars, one red, one white, and the other blue. It was the Tricolor in the air, and the signal from the French Admiral to commence the attack. Castellan's orders were to cripple or sink the battleships of the Reserve Fleet which was moored in two divisions in Spithead and the Solent.

The Spithead Division lay in column of line abreast between Gilkicker Point and Ryde Pier. It consisted of the *Formidable*, *Irresistible*, *Implacable*, *Majestic* and *Magnificent*, and the cruisers *Hogue*, *Sutlej*, *Ariadne*, *Argonaut*, *Diadem* and *Hawke*. The western Division consisted of the battleships *Prince George*, *Victoria*, *Jupiter*, *Mars* and *Hannibal*, and the cruisers *Amphitrite*, *Spartiate*, *Andromeda*, *Europa*, *Niobe*, *Blenheim*, and *Blake*.

It had of course been perfectly easy for Castellan to mark the position of the two squadrons from the air, and he knew that though they were comparatively old vessels they were quite powerful enough, with the assistance of the shore batteries, to hold even Admiral Durenne's splendid fleet until the Channel Fleet, which for the time being seemed to have vanished from the face of the waters, came up and took the French in the rear.

In such a case, the finest fleet of France would be like a nut in a vice, and that was the reason for the remorseless orders which had been given to him, orders which he was prepared to carry out to the letter, in spite of the appalling loss of life which they entailed; for, as the *Flying Fish* sank down into the water, he thought of that swimming race in Clifden Bay and of the girl whose marriage with himself, willing or unwilling, was to be one of the terms of peace when the British Navy lay shattered round her shores, and the millions of the Leagued Nations had trampled the land forces of Britain into submission.

Just as she touched the water a brilliant flash of pink flame leapt up from the eastern fort on the Hillsea Lines, followed by a sharp crash which shook the atmosphere. A thin ray of light fell from the clouds, then came a quick succession of flashes moving in the direction of the great fort on Portsdown, until two rose in quick succession from Portsdown itself, and almost at the same moment another from Hurst Castle, and yet another from the direction of Fort Victoria.

"God bless my soul, what's that?" exclaimed the Commander-in-Chief, Admiral Sir Compton Domville, who had just completed his final inspection of the defenses of Portsmouth Harbor, and was standing on the roof of Southsea Castle, taking a general look round before going back to headquarters. "Here, Markham," he said, turning to the Commander of the Fort, "just telephone up to Portsdown at once and ask them what they're up to."

An orderly instantly dived below to the telephone room. The Fort Commander took Sir Compton aside and said in a low voice:

"I am afraid, sir, that the forts are being attacked from the air."

"What's that?" replied Sir Compton, with a start. "Do you mean that infernal thing that Erskine and Castellan and the watch of the *Cormorant* saw in the North Sea?"

"Yes, sir," was the reply. "There is no reason why the enemy should not possess a whole fleet of these craft by this time, and naturally they would act in concert with the attack of the French Fleet. I've heard rumors of a terrible new explosive they've got, too, which shatters steel into splinters and poisons everyone within a dozen yards of it. If that's true and they're dropping it on the forts, they'll probably smash the guns as well. For heaven's sake, sir, let me beg of you to go back at once to headquarters! It will probably be our turn next. You will be safe there, for they're not likely to waste their shells on Government buildings."

"Well, I suppose I shall be of more use there," growled Sir Compton.

At this moment the orderly returned, looking rather scared. He saluted and said:

"If you please, sir, they've tried Portsdown and all the Hillsea forts and can't get an answer."

"Good heavens!" said the Commander-in-Chief, "that looks almost as if you were right, Markham. Signal to Squadron A to up-anchor at once and telephone to Squadron B to do the same. Telephone Gilkicker to turn all searchlights on. Now I must be off and have a talk with General Hamilton."

He ran down to his pinnace and went away full speed for the harbor, but before he reached the pier another flash burst out from the direction of Fort Gilkicker, followed by a terrific roar. To those standing on the top of Southsea Castle the fort seemed turned into a volcano, spouting flame and clouds of smoke, in the midst of which they could see for an instant whirling shapes, most of which would probably be the remains of the gallant defenders, hurled into eternity before they had a chance of firing a shot at the invaders. The huge guns roared for the first and last time in the war, and the great projectiles plunged aimlessly among the ships of the squadron, carrying wreck and ruin along the line.

"Our turn now, I suppose," said the Fort Commander, quietly, as he looked up and by a chance gleam of moonlight through the breaking clouds saw a dim grey, winged shape drift across the harbor entrance.

They were the last words he ever spoke, for the next moment the roof crumbled under his feet, and his body was scattered in fragments through the air, and in that moment Portsmouth had ceased to be a fortified stronghold.

Chapter XI

THE TRAGEDY OF THE TWO SQUADRONS

It takes a good deal to shake the nerves of British naval officer or seaman, but those on board the ships of the Spithead Squadron would have been something more than human if they could have viewed the appalling happenings of the last few terrible minutes with their accustomed coolness. They were ready to fight anything on the face of the waters or under them, but an enemy in the air who could rain down shells, a couple of which were sufficient to destroy the most powerful forts in the world, and who could not be hit back, was another matter.

It was a bitter truth, but there was no denying it. The events of the last ten years had clearly proved that a day must come when the flying machine would be used as an engine of war, and now that day had come – and the fighting flying machine was in the hands of the enemy.

The anchors were torn from the ground, signals were flashed from the flagship, the *Prince George*, and within four minutes the squadron was under way to the southeastward. After what had happened the Admiral in command promptly and rightly decided that to keep his ships cramped up in the narrow waters was only to court further disaster. His place was now the open sea, and a general fleet action offered the only means of preventing an occupation of almost defenseless Portsmouth, and the landing of hostile troops in the very heart of England's southern defenses.

Fifteen first-class torpedo boats and ten destroyers ran out from the Hampshire and Isle of Wight coasts, ran through the ships, and spread themselves out in a wide curve ahead, and at the same time twenty submarines crept out from the harbor and set to work laying contact mines in the appointed fields across the harbor mouth and from shore to shore behind the Spithead forts.

But the squadron had not steamed a mile beyond the forts before a series of frightful disasters overtook them. First, a huge column of water rose under the stern of the *Jupiter*. The great ship stopped and shuddered like a stricken animal, and began to settle down stern first. Instantly the *Mars* and *Victorious* which were on either side of her slowed down, their boats splashed into the water and set to work to rescue those who managed to get clear of the sinking ship.

But even while this was being done, the *Banshee*, the *Flying Fish* which had destroyed the forts, had taken up her position a thousand feet above the doomed squadron. A shell dropped upon the deck of the *Spartiate*, almost amidships. The pink flash blazed out between her two midship funnels. They crumpled up as if they had been made of brown paper. The six-inch armored casemates on either side seemed to crumble away. The four-inch steel deck gaped and split as though it had been made of matchboard. Then the *Banshee* dropped to within five hundred feet and let go another shell almost in the same place. A terrific explosion burst out in the very vitals of the stricken ship, and the great cruiser seemed to split asunder. A vast volume of mingled smoke and flame and steam rose up, and when it rolled away, the *Spartiate* had almost vanished.

But that was the last act of destruction that the *Banshee* was destined to accomplish. That moment the moon sailed out into a patch of clear sky. Every eye in the squadron was turned upward. There was the airship plainly visible. Her captain instantly saw his danger and quickened up his engines, but it was too late. He was followed by a hurricane of shells from the three-pound quick-firers in the upper tops of the battleships. Then came an explosion in mid-air which seemed to shake the very firmament itself. She had fifty or sixty of the terrible shells which had wrought so much havoc on board, and as a dozen shells pierced her hull and burst, they too exploded with the shock. A vast blaze of pink flame shone out.

"Talk about going to glory in a blue flame," said Seaman Gunner Tompkins, who had aimed one of the guns in the fore-top of the *Hannibal*, and of course, like everybody else, piously believed that his was one of the shells that got there. "That chap's gone to t'other place in a red'un. War's war, but I don't hold with that sort of fighting; it doesn't give a man a chance. Torpedoes is bad enough, Gawd knows –"

The words were hardly out of his mouth when a shock and a shudder ran through the mighty fabric of the battleship. The water rose in a foam-clad mountain under her starboard quarter. She heeled over to port, and then rolled back to starboard and began to settle.

"Torpedoed, by George! What did I tell you?" gasped Gunner Tompkins. The next moment a lurch of the ship hurled him and his mates far out into the water.

Even as his ship went down, Captain Barclay managed to signal to the other ships, "Don't wait – get out." And when her shattered hull rested on the bottom, the gallant signal was still flying from the upper yard.

It was obvious that the one chance of escaping their terrible unseen foe was to obey the signal. By this time crowds of small craft of every description had come off from both shores to the rescue of those who had gone down with the ships, so the Admiral did what was the most practical thing to do under the circumstances – he dropped his own boats, each with a crew, and ordered the *Victorious* and *Mars* to do the same, and then gave the signal for full speed ahead. The great engines panted and throbbed, and the squadron moved forward with ever-increasing speed, the cruisers and destroyers, according to signal, running ahead of the battleships; but before full speed was reached, the *Mars* was struck under the stern, stopped, shuddered, and went down with a mighty lurch.

This last misfortune convinced the Admiral that the destruction of his battleships could not be the work of any ordinary submarine, for at the time the *Mars* was struck she was steaming fifteen knots and the underwater speed of the best submarine was only twelve, saving only the *Ithuriel*, and she did not use torpedoes. The two remaining battleships had now reached seventeen knots, which was their best speed. The cruisers and their consorts were already disappearing round Foreland.

There was some hope that they might escape the assaults of the mysterious and invisible enemy now that the airship had been destroyed, but unless the submarine had exhausted her torpedoes, or some accident had happened to her, there was very little for the *Prince George* and the *Victorious,* and so it turned out. Castellan's strict orders had been to confine his attentions to the battleships, and he obeyed his pitiless instructions to the letter. First the *Victorious* and then the flagship, smitten by an unseen and irresistible bolt in their weakest parts, succumbed to the great gaping wounds torn in the thin under-plating, reeled once or twice to and fro like leviathans struggling for life, and went down. And so for the time being, at least, ended the awful work of the *Flying Fish.*

Leaving the cruisers and smaller craft to continue their dash for the open Channel, we must now look westward.

When Vice-Admiral Codrington, who was flying his flag on the *Irresistible,* saw the flashes along the Hillsea ridge and Portsdown height and heard the roar of the explosions, he at once up-anchor and got his squadron under way. Then came the appallingly swift destruction of Hurst Castle and Fort Victoria. Like all good sailors, he was a man of instant decision. His orders were to guard the entrance to the Solent, and the destruction of the forts made it impossible for him to do this inside. How that destruction had been wrought, he had of course no idea, beyond a guess that the destroying agent must have come from the air, since it could not have come from sea or land without provoking a very vigorous reply from the forts. Instead of that they had simply blown up without firing a shot.

He therefore decided to steam out through the narrow channel between Hurst Castle and the Isle of Wight as quickly as possible.

It was a risky thing to do at night and at full speed, for the Channel and the entrance to it was strewn with contact mines, but one of the principal businesses of the British Navy is to take risks where necessary, so he put his own ship at the head of the long line, and with a mine chart in front of him went ahead at eighteen knots.

When Captain Adolph Frenkel, who was in command of the *See Adler,* saw the column of warships twining and wriggling its way out through the Channel, each ship handled with consummate skill and keeping its position exactly, he could not repress an admiring "Ach!" Still it was not his business to admire, but destroy.

He rose to a thousand feet, swung round to the northeastward until the whole line had passed beneath him, and then quickened up and dropped to seven hundred feet, swung round again and crept up over the *Hogue*, which was bringing up the rear. When he was just over her fore part, he let go a shell, which dropped between the conning-tower and the forward barbette.

The navigating bridge vanished; the twelve-inch armored conning-tower cracked like an eggshell; the barbette collapsed like the crust of a loaf, and the big 9.2 gun lurched backwards and lay with its muzzle staring helplessly at the clouds. The deck crumpled up as though it had been burned parchment, and the ammunition for the 9.2 and the forward six-inch guns which had been placed ready for action exploded, blowing the whole of the upper forepart of the vessel into scrap-iron.

But an even worse disaster than this was to befall the great twelve-thousand-ton cruiser. Her steering gear was, of course, shattered. Uncontrolled and uncontrollable, she swung swiftly round to starboard, struck a mine, and inside three minutes she was lying on the mud.

Almost at the moment of the first explosion, the beams of twenty searchlights leapt up into the air, and in the midst of the broad white glare hundreds of keen angry eyes saw a winged shape darting up into the air, heading southward as though it would cross the Isle of Wight over Yarmouth. Almost simultaneously, every gun from the tops of the battleships spoke, and a storm of shells rent the air.

But Captain Frenkel had already seen his mistake. The *See Adler's* wings were inclined at an angle of twenty degrees, her propellers were revolving at their utmost velocity, and at a speed of nearly a hundred miles an hour, she took the Isle of Wight in a leap. She slowed down rapidly over Freshwater Bay. Captain Frenkel took a careful observation of the position and course of the squadron, dropped into the water, folded his wings and crept round the Needles with his conning-tower just awash, and lay in wait for his prey about two miles off the Needles.

The huge black hull of the *Irresistible* was only a couple of hundred yards away. He instantly sank and turned on his water-ray. As the flagship passed within forty yards he let go his first torpedo. It hit her sternpost, smashed her rudder and propellers, and tore a great hole in her run. The steel monster stopped, shuddered, and slid sternward with her mighty ram high in the air into the depths of the smooth grey sea.

There is no need to repeat the ghastly story which has already been told – the story of the swift and pitiless destruction of these miracles of human skill, huge in size and mighty in armament and manned by the bravest men on land or sea, by a foe puny in size but of awful potentiality. It was a fight, if fight it could be called, between the visible and the invisible, and it could only have one end. Battleship after battleship received her death-wound, and went down without being able to fire a shot in defense, until the *Magnificent,* smitten in the side under her boilers, blew up and sank amidst a cloud of steam and foam, and the Western Squadron had met the fate of the Eastern.

While this tragedy was being enacted, the cruisers scattered in all directions and headed for the open at their highest speed. It was a bitter necessity, and it was bitterly felt by every man and boy on board them; but the captains knew that to stop and attempt the rescue of even some of their comrades meant losing the ships which it was their duty at all costs to preserve, and so they took the only possible chance to escape from this terrible unseen foe which struck out of the silence and the darkness with such awful effect.

But despite the tremendous disaster which had befallen the Reserve Fleet, the work of death and destruction was by no means all on one side. When he sank the *Leger,* Erskine had done a great deal more damage to the enemy than he knew, for she had been sent not for fighting purposes, but as a dépôt ship for the *Flying Fishes,* from which they could renew their torpedoes and the gas cylinders which furnished their driving power. Being a light craft, she was to take up an agreed position off Bracklesham Bay three miles to the northwest of Selsey Bill, the loneliest and shallowest part of the coast, with all lights out, ready to supply all that was wanted or to make any repairs that might be necessary. Her sinking, therefore, deprived John Castellan's craft of their base.

After the *Dupleix* had gone down, the *Ithuriel* rose again, and Erskine said to Lennard:

"There must be more of them outside, they wouldn't be such fools as to rush Portsmouth with three destroyers and a couple of cruisers. We'd better go on and reconnoiter."

The *Ithuriel* ran out southeastward at twenty knots in a series of broad curves, and she was just beginning to make the fourth of these when six black shapes crowned with wreaths of smoke loomed up out of the semi-darkness.

"Thought so – destroyers," said Erskine. "Yes, and look there, behind them – cruiser supports, three of them – these are for the second rush. Coming up pretty fast, too; they'll be there in half an hour. We shall have something to say about that. Hold on, Lennard."

"Same tactics, I suppose," said Lennard.

"Yes," replied Erskine, taking down the receiver. "Are you there, Castellan? All right. We've six more destroyers to get rid of. Full speed ahead, as soon as you like – guns all ready, I suppose? Good – go ahead."

The *Ithuriel* was now about two miles to the westward and about a mile in front of the line of destroyers, which just gave her room to get up full speed. As she gathered way, Lennard saw the nose of the great ram rise slowly out of the water. The destroyer's guns crackled, but it is not easy to hit a low-lying object moving at fifty miles an hour, end on, when you are yourself moving nearly twenty-five. Just the same thing happened as before. The point of the ram passed over the destroyer's bows, crumpled them up and crushed them down, and the *Ithuriel* rushed on over the sinking wreck, swerved a quarter turn, and bore down on her next victim. It was all over in ten minutes. The *Ithuriel* rushed hither and thither among the destroyers like some leviathan of the deep. A crash, a swift grinding scrape, and a mass of crumpled steel was dropping to the bottom of the Channel.

While the attack on the destroyers was taking place, the cruisers were only half a mile away. Their captains had found themselves in curiously difficult positions. The destroyers were so close together, and the movements of this strange monster which was running them down so rapidly, that if they opened fire they were more likely to hit their own vessels than it, but when the last had gone down, every available gun spoke, and a hurricane of shells, large and small, plowed up the sea where the *Ithuriel had* been. After the first volley, the captains looked at their officers and the officers looked at the captains, and said things which strained the capabilities of the French language to the utmost. The monster had vanished.

The fact was that Erskine had foreseen that storm of shell, and the pumps had been working hard while the ramming was going on. The result was that the *Ithuriel* sank almost as soon as her last victim, and in thirty seconds there was nothing to shoot at.

"I shall ram those chaps from underneath," he said. "They've too many guns for a shooting match."

He reduced the speed to thirty knots, rose for a moment till the conning-tower was just above the water, took his bearings, sank, called for full speed, and in four minutes the ram crashed into the *Alger's* stern, carried away her sternpost and rudder, and smashed her propellers. The *Ithuriel* passed on as if she had hit a log of wood and knocked it aside. A slight turn of the steering-wheel, and within four minutes the ram was buried in the vitals of the *Suchet.* Then the *Ithuriel* reversed engines, the fore screw sucked the water away, and the cruiser slid off the ram as she might have done off a rock. As she went down, the *Ithuriel* rose to the surface. The third cruiser, the *Davout,* was half a mile away. She had changed her course and was evidently making frantic efforts to get back to sea.

"Going to warn the fleet, are you, my friend?" said Erskine, between his teeth. "Not if I know it!"

He asked for full speed again and the terror-stricken Frenchmen saw the monster, just visible on the surface of the water, flying towards them in the midst of a cloud of spray. A sheep might as well have tried to escape from a tiger. Many of the crew flung themselves overboard in the madness of despair. There was a shock and a grinding crash, and the ram bored its way twenty feet into the unarmored quarter. Then the *Ithuriel's* screws dragged her free, and the *Davout* followed her sisters to the bottom of the Channel.

Chapter XII

HOW LONDON TOOK THE NEWS

The awaking of England on the morning of the twenty-sixth of November was like the awaking of a man from a nightmare. Everyone who slept had gone to sleep with one word humming in his brain – war – and war at home, that was the terrible thought which robbed so many millions of eyes of sleep. But even those who slept did not do so for long.

At a quarter to one a sub-editor ran into the room of the chief News Editor of the *Daily Telegraph,* without even the ceremony of a knock.

"What on earth's the matter, Johnson?" exclaimed the editor. "Seen a ghost?"

"Worse than that, sir. Read this!" said the sub-editor, in a shaking voice, throwing the slip down on the desk.

"My God, what's this?" said the editor, as he ran his eye along the slip. "'Portsmouth bombarded from the air. Hillsea, Portsmouth, Gilkicker and Southsea Castle destroyed. Practically defenseless. Fleet Reserve Squadrons sailing.'"

The words were hardly out of his mouth before another man came running in with a slip. "'*Jupiter* and *Hannibal* torpedoed by submarine. *Spartiate* blown up by aërial torpedo.'" Then there came a gap, as though the men at the other end had heard of more news, then followed – "'*Mars, Prince George, Victorious,* all torpedoed. Cruisers escaped to sea. No news of *Ithuriel,* no torpedo attack up to present.'"

"Oh, that's awful," gasped the editor, and then the professional instinct reasserted itself, for he continued, handing the slip back: "Rush out an edition straight away, Johnson. Anything, if it's only a half-sheet – get it on the streets as quick as you can – there'll be plenty of people about still. If anything else comes bring it up."

In less than a quarter of an hour a crowd of newsboys were fighting in the passage for copies of the single sheet which contained the momentous news, just as it had come over the wire. The *Daily Telegraph* was just five minutes ahead, but within half an hour every London paper, morning and evening, and all the great provincial journals had rushed out their midnight specials, and from end to end of England and Scotland, and away to South Wales, and over the narrow seas to Dublin and Cork, the shrill screams of the newsboys, and the hoarse, raucous howls of the newsmen were spreading the terrible tidings over the land. What the beacon fires were in the days of the Armada, these humble heralds of Fate were in the twentieth century.

"War begun – Portsmouth destroyed – Fleet sunk."

The six terrible words were not quite exact, of course, but they were near enough to the truth to sound like the voice of Fate in the ears of the millions whose fathers and fathers' fathers back through six generations had never had their midnight rest so rudely broken.

Lights gleamed out of darkened windows, and front doors were flung open in street after street, as the war-cry echoed down it. Any coin that came first to hand, from a penny to a sovereign, was eagerly offered for the single, hurriedly-printed sheets, but the business instincts of the newsboys rose superior to the crisis, and nothing less than a shilling was accepted. Streams of men and boys on bicycles with great bags of specials slung on their backs went tearing away, head down and pedals whirling, north, south, east and west into the suburbs. Newsagents flung their shops open, and in a few minutes were besieged by eager, anxious crowds, fighting for the first copies. There was no more sleep for man or woman in London that night, though the children slept on in happy unconsciousness of what the morrow was to bring forth.

What happened in London was happening almost simultaneously all over the kingdom. For more than a hundred years the British people had worked and played and slept in serene security, first behind its wooden walls, and then behind the mighty iron ramparts of its invincible Fleets, and now, like a thunderbolt from a summer sky, came the paralyzing tidings that the first line of defense had been pierced by a single blow, and the greatest sea stronghold of England rendered defenseless – and all this between sunset and midnight of a November day.

Was it any wonder that men looked blankly into each other's eyes, and asked themselves and each other how such an unheard-of catastrophe had come about, and what was going to happen next? The first and universal feeling was one of amazement, which amounted almost to mental paralysis, and then came a sickening sense of insecurity. For two generations the Fleet had been trusted implicitly, and invasion had been looked upon merely as the fad of alarmists, and the theme of sensational story-writers. No intelligent person really trusted the army, although its ranks, such as they were, were filled with as gallant soldiers as ever carried a rifle, but it had been afflicted ever since men could remember with the bane and blight of politics and social influence. It had never been really a serious profession, and its upper ranks had been little better than the playground of the sons of the wealthy and well-born.

Politician after politician on both sides had tried his hand at scheme after scheme to improve the army. What one had done, the next had undone, and the permanent War Office Officials had given more attention to buttons and braids and caps than to businesslike organizations of fighting efficiency. The administration was, as it always had been, a chaos of muddle. The higher ranks were rotten with inefficiency, and the lower, aggravated and bewildered by change after change, had come to look upon soldiering as a sort of game, the rules of which were being constantly altered.

The Militia, the Yeomanry, and the Volunteers had been constantly snubbed and worried by the authorities of Pall Mall. Private citizens, willing to give time and money in order to learn the use of the rifle, even if they could not join the Yeomanry or Volunteers, had been just ignored. The War Office could see no use for a million able-bodied men who had learned to shoot straight, besides they were only "damned civilians," whose proper place was in their offices and shops. What right had they with rifles? If they wanted exercise, let them go and play golf, or cricket, or football. What had they to do with the defense of their country and their homes?

But that million of irregular sharpshooters were badly wanted now. They could have turned every hedgerow into a trench and cover against the foe which would soon be marching over the fields and orchards and hop-gardens of southern England. They would have known every yard of the ground, and the turn of every path and road, and while the regular army was doing its work they could have prevented many a turning movement of the superior forces, shot down the horses of convoys and ammunition trains, and made themselves generally objectionable to the enemy.

Now the men were there, full of fight and enthusiasm, but they had neither ammunition nor rifles, and if they had had them, ninety percent would not have known how to use them. Wherefore, those who were responsible for the land defenses of the country found themselves with less than three hundred thousand trained and half-trained men, of all arms, to face invading forces which would certainly not number less than a million, every man of which had served his apprenticeship to the grim trade of war, commanded by officers who had taken that same trade seriously, studied it as a science, thinking it of considerably more importance than golf or cricket or football.

It had been said that the British Nation would never tolerate conscription, which might or might not have been true; but now, when the next hour or so might hear the foreign drums thrumming and the foreign bugles blaring, conscription looked a very different thing. There wasn't a loyal man in the kingdom who didn't bitterly regret that he had not been taken in the prime of his young manhood, and taught how to defend the hearth and home which were his, and the wife and children which were so dear to him.

But it was too late now. Neither soldiers nor sharpshooters are made in a few hours or days, and within a week the first battles that had been fought on English ground for nearly eight hundred years would have been lost and won, and nine-tenths of the male population of England would be looking on in helpless fury.

There had been plenty of theorists, who had said that the British Islands needed no army of home defense, simply because if she once lost command of the sea it would not be necessary for an enemy to invade her, since a blockade of her ports would starve her into submission in a month – which, thanks to the decay of agriculture and the depopulation of the country districts, was true enough. But it was not all the truth. Those who preached these theories left out one very important factor, and that was human nature.

For over a century the Continental nations had envied and hated Britain, the land-grabber; Britain who had founded nations while they had failed to make colonies; Britain, who had made the Seven Seas her territories, and the coasts of other lands her frontiers. Surely the leaders of the leagued nations would have been more or less than human had they resisted, even if their people had allowed them to do it, the temptation of trampling these proud Islanders into the mud and mire of their own fields and highways, and dictating terms of peace in the ancient halls of Windsor.

These were the bitter thoughts which were rankling in the breast of every loyal British man during the remainder of that night of horrible suspense. Many still had reason to remember the ghastly blunders and the muddling which had cost so many gallant lives and so many millions of treasure during the Boer War, when it took three hundred thousand British troops to reduce eighty thousand undrilled farmers to submission. What if the same blundering and muddling happened now? And it was just as likely now as then.

Men ground their teeth, and looked at their strong, useless hands, and cursed theorist and politician alike. And meanwhile the Cabinet was sitting, deliberating, as best it might, over the tidings of disaster. The House of Commons, after voting full powers to the Cabinet and the Council of Defense, had been united at last by the common and immediate danger, and members of all parties were hurrying away to their constituencies to do what they could to help in organizing the defense of their homeland.

There was one fact which stood out before all others, as clearly as an electric light among a lot of candles, and, now that it was too late, no one recognized it with more bitter conviction than those who had made it the consistent policy of both Conservative and Liberal Governments, and of the Executive Departments, to discourage invention outside the charmed circle of the Services, and to drive the civilian inventor abroad.

Again and again, designs of practical airships – not gas-bags which could only be dragged slowly against a moderate wind, but flying machines which conquered the wind and used it as a bird does – had been submitted to the War Office during the last six or seven years, and had been pooh-poohed or pigeon-holed by some sapient permanent official – and now the penalty of stupidity and neglect had to be paid.

The complete descriptions of the tragedy that had been and was being enacted at Portsmouth that were constantly arriving in Downing Street left no possibility of doubt that the forts had been destroyed and the *Spartiate* blown up by torpedoes from the air – from which fact it was necessary to draw the terrible inference that the enemy had possessed themselves of the command of the air.

What was the command of the sea worth after that? What was the fighting value of the mightiest battleship that floated when pitted against a practically unassailable enemy, which had nothing to do but drop torpedoes, loaded with high explosives, on her decks and down her funnels until her very vitals were torn to pieces, her ammunition exploded, and her crew stunned by concussion or suffocated by poisonous gas?

It was horrible, but it was true. Inside an hour the strongest fortifications in England had been destroyed, and ten first-class battleships and a cruiser had been sent to the bottom of the sea, and so at last her ancient scepter was falling from the hand of the Sea Queen, and her long inviolate domain was threatened by the armed legions of those whose forefathers she had vanquished on many a stricken field by land and sea.

"Well, gentlemen," said the Prime Minister to the other members of the Cabinet Council, who were sitting round that historic oval table in the Council Chamber in Downing Street, "we may as well confess that this is a great deal more serious than we expected it to be, and that is to my mind all the better reason why we should strain every nerve to hold intact the splendid heritage which our fathers have left to us –"

Boom! A shudder ran through the atmosphere as he spoke the last words, and the double windows in Downing Street shook with the vibration. The members of the Cabinet started in their seats and looked at each other. Was this the fulfillment of the half prophecy which the Prime Minister had spoken so slowly and so clearly in the silent, crowded House of Commons?

Almost at the same moment the electric bell at the outer of the double doors rang. The doors were opened, and a messenger came in with a telegram which he handed to the Prime Minister, and then retired. He opened the envelope, and for nearly five minutes of intense suspense he mentally translated the familiar cypher, and then he said, as he handed the telegram to the Secretary for War:

"Gentlemen, I deeply regret to say that the possible prospect which I outlined in the House tonight has become an accomplished fact. Two hundred and forty-three years ago London heard the sound of hostile guns. We have heard them tonight. This telegram is from Sheerness, and it tells, I most deeply regret to say, the same story, or something like it, as the messages from Portsmouth. A Russo-German-French fleet of battleships, cruisers and destroyers, assisted by four airships and an unknown number of submarines, has defeated the Southern portion of the North Sea Squadron, and is now proceeding in two divisions, one up the Medway towards Chatham, and the other up the Thames towards Tilbury. Garrison Fort is now being bombarded from the sea and the air, and will probably be in ruins within an hour."

Chapter XIII

A CRIME AND A MISTAKE

When the destruction of the forts and the sinking of the battleships at Portsmouth had been accomplished, John Castellan made about the greatest mistake in his life, a mistake which had very serious consequences for those to whom he had sold himself and his terrible invention.

He and his brother Denis formed a very curious contrast, which is nevertheless not uncommon in Irish families. The British army and navy can boast no finer soldiers or sailors, and the Empire no more devoted servants than those who claim Ireland as the land of their birth, and Denis Castellan was one of these. As the reader may have guessed already, he and Erskine had only been on the *Cormorant* because it was the policy of the Naval Council to keep two of the ablest men in the service out of sight for a while. Denis, who had a remarkable gift of tongues, was really one of the most skillful naval *attachés* in service, and what he didn't know about the naval affairs of Europe was hardly worth learning. Erskine had been recognized by the Naval Council which, under Sir John Fisher, had raised the British Navy to a pitch of efficiency that was the envy of every nation in the world, except Japan, as an engineer and inventor of quite extraordinary ability, and while the *Ithuriel* was building, they had given him the command of the *Cormorant,* chiefly because there was hardly anything to do, and therefore he had ample leisure to do his thinking.

On the other hand John Castellan was an unhappily brilliant example of that type of Keltic intellect which is incapable of believing the world-wide truism that the day of small states is passed. He had two articles of political faith. One was an unshakable belief in the possibility of Irish independence, and the other, which naturally followed from the first, was implacable hatred of the Saxon oppressor whose power and wealth had saved Ireland from invasion for centuries. He was utterly unable to grasp the Imperial idea, while his brother was as enthusiastic an Imperialist as ever sailed the seas.

Had it not been for this blind hatred, the disaster which had befallen the Reserve Fleet would have been repeated at sea on a much vaster scale; but he allowed his passions to overcome his judgment, and so saved the Channel Fleet. There lay beneath him defenseless the greatest naval port of England, with its docks and dockyards, its barracks and arsenals, its garrisons of soldiers and sailors, and its crowds of workmen. The temptation was too strong for him, and he yielded to it.

When the *Prince George* had gone down he rose into the air, and ran over the Isle of Wight, signaling to the *See Adler.* The signals were answered, and the two airships met about two miles southwest of the Needles, and Castellan informed Captain Frenkel of his intention to destroy Portsmouth and Gosport. The German demurred strongly. He had no personal hatred to satisfy, and he suggested that it would be much better to go out to sea and discover the whereabouts of the Channel Fleet; but Castellan was Commander-in-Chief of the Aërial Squadrons of the Allies, and so his word was law, and within the next two hours one of the greatest crimes in the history of civilized warfare was committed.

The two airships circled slowly over Gosport and Portsmouth, dropping their torpedoes wherever a worthy mark presented itself. The first one discharged from the *Flying Fish* fell on the deck of the old *Victory.* The deck burst up, as though all the powder she had carried at Trafalgar had exploded beneath it, and the next moment she broke out in inextinguishable flames. The old *Resolution* met the same fate from the *See Adler,* and then the pitiless hail of destruction fell on the docks and jetties. In a few minutes the harbor was ringed with flame. Portsmouth Station, built almost entirely of wood, blazed up like matchwood; then came the turn of the dockyards at Portsea, which were soon ablaze from end to end.

Then the two airships spread their wings like destroying angels over Portsmouth town. Half a dozen torpedoes wrecked the Town Hall and set the ruins on fire. This was the work of the *See Adler.* The *Flying Fish* devoted her attention to the naval and military barracks, the Naval College and the Gunnery School on Whale Island. As soon as these were reduced to burning ruins, the two airships scattered their torpedoes indiscriminately over churches, shops and houses, and in the streets crowded by terrified mobs of soldiers, sailors and civilians.

The effect of the torpedoes in the streets was too appalling for description. Everyone within ten or a dozen yards of the focus of the explosion was literally blown to atoms, and for fifty yards round every living creature dropped dead, killed either by the force of the concussion or the poisonous gases which were liberated by the explosion. Hundreds fell thus without the mark of a wound, and when some of their bodies were examined afterwards, it was found that their hearts were split open as cleanly as though they had been divided with a razor, just as are the hearts of fishes which have been killed with dynamite.

John Castellan and his lieutenant, M'Carthy, for the time being gloried in the work of destruction. Captain Frenkel was a soldier and a gentleman, and he saw nothing in it save wanton killing of defenseless people and a wicked waste of ammunition; but the terrible War Lord of Germany had given Castellan supreme command, and to disobey meant degradation, and possibly death, and so the *See Adler* perforce took her share in the tragedy.

In a couple of hours Portsmouth, Gosport and Portsea had ceased to be towns. They were only areas of flaming ruins; but at last the ammunition gave out, and Castellan was compelled to signal the *See Adler* to shape her course for Bracklesham Bay in order to replenish the magazines. They reached the bay, and descended at the spot where the *Leger* ought to have been at anchor. She was not there, for the sufficient reason that the *Ithuriel's* ram had sent her to the bottom of the Channel.

For half an hour the *Flying Fish* and the *See Adler* hunted over the narrow waters, but neither was the *Leger* nor any other craft to be seen between the Selsey coast and the Isle of Wight. When they came together again in Bracklesham Bay, John Castellan's rage against the hated Saxon had very considerably cooled. Evidently something serious had happened, and something that he knew nothing about, and now that the excitement of destruction had died away, he remembered more than one thing which he ought to have thought of before.

The two rushes of the torpedo boats, supported by the swift cruisers, had not taken place. Not a hostile vessel had entered either Spithead or the Solent, and the British cruisers, which he had been ordered to spare, had got away untouched. It was perfectly evident that some disaster had befallen the expedition, and that the *Leger* had been involved in it. In spite of the terrible destruction that the *Flying Fish,* the *See Adler* and the *Banshee* had wrought on sea and land, it was plain that the first part of the invader's program had been brought to nothing by some unknown agency.

He was, of course, aware of the general plan of attack. He had destroyed the battleships of the Fleet Reserve. While he was doing that the destroyers should have been busy among the cruisers, and then the main force, under Admiral Durenne, would follow, and take possession of Southampton, Portsmouth and the Isle of Wight. A detachment of cruisers and destroyers was then to be dispatched to Littlehampton, and land a sufficient force to seize and hold the railway at Ford and Arundel, so that the coast line of the L.B.S.C.R., as well as the main line to Horsham and London, should be at the command of the invaders.

Littlehampton was also particularly valuable on account of its tidal river and harbor, which would give shelter and protection to a couple of hundred torpedo boats and destroyers, and its wharves from which transports could easily coal. It is hardly worth while to add that it had been left entirely undefended. It had been proposed to mount a couple of 9.2 guns on the old fort on the west side of the river mouth, with half a dozen twelve-pound quick-firers at the Coast-Guard station on the east side to repel torpedo attack, but the War Office had laughed at the idea of an enemy getting within gunshot of the inviolate English shore, and so one of the most vulnerable points on the south coast had been left undefended.

What would Castellan have given now for the torpedoes which the two ships had wasted in the wanton destruction of Portsmouth, and the murder of its helpless citizens. The main French Fleet by this time could not be very far off. Behind it, somewhere, was the British Channel Fleet, the most powerful sea force that had ever ridden the subject waves, and here he was without a torpedo on either of his ships, and no supplies nearer than Kiel. The *Leger* had carried two thousand torpedoes and five hundred cylinders of the gases which supplied the motive power. She was gone, and for all offensive purposes the *Flying Fish* and *See Adler* were as harmless as a couple of balloons.

When it was too late, John Castellan remembered in the bitterness of his soul that the torpedoes which had destroyed Portsmouth would have been sufficient to have wrecked the Channel Fleet, and now there was nothing for it but to leave Admiral Durenne to fight his own battle against the most powerful fleet in the world, and to use what was left of the motive power to get back to Kiel, and replenish their magazines.

Horrible as had been the fate which had fallen on the great arsenal of southern England, it had not been sacrificed in vain, and very sick at heart was John Castellan when he gave the order for the two vessels, which a few hours ago had been such terrible engines of destruction, to rise into the air and wing their harmless flight towards Kiel.

When the *Flying Fish* and the *See Adler* took the air, and shipped their course eastward, the position of the opposing fleets was somewhat as follows: The cruisers of the A Squadron, *Amphitrite, Andromeda, Europa, Niobe, Blenheim* and *Blake,* with fifteen first-class torpedo boats and ten destroyers, had got out to sea from Spithead unharmed. All these cruisers were good for twenty knots, the torpedo boats for twenty-five, and the destroyers for thirty. The *Sutlej, Ariadne, Argonaut* and *Diadem* had got clear away from the Solent, with ten first-class torpedo boats and five destroyers. They met about four miles southeast of St. Catherine's Point. Commodore Hoskins of the *Diadem* was the senior officer in command, and so he signaled for Captain Pennell, of the *Andromeda,* to come on board, and talk matters over with him, but before the conversation was halfway through, a black shape, with four funnels crowned with smoke and flame, came tearing up from the westward, made the private signal, and ran alongside the *Diadem.*

The news that her commander brought was this – Admiral Lord Beresford had succeeded in eluding the notice of the French Channel Fleet, and was on his way up the southwest with the intention of getting behind Admiral Durenne's fleet, and crushing it between his own force to seaward and the batteries and Reserve Fleet on the landward side. The Commander of the destroyer was, of course, quite ignorant of the disaster which had befallen the battleships of the Reserve Fleet and Portsmouth, and when the captain of the cruiser told him the tidings, though he received the news with the almost fatalistic *sangfroid* of the British naval officer, turned a shade or two paler under the bronze of his skin.

"That is terrible news, sir," he said, "and it will probably alter the Admiral's plans considerably. I must be off as soon as possible, and let him know: meanwhile, of course, you will use your own judgment."

"Yes," replied the Commodore, "but I think you had better take one of our destroyers, say the *Greyhound,* back with you. She's got her bunkers full, and she can manage thirty-two knots in a sea like this."

At this moment the sentry knocked at the door of the Commodore's room.

"Come in," said Commodore Hoskins. The door opened, a sentry came in and saluted, and said:

"The *Ithuriel's* alongside, sir, and Captain Erskine will be glad to speak to you."

"Ah!" exclaimed the Commodore, "the very thing. I wonder what that young devil has been up to. Send him in at once, sentry."

The sentry retired, and presently Erskine entered the room, saluted, and said:

"I've come to report, sir, I have sunk everything that tried to get in through Spithead. First division of three destroyers, the old *Leger,* the *Dupleix* cruiser, six destroyers of the second division, and three cruisers, the *Alger, Suchet* and *Davout.* They're all at the bottom."

The Commodore stared for a moment or two at the man who so quietly described the terrific destruction that he had wrought with a single ship, and then he said:

"Well, Erskine, we expected a good deal from that infernal craft of yours, but this is rather more than we could have hoped for. You've done splendidly. Now, what's your best speed?"

"Forty-five knots, sir."

"Good Lord!" exclaimed the Commander of the *Greyhound.* "You don't say so."

"Oh, yes," said Erskine with a smile. "You ought to have seen us walk over those destroyers. I hit them at full speed, and they crumpled up like paper boats."

By this time the Commodore had sat down, and was writing his report as fast as he could get his pencil over the paper. It was a short, terse, but quite comprehensive account of the happenings of the last three hours, and a clear statement of the strength and position of the torpedo and cruiser squadron under his command. When he had finished, he put the paper into an envelope, and said to the Commander of the *Greyhound*:

"I am afraid you are no good here, Hawkins. I shall have to give the message to Captain Erskine, he'll be there and back before you're there. Just give him the bearings of the Fleet and he'll be off at once. There you are, Erskine, give that to the Admiral, and bring me instructions back as soon as you can. You've just time for a whisky-and-soda, and then you must be off."

Erskine took the letter, and they drank their whisky-and-soda. Then they went on deck. The *Ithuriel* was lying outside the *Greyhound,* half submerged – that is to say, with three feet of freeboard showing. Commander Hawkins looked at her with envious eyes. It is an article of faith with all good commanders of destroyers that their own craft is the fastest and most efficient of her class. At a pinch he could get thirty-two knots out of the *Greyhound,* and here was this quiet, determined-looking young man, who had created a vessel of his own, and had reached the rank of captain by sheer genius over the heads of men ten years older than himself, talking calmly of forty-five knots, and of the sinking of destroyers and cruisers, as though it was a mere matter of cracking egg-shells. Wherefore there was wrath in his soul when he went on board and gave the order to cast loose. Erskine went with him. They shook hands on the deck of the *Greyhound,* and Erskine went aboard of the *Ithuriel,* saying:

"Well, Hawkins, I expect I shall meet you coming back."

"I'm damned if I believe in your forty-five knots," replied Captain Hawkins, shortly.

"Cast off, and come with me then," laughed Erskine, "you soon will."

Inside three minutes the two craft were clear of the *Diadem.* Erskine gave the *Greyhound* right of way until they had cleared the squadron. The sea was smooth, and there was scarcely any wind, for it had been a wonderfully fine November. The *Greyhound* got on her thirty-two knots as soon as there was no danger of hitting anything.

"That chap thinks he can race us," said Erskine to Lennard, as he got into the conning-tower, "and I'm just going to make him the maddest man in the British navy. He's doing thirty-two – we're doing twenty-five. Now that we're clear I'll wake him up." He took down the receiver and said:

"Pump her out, Castellan, and give her full speed as soon as you can."

The *Ithuriel* rose in the water, and began to shudder from stem to stern with the vibrations of the engines, as they gradually worked up to their highest capacity. Commander Hawkins saw something coming up astern, half hidden by a cloud of spray and foam. It went past him as though he had been standing still instead of steaming at thirty-two knots. A few moments more and it was lost in the darkness.

Chapter XIV

THE EVE OF BATTLE

In twenty minutes the *Ithuriel* ran alongside the *Britain,* which was one of the five most formidable battleships in existence. For five years past a new policy had been pursued with regard to the navy. The flagships, which of course contained the controlling brains of the fleets, were the most powerful afloat. By the time war broke out five of them had been launched and armed, and the *Britain* was the newest and most powerful of them.

Her displacement was twenty-two thousand tons, and her speed twenty-four knots. She was armored from end to end with twelve-inch plates against which ordinary projectiles smashed as harmlessly as egg-shells. Twelve fourteen-inch thousand-pounder guns composed her primary battery; her secondary consisted of ten 9.2 guns, and her tertiary of twelve-pounder Maxim-Nordenfeldts in the fighting tops.

It was the first time that Erskine had seen one of these giants of the ocean, and when they got alongside he said to Denis Castellan:

"There's a fighting machine for you, Denis. Great Scott, what wouldn't I give to see her at work in the middle of a lot of Frenchmen and Germans, as the *Revenge* was among the Spaniards in Grenville's time. Just look at those guns."

"Yes," replied Castellan, "she's a splendid ship, and those guns look as though they could talk French to the Frenchies and German to the Dutchmen and plain English to the lot in a way that wouldn't want much translating. And what's more, they have the right men behind them, and the best gun in the world isn't much good without that."

At this moment they heard a shrill voice from the forecastle of the nearest destroyer.

"Hulloa there, what's the matter?" came from the deck of the *Britain.*

"Four French destroyers coming up pretty fast from the south'ard, sir. Seem to be making for the flagship," was the reply.

"That's a job for us," said Erskine, who was standing on the narrow deck of the *Ithuriel,* waiting to go on board the *Britain.* "Commander, will you be good enough to deliver this to the Admiral? I must be off and settle those fellows before they do any mischief."

The commander of the destroyer took the letter, Erskine dived below, a steel plate slid over the opening to the companion way, and when he got into the conning-tower he ordered full speed.

Four long black shapes were stealing slowly towards the British center, and no one knew better than he did that a single torpedo well under waterline would send Admiral Beresford's floating fortress to the bottom inside ten minutes, and that was the last thing he wanted to see.

A quartermaster ran down the ladder and caught the letter from the commander just as the *Ithuriel* moved off.

"Tell the Admiral, with Captain Erskine's compliments, that he'll be back in a few minutes, when he's settled those fellows."

The quartermaster took the letter, and by the time he got to the top of the ladder, the *Ithuriel* was flying through a cloud of foam and spray towards the first of the destroyers. He heard a rattle of guns, and then the destroyer vanished. The *Ithuriel* swung round, hit the next one in the bows, ground her under the water, turned almost at right angles, smashed the stern of the third one into scrap iron, hit the fourth one abreast of the conning-tower, crushed her down and rolled her over, and then slowed down and ran back to the flagship at twenty knots.

"Well!" said Quartermaster Maginniss, who for the last few minutes had been held spellbound at the top of the ladder, in spite of the claims of discipline, "of all the sea-devils of crafts that I've ever heard of, I should say that was the worst. Four destroyers gone in five minutes, and here he is coming back before I've delivered the letter. If we only have a good square fight now, I'll be sorry for the Frenchies."

The next moment he stiffened up and saluted. "A letter for you, Admiral, left by Captain Erskine before he went away to destroy those destroyers."

"And you've been watching the destruction instead of delivering the letter," laughed Lord Beresford, as he took it from him. "Well, I'll let you off this time. When Captain Erskine comes alongside, ask him to see me in my room at once."

The *Ithuriel* ran alongside even as he was speaking. The gangway was manned, and when he reached the deck, Admiral Beresford held out his hand, and said with a laugh:

"Well, Captain Erskine, I understood that you were bringing me a message from Commodore Hoskins, but you seem to have had better game to fly for."

"My fault, sir," said Erskine, "but I hope you won't court-martial me for it. You see, there were four French destroyers creeping round, and mine was the only ship that could tackle them, so I thought I'd better go and do it before they did any mischief. Anyhow, they're all at the bottom now."

"I don't think I should have much case if I court-martialled you for that, Captain Erskine," laughed the Admiral, "especially after what you've done already, according to Commodore Hoskins' note. That must be a perfect devil of a craft of yours. Can you sink anything with her?"

"Anything, sir," replied Erskine. "This is the most powerful fighting ship in the world, but I could put you at the bottom of the Channel in ten minutes."

"The Lord save us! It's a good job you're on our side."

"And it's a very great pity," said Erskine, "that the airships are not with us too. I had a very narrow squeak in Spithead about three hours ago from one of their aërial torpedoes. It struck part of a destroyer that I'd just sunk, and although it was nearly fifty yards away, it shook me up considerably."

"Have you any idea of the whereabouts and formation of the French Fleet? I must confess that I haven't. These infernal airships have upset all the plans for catching Durenne between the Channel Fleet and the Reserve, backed up by the Portsmouth guns, so that we could jump out and catch him between the fleet and the forts. Now I suppose it will have to be a Fleet action at sea."

"If you care to leave your ship for an hour, sir," replied Erskine, "I will take you round the French fleet and you shall see everything for yourself. We may have to knock a few holes in something, if it gets in our way, but I think I can guarantee that you shall be back on the *Britain* by the time you want to begin the action."

"Absolutely irregular," said Lord Beresford, stroking his chin, and trying to look serious, while his eyes were dancing with anticipation. "An admiral to leave his flagship on the eve of an engagement! Well, never mind, Courtney's a very good fellow, and knows just as much about the ship as I do, and he's got all sailing orders. I'll come. He's on the bridge now, I'll go and tell him."

The Admiral ran up on to the bridge, gave Captain Courtney Commodore Hoskins' letter, added a few directions, one of which was to keep on a full head of steam on all the ships, and look out for signals, and five minutes later he had been introduced to Lennard, and was standing beside him in the conning-tower of the *Ithuriel* listening to Erskine, as he said into the telephone receiver:

"Sink her to three feet, Castellan, and then ahead full speed."

The pumps worked furiously for a few minutes, and the *Ithuriel* sank until only three feet of her bulk appeared above the water. Then the Admiral felt the floor of the conning-tower shudder and tremble under his feet. He looked out of the side porthole on the starboard bow, and saw his own fleet dropping away into the distance and the darkness of the November night. The water ahead curled up into two huge swathes, which broke into foam and spray, which lashed hissing along the almost submerged decks.

"You have a pretty turn of speed on her, I must say, Captain Erskine," said the Admiral, after he had taken a long squint through the semicircular window. "I'm sorry we haven't got a score of craft like this."

"And we should have had, your lordship," replied Erskine, "if the Council had only taken the opinion that you gave after you saw the plans."

"I'd have a hundred like her," laughed the Admiral, "only you see there's the Treasury, and behind that the most noble House of Commons, elected mostly by the least educated and most short-sighted people in the nation, who scarcely know a torpedo from a common shell, and we should never have got them. We had hard enough work to get this one as an experiment."

"I quite agree with you, sir," said Erskine, "and I think Lennard will too. There has never been an instance in history in which democracy did not spell degeneration. It's a pity, but I suppose it's inevitable. As far as my reading has taken me, it seems to be the dry-rot of nations. Halloa, what's that? Torpedo gunboat, I think! Ah, there's the moon. Now, sir, if you'll just come and stand to the right here, for'ard of the wheel, I'll put the *Ithuriel* through her paces, and show you what she can do."

A long grey shape, with two masts and three funnels between them, loomed up out of the darkness into a bright patch of moonlight. Erskine took the receiver from the hooks and said:

"Stand by there, Castellan. Forward guns fire when I give the word – then I shall ram."

The Admiral saw the three strangely shaped guns rise from the deck, their muzzles converging on the gunboat. He expected a report, but none came; only a gentle hiss, scarcely audible in the conning-tower. Then three brilliant flashes of flame burst out just under the Frenchman's topworks. Erskine, with one hand on the steering-wheel, and the other holding the receiver, said:

"Well aimed – now full speed. I'm going over him."

"Over him!" echoed the Admiral. "Don't you ram under the water-line?"

"If it's the case of a big ship, sir," replied Erskine, "we sink and hit him where it hurts most, but it isn't worth while with these small craft. You will see what I mean in a minute."

As he spoke a shudder ran through the *Ithuriel.* The deck began to quiver under the Admiral's feet; the ram rose six feet out of the water. The shape of the gunboat seemed to rush towards them; the ram hit it squarely amidships; then came a shock, a grinding scrape, screams of fear from the terrified sailors, a final crunch, and the gunboat was sinking fifty yards astern.

"That's awful," said the Admiral, with a perceptible shake in his voice. "What speed did you hit her at?"

"Forty-five knots," replied Erskine, giving a quarter turn to the wheel, and almost immediately bringing a long line of battleships, armored cruisers, protected cruisers and destroyers into view.

The French Channel Fleet was composed of the most powerful ships in the navy of the Republic. The two portions from Brest and Cherbourg had now united their forces. The French authorities had at last learned the supreme value of homogeneity. The center was composed of six ships of the *Republique* class, all identical in size, armor and armament, as well as speed. They were the *Republique, Patrie* flagship, *Justice, Democratie, Liberte* and *Verite.* They were all of fifteen thousand tons and eighteen knots. To these was added the *Suffren,* also of eighteen knots, but only twelve thousand seven hundred tons: she had come from Brest with a flotilla of torpedo boats.

There were six armored cruisers, *Jules Ferry, Leon Gambetta, Victor Hugo, Jeanne d'Arc, Aube* and *Marseillaise.* These were all heavily armed and armored vessels, all of them capable of maneuvering at a speed of over twenty knots. A dozen smaller protected and unprotected cruisers hung on each flank, and a score of destroyers and torpedo boats lurked in between the big ships.

The *Ithuriel* ran quietly along the curving line of battleships and cruisers, turned and came back again without exciting the slightest suspicion.

Erskine would have dearly loved to sink a battleship or one or two cruisers, just to show his lordship how it was done, but the Admiral forbade this, as he wanted to get the Frenchmen, who still thought they were going to easy victory, entangled in the shallows of the narrow waters, and therefore with the exception of rolling over and sinking three submarines which happened to get in the way, no damage was done.

The British Channel Fleet, even not counting the assistance of the terrible *Ithuriel,* was the most powerful squadron that had ever put to sea under a single command. The main line of battle consisted of the flagship *Britain,* and seven ships of the *King Edward* class, *King Edward the Seventh, Dominion, Commonwealth, Hindustan, New Zealand, Canada* and *Newfoundland*; all over sixteen thousand tons, and of nineteen knots speed. With the exception of the giant flagships, of which there were five in existence – the *Britain, England, Ireland, Scotland* and *Wales* – and two nineteen thousand ton monsters which had just been completed for Japan, these were the fastest and most heavily-armed battleships afloat.

The second line was composed of the armored cruisers, *Duke of Edinburgh, Black Prince, Henry the Fourth, Warwick, Edward the Third, Cromwell,* all of over thirteen thousand tons, and twenty-two knots speed; the *Drake, King Alfred, Leviathan* and *Good Hope,* of over fourteen thousand tons and twenty-four knots speed; and the reconstructed *Powerful,* and *Terrible,* of fourteen thousand tons and twenty-two knots. There was, of course, the usual swarm of destroyers and torpedo boats; and in addition must be counted the ten cruisers, ten destroyers, and fifteen torpedo boats, which had escaped from Spithead and the Solent.

These had already formed a junction with the left wing of the British force.

For nearly two hours the two great fleets slowly approached each other almost at a right angle. As the grey dawn of the November morning began to steal over the calm blue-grey water, they came in plain sight of each other, and at once the signal flew from the foreyard of the *Britain,* "Prepare for action – battleships will cross front column of line ahead – cruisers will engage cruisers individually at discretion of Commanders – destroyers will do their worst."

Chapter XV

THE STRIFE OF GIANTS

As it happened, it was a fine, cold wintry day that dawned as the two great fleets drew towards each other. As Denis Castellan said, "It was a perfect jewel of a day for a holy fight," and so it was. The French fleet was advancing at twelve knots. Admiral Beresford made his fifteen, and led the line in the *Britain.* Erskine had been ordered to go to the rear of the French line and sink any destroyer or torpedo boat that he could get hold of, but to let the battleships and cruisers alone, unless he saw a British warship hard pressed, in which case he was to ram and sink the enemy if he could.

One division of cruisers, consisting of the fastest and most powerful armored vessels, was to make a half-circle two miles in the rear of the French Fleet. The ships selected for this service were the *Duke of Edinburgh, Warwick, Edward III., Cromwell* and *King Alfred.* Outside them, two miles again to the rear, the *Leviathan, Good Hope, Powerful* and *Terrible,* the fastest ships in the Fleet, were to take their station to keep off stragglers.

For the benefit of the non-nautical reader, it will be as well to explain here the two principal formations in which modern fleets go into action.

As a matter of fact, they are identical with the tactics employed by the French and Spanish on the one side and Nelson on the other during the Napoleonic wars. Before Nelson's time, it was the custom for two hostile fleets to engage each other in column of line abreast, which means that both fleets formed a double line which approached each other within gunshot, and then opened fire.

At Trafalgar, Nelson altered these tactics completely, with results that everybody knows. The allied French and Spanish fleets came up in a crescent, just in the same formation as Admiral Durenne was advancing on Portsmouth. Nelson took his ships into action in column of line ahead, in other words, in single file, the head of the column aiming for the center of the enemy's battle line.

The main advantage of this was, first, that it upset the enemy's combination, and, secondly, that each ship could engage two, since she could work both broadsides at once, whereas the enemy could only work one broadside against one ship. These were the tactics which, with certain modifications made necessary by the increased mobility on both sides, Lord Beresford adopted.

With one exception, no foreigner had ever seen the new class of British flagship, and that exception, as we know, was safely locked up on board the *Ithuriel*, and his reports were even now being carefully considered by the Naval Council.

There are no braver men on land and sea than the officers and crews of the French Navy, but when the giant bulk of the *Britain* loomed up out of the westward in the growing light, gradually gathering way with her stately train of nineteen-knot battleships behind her, and swept down in front of the French line, many a heart stood still for the moment, and many a man asked himself what the possibilities of such a Colossus of the ocean might be.

They had not long to wait. As the British battleships came on from the left with ever-increasing speed, the whole French line burst into a tornado of thunder and flame, but not a shot was fired from the English lines. Shells hurtled and screamed through the air, topworks were smashed into scrap-iron, funnels riddled, and military masts demolished; but until the *Britain* reached the center of the French line not a British gun spoke.

Then the giant swung suddenly to starboard, and headed for the space between the *Patrie* and the *Republique*. The *Canada*, *Newfoundland*, *New Zealand* and *Hindustan* put on speed, passed under her stern, and headed in between the *Suffren*, *Liberte*, *Verite* and *Patrie*, while the *Edward VII.*, *Dominion* and *Commonwealth* turned between the *Justice*, *Democratie*, the *Aube* and *Marseillaise*.

Within a thousand yards the British battleships opened fire. The first gun from the *Britain* was a signal which turned them all into so many floating volcanoes. The *Britain* herself ran between the *Patrie* and the *Republique,* vomiting storms of shell, first ahead, then on the broadside and then astern. Her topworks were of course crumpled out of all shape – that was expected, for the range was now only about five hundred yards – but the incessant storm of thousand-pound shells from the fourteen-inch guns, followed by an unceasing hail of three hundred and fifty pound projectiles from the 9.2 quick-firers, reduced the two French battleships to little better than wrecks. The *Britain* steamed through and turned, and again the awful hurricane burst out from her sides and bow and stern. She swung round again, but now only a few dropping shots greeted her from the crippled Frenchmen.

"I don't think those chaps have much more fight left in them," said the Admiral to the Captain as they passed through the line for the third time. "We'll just give them one more dose, and then see how the other fellows are getting on."

Once more the monster swept in between the doomed ships; once more her terrible artillery roared. Two torpedo boats, five hundred yards ahead, were rushing towards her. A grey shape rose out of the water, flinging up clouds of spray and foam, and in a moment they were ground down into the water and sunk. The hastily-fired torpedoes diverged and struck the two French battleships instead of the *Britain.* Two mountains of foam rose up under their sterns, their bows went down and rose again, and with a sternward lurch they slid down into the depths.

The *Britain* swung round to port, and poured a broadside into the *Liberte,* which had just crippled the *Hindustan,* and sunk her with a torpedo. The *New Zealand* was evidently in difficulties between the *Liberte* and the *Verite.* Her upper works were a mass of ruins, but she was still blazing away merrily with her primary battery. The Admiral slowed down to ten knots, and got between the two French battleships; then her big guns began to vomit destruction again, and in five minutes the two French battleships, caught in the triangular fire and terribly mauled, hauled their flags down, and so Lord Beresford's scheme was accomplished. The *Dominion* and *Edward VII.* had got between their ships at the expense of a severe handling, and were giving a very good account of them, and the *Canada* had sunk the *Suffren* with a lucky shell which exploded in her forward torpedo room and blew her side out.

It was broad daylight by this time, and it was perfectly plain, both to friend and foe, that the French center could no longer be counted upon as a fighting force. One of the circumstances which came home hardest afterwards to the survivors of the French force was the fact that, as far as they knew, not a single British battleship or cruiser had been struck by a French destroyer or torpedo boat. The reason for this was the very simple fact that Erskine had taken these craft under his charge, and, while the big ships had been thundering away at each other, he had devoted himself to the congenial sport of smashing up the smaller fry. He sent the *Ithuriel* flying hither and thither at full speed, tearing them into scrap-iron and sending them to the bottom, as if they had been so many penny steamers. He could have sent the battleships to the bottom with equal ease, but orders were orders, and he respected them until his chance came.

The *Verite* was now the least injured of the French battleships. To look at she was merely a floating mass of ruins, but her engines were intact, and her primary battery as good as ever. Her captain, like the hero that he was, determined to risk his ship and everything in her in the hope of destroying the monster which had wrought such frightful havoc along the line. She carried two twelve-inch guns ahead, a 6.4 on each side of the barbette, and four pairs of 6.4 guns behind these, and the fire of all of them was concentrated ahead.

As the *Britain* came round for the third time every one of the guns was laid upon her. He called to the engine-room for the utmost speed he could have, and at nineteen knots he bore down upon the leviathan. The huge guns on the *Britain* swung round, and a tempest of shells swept the *Verite* from end to end. Her armor was gashed and torn as though it had been cardboard instead of six-and eleven-inch steel; but still she held on her course. At five hundred yards her guns spoke, and the splinters began to fly on board the *Britain.* The Captain of the *Verite* signaled for the last ounce of steam he could have – he was going to appeal to the last resort in naval warfare – the ram. If he could once get that steel spur of his into the *Britain's* hull under her armor, she would go down as certainly as though she had been a first-class cruiser.

When the approaching vessels were a little more than five hundred yards apart, the *Ithuriel,* who had settled up with all the destroyers and torpedo boats she could find, rose to the north of the now broken French line. Erskine took in the situation at a glance. He snatched the receiver from the hooks, shouted into it:

"Sink – full speed – ram!"

The *Ithuriel* dived and sprang forward, and when the ram of the *Verite* was within a hundred yards of the side of the *Britain* his own ram smashed through her stern, cracked both the propeller shafts, and tore away her rudder as if it had been a piece of paper. She stopped and yawed, broadside on to the *Britain.* The chases of the great guns swung round in ominous threatening silence, but before they could be fired the Tricolor fluttered down from the flagstaff, and the *Verite,* helpless for all fighting purposes, had surrendered.

It was now the turn of the big armored cruisers. They were practically untouched, for the heaviest of the fighting had fallen on the battleships. A green rocket went up from the deck of the *Britain,* and was followed in about ten seconds by a blue one. The inner line of cruisers made a quarter turn to port, and began hammering into the crippled battleships and cruisers indiscriminately, while the *Leviathan, Good Hope, Powerful* and *Terrible* took stations between the Isle of Wight and the Sussex coast.

The *Ithuriel* rose to her three-foot freeboard, and put in some very pretty practice with her pneumatic guns on the topworks of the cruisers. The six-funneled *Jeanne d'Arc* got tired of this, and made a rush at her at her full speed of twenty-three knots, with the result that the *Ithuriel* disappeared, and three minutes afterwards there came a shock under the great cruiser's stern which sent a shudder through her whole fabric. The engines whirled furiously until they stopped, and a couple of minutes later her captain recognized that she could neither steam nor steer. Meanwhile, the tide was setting strongly in towards Spithead, and the disabled ships were drifting with it, either to capture or destruction.

The French center had now, to all intents and purposes, ceased to exist. Four out of six battleships were sunk, and one had surrendered, and the *Jeanne d'Arc* had gone down.

On the British side the *Hindustan* had been sunk, and the *Dominion, Commonwealth* and *Newfoundland* very badly mauled, so badly indeed that it was a matter of dry-dock as quickly as possible for them. All the other battleships, including even the *Britain* herself, were little better than wrecks to look at, so terrible had been the firestorms through which they had passed.

But for the presence of the *Ithuriel,* the British loss would of course have been much greater. It is not too much to say that her achievements spread terror and panic among the French torpedo flotilla. Under ordinary circumstances they would have taken advantage of the confusion of the battleship action to attack the line of armored cruisers behind, but between the two lines there was the ever-present destroying angel, as they came to call her, with her silent deadly guns, her unparalleled speed, and her terrible ram. No sooner did a destroyer or torpedo boat attempt to make for a cruiser, than a shell came hissing along the water, and blew the middle out of her, or the ram crashed through her sides, and sent her in two pieces to the bottom.

The result was that when the last French cruiser had hauled down her flag, Admiral Beresford found himself in command of a fleet which was still in being. Of the French battleships the *Justice* and the *Democratie* were still serviceable, and of the cruisers, the *Jules Ferry, Leon Gambetta, Victor Hugo, Aube* and *Marseillaise* were still in excellent fighting trim, although of course they were in no position to continue the struggle against the now overwhelming force of British battleships and armored cruisers. This was what Admiral Beresford had fought for: to break the center and put as many battleships as possible out of action. His orders had been to spare the cruisers as much as possible, because, he said, with a somewhat grim laugh, they might be useful later on.

The idea of their escaping to sea through the double line of British cruisers, to say nothing of the *Ithuriel,* with her speed of over fifty miles an hour, and her ability to ram them in detail before they were halfway across the Channel, was entirely out of the question. To have attempted such a thing would have been simply a form of collective suicide, so the flags were hauled down, and all that was left of the fleet surrendered.

Another circumstance which had placed the French fleet at a tremendous disadvantage was the absence of the three *Flying Fishes,* which were to have co-operated with the invading fleet, but of course neither Admiral Durenne, who had gone down with his ship, nor any other of his officers knew that the *Banshee* had been blown up in mid-air, or that the *Ithuriel* had destroyed the dépôt ship, and so forced Castellan, after his mad waste of ammunition in the destruction of Portsmouth, to wing his way to Kiel, with the *See Adler,* in order to replenish his magazines. Had those two amphibious craft been present at the battle, the issue might have been something very different.

The whole fight had only taken a couple of hours from the firing of the first shot to the hauling down of the last flag. Admiral Beresford made direct for Portsmouth to get his lame ducks into dock if possible, and to discover the amount of damage done. As they steamed in through the Spithead Forts, flags went up all along the northern shore of the Isle of Wight, and the guns on the Spithead Forts and Fort Monckton, which the *Banshee* had been commissioned to destroy, roared out a salute of welcome.

The signal masts of the sunk battleships showed where their shattered hulls were lying, and as the *Britain* led the way in between them, Lord Beresford rubbed his hands across his eyes, and said to his Commodore, who was standing on what was left of the navigating bridge:

"Poor fellows, it was hardly fair fighting. We might have had something very like those infernal craft if we'd had men of decent brains at the War Office. Same old story – anything new must be wrong in Pall Mall. Still we've got something of our own back this morning. I hope we shall be able to use some of the docks; if I'm not afraid our lame ducks will have to crawl round to Devonport as best they can. The man in command of those airships must have been a perfect devil to destroy a defenseless town in this fashion. The worst of it is that if they can do this sort of thing here they can do it just as easily to London or Liverpool, or Manchester or any other city. I hope there won't be anymore bad news when we get ashore."

Chapter XVI

HOW THE FRENCH LANDED AT PORTSMOUTH

All the ships able to take their place in the fighting-line were left outside. The French prisoners were disembarked and their places taken by drafts from the British warships, who at once set about making such repairs as were possible at sea. Admiral Beresford boarded the *Ithuriel*, which, until the next fight, he proposed to use as a dispatch-boat, and ran up the harbor.

He found every jetty, including the North and South Railway piers, mere masses of smoking ruins: but the Ordnance Dépôt on Priddy's Hard had somehow escaped, probably through the ignorance of the assailants. He landed at Sheer Jetty opposite Coaling Point, and before he was halfway up the steps a short, rather stout man, in the undress uniform of a General of Division, ran down and caught him by the hand. After him came a taller, slimmer man with eyes like gimlets and a skin wrinkled and tanned like Russian leather.

The first of the two men was General Sir John French, Commander-in-Chief at Aldershot, and the second was General Sir Ian Hamilton, Commander of the Southern Military District.

"Bravo, Beresford!" said General French, quietly. "Scooped the lot, didn't you?"

"All that aren't at the bottom of the Channel. Good-morning, Hamilton. I've heard that you're in a pretty bad way with your forts here," replied the Admiral. "By the way, how are the docks? I've got a few lame ducks that want looking after badly."

"We've just been having a look round," replied General Hamilton. "The town's in an awful state, as you can see. The Naval and Military barracks, and the Naval School are wrecked, and we haven't been able to save very much from the yards, but I don't think the docks are hurt much. The sweeps went more for the buildings. We can find room for half a dozen, I think, comfortably."

"That's just about what I want," said the Admiral. "We've lost the *Hindustan* and *New Zealand.* The *Canada* and *Newfoundland* are pretty badly mauled, and I've got half a dozen Frenchmen that would be all the better for a look over. The *Britain, Edward VII., Dominion* and *Commonwealth* are quite seaworthy, although, as you see, they've had it pretty hot in their topworks. The cruiser squadron is practically untouched. We've got the *Verite, Justice* and *Democratie,* but the *Verite* has got her propellers and rudders smashed. By the way, that ship of Erskine's, the *Ithuriel,* has turned out a perfect demon. She smashed up the first attack, sank nine destroyers and two cruisers, one of them was that big chap the *Dupleix,* before we came on the scene. During the action she wiped out I don't know how many destroyers and torpedo boats, sank the *Jeanne d'Arc* and saved my ship from being rammed by crippling the *Verite* just in the nick of time. If we only had a squadron of those boats and made Erskine Commodore, we'd wipe the fleets of Europe out in a month. Now that's my news. What's yours?"

"Bad enough," replied General French. "A powerful combined fleet of Germans and French, helped by some of these infernal things that seem as much at home in the air as they are in the water, are making a combined attack on Dover, and we seem to be getting decidedly the worst of it. Dover Castle is in flames, and nearly all the forts are in a bad way; so are the harbor fortifications. The Russians and Dutch are approaching London with a string of transports behind them, and four airships above them. Their objectives are supposed to be Tilbury and Woolwich on one hand, and Chatham on the other. By the way, weren't there any transports behind this French Fleet that you've settled up with?"

He had scarcely uttered the last word when a helio began to twinkle from the hill above Foreland.

"That's bad news," said the Admiral, "but wait now, there's something else. It's a good job the sun's come out, though it doesn't look very healthy."

The message that the helio twinkled out was as follows:

"Thirty large vessels, apparently transports, approaching from direction of Cherbourg and Brest about ten miles southeast by south."

"Very good," said the Admiral, rubbing his hands. "Of course they think we're beaten. I've got five French cruisers that they'll recognize. I'll get crews aboard them at once and convoy those transports in, and the Commanders will be about the most disgusted men in Europe when they get here."

Acting on the principle that all is fair in love and war, Admiral Beresford and the two Generals laid as pretty a trap for the French transports as the wit of man ever devised. Ten minutes' conversation among them sufficed to arrange matters. Then the Admiral, taking a list of the serviceable docks with him, went back on board the *Ithuriel* and ran out to the Fleet. He handed over the work of taking care of the lame ducks to Commodore Courtney of the *Britain*; then from the damaged British ships he made up the crews of the French cruisers, the *Jules Ferry, Leon Gambetta, Victor Hugo, Aube* and *Marseillaise.* He took command of the squadron on board the *Victor Hugo,* and to the amazement of officers and men alike, he ordered the Tricolor to be hoisted. At the same time, the White Ensign fluttered down from all the British ships that were not being taken into the dockyard and was replaced by the Tricolor. A few minutes afterward the French flag rose over Fort Monckton and upon a pole mast which had been put up amidst the ruins of Southsea Castle.

The French prisoners of course saw the ruse and knew that its very daring and impudence would command success. Some of them wrung their hands and danced in fury, others wept, and others cursed to the full capability of the French language, but there was no help for it. What was left of Portsmouth was already occupied by twenty thousand men of all arms from the Southern Division. The prisoners were disarmed and their ships were in the hands of the enemy to do what they pleased with, and so in helpless rage they watched the squadron of cruisers steam out to meet the transports, flying the French flag and manned by British crews. It meant either the most appalling carnage, or the capture of the First French Expeditionary Force consisting of fifty thousand men, ten thousand horses, and two hundred guns.

The daringly original stratagem was made all the easier of achievement by the fact that the Commanders of the French transports, counting upon the assistance of the airships and the enormous strength of the naval force which had been launched against Portsmouth, had taken victory for granted, and when the first line came in sight of land,

and officers and men saw the smoke-cloud that was still hanging over what twenty-four hours before had been the greatest of British strongholds, cheer after cheer went up. Portsmouth was destroyed and therefore the French Fleet must have been victorious. All that they had to do, therefore, was to steam in and take possession of what was left. At last, after all these centuries, the invasion of England had been accomplished, and Waterloo and Trafalgar avenged!

Happily, in the turmoil of the fight and the suddenness in which the remains of the French Fleet had been forced to surrender, the captain of the *Victor Hugo* had forgotten to sink his Code Book. The result was that when the cruiser squadron steamed out in two divisions to meet the transports, the French private signal, "Complete victory – welcome," was flying from the signalyard of the *Victor Hugo.* Again a mighty cheer thundered out from the deck of every transport. The cruisers saluted the transports with seventeen guns, and then the two divisions swung out to right and left, and took their stations on either flank of the transports.

And so, all unsuspecting, they steamed into Spithead, and when they saw the British ships lying at anchor, flying the Tricolor and the same flag waving over Fort Monckton and Southsea Castle, as well as from half a dozen other flagstaffs about the dockyards, there could be no doubt as to the magnitude and completeness of the victory which the French Fleet had gained, and moreover, were not those masts showing above the waters of Spithead, the masts of sunken British battleships.

Field-Marshal Purdin de Trevillion, Commander of the Expeditionary Force, accompanied by his staff, was on board the Messageries liner *Australien,* and led the column of transports. In perfect confidence he led the way in between the Spithead Forts, which also flew the Tricolor and saluted him as he went past. As the other vessels of the great flotilla followed in close order, Fort Monckton and the rest of the warships saluted; and then as the last transport entered the narrow waters, a very strange thing happened. The cruisers that had dropped behind spread themselves out in a long line behind the forts; the British ships slipped their moorings and steamed out from Stokes Bay and made a line across to Ryde. Destroyers and torpedo boats suddenly dotted the water with their black shapes, appearing as though from nowhere; then came down every Tricolor on fort and ship, and the White Ensign ran up in its place, and the same moment, the menacing guns swung round and there was the French flotilla, unarmed and crowded with men, caught like a flock of sheep between two packs of wolves.

Every transport stopped as if by common instinct. The French Marshal turned white to the lips. His hands went up in a gesture of despair, and he gasped to his second-in-command, who was standing beside him:

"Mon Dieu! Nous sommes trahis! Ces sacrés perfides Anglais! We are helpless, like rats in a trap. With us it is finished, we can neither fight nor escape."

While he was speaking, the huge bulk of the *Britain* steamed slowly towards the *Australien,* flying the signal "Do you surrender?" Within five hundred yards, the huge guns in her forward barbette swung round and the muzzles sank until the long chases pointed at the *Australien's* water-line. The Field-Marshal knew full well that it only needed the touch of a finger on a button to smash the *Australien* into fragments, and he knew too that the first shot from the flagship would be the signal for the whole Fleet to open fire, and that would mean massacre unspeakable. He was as brave a man as ever wore a uniform, but he knew that on the next words he should speak the lives of fifty thousand men depended. He took one more look round the ring of steel which enclosed him on every side, and then with livid lips and grinding teeth gave the order for the flag to be hauled down. The next moment he unbuckled his sword and hurled it into the sea; then with a deep groan he dropped fainting to the deck.

It would be useless to attempt to describe the fury and mortification with which the officers and men of the French Force saw the flags one by one flutter down from end to end of the long line of transports, but it was plain even to the rawest conscript that there was no choice save between surrender and massacre. They cursed and stamped about the decks or sat down and cried, according to temperament, and that, under the circumstances, was about all they could do.

Meanwhile, a steam pinnace came puffing out from the harbor, and in a few minutes General French was standing on the promenade deck of the *Australien.* The Field Marshal had already been carried below. A grey-haired officer in the uniform of a general came forward with his sword in his hand and said in excellent English, but with a shake in his voice:

"You are General French, I presume? Our Commander, Field-Marshal Purdin de Trevillion had such an access of anger when he found how we had been duped that he flung his sword into the sea. He then fainted, and is still unconscious. You will, therefore, perhaps accept my sword instead of his."

General French touched the hilt with his hand, and said:

"Keep it. General Devignes, and I hope your officers will do the same. I will accept your parole for all of them. You are the Field-Marshal's

Chief-of-Staff, I believe, and therefore, of course, your word is his. I am very sorry to hear of his illness."

"You have my word," replied General Devignes, "for myself and those of my officers who may be willing to give their parole, but for those who prefer to remain prisoners I cannot, of course, answer."

"Of course not," replied General French, with a rather provoking genial smile. "Now I will trouble you to take your ships into the harbor. I will put a guard on each as she passes; meanwhile, your men will pile arms and get ready to disembark. We cannot offer you much of a welcome, I'm afraid, for those airships of yours have almost reduced Portsmouth to ruins, to say nothing of sending ten of our battleships and cruisers to the bottom. I can assure you, General, that the losses are not all on your side."

"No, General," replied the Frenchman, "but for the present, at least, the victory is on yours."

Then transport after transport filed into the harbor, and General Hamilton and his staff took charge of the disembarkation. Six of the British lame ducks had been got safely into dock, and every available man was slaving away in deadly earnest to repair the damage done in those terrible two hours. Repairs were also being carried out as rapidly as possible on the cruisers and battleships lying in Spithead, and as shipload after shipload of the disarmed French soldiers were landed, they were set to work, first at clearing up the dockyards and getting them into something like working order, and then clearing up the ruins of the three towns.

The news of Admiral Beresford's magnificent coup had already reached London, and the reply had come back terse and to the point:

> "Excellently well done. Congratulate Admiral Beresford and all concerned. We are hard pressed at Dover, and London is threatened. Send *Ithuriel* to Dover as soon as possible, and let her come on here when she has given any possible help. Land and sea defense of south and southeast at discretion of yourself, Domville and Beresford.
>
> "CONNAUGHT"

By some miracle, the Keppel's Head, perhaps the most famous naval hostelry in the south of England, had escaped the shells from the airships, and so General French had made it his headquarters for the time being. Sir Compton Domville had received a rather serious injury from a splinter in the left arm during the destruction of the Naval Barracks, but he had had his wounds dressed and insisted, against the advice of the doctors, in driving down to the Hard and talking matters over with General French. They were discussing the disposition of the French prisoners and the huge amount of war material which had been captured, when the telegram was delivered. They had scarcely read it when there was a knock at the door and an orderly entered, and said:

"Captain Erskine, of the *Ithuriel,* would be pleased to see the General when he's at liberty."

"The very man!" said General French. "This is the young gentleman," he continued, turning to Admiral Domville, "who practically saved us from two torpedo attacks, won the Fleet action for us, and saved Beresford from being rammed at the moment of victory."

The door opened again, and Erskine came in. He saluted and said:

"General, if I may suggest it, I shall not be much more use here, and my lieutenant, Denis Castellan, has just had a telegram from his aunt and sister, who are in London, saying that things are pretty bad there. I fancy I might be of some use if you would let me go, sir."

"Let you go!" laughed the General. "Why, my dear sir, you've got to go. Here's a telegram that I've just had from His Royal Highness the Commander-in-Chief, saying that Dover and London are in a bad way, and telling me to send you round at once. When can you start?"

"Well, sir," replied Erskine, after a moment's thought, "we're not injured in any way, but it will take a couple of hours, I'm afraid, to replenish our motive power, and fill up with shell, and added to that, I should like to have a good overhaul of the machinery."

"Just listen to that, now!" exclaimed Admiral Beresford, who had entered the room while he was speaking. "Here's a man who has done nearly as much single-handed as the rest of us put together and fought through as stiff a Fleet action as the hungriest fire-eater in the navy wants to see, and tells you he isn't injured, while half of us are knocked to scrap-iron. I wish we had fifty *Ithuriels,* there'd be very little landing on English shores."

"I don't think you have very much to complain of in the French landing at Portsmouth, Beresford," laughed Sir Compton Domville. "I don't want to flatter you, but it was an absolute stroke of genius. We shall have to set those fellows to work on the forts and yards, and get some guns into position again. It isn't exactly what they came for but they'll come in very useful. But that can wait. Here's the wire from the Commander-in-Chief. Captain Erskine, you are to get round to Dover and London as soon as possible, and, I presume, do all the damage you can on the way. General French is going to London as soon as a special can be got ready for him."

"May I ask a great favor, sir?" said Erskine.

"Anything, after what you've done," replied Sir Compton. "What is it?"

General French and Lord Beresford nodded in agreement, and Erskine continued, addressing Lord Beresford: "That Mr. Lennard, whom your lordship met on board the *Ithuriel*, has given me the formula of a new high explosive. Absurdly simple, but simply terrific in its effect. I made up half a dozen shells with it and tried them. I gave the *Dupleix* three rounds. They seem to reduce steel to dust, and, as far as we could see every man on the decks dropped as if he had been struck by lightning. From what we have done with them I think they will be of enormous value. Now Mr. Lennard is very anxious to get to London and the north of England, and if General French could find him a place in his special –"

"My dear sir," interrupted the General, "I shall be only too delighted to know your maker of thunderbolts. Is he here now?"

"Yes, sir, he's in the smoking-room with Lieutenant Castellan. And that reminds me, if I am to go to London, I hope you will allow me to hand over the German spy that we caught here as soon as convenient."

"Bring them both in," said General French. "Sir Compton and General Hamilton will court-martial your spy this morning, and, I hope, shoot him this evening."

Within an hour, Lennard, who had something more serious now to think about than even war, was flying away Londonwards in General French's special, with a letter of introduction from Denis Castellan to his aunt and sister, and an hour after the special had started, the *Ithuriel* had cleared the narrow waters and was tearing up the Channel at fifty miles an hour, to see what havoc she could work on the assailants of London and Dover.

Chapter XVII

AWAY FROM THE WARPATH

When Lennard entered the little drawing room in the house in Westbourne Terrace, where Norah Castellan and her aunt were staying, he had decided to do something which, without his knowing it, probably made a very considerable difference in his own fortunes and those of two or three other people.

During his brief but exciting experiences on board the *Ithuriel,* he had formed a real friendship for both Erskine and Castellan, and he had come to the conclusion that Denis's sister and aunt would be very much safer in the remote seclusion of Whernside than in a city which might within the next few days share the fate of Portsmouth and Gosport. He was instantly confirmed in this resolution when Mrs. O'Connor and her niece came into the room. Never had he seen a more perfect specimen of the Irishwoman, who is a lady by Nature's own patent of nobility, than Mrs. O'Connor, and, with of course one exception, never had he seen such a beautiful girl as Norah Castellan.

He was friends with them in half an hour, and inside an hour he had accepted their invitation to dine and sleep at the house and help them to get ready for their unexpected journey to the North the next morning.

He went back to the Grand and got his portmanteau and Gladstone bag and returned to Westbourne Terrace in time for afternoon tea. Meanwhile, he had bought the early copies of all the evening papers and read up the condition of things in London, which, in the light of his experiences at Portsmouth, did not appear to him to be in any way promising. He gave Norah and her aunt a full, true and particular account of the assault on Portsmouth, the doings of the *Ithuriel,* the great Fleet action, and the brilliant *ruse de guerre* which Admiral Beresford had used to capture the First French Army Corps that had landed in England – and landed as prisoners.

The news in the afternoon papers, coupled with what he already knew of the tactics of the enemy, impressed Lennard so gravely that he succeeded in persuading Mrs. O'Connor and Norah to leave London by the midnight sleeping-car train from St. Pancras for Whernside, since no one knew at what time during the night John Castellan or his lieutenants might not order an indiscriminate bombardment of London from the air. He was also very anxious, for reasons of his own, to get back to his work at the observatory and make his preparations for the carrying out of an undertaking compared with which the war, terrible as it was and would be, could only be considered as the squabblings of children or lunatics.

His task was not one of aggression or conquest, but of salvation, and the enemy he was going to fight was an invader not of states or countries, but of a whole world, and unless the assault of this invader from the outer wilderness of Space were repelled, the result would not be merely the destruction of ships and fortresses, or the killing of a few hundreds or thousands of men on the battlefield; it would mean nothing less than a holocaust which would involve the whole human race, and the simultaneous annihilation of all that the genius of man had so laboriously accumulated during the slow, uncounted ages of his progress from the brute to the man.

They left the train at Settle at six o'clock the next morning, and were at once taken charge of by the station-master, who had had his instructions by telephone from the Parmenter mansion on the slopes of Great Whernside. He conducted them at once to the Midland Hotel, where they found a suite of apartments, luxuriously furnished, with fires blazing in the grates, and everything looking very cozy under the soft glow of the shaded electric lights. Baths were ready and breakfast would be on the table at seven. At eight, Mr. Parmenter, who practically owned this suite of rooms, would drive over with Miss Parmenter in a couple of motorcars and take the party to the house.

"Sure, then," said Mrs. O'Connor, when the arrangements had been explained to her, "it must be very comfortable to have all the money to buy just what you want, and make everything as easy as all this, and it's yourself, Mr. Lennard, we have to thank for making us the guests of a millionaire, when neither Norah nor myself have so much as seen one. Is he a very great man, this Mr. Parmenter? It seems to me to be something like going to dine with a duke."

"My dear Mrs. O'Connor," laughed Lennard, "I can assure you that you will find this master of millions one of Nature's own gentlemen. Although he can make men rich or poor by a stroke of his pen, and, with a few others like him, wield such power as was never in the hands of kings, you wouldn't know him from a plain English country gentleman if it wasn't for his American accent, and there's not very much of that."

"And his daughter, Miss Auriole, what's she like?" said Norah. "A beauty, of course."

Lennard flushed somewhat suspiciously, and a keen glance of Norah's Irish eyes read the meaning of that flush in an instant.

"Miss Parmenter is considered to be very beautiful," he replied, "and I must confess that I share the general opinion."

"I thought so," said Norah, with a little nod that had a great deal of meaning in it. "Now, I suppose we'd better go and change, or we'll be late for breakfast. I certainly don't want the beautiful Miss Parmenter to see me in this state for the first time."

"My dear Miss Castellan, I can assure you that you have not the faintest reason to fear any comparison that might be made," laughed Lennard as he left the room and went to have his tub.

Punctually at eight a double "Toot-toot" sounded from the street in front of the main entrance to the hotel. Norah ran to the window and saw two splendidly-appointed Napier cars – although, of course, she didn't know a Napier from a Darracq. Something in female shape with peaked cap and goggles, gauntleted and covered from head to foot in a heavy fur coat, got out of the first car, and another shape, rather shorter but almost similarly clad, got out of the second. Five minutes later there was a knock at the door of the breakfast-room. It opened, and Norah saw what the cap and the goggles and the great fur coat had hidden. During the next few seconds, two of the most beautiful girls in the two hemispheres looked at each other, as only girls and women can look. Then Auriole put out both her hands and said, quite simply:

"You are Norah Castellan. I hope we shall be good friends. If we're not, I'm afraid it will be my fault."

Norah took her hands and said:

"I think it would more likely be mine, after what Mr. Lennard has been telling us of yourself and your father."

At this moment Lennard saved the situation as far as he was concerned by making the other introductions, and Mrs. O'Connor took the hand which wielded the terrible power of millions and experienced a curious sort of surprise at finding that it was just like other hands, and that the owner of it was bending over hers with one of those gestures of simple courtesy which are the infallible mark of the American gentleman. In a few minutes they were all as much at home together as though they had known each other for weeks. Then came the preparation of Norah and her aunt for the motor ride, and then the ride itself.

The sun had risen clearly, and there was a decided nip of frost in the keen Northern air. The roads were hard and clean, and the twenty-five-mile run over them, winding through the valleys and climbing the ridges with the heather-clad, rock-crowned hills on all sides, now sliding down a slope or shooting along a level, or taking a rise in what seemed a flying leap, was by far the most wonderful experience that Norah and her aunt had ever had.

Auriole drove the first car, and had Norah sitting beside her on the front seat. Her aunt and the mechanician were sitting in the tonneau behind. Mr. Parmenter drove the second car with Lennard beside him. His tonneau was filled with luggage.

At the end of the eighteenth mile the cars, going at a quite illegal speed, jumped a ridge between two heather-clad moors, which in South Africa would have been called a nek, and dived down along a white road leading into a broad forest track, sunlit now, but bordered on either side by the twilight of towering pines and firs through which the sunlight filtered only in little flakes, which lay upon the last year's leaves and cones, somewhat as an electric light might have fallen on a monkish manuscript of the thirteenth century.

Then came two more miles on hard, well-kept roads, so perfectly graded that the upward slope was hardly perceptible.

"We're on our own ground now and I guess I'll let her out," said Miss Auriole. "Don't be frightened, Norah. These things look big and strong, but it's quite wonderful what they'll do when there's a bit of human sense running them. See that your goggles are right and twist your veil in a bit tighter, I'm going to give you a new sensation."

She waved her hand to her father in the car behind and put on the fourth speed lever, and said: "Hold tight now."

Norah nodded, for she could hardly breathe as it was. Then the pines and firs on either side of the broad drive melted into a green-grey blur. The road under them was like a rapidly unwinding ribbon. The hilltops which showed above the trees rose up now to the right hand and now to the left, as the car swung round the curves. Every now and then Norah looked at the girl beside her, controlling the distance-devouring monster with one hand on a little wheel, her left foot on a pedal and her right hand ready to work the levers if necessary.

The two miles of the drive from the gates to the front door of Whernside House, a long, low-lying two-storeyed, granite-built house, which was about as good a combination of outward solidity and indoor comfort as you could find in the British Islands, was covered in two and a half minutes, and the car pulled up, as Norah thought, almost at full speed and stopped dead in front of the steps leading up from the broad road to the steps leading up to the terrace which ran along the whole southward front of Whernside House.

"I reckon, Miss Castellan –"

"If you say Miss Castellan, I shall get back to Settle by the first conveyance that I can hire."

"Now, that's just nice of you, Norah. What I was going to say, if I hadn't made that mistake, was, that this would be about the first time that you had covered two miles along a road at fifty miles an hour, and that's what you've just done. Pretty quick, isn't it? Oh, there's Lord Westerham on the terrace! Come for lunch, I suppose. He's a very great man here, you know. Lord-Lieutenant of the West Riding of Yorkshire, fought through the Boer War, got made a Colonel by some miracle when he was only about twenty-eight, went to Lhassa, and now he's something like Commander-in-Chief of the Yeomanry and Volunteers round here – and without anything of that sort, he's just about the best sort of man you want to meet. Come along, I'll introduce you."

The two cars stopped at the steps leading up to the terrace, a man in khaki, with a stretch of a dozen ribbons across the left side of his tunic, came bareheaded down the steps and opened the side door of Auriole's motorcar. Auriole pushed her goggles up and held out her gauntleted hand, and said:

"What! Lord Westerham! Well now, this is nice of you. Come to lunch, of course. And how's the recruiting going on?"

Then without waiting for a reply, she went on: "Norah, dear, this is Lord Westerham, Lord-Lieutenant of this part of the County of York, Colonel commanding the West Riding Yeomanry and lots of other things that I don't understand."

Norah pushed her goggles up and tilted her hat back. Auriole saw a flash of recognition pass like lightning between their eyes. She noticed that Norah's cheeks were a little bit brighter than even the speed of the car could account for. She saw, too, that there was a flush under the tan of Lord Westerham's face, and to her these were signs of great comfort.

"I don't know how this particular miracle has been arranged," said Lord Westerham, as he gave his hand to Norah and took her out of the car, "but a re-introduction is, if you will allow me to say so, Miss Parmenter, rather superfluous. I have known Miss Castellan for quite two years, at least, I had the pleasure of meeting her in Connemara, and we have fished and shot and sailed together until we became almost friends."

Auriole's eyes, observant at all times, had been working hard during the last two or three minutes, and in those few minutes she had learned a great deal. Arthur Lennard, who also had his eyes wide open, had learnt in his own slow, masculine way about as much, and perhaps a little more. He and Lord Westerham had been school-fellows and college chums and good friends for years, but of late a shadow had come between them, and it's hardly necessary to say that it was the shadow of a woman. He knew perfectly well by this time that Lord Westerham was, in the opinion of Mr. Parmenter, the husband-designate, one might say, of Auriole. Young as he was, he already had a distinguished record as a soldier and an administrator, but he was also heir to one of the oldest Marquisates in England with a very probable reversion to a dukedom.

This was what he had been thinking of that night in the observatory when he told Auriole of the fate that was approaching the world. No one knew better than he how brilliant a figure she would make in Society as the Marchioness of Westerham, granted always that the Anglo-Saxon would do now as he had ever done, fling the invader back upon his own shores or into the sea which he had crossed: but that swift flash of recognition seen as his car came up behind Auriole's, and the slight but most significant change which had come over the features of both of them as he handed her out of the car, had instantly banished the shadow and made him a happier man than he had been for a good many months past.

Still he was one of those hard-headed, practical men who rightly consider that the very worst enemy either to friendship between man and man, or love between man and woman, is an unexplained misunderstanding, and so in that moment he decided to "have it out" with his lordship on the first possible opportunity.

Chapter XVIII

A GLIMPSE OF THE PERIL

The morning was spent in a general overhaul of the observatory and the laboratory in which Lennard had discovered and perfected the explosive which had been used with such deadly effect in the guns of the *Ithuriel.* Lunch was an entirely delightful meal, and when it was over Auriole took Mrs. O'Connor and Norah up to her own particular domain in the house to indulge in that choicest of feminine luxuries, a good long talk. Mr. Parmenter excused himself and disappeared into his study to get ready for the evening mail, and so Lord Westerham and Lennard were left to their own devices for a couple of hours or so. This was just what Lennard wanted, and so he proposed a stroll and a smoke in the Park.

They lit their cigars and walked for a few minutes along a pine-shaded path. His lordship had an intuitive idea that his companion had something to say to him – albeit he was very far from imagining what that something was to be – and so he thought he had better let him begin. When they were out of sight or hearing of anyone, Lennard slowed down his pace a little and said somewhat abruptly:

"Westerham, I am going to ask you a question which you will probably think a rather impertinent one, and, moreover, whether you choose to answer it or not, I hope you will not for the present ask me why I ask it. Now there are a good many 'asks' in that, but as the matter is somewhat important to both of us, I wanted to put the thing plainly, even at the expense of a little tautology."

Lord Westerham, in addition to being a gentleman and a soldier, was also one of the most frankly open-minded men that another honest man could wish to have anything to do with, and so, after a long pull at his cigar, he looked round and said:

"My dear Lennard, we were school-fellows once, and we managed to worry through Cambridge together – you with a great deal more kudos than I did – and we have been very good friends since, so there can't be any question of impertinence between us, although there might be some unpleasantness for one or both of us. But, anyhow, whatever it is, out with it. Honestly, I don't think you could offend me if you tried."

"That's just what I thought you would say," replied Lennard. "And I think you are about the only man I should like to ask such a question; but after what you've just said I'll put it just as shortly as it can be made."

"And the question is?" asked Lord Westerham, blowing a long stream of blue smoke up through the still air towards the tops of the pine trees.

There was a little pause, during which Lennard bit off about half an inch of the end of his cigar, spat it out, and took two or three more puffs from what was left. Then he said, in a dry, almost harsh tone:

"The question is quite a short one, Westerham, and you can answer it by a simple yes or no. It's just this: Do you intend to make Miss

Parmenter Marchioness of Westerham or not? Other things of course being equal, as we used to say at school."

Somewhat to Lennard's astonishment, Lord Westerham's cigar shot from his lips like a torpedo from a tube, and after it came an explosion of laughter, which fully accounted for its sudden ejectment. His lordship leant up against a convenient pine and laughed till he was almost speechless.

"What the devil's the matter with you, Westerham?" said Lennard, with a note of anger in his voice. "You'll excuse my saying so, but it seems hardly a question for a sort of explosion like that. I have been asking you a question which, as you might have seen, concerns me rather closely."

Lord Westerham sobered down at once, although his voice was still somewhat tremulous with suppressed laughter when he said:

"My dear chap, I'm very sorry. It was beastly rude of me to laugh, but I'm quite sure you'll forgive me when you know the facts or, at least, *the* fact, and that is as follows, as they say in the newspapers. When I tell you that your sweetheart drove my sweetheart up to the house today from Settle –"

"What, Norah Castellan!" exclaimed Lennard. "I didn't even know that you had met her before."

"Haven't I!" replied Lord Westerham. "Look here, it was this way."

And then he began a story of a fishing and shooting trip to Connemara, where he had rented certain salmon streams and shooting moors from a squire of the county, named Lismore, who was very much in love with Norah Castellan, and how he had fished and shot and yachted with her and the brother who had sold his diabolical inventions to the enemies of England, until he had come to love the sister as much as he hated the brother. And when he had done, Lennard told him of the swimming race in Clifden Bay, and many other things to which Lord Westerham listened with an interest which grew more and more intense as every minute passed; until when Lennard stopped, he crossed the road and held out his hand and said:

"I've got the very place to suit you. A cannel-coal mine near Bolton in Lancashire with a perpendicular shaft, twelve hundred feet deep. The very place to do your work. It's yours from today, and if the thing comes off, Papa Parmenter shall give a couple of hundred thousand dowry instead of buying the mine. I don't think he'll kick at that. Now, let's go back and have a whisky-and-soda. I've got to be off recruiting tomorrow."

"I wish I could join the Yeomanry and come with you, if you would have me," laughed Lennard, whose spirits had been rising rapidly during the last half-hour or so, "only I reckon, as Mr. Parmenter would put it, that I shall have all my work cut out getting ready to give our celestial invader a warm reception. To begin with, it won't exactly be child's play building a cannon twelve hundred feet long."

"I wonder what they'd think of a proposition like that at the War Office?" laughed Lord Westerham in reply. "Several permanent officials would certainly faint on the spot."

A sharp frost set in during the night, and the sky was brilliantly clear. After dinner, when the ladies had left the table, Lennard said to Mr. Parmenter:

"I am going to renew my acquaintance with our celestial visitor tonight. I shall want a couple of hours to run over my calculations and verify the position of the comet up to date; and then, say at eleven o'clock, I should like you and Lord Westerham to come up to the observatory and have a somewhat serious talk."

The owner of the great reflector looked up quickly over his wine-glass and said:

"Look here, Mr. Lennard, I guess this poor old country of yours has about enough serious matters on hand just now without worrying about comets. What's the trouble now?"

"My dear sir," replied Lennard, gravely, "this is a matter which not only England, but every other country in the world, will have to trouble about before very long."

"Say, that sounds pretty serious," said Mr. Parmenter. "What's the worry with this old comet of yours, anyhow?"

Lord Westerham smiled, and Lennard could not help smiling too as he replied:

"It is too long a story to tell now, sir, and what is more, I cannot tell it until I have reverified my observations and figures, and, besides, the ladies will be expecting us. I shall be quite ready for you by eleven. By the way, I haven't told you yet that those shells were a perfect success, from our point of view, at least. It seems rather curious how that all came about, I must say. Here's Denis Castellan, the brother of the traitor, a British naval officer, and like his sister an acquaintance of Westerham's. I discover the explosive, tell you about it, you tell Westerham, and send me off to try it on the *Ithuriel*, and here I come back from London with Miss Castellan and her aunt."

"Quite an excellent arrangement of things on the part of the Fates," remarked Lord Westerham, with a meaning which Mr. Parmenter did not understand.

"Why, yes," said their host, "quite like a piece out of a story, isn't it? And so that explosive got its work in all right, Mr. Lennard?"

"As far as we could see," replied Lennard. "It tore steel armor into shreds as if it had been cardboard, and didn't leave a living thing anywhere within several yards of the focus of the explosion. Erskine and Castellan are filling up with it, and I expect we shall hear something about it from London before long. I am glad to say that Lord Beresford told me that after what he had seen of our fire, Government and private gun factories were going to work night and day turning out pneumatic guns to use it. The effect of it on land if a battery once gets within reach of large masses of men will be something frightful."

"Sounds pretty useful," said Lord Westerham, who was one of those soldiers who rightly believe that the most merciless methods of waging war are in the end most merciful.

By nine o'clock Lennard was in the equatorial chamber of the observatory, taking his first observations since he had left for Portsmouth the week before. The ghostly shape pictured on the great reflector was bigger and brighter now, although, to his great comfort, none of the scientific papers had made any mention of its discovery by other observers. When he had noted its exact position, he went to his desk and plunged into a maze of calculations.

Precisely at eleven there was a tap at the door and Mr. Parmenter and Lord Westerham came in. Lord Westerham, as the guest, had the first look at the approaching World Peril; then Mr. Parmenter took a long squint into the eye-piece and then they sat down, and Lennard told Mr. Parmenter, in the cold, precise language of science, the story which he had already told to Auriole and Lord Westerham.

The millionaire, who had listened with an attention that even he had never given to any subject before, smoked in silence for a few moments after Lennard had finished, and then he said quietly:

"Well, I reckon that's about the biggest order that two or three human beings have ever been called upon to fill. One thing's certain. It'd make these fighting fellows feel pretty foolish if they could be got to believe it, which they couldn't. No disrespect to you, Lord Westerham, because I take it you do believe it."

"Certainly I do," he replied. "Lennard was never known to make a mistake in figures, and I am perfectly certain that he would not make any in working out such a terrific problem as this. I think I may also say that I have equal confidence in his plan for saving humanity from the terrible fate which threatens it."

"That's good hearing," said Mr. Parmenter, dryly. "Personally, I don't quite feel that I've finished up with this old world yet, and if it's a question of dollars – as far as I'm concerned, as I've got a few millions hanging around loose, I might as well use them to help to save the human race from being burned to death as to run corners and trusts, which won't be much use anyhow if we can't stop this comet, or whatever it is. Now, Mr. Lennard, what's your plan for the scientific salvation of the world?"

"There is nothing new about the idea," replied Lennard, "except its application to the present circumstances. Of course you have read Jules Verne's *Journey to the Moon?* Well, my plan is simply to do the same thing on a much bigger scale, only instead of firing men and dogs and chickens out of my cannon, I am going to fire something like a ton and a half of explosives.

"The danger is in the contact of the nucleus of the comet with the earth's atmosphere. If that can be prevented there is no further cause for alarm; so, to put the matter quite shortly, my projectile will have an initial velocity of ten miles a second, and therefore a range that is practically infinite, for that velocity will carry it beyond the sphere of the earth's attraction.

"Hence, if the gun is properly trained and fired at precisely the right moment, and if the fuse does its work, the projectile will pass into the nucleus of the comet, and, before the heat has time to melt the shell, the charge will explode and the nucleus – the only dangerous part – will either be blown to fragments or dissipated in gas. Therefore, instead of what I might be allowed to call a premature Day of Judgment, we shall simply have a magnificent display of celestial fireworks, which will probably amount to nothing more than an unparalleled shower of shooting stars, as they are popularly called.

"The details of the experiment will be practically the same as those Jules Verne described – I mean as regards the making and firing of the cannon – only, as we haven't time to get a big enough hole dug, I should strongly advise the acceptance of Lord Westerham's very opportune offer."

"That's so," said Mr. Parmenter, quietly, "but I've got a sort of fancy for running this business myself. My reflector discovered this comet, thanks, of course, to the good use you made of it, and it seems to me that I'm in a way responsible for making it harmless if that can be done, and so I'm not disposed to take that convenient colliery as a gift from anyone, no, not even you, Lord Westerham. You see, my lord, all that I can do here is just finding the dollars, and to a man in your position, doing his best to get as many men and horses and guns together for the defense of his country, money is money. Will you take a quarter of a million pounds for that colliery?"

"No, I won't, Mr. Parmenter," laughed Lord Westerham. "In the first place, the colliery isn't worth a tenth of that, and this country can very well afford to pay for her own defense. Besides, you must remember that you will have to pay for the work: I mean casing the pit-shaft, smelting the metal and building the shell, to say nothing of the thousand and one other expenses of which Lennard can tell you more than I. For one thing, I expect you will have a hundred thousand or so to pay in damage to surrounding property after that cannon has gone off. In other words, if you do save the world you'll probably have to pay pretty stiffly for doing it. They're excellent business people in Lancashire, you know."

"I don't quite see the logic of that, Lord Westerham," replied Mr. Parmenter a little testily. "If we can put this business through, the dollars couldn't be much better used, and if we can't they won't be much use to me or anyone else. It's worth doing, anyhow, if it's only to show what new-world enterprise helped with old-world brains can do in bringing off a really big thing, and that's why I want to buy that colliery."

"Well, Mr. Parmenter," laughed Lord Westerham again, "we won't quarrel over that. I'm not a business man, but I believe it's generally recognized that the essence of all business is compromise. I'll meet you halfway. For the present you shall take the pit for nothing and pay all expense connected with making a cannon of it. If that cannon does its work you shall pay me two hundred thousand pounds for the use of it – and I'll take your I.O.U. for the amount now. Will that suit you?"

"That's business," said Mr. Parmenter, getting up and going to Lennard's desk. "There you are, my lord," he continued, as he came back with a half sheet of notepaper in his hand, "and I only hope I shall have to pay that money."

Chapter XIX

A CHANGE OF SCENE

The *Ithuriel* had orders to call at Folkestone and Dover in order to report the actual state of affairs there to the Commander-in-Chief by telegraph if Erskine could get ashore or by flash-signal if he could not, and incidentally to do as much damage as he could without undue risk to his craft if he considered that circumstances demanded it.

He arrived off Folkestone just before dusk, and, as he expected, found that there were half a dozen large transports, carrying probably eight thousand men and a proportionate number of horses and quick-firing guns, convoyed by four cruisers and ten destroyers, lying off the harbor. There were evidently no airships with the force, as, if there had been, they would certainly have been hovering over the town and shelling Shorncliffe Barracks and the forts from the air. A brisk artillery duel was proceeding between the land batteries and the squadron, and the handsome town was already in flames in several places.

Erskine, of course, recognized at once that this attack was simultaneous with that on Dover; the object of the enemy being obviously the capture of the shore line of railway between the two great Channel ports, which would provide the base of a very elongated triangle, the sides of which would be roughly formed by the roads and railways running to the westward and southward through Ashford and Maidstone, and to the northward and eastward through Canterbury, Faversham and Sittingbourne, and meeting at Rochester and Chatham, where the land forces of the invaders would, if all went well, co-operate with the sea forces in a combined attack on London, which would, of course, be preceded by a bombardment of fortified positions from the air.

Knowing what he did of the disastrous results of the battle of Portsmouth, he came to the conclusion that it was his duty to upset this plan of attack at all hazards, so he called Castellan up into the conning-tower and asked his advice on the situation.

"I see just what you mean, Erskine," replied the Lieutenant, when he had taken a good look at the map of Kent, "and it's my opinion that you'll do more to help London from here and Dover just now than you will from the Thames. Those French cruisers are big ones, though I don't quite recognize which they are, and they carry twice or three times the metal that those miserable forts do – which comes of trusting everything to the Fleet, as though these were the days of wooden walls and sails instead of steam battleships, fast cruisers and destroyers, to say nothing of submarines and airships. These Frenchies here don't know anything about the hammering they've got at Portsmouth and the capture of the transports, so they'll be expecting that force to be moving on London by the Brighton and South Coast line instead of re-building our forts and dockyards; so you go in and sink and smash everything in sight. That's just my best advice to you."

"It seems pretty rough on those chaps on the transports, doesn't it?" said Erskine, with a note of regret in his voice. "We shan't be able to pick up any of them. It will be pretty like murder."

"And what's that?" exclaimed Castellan, pointing to the fires in the town. "Don't ye call shelling a defenseless watering-place and burning unarmed people to death in their own homes murder? What if ye had your sister, or your mother, or your sweetheart there? How would ye feel about murder then?"

Denis Castellan spoke feelingly, for his captain possessed not only a mother, but also a very charming sister in connection with whom he cherished certain not altogether ill-founded hopes which might perchance be realized now that war had come and promotion was fairly sure for those who "got through all right."

Erskine nodded and said between his teeth:

"Yes, you're right, old man. Such mercy as they give – such shall they have. Get below and take charge. We'd better go for the cruisers first and sink them. That'll stop the shelling of the town anyhow. Then we'll tackle the destroyers, and after that, if the transports don't surrender – well, the Lord have mercy on them when those shells of Lennard's get among them, for they'll want it."

"And divil a bit better do they deserve. What have we done to them that they should all jump on us at once like this?" growled Denis as the platform sank with him. "There isn't one, no, nor two of them that dare tackle the old sea-dog alone."

Which remark was Irish but perfectly true.

By this time it was dusk enough for the *Ithuriel* to approach the unsuspecting cruisers unseen, as nothing but her conning-tower was soon visible, even at five hundred yards, and this would vanish when she sank to make her final rush.

The cruisers were the *Charner, Chanzy, Bruix* and *Latouche-Treville,* all of about five thousand tons, and carrying two 7.6 in., six 5.5 in. and six 9 pounders in addition to their small quick-firers. They were steaming in an oval course of about two miles long in line ahead, delivering their bow, stern and broadside fire as they circled. The effect of the shells along the strip of coast was terrible, and by the time the *Ithuriel* came on the scene of action Sandgate, Shorncliffe and Folkestone were ablaze. The destroyers were of course shepherding the transports until the cruisers had silenced the shore batteries and prepared the way for the landing.

The *Latouche-Treville* was leading the French line when Erskine gave the order to sink and ram. Her captain never so much as suspected the presence of a British warship until his vessel reeled under the shock of the ram, trembled from stem to stern, and began to settle quickly by the head. Before she had time to sink the *Ithuriel* had shaken herself free, swung round in half a curve, and ripped the port quarter of the *Chanzy* open ten feet below the water line. Then she charged the *Bruix* amidships and nearly cut her in half, and as the *Charner* steamed up to the rescue of her stricken consorts her screws dragged her back from the sinking ship and her stern ram crashed into the Frenchman's starboard side under the foremast, and in about a quarter of an hour from the delivery of the mysterious attack the four French cruisers were either sunk or sinking.

It would be almost impossible to describe the effect which was produced by this sudden and utterly unexpected calamity, not only upon the astounded invaders, but upon the defenders, who, having received the welcome tidings of the tremendous disaster which had befallen the French Expedition at Portsmouth, were expecting aid in a very different form. Like their assailants, they had seen nothing, heard nothing, until the French cruisers suddenly ceased fire, rolled over and disappeared.

But a few minutes after the *Charner* had gone down, all anxiety on the part of the defenders was, for the time being, removed. The *Ithuriel* rose to the surface; her searchlight projector turned inshore, and she flashed in the Private Code:

> "Suppose you have the news from Portsmouth. I am now going to smash destroyers and sink transports if they don't surrender. Don't shoot: might hurt me. Get ready for prisoners.
>
> "Erskine, *Ithuriel*"

It was perhaps the most singular message that had ever been sent from a sea force to a land force, but it was as well understood as it was welcome, and soon the answering signals flashed back:

> "Well done, *Ithuriel.* Heard news. Go ahead!"

Then came the turn of the destroyers. The *Ithuriel* rose out of the water till her forward ram showed its point six feet above the waves. Erskine ordered full speed, and within another twenty-five minutes the tragedy of Spithead had been repeated on a smaller scale. The destroying monster rushed round the transports, hunting the *torpilleurs de haute mer* down one after the other as a greyhound might run rabbits down, smashed them up and sank them almost before their officers and crew had time to learn what had happened to them – and then with his searchlight Erskine signaled to the transports in the International Code, which is universally understood at sea:

> "Transports steam quarter speed into harbor and surrender. If a shot is fired shall sink you as others."

Five of the six flags came down with a run and all save one of the transports made slowly for the harbor. Their commanders were wise enough to know that a demon of the deep which could sink cruisers before they could fire a shot and smash destroyers as if they were pleasure boats could make very short work of liners and cargo steamers, so they bowed to the inevitable and accepted with what grace they could defeat and capture instead of what an hour or so ago looked like certain victory. But the captain of the sixth, the one that was farthest out to sea, made a dash for liberty – or Dover.

Erskine took down the receiver and said quietly:

> "Center forward gun. Train: fire!"

The next moment a brilliant blaze of flame leapt up between the transport's funnels. They crumpled up like scorched parchment. Her whole super-structure seemed to take fire at once and she stopped.

Again flashed the signal:

> "Surrender or I'll ram."

The Tricolor fluttered slowly down through the damp, still evening air from the transport's main truck, and almost at the same moment a fussy little steam pinnace – which had been keeping itself snugly out of harm's way since the first French cruiser had gone down – puffed busily out of the harbor, and the proudest midshipman in the British Navy – for the time being, at least – ran from transport to transport, crowded with furious and despairing Frenchmen, and told them, individually and collectively, the course to steer if they wanted to get safely into Folkestone harbor and be properly taken care of.

Then out of the growing darkness to the westward long gleams of silver light flashed up from the dull grey water and wandered about the under-surface of the gathering clouds, coming nearer and growing brighter every minute, jumping about the firmament as though the men behind the projectors were either mad or drunk; but the signals spelt out to those who understood them the cheering words:

> "All right. We'll look after these fellows. Commander-in-Chief's orders: Concentrate on Chilham, Canterbury and Dover."

"That's all right," said Erskine to himself, as he read the signals. "Beresford's got them comfortably settled already, and he's sending someone to help here. Well, I think we've done our share and we'd better get along to Dover and London."

He flashed the signal: "Good-bye and good luck!" to the shore, and shaped his course for Dover.

So far, in spite of the terrible losses that had been sustained by the Reserve Fleet and the Channel Fleet, the odds of battle were still a long way in favor of Britain, in spite of the enormous forces ranged against her. At least so thought both Erskine and Castellan until they got within about three miles of Dover harbor, and Castellan, looking on sea and land and sky, exclaimed:

"Great Heaven help us! This looks like the other place let loose!"

Chapter XX

THE NIGHT OF TERROR BEGINS —

Denis Castellan had put the situation tersely, but with a considerable amount of accuracy. Earth and sea and sky were ablaze with swarms of shooting, shifting lights, which kept crossing each other and making ever-changing patterns of a magnificent embroidery, and amidst these, huge shells and star-rockets were bursting in clouds of smoke and many-colored flame. The thunder of the big guns, the grinding rattle of the quick-firers, and the hoarse, whistling shrieks of the shells, completed the awful pandemonium of destruction and death that was raging round Dover.

The truth was that the main naval attack of the Allies was being directed on the southeastern stronghold. I am aware that this is not the usual plan followed by those who have written romantic forecasts of the invasion of England. It seems at first sight, provided that the enemy could pass the sentinels of the sea unnoticed, easy to land troops on unprotected portions of our shores; but, in actual warfare, this would be the most fatal policy that could be pursued, simply because, whatever the point selected, the invaders would always find themselves between two strong places, with one or more ahead of them. They would thus be outflanked on all sides, with no retreat open but the sea, which is the most easily closed of all retreats.

From their point of view, then, the Allies were perfectly right in their project of reducing the great strongholds of southern and eastern England, before advancing with their concentrated forces upon London. It would, of course, be a costly operation. In fact Britain's long immunity from invasion went far to prove that, to enemies possessing only the ordinary means of warfare, it would have been impossible, but, ever since the success of the experiment at Potsdam, German engineering firms had been working hard under John Castellan's directions turning out improved models of the *Flying Fish.* The various parts were manufactured at great distances apart, and no one firm knew what the others were doing. It was only when the parts of the vessels and the engines were delivered at the closely-guarded Imperial factory at Potsdam, that, under Castellan's own supervision, they became the terrible fighting machines that they were.

The Aërial Fleet numbered twenty when war broke out, and of these five had been detailed for the attack on Dover. They were in fact the elements which made that attack possible, and, as is already known, four were co-operating with the Northern Division of the Allied Fleets against the forts defending Chatham and London.

Dover was at that time one of the most strongly fortified places in the world. Its magnificent new harbor had been completed, and its fortifications vastly strengthened and re-armed with the new fourteen-inch gun which had superseded the old sixteen-inch gun of position, on account of its greater handiness, combined with greater penetrating power.

But at Dover, as at Portsmouth, the forts were powerless against the assaults of these winged demons of the air. They were able to use their terrible projectiles with reckless profusion, because only twenty-two miles away at Calais there were inexhaustible stores from which they could replenish their magazines. Moreover, the private factory at Kiel, where alone they were allowed to be manufactured, were turning them out by hundreds a day.

They had, of course, formed the vanguard of the attacking force which had advanced in three divisions in column of line abreast from Boulogne, Calais and Antwerp. The Boulogne and Calais divisions were French, and each consisted of six battleships with the usual screens of cruisers, destroyers and torpedo boats: these two divisions constituted the French North Sea Squadron, whose place had been taken by the main German Fleet, assisted by the Belgian and Dutch squadron.

Another German and Russian division was advancing on London. It included four first-class battleships, and two heavily-armed coast defense ships, huge floating fortresses, rather slow in speed, but tremendous in power, which accompanied them for the purpose of battering the fortifications, and doing as much damage to Woolwich and other important places on both sides as their big guns could achieve. Four *Flying Fishes* accompanied this division.

Such was the general plan of action on that fatal night. Confident in the terrific powers of their Aërial Squadrons, and ignorant of the existence of the *Ithuriel*, the Allied Powers never considered the possibilities of anything but rapid victory. They knew that the forts could no more withstand the shock of the bombardment from the air than battleships or cruisers could resist the equally deadly blow which these same diabolical contrivances could deliver under the water.

They had not the slightest doubt but that forts would be silenced and fleets put out of action with a swiftness unknown before, and then the crowded transports would follow the victorious fleets, and the military promenade upon London would begin, headed by the winged messengers of destruction, from which neither flight nor protection was possible.

Of course, the leaders of the Allies were in ignorance of the misfortunes they had suffered at Portsmouth and Folkestone. All they knew they learned from aerograms, one from Admiral Durenne off the Isle of Wight saying that the Portsmouth forts had been silenced and the Fleet action had begun, and another from the Commodore of the squadron off Folkestone saying that all was going well, and the landing would shortly be effected: and thus they fully expected to have the three towns and the entrance to the Thames at their mercy by the following day.

Certainly, as far as Dover was concerned, things looked very much as though their anticipations would be realized, for when the *Ithuriel* arrived upon the scene, Dover Castle and its surrounding forts were vomiting flame and earth into the darkening sky, like so many volcanoes. The forts on Admiralty Pier, Shakespeare Cliff, and those commanding the new harbor works, had been silenced and blown up, and the town and barracks were in flames in many places.

The scene was, in short, so inhumanly appalling, and horror followed horror with such paralyzing rapidity, that the most practiced correspondents and the most experienced officers, both afloat and ashore, were totally unable to follow them and describe what was happening with anything like coherence. It was simply an inferno of death and destruction, which no human words could have properly described, and perhaps the most ghastly feature of it was the fact that there was no human agency visible in it at all. There was no Homeric struggle of man with man, although many a gallant deed was done that night which never was seen nor heard of, and many a hero went to his death without so much as leaving behind him the memory of how he died.

It was a conflict of mechanical giants – giant ships, giant engines, giant guns, and explosives of something more than giant strength. These were the monsters which poor, deluded Humanity, like another Frankenstein, had thought out with infinite care and craft, and fashioned for its own mutual destruction. Men had made a hell out of their own passions and greed and jealousies, and now that hell had opened and mankind was about to descend into it.

The sea-defense of Dover itself consisted of the Home Fleet in three divisions, composed respectively of the *England, London, Bulwark* and *Venerable, Queen* and *Prince of Wales* battleships, and ten first-class armored cruisers, the *Duncan, Cornwallis, Exmouth* and *Russell* battleships, with twelve armored cruisers, and thirdly, the reconstructed and rearmed *Empress of India, Revenge, Repulse* and *Resolution,* with eight armored cruisers. To the north between Dover and the North Foreland lay the Southern Division of the North Sea Squadron.

When the battle had commenced these three divisions were lying in their respective stations, in column of line ahead about six miles from the English shore. Behind them lay a swarm of destroyers and torpedo boats, ready to dart out and do their deadly work between the ships, and ten submarines were attached to each division. The harbor and approaches were, of course, plentifully strewn with mines.

"It's an awful sight," said Castellan, with a note of awe in his voice, when they had taken in the situation with the rapidity and precision of the professional eye. "And to me the worst of it is that it won't be safe for us to take a share in the row."

"What!" exclaimed Erskine, almost angrily. "Do you mean to tell me we shan't be able to help our fellows? Then what on earth have we come here for?"

"Just look there, now!" said Castellan, pointing ahead to where huge shapes, enveloped in a mist of flame and smoke, were circling round each other, vomiting their thunderbolts, like leviathans engaged in a veritable dance of death.

"D'ye see that!" continued Denis. "What good would we be among that lot? The *Ithuriel* hasn't eyes on her that can see through the dark water, and if she had, how would we tell the bottom of a French or German ship from a Britisher's, and a nice thing it would be for us to go about sinking the King's ships, and helping those foreign devils to land in old England! No, Erskine, this ship of yours is a holy terror, but she's a daylight fighter. Don't you see that we came too late, and wait till tomorrow we can't, and there's the Duke's orders.

"I'll tell you what," he continued more cheerfully, as the *Ithuriel* cleared the southern part of the battle, "if we could get at the transports we might have some fun with them, but they'll all be safe enough in port, loading up, and there's not much chance that they'll come out till our boys have been beaten and the roads are clear for them. Then they'll go across thinking they'll meet their pals from Portsmouth and Folkestone. Now, you see that line out there to the northeastward?"

"Yes," said Erskine, looking towards a long row of dim shapes which every now and then were brought out into ominous distinctness by the flashes of the shells and searchlights.

"Well," continued Castellan, "if I know anything of naval tactics, that's the Reserve lot waiting till the battle's over. They think they'll win, and I think so too, thanks to those devil-ships my brother has made for them. Even if Beresford does come up in time, he can no more fight against them than anybody else. Now, there's just one chance that we can give him, and that is sinking the Reserve; for, you see, if we've only half a dozen ships left that can shoot a bit in the morning, they won't dare to put their transports out without a convoy, and unless they land them, well, they're no use."

"Castellan," said Erskine, putting his hand on his shoulder, "you'll be an admiral some day. Certainly, we'll go for the convoy, for I'll be kicked if I can stand here watching all that going on and not have a hand in it. We'd better sink, and use nothing but the ram, I suppose."

"Why, of course," replied Castellan. "It would never do to shoot at them. There are too many, and besides, we don't want them to know that we're here until we've sent them to the bottom."

"And a lot they'll know about it then!" laughed Erskine. "All right," he continued, taking down the receiver. "Courtney and Mac can see to the sinking, so you'd better stop here with me and see the fun."

"That I will, with all the pleasure in life and death," said Castellan grimly, as Erskine gave his orders and the *Ithuriel* immediately began to sink.

Castellan was perfectly right in his conjecture as to the purpose of the Reserve.

The French and German Squadron, which was intended for the last rush through the remnants of the crippled British fleet, consisted of four French and three German battleships, old and rather slow, but heavily armed, and much more than a match for the vessels which had already passed through the terrible ordeal of battle. In addition there were six fast second-class cruisers, and about a score of torpedo boats.

With her decks awash and the conning-tower just on a level with the short, choppy waves, the *Ithuriel* ran round to the south of the line at ten knots, as they were anxious not to kick up any fuss in the water, lest a chance searchlight from the enemy might fall upon them, and lead to trouble. She got within a mile of the first cruiser unobserved, and then Erskine gave the order to quicken up. They had noticed that the wind was rising, and they knew that within half an hour the tide would be setting southward like a mill-race through the narrow strait.

Their tactics therefore were very simple. Every cruiser and battleship was rammed in the sternpost; not very hard, but with sufficient force to crumple up the sternpost, and disable the rudder and the propellers, and with such precision was this done, that, until the signals of distress began to flash, the uninjured ships and the nearest of those engaged in the battle were under the impression that orders had been given for the Reserve to move south. But this supposition very soon gave place to panic as ship after ship swung helplessly inshore, impelled by the ever-strengthening tide towards the sands of Calais and the rocks of Gris Nez.

Searchlights flashed furiously, but Erskine and Castellan had already taken the bearings of the remaining ships, and the *Ithuriel,* now ten feet below the water, and steered solely by compass, struck ship after ship, till the whole of the Reserve was drifting helplessly to destruction.

This, as they had both guessed, produced a double effect on the battle. In the first place it was impossible for the Allies to see their Reserve, upon which so much might depend, in such a helpless plight, and the admirals commanding were therefore obliged to detach ships to help them; and on the other hand, the British were by no means slow to take advantage of the position. A score of torpedo boats, and half as many destroyers, dashed out from behind the British lines, and, rushing through the hurricane of shell that was directed upon them, ran past the broken line of unmanageable cruisers and battleships, and torpedoed them at easy range. True, half of them were crumpled up, and sent to the bottom during the process, but that is a contingency which British torpedo officers and men never take the slightest notice of. The disabled ships were magnificent marks for torpedoes, and they had to go down, wherefore down they went.

Meanwhile the *Ithuriel* had been having a merry time among the torpedo flotilla of the Reserve Squadron. She rose flush with the water, put on full speed, and picked them up one after another on the end of her ram, and tossed them aside into the depths as rapidly as an enraged whale might have disposed of a fleet of whaleboats.

The last boat had hardly gone down when signals were seen flashing up into the sky from over Dungeness.

"That's Beresford to the rescue," said Castellan, in a not overcheerful voice. "Now if it wasn't for those devil-ships of my brother's there'd be mighty little left of the Allied Fleet tomorrow morning; but I'm afraid he won't be able to do anything against those amphibious *Flying Fishes,* as he calls them. Now, we'd better be off to London."

Chapter XXI

— AND ENDS

The defenders of Dover, terribly as they had suffered, and hopeless as the defense really now seemed to be, were still not a little cheered by the tidings of the complete and crushing defeat which had been inflicted by Admiral Beresford and the *Ithuriel* on the French at Portsmouth and Folkestone, and the brilliant capture of the whole of the two Expeditionary Forces. Now, too, the destruction of the Allied Reserve made it possible to hope that at least a naval victory might be obtained, and the transports prevented from crossing until the remains of the British Fleet Reserve could be brought up to the rescue.

At any rate it might be possible, in spite of sunken ships and shattered fortifications, to prevent, at least for a while, the pollution of English soil by the presence of hostile forces, and to get on with the mobilization of regulars, militia, yeomanry and volunteers, which, as might have been expected, this sudden declaration of war found in the usual state of hopeless muddle and chaos.

But, even in the event of complete victory by sea, there would still be those terrible cruisers of the air to be reckoned with, and they were known to be as efficient as submarines as they were as airships.

Still, much had been done, and it was no use going to meet trouble halfway. Moreover, Beresford's guns were beginning to talk down yonder to the southward, and it was time for what was left of the North Sea Squadron and the Home Fleet to reform and maneuver, so as to work to the northeastward, and get the enemy between the two British forces.

A very curious thing came to pass now. The French and German Fleets, though still much superior to the defenders, had during that first awful hour of the assault received a terrible mauling, especially from the large guns of the *England* and the *Scotland* – sisters of the *Britain,* and the flagships respectively of the North Sea Squadron and the Home Fleet – and the totally unexpected and inexplicable loss of their reserve; but the guns booming to the southwestward could only be those of

Admiral Durenne's victorious fleet. He would bring them reinforcements more than enough, and with him, too, would come the three *Flying Fishes,* which had been commissioned to destroy Portsmouth and the battleships of the British Reserve. There need be no fear of not getting the transports across now, and then the march of victory would begin.

In a few minutes the fighting almost entirely ceased. The ships which had been battering each other so heartily separated as if by mutual consent, and the French and German admirals steamed to the southwestward to join their allies and sweep the Strait of Dover clear of those who had for so many hundred years considered – yes, and kept it – as their own sea-freehold.

At the same time private signals were flashed through the air to the *Flying Fishes* to retire on Calais, replenish their ammunition and motive power, which they had been using so lavishly, and return at daybreak.

Thus what was left of Dover, its furiously impotent soldiery, and its sorely stricken inhabitants, had a respite at least until day dawned and showed them the extent of the ruin that had been wrought.

It was nearly midnight when the three fleets joined, and just about eight bells the clouds parted and dissolved under the impact of a stiff nor'easter, which had been gathering strength for the last two hours. The war smoke drifted away, and the moon shone down clearly on the now white-crested battlefield.

By its light and their own searchlights the French and German admirals, steaming as they thought to join hands with their victorious friends, saw the strangest and most exasperating sight that their eyes had ever beheld. The advancing force was a curiously composed one. Trained, as they were, to recognize at first sight every warship of every nation, they could nevertheless hardly believe their eyes. There were six battleships in the center of the first line. One was the *Britain,* three others were of the *Edward the Seventh* class; two were French. Of the sixteen cruisers which formed the wings, seven were French – and every warship of the whole lot was flying the White Ensign!

Did it mean disaster – almost impossible disaster – or was it only a *ruse de guerre?*

They were not left very long in doubt. At three miles from a direction almost due southeast of Dover, the advancing battleships opened fire with their heavy forward guns, and the cruisers spread out in a fan on either side of the French and German Fleets. The *Britain,* as though glorying in her strength and speed, steamed ahead in solitary pride right into the midst of the Allies, thundering and flaming ahead and from each broadside. The *Braunschweig* had the bad luck to get in her way.

She made a desperate effort to get out of it; but eighteen knots was no good against twenty-five. The huge ram crashed into her vitals as she swerved, and reeling and pitching like some drunken leviathan, she went down with a mighty plunge, and the *Britain* plowed on over the eddies that marked her ocean grave.

This was the beginning of the greatest and most decisive sea-fight that had been fought since Trafalgar. The sailors of Britain knew that they were fighting not only for the honor of their King and country, but, as British sailors had not done for a hundred and four years, for the very existence of England and the Empire. On the other hand, the Allies knew that this battle meant the loss or the keeping of the command of the sea, and therefore the possibility or otherwise of starving the United Kingdom into submission after the landing had been effected.

So from midnight until dawn battleship thundered against battleship, and cruiser engaged cruiser, while the torpedo craft darted with flaming funnels in and out among the wrestling giants, and the submarines did their deadly work in silence. Miracles of valor and devotion were achieved on both sides. From admiral and commodore and captain in the conning-towers to officers and men in barbettes and casemates, and the sweating stokers and engineers in their steel prisons – which might well become their tombs – every man risked and gave his life as cheerfully as the most reckless commander or seaman on the torpedo flotillas.

It was a fight to the death, and every man knew it, and accepted the fact with the grim joy of the true fighting man.

Naturally, no detailed description of the battle of Dover would be possible, even if it were necessary to the narrative. Not a man who survived it could have written such a description. All that was known to the officials on shore was that every now and then an aerogram came, telling in broken fragments of the sinking of a battleship or cruiser on one side or the other, and the gradual weakening of the enemy's defense; but to those who were waiting and watching so anxiously along the line of cliffs, the only tidings that came were told by the gradual slackening of the battle-thunder, and the ever-diminishing frequency of the pale flashes of flame gleaming through the drifting gusts of smoke.

Then at last morning dawned, and the pale November sun lit up as sorry a scene as human eyes had ever looked upon. Not a fourth of the ships which had gone into action on either side were still afloat, and these were little better than drifting wrecks.

All along the shore from East Wear Bay to the South Foreland lay the shattered, shell-riddled hulks of what twelve hours before had been the finest battleships and cruisers afloat, run ashore in despair to save the lives of the few who had come alive through that awful battle-storm. Outside them showed the masts and fighting-tops of those which had sunk before reaching shore, and outside these again lay a score or so of battleships and a few armored cruisers, some down by the head, some by the stern, and some listing badly to starboard or port – still afloat, and still with a little fight left in them, in spite of their gashed sides, torn decks, riddled topworks and smashed barbettes.

But, ghastly as the spectacle was, it was not long before a mighty cheer went rolling along the cliffs and over the ruined town for, whether flew the French or German flag, there was not a ship that French or German sailor or marine had landed on English soil save as prisoners.

The old Sea Lion had for the first time in three hundred and fifty years been attacked in his lair, and now as then he had turned and rent the insolent intruder limb from limb.

The main German Fleet and the French Channel Fleet and North Sea Squadrons had ceased to exist within twenty-four hours of the commencement of hostilities.

Once more Britain had vindicated her claim to the proud title of Queen of the Seas; once more the thunder of her enemies' guns had echoed back from her white cliffs – and the echo had been a message of defeat and disaster.

If the grim game of war could only have been played now as it had been even five years before, the victory would have already been with her, for the cable from Gibraltar to the Lizard had that morning brought the news from Admiral Commerell, Commander-in-Chief in the Mediterranean, that he had been attacked by, and had almost destroyed, the combined French Mediterranean and Russian Black Sea Fleets, and that, with the aid of an Italian Squadron, he was blockading Toulon, Marseilles and Bizerta. The captured French and Russian ships capable of repair had been sent to Malta and Gibraltar to refit.

This, under the old conditions, would, of course, have meant checkmate in the game of invasion, since not a hostile ship of any sort would have dared to put to sea, and the crowded transports would have been as useless as so many excursion steamers, but –

Chapter XXII

DISASTER

About eight o'clock, as the half-wrecked victors and vanquished were slowly struggling into the half-ruined harbor, five winged shapes became visible against the grey sky over Calais, rapidly growing in size, and a few minutes later two more appeared, approaching from the northeast. They, alas, were the heralds of a fate against which all the gallantry and skill of Britain's best sailors and soldiers would fight in vain.

The two from the northeast were, of course, the *Flying Fish* and the *See Adler*; the others were those which had been ordered to load up at the Calais depot, and complete that victory of the Allied Fleets which the science and devotion of British sailors had turned into utter defeat.

John Castellan, standing in the conning-tower of the *Flying Fish,* looking down over sea and land through his prismatic binoculars, suddenly ground his teeth hard together, and sent a hearty Irish curse hissing between them. He had a complete plan of the operations in his possession, and knew perfectly what to expect – but what was this?

Dover and its fortifications were in ruins, as they ought to have been by this time; but the British Flag still floated over them! The harbor was almost filled with mutilated warships, and others were slowly steaming towards the two entrances; but every one of these was flying the White Ensign of England! There was not a French or German flag to be seen – and there, all along the coast, which should have been in the possession of the Allies by now, lay the ragged line of helpless hulks which would never take the sea again.

What had happened? Where were the splendid fleets which were to have battered the English defense into impotence? Where was the Reserve, which was to have convoyed the transports across the narrow waters? Where were the transports themselves and the half million men, horses and artillery which today they were to land upon the stricken shores of Kent?

With that marvelous intuition which is so often allied with the Keltic genius, he saw in a flash all, or something like all, that had really happened as a consequence of the loss of the depot ship at Spithead, and the venting of his own mad hatred of the Saxon on the three defenseless towns. The Channel Fleet had come, after all, in time, and defeated Admiral Durenne's fleet; the Reserve cruisers had escaped, and Portsmouth had been re-taken!

Would that have happened if he had used the scores of shells which he had wasted in mere murder and destruction against the ships of the Channel Fleet? It would not, and no one knew it better than he did.

Still, even now there was time to retrieve that ghastly mistake which had cost the Allies a good deal more than even he had guessed at. He was Admiral of the Aërial Squadrons, and, save under orders from headquarters, free to act as he thought fit against the enemy. If his passion had lost victory he could do nothing less than avenge defeat.

He ran up his telescopic mast and swerved to the southward to meet the squadron from Calais, flying his admiral's flag, and under it the signal:

"I wish to speak to you."

The *Flying Fish* and the *See Adler* quickened up, and the others slowed down until they met about two thousand feet above the sea. Castellan ran the *Flying Fish* alongside the Commodore of the other Squadron, and in ten minutes he had learned what the other had to tell, and arranged a plan of operations.

Within the next five minutes three of the seven craft had dropped to the water and disappeared beneath it. The other four, led by the *Flying Fish,* winged their way towards Dover.

The aërial section of the squadron made straight for the harbor. The submarine section made southwestward to cut off the half dozen "lame ducks" which were still struggling towards it. With these, unhappily, was the *Scotland,* the huge flagship of the North Sea Squadron, which still full of fight, was towing the battleship *Commonwealth,* whose rudder and propellers had been disabled by a torpedo from a French submarine.

She was, of course, the first victim selected. Two *Flying Fishes* dived, one under her bows and one under her stern, and each discharged two torpedoes.

No fabric made by human hands could have withstood the shock of the four explosions which burst out simultaneously. The sore-stricken leviathan stopped, shuddered and reeled, smitten to death. For a few moments she floundered and wallowed in the vast masses of foaming water that rose up round her – and when they sank she took a mighty sideward reel and followed them.

The rest met their inevitable fate in quick succession, and went down with their ensigns and pennants flying – to death, but not to defeat or disgrace.

The ten British submarines which were left from the fight had already put out to try conclusions with the *Flying Fishes*; but a porpoise might as well have tried to hunt down a northern diver. As soon as each *Flying Fish* had finished its work of destruction it spread its wings and leapt into the air – and woe betide the submarine whose periscope showed for a moment above the water, for in that moment a torpedo fell on or close to it, and that submarine dived for the last time.

Meanwhile the horrors of the past afternoon and evening were being repeated in the crowded harbor, and on shore, until a frightful catastrophe befell the remains of the British Fleet.

John Castellan, with two other craft, was examining the forts from a height of four thousand feet, and dropping a few torpedoes into any which did not appear to be completely wrecked. The captain of another was amusing himself by dispersing, in more senses than one, the helpless, terror-stricken crowds on the cliffs whence they had lately cheered the last of Britain's naval victories, and the rest were circling over the harbor at a height of three thousand feet, letting go torpedoes whenever a fair mark presented itself.

Of course the fight, if fight it could be called, was hopeless from the first; but your British sailor is not the man to take even a hopeless fight lying down, and so certain gallant but desperate spirits on board the *England*, which was lying under what was left of the Admiralty Pier, got permission to dismount six 3-pounders and remount them as a battery for high-angle fire. The intention, of course, was, as the originator of the idea put it: "To bring down a few of those flying devils before they could go inland and do more damage there."

The intention was as good as it was unselfish, for the ingenious officer in charge of the battery knew as well as his admiral that the fleet was doomed to destruction in detail – but the first volley that battery fired was the last.

A few of the shells must have hit a French *Flying Fish*, which was circling above the center of the harbor, and disabled the wings and propellors on one side, for she lurched and wobbled for an instant like a bird with a broken wing. Then she swooped downwards in a spiral course, falling ever faster and faster, till she struck the deck of the *Britain*.

What happened the next instant no one ever knew. Those who survived said that they heard a crashing roar like the firing of a thousand cannon together; a blinding sheet of flame overspread the harbor; the water rose into mountains of foam, ships rocked and crashed against each other – and then came darkness and oblivion.

When human eyes next looked on Dover Harbor there was not a ship in it afloat.

Dover, the great stronghold of the southeast, was now as defenseless as a fishing village, and there was nothing to prevent a constant stream of transports filled with men and materials of war being poured into it, or any other port along the eastern Kentish coast. Then would come seizure of railway stations and rolling stock, rapid landing of men and horses and guns, and the beginning of the great advance.

On the whole, John Castellan was well satisfied with his work. He regretted the loss of his consort; but she had not been wasted. The remains of the British fleets had gone with her to destruction.

Certainly what had been done had brought nearer the time when he, the real organizer of victory, the man who had made the conquest of England possible, would be able to claim his double reward – the independence of Ireland, and the girl whom he intended to make the uncrowned Queen of Erin.

It was a splendid and, to him, a delicious dream as well; but between him and its fulfillment, what a chaos of bloodshed, ruin and human misery lay! And yet he felt not a tremor of compunction or of pity for the thousands of brave men who would be flung dead and mangled and tortured into the bloody mire of battle, for the countless homes that would be left desolate, or for the widows and the fatherless whose agony would cry to Heaven for justice on him.

No; these things were of no account in his eyes. Ireland must be free, and the girl he had come to love so swiftly, and with such consuming passion, must be his. Nothing else mattered. Was he not Lord of the Air, and should the desire of his heart be denied him?

Thus mused John Castellan in the conning-tower of the *Flying Fish,* as he circled slowly above the ruins of Dover, while the man who had beaten him in the swimming-race was sitting in the observatory on far-off Whernside, verifying his night's observations and calculating for the hundredth time the moment of the coming of an Invader, compared with which all the armed legions of Europe were of no more importance than a swarm of flies.

When he had satisfied himself that Dover was quite defenseless he sent one of the French *Flying Fishes* across to Calais with a letter to the District Commander, describing briefly what had taken place, and telling him that it would be now quite safe for the transports to cross the Straits and land the troops at Portsmouth, Newhaven, Folkestone, Dover and Ramsgate.

He would station one of his airships over each of these places to prevent any resistance from land or sea, and would himself make a general reconnaissance of the military dispositions of the defenders. He advised that the three *Flying Fishes,* which had been reserved for the defense of the Kiel Canal, should be telegraphed for as convoys, as there was now no danger of attack, and that the depot of torpedoes and motive power for his ships should be transferred from Calais to Dover.

As soon as he had dispatched this letter, Castellan ordered two of his remaining ships to cruise northward to Ramsgate, keeping mainly along the track of the railway, one on each side of it, and to wreck the first train they saw approaching Dover, Deal, Sandwich and Ramsgate from the north. The other two he ordered to take the Western Coast line as far as Portsmouth, and do the same with trains coming east.

Then he swung the *Flying Fish* inland, and took a run over Canterbury, Ashford, Maidstone, Tonbridge, Guildford and Winchester, to Southampton and Portsmouth, returning by Chichester, Horsham and Tunbridge Wells.

It was only a tour of observation for the purpose of discovering the main military dispositions of the defenders – who were now concentrating as rapidly as possible upon Folkestone and Dover – but he found time to stop and drop a torpedo or two into each town or fort that he passed over – just leaving cards, as he said to M'Carthy – as a promise of favors to come.

He also wrecked half a dozen long trains, apparently carrying troops, and incidentally caused a very considerable loss of good lives and much confusion, to say nothing of the moral effect which this new and terrible form of attack produced upon the nerves of Mr. Thomas Atkins.

When he got back to Dover he found a letter waiting for him from the General informing him that the transports would sail at once, and that his requests would be complied with.

Chapter XXIII

THE OTHER CAMPAIGN BEGINS

It was on the day following the destruction of Dover that the news of the actual landing of the French and German forces had really taken place at the points selected by Castellan reached Whernside. The little house party were at lunch, and the latest papers had just come over from Settle. Naturally what they contained formed the sole topic of conversation.

"Really, Arnold, I think even you must confess that things are a great deal more serious than anyone could have imagined a few days ago. The very idea – an invasion accomplished in forty-eight hours – Portsmouth, Dover, Sheerness and Tilbury destroyed, and French and German and Russian soldiers actually in arms on English soil. The thing would be preposterous if it were not true!

"And what are we to do now, I should like to know? The Fleet doesn't exist – we have no army in the Continental sense of the word, which of course is the real military sense, thanks to a lot of politicians calling themselves statesmen who have been squabbling about what an army ought to be for the last ten years.

"You will be able to put a million trained and half-trained – mostly half-trained – men into the field, to face millions of highly-trained French, German, Russian and Austrian troops, led by officers who have taken their profession seriously, and not by gentlemen who have gone into the army because it was a nice sort of playground, where you could have lots of fun, and a little amateur fighting now and then. I wonder what they will do now against the men who have made war a science instead of sport!

"I should like to know what the good people who have made such a fuss about the 'tyranny of Conscription' will say now, when they find that we haven't trained men enough to defend our homes. Just as if military service was not the first duty a man owes to his country and to his home. A man has no right to a country nor a home if he isn't able to defend them. Kipling was perfectly right when he said:

"'What is your boasting worth
If you grudge a year of service to the lordliest life on earth?'"

This little lecture was delivered with trembling lips, flushed cheeks and flashing eyes by Lady Margaret Holker, Lord Westerham's sister, who had joined the party that morning to help her brother in his recruiting.

She was an almost perfect type of the modern highly-bred Englishwoman, who knows how to be entirely modern without being vulgarly "up-to-date." She was a strong contrast to her brother, in that she was a bright brunette – not beautiful, perhaps not even pretty, but for all that distinctly good-looking. Her hair and eyebrows were black, her eyes a deep pansy-blue. A clear complexion, usually pale but decidedly flushed now, and, for the rest, somewhat irregular features which might have been almost plain, but for that indefinable expression of combined gentleness and strength which only the careful selection of long descent can give.

As for her figure, it was as perfect as absolute health and abundant exercise could make it. She could ride, shoot, throw a fly and steer a yacht better than most women and many men of her class; but for all that she could grill steaks and boil potatoes with as much distinction as she could play the piano and violin, and sing in three or four languages.

She also had a grip, not on politics, for which she had a wholesome contempt, but on the affairs of the nations – the things which really mattered. And yet withal she was just an entirely healthy young Englishwoman, who was quite as much at home in the midst of a good swinging waltz as she was in an argument on high affairs of State.

"My dear Madge," said her brother, who had been reading the reports in the second morning edition of the *Times* aloud, "I am afraid that, after all, you are right. But then, you must not forget that a new enemy has come into the field. I hardly like to say so in Miss Castellan's presence, but it is perfectly clear that, considering what the Fleet did, there would have been no invasion if it had not been for those diabolical contrivances that John Castellan took over to the German Emperor."

"You needn't have any hesitation in saying what you like about him before me, Lord Westerham," said Norah, flushing. "It's no brother he is of mine now, as I told him the day he went aboard the German yacht at Clifden. I'd see him shot tomorrow without a wink of my eyes. The man who does what he has done has no right to the respect of any man nor the love of any woman – no, not even if the woman is his sister. Think of all the good, loyal Irishmen, soldiers and sailors, that he has murdered by this time. No, I have no brother called John Castellan."

"But you have another called Denis," said Auriole, "and I think you may be well content with him!"

"Ah, Denis!" said Norah, flushing again, but for a different reason, "Denis is a good and loyal man; yes, I am proud of him – God bless him!"

"And I should reckon that skipper of his, Captain Erskine, must be a pretty smart sort of man," said Mr. Parmenter, who so far had hardly joined in the conversation, and who had seemed curiously indifferent to the terrible exploits of the *Flying Fishes* and all that had followed them. "That craft of his seems to be just about as businesslike as anything that ever got into the water or under it. I wonder what he is doing with the Russian and German ships in the Thames now. I guess he won't let many of them get back out of there. Quite a young man, too, according to the accounts."

"Oh, yes," said Lady Margaret, "he isn't twenty-nine yet. I know him slightly. He is a son of Admiral Erskine, who commanded the China Squadron about eight years ago, and died of fever after a pirate hunt, and he is the nephew of dear old Lady Caroline Anstey, my other mother as I call her. He is really a splendid fellow, and some people say as good-looking as he is clever; although, of course, there was a desperate lot of jealousy when he was promoted Captain straight away from Lieutenant-Commander of a Fishery cruiser, but I should like to know how many of the wiseacres of Whitehall could have designed that *Ithuriel* of his."

"It's a pity she can't fly, though, like those others," said Mr. Parmenter, with a curious note in his voice which no one at the table but Lennard understood. "She's a holy terror in the water, but the other fellow's got all the call on land. If they get a dozen or so of these aërial submarines as you might call them, in front of the invading forces, I can't see what's going to stop a march on London, and right round it. Your men are just as brave as any on earth, and a bit more than some, if their officers are a bit more gentlemen and sportsmen than soldiers; but no man can fight a thing he can't hit back at, and so I reckon the next thing we shall hear of will be the siege of London. What do you think, Lennard?"

Lennard, who had hardly spoken a word during the meal, looked up, and said in a voice which Lady Madge thought curiously unsympathetic:

"I shouldn't think it would take more than a fortnight at the outside, even leaving these airships out of the question. We haven't three hundred thousand men of all sorts to put into the field, who know one end of a gun from another, or who can sit a horse; and now that the sea's clear the enemy can land two or three millions in a fortnight."

"All our merchant shipping will be absolutely at their mercy, and they will simply have to take them over to France and Germany and load them up with men and horses, and bring them over as if they were coming to a picnic. But, of course, with the airships to help them the thing's a foregone conclusion, and to a great extent it is our own fault. I thoroughly agree with what Lady Margaret says about conscription. If we had had it only five years ago, we should now have three million men, instead of three hundred thousand, trained and ready to take the field. Though, after all –"

"After all – what?" said Lady Margaret, looking sharply round at him.

"Oh, nothing of any importance," he said. "At least, not just at present. I daresay Lord Westerham will be able to explain what I might have said better than I could. There's not time for it just now, I've got to get a train to Bolton in an hour's time."

"And I'll have to be in Glasgow tonight," said Mr. Parmenter, rising. "I hope you won't think it very inhospitable of us, Lady Margaret: but business is business, you know, and more so than usual in times like these.

"Now, I had better say good-bye. I have a few things to see to before Mr. Lennard and I go down to Settle, but I've no doubt Auriole will find some way of entertaining you till you want to start for York."

At half-past two the motor was at the door to take Mr. Parmenter and Lennard to Settle. That evening, in Glasgow, Mr. Parmenter bought the *Minnehaha*, a steel turbine yacht of two thousand tons and twenty-five knots speed, from Mr. Hendray Chinnock, a brother millionaire, who had laid her up in the Clyde in consequence of the war the day before. He re-engaged her officers and crew at double wages to cover war risks, and started for New York within an hour of the completion of the purchase.

Lennard took the express to Bolton, with letters and a deed of gift from Lord Westerham, which gave him absolute ownership of the cannel mine with the twelve-hundred-foot vertical shaft at Farnworth.

That afternoon and evening Lady Margaret was more than entertained, for during the afternoon she learned the story of the approaching cataclysm, in comparison with which the war was of no more importance than a mere street riot; and that night Auriole, who had learned to work the great reflector almost as well as Lennard himself, showed her the ever-growing, ever-brightening shape of the Celestial Invader.

Chapter XXIV

TOM BOWCOCK — PITMAN

Lennard found himself standing outside the Trinity Street Station at Bolton a few minutes after six that evening.

Of course it was raining. Rain and fine-spun cotton thread are Bolton's specialities, the two chief pillars of her fame and prosperity, for without the somewhat distressing superabundance of the former she could not spin the latter fine enough. It would break in the process. Wherefore the good citizens of Bolton cheerfully put up with the dirt and the damp and the abnormal expenditure on umbrellas and mackintoshes in view of the fact that all the world must come to Bolton for its finest threads.

He stood for a moment looking about him curiously, if with no great admiration in his soul, for this was his first sight of what was to be the scene of the greatest and most momentous undertaking that human skill had ever dared to accomplish.

But the streets of Bolton on a wet night do not impress a stranger very favorably, so he had his flat steamer-trunk and hat-box put on to a cab and told the driver to take him to the Swan Hotel, in Deansgate, where he had a wash and an excellent dinner, to which he was in a condition to do full justice – for though nation may rage against nation, and worlds and systems be in peril, the healthy human digestion goes on making its demands all the time, and, under the circumstances, blessed is he who can worthily satisfy them.

Then, after a cup of coffee and a meditative cigar, he put on his mackintosh, sent for a cab, and drove to number 134 Manchester Road, which is one of a long row of small, two-storeyed brick houses, as clean as the all-pervading smoke and damp will permit them to be, but not exactly imposing in the eyes of a newcomer.

When the door opened in answer to his knock he saw by the light of a lamp hanging from the ceiling of the narrow little hall a small, slight, neatly-dressed figure, and a pair of dark, soft eyes looked up inquiringly at him as he said:

"Is Mr. Bowcock at home?"

"Yes, he is," replied a voice softly and very pleasantly tinged with the Lancashire accent. Then in a rather higher key the voice said:

"Tom, ye're wanted."

As she turned away Lennard paid his cabman, and when he went back to the door he found the passage almost filled by a tall, square-shouldered shape of a man, and a voice to match it said:

"If ye're wantin' Tom Bowcock, measter, that's me. Will ye coom in? It's a bit wet i' t' street."

Lennard went in, and as the door closed he said:

"Mr. Bowcock, my name is Lennard –"

"I thou't it might be," interrupted the other. "You'll be Lord Westerham's friend. I had a wire from his lordship's morning telling me t' expect you tonight or tomorrow morning. You'll excuse t' kitchen for a minute while t' missus makes up t' fire i' t' sittin' room."

When Lennard got into the brightly-lighted kitchen, which is really the living room of small Lancashire houses, he found himself in an atmosphere of modest cozy comfort which is seldom to be found outside the North and the Midland manufacturing districts. It is the other side of the hard, colorless life that is lived in mill and mine and forge, and it has a charm that is all its own.

There was the big range, filling half the space of one of the side-walls, its steel framings glittering like polished silver; the high plate-rack full of shining crockery at one end by the door, and the low, comfortable couch at the other; two lines of linen hung on cords stretched under the ceiling airing above the range, and the solid deal table in the middle of the room was covered with a snow-white cloth, on which a pretty tea-service was set out.

A brightly polished copper kettle singing on the range, and a daintily furnished cradle containing a sleeping baby, sweetly unconscious of wars or world-shaking catastrophes, completed a picture which, considering his errand, affected Gilbert Lennard very deeply.

"Lizzie" said the giant, "this is Mr. Lennard as his lordship telegraphed about today. I daresay yo can give him a cup of tay and see to t' fire i' t' sittin' room. I believe he's come to have a bit of talk wi' me about summat important from what his lordship said."

"I'm pleased to see you, Mr. Lennard," said the pleasant voice, and as he shook hands he found himself looking into the dark, soft eyes of a regular "Lancashire witch," for Lizzie Bowcock had left despair in the heart of many a Lancashire lad when she had put her little hand into big Tom's huge fist and told him that she'd have him for her man and no one else.

She left the room for a few minutes to see to the sitting room fire, and Lennard turned to his host and said:

"Mr. Bowcock, I have come to see you on a matter which will need a good deal of explanation. It will take quite a couple of hours to put the whole thing before you, so if you have any other engagements for tonight, no doubt you can take a day off tomorrow – in fact, as the pit will have to stop working –"

"T' 'pit stop working, Mr. Lennard!" exclaimed the manager. "Yo' dunno say so. Is that his lordship's orders? Why, what's up?"

"I will explain everything, Mr. Bowcock," replied Lennard, "only, for her own sake, your wife must know nothing at present. The only question is, shall we have a talk tonight or not?"

"If it's anything that's bad," replied the big miner with a deeper note in his voice, "I'd soonest hear it now. Mysteries don't get any t' better for keepin'. Besides, it'll give me time to sleep on't; and that's not a bad thing to do when yo've a big job to handle."

Mrs. Bowcock came back as he said this, and Lennard had his cup of tea, and they of course talked about the war. Naturally, the big miner and his pretty little wife were the most interested people in Lancashire just then, for to no one else in the County Palatine had been given the honor of hearing the story of the great battle off the Isle of Wight from the lips of one who had been through it on board the now famous *Ithuriel.*

But when Tom Bowcock came out of the little sitting room three hours later, after Lennard had told him of the approaching doom of the world and had explained to him how his pit-shaft was to be used as a means of averting it – should that, after all, prove to be possible – his interest in the war had diminished very considerably, for he had already come to see clearly that this was undeniably a case of the whole being very much greater than the part.

Tom Bowcock was one of those men, by no means rare in the north, who work hard with hands and head at the same time. He was a pitman, but he was also a scientific miner, almost an engineer, and so Lennard had found very little difficulty in getting him to grasp the details of the tremendous problem in the working out of which he was destined to play no mean part.

"Well, Measter Lennard," he said, slowly, as they rose from the little table across which a very large amount of business had been transacted. "It's a pretty big job this that yo've putten into our hands, and especially into mine; but I reckon they'll be about big enough for it; and yo've come to t' right place, too. I've never heard yet of a job as Lancashire took on to as hoo didn't get through wi'.

"Now, from what yo've been telling me, yo' must be a bit of an early riser sometimes, so if yo'll come here at seven or so i' t' mornin', I'll fit yo' out wi' pit clothes and we'll go down t' shaft and yo' can see for yoursel' what's wantin' doin'. Maybe that'll help yo' before yo' go and make yo'r arrangements wi' Dobson & Barlow and t'other folk as yo'll want to help yo'."

"Thank you very much, Mr. Bowcock," replied Lennard. "You will find me here pretty close about seven. It's a big job, as you say, and there's not much time to be lost. Now, if Mrs. Bowcock has not gone to bed, I'll go and say good-night."

"She's no'on to bed yet," said his host, "and yo'll take a drop o' summat warm before yo' start walkin' to t' hotel, for yo'll get no cab up this way toneet. She'll just have been puttin' t' youngster to bed –"

Tom Bowcock stopped suddenly in his speech as a swift vision of that same "youngster" and his mother choking in the flames of the Fire-Mist passed across his senses. Lennard had convinced his intellect of the necessity of the task of repelling the Celestial Invader and of the possibility of success; but from that moment his heart was in the work.

It had stopped raining and the sky had cleared a little when they went to the door half an hour later. To the right, across the road, rose a tall gaunt shape like the skeleton of an elongated pyramid crowned with two big wheels. Lights were blazing round it, for the pit was working night and day getting the steam coal to the surface.

"Yonder's t' shaft," said Tom, as they shook hands. "It doesn't look much of a place to save the world in, does it?"

Chapter XXV

PREPARING FOR ACTION

The next day was a busy one, not only for Lennard himself but for others whose help he had come to enlist in the working out of the Great Experiment.

He turned up at Bowcock's house on the stroke of seven, got into his pit clothes, and was dropped down the twelve-hundred-foot shaft in the cage. At the bottom of the shaft he found a solid floor sloping slightly eastward, with three drives running in fan shape from northeast and southeast. There were two others running north and northwest.

After ten minutes' very leisurely walk round the base of the shaft, during which he made one or two observations by linear and perpendicular compass, he said to Tom Bowcock:

"I think this will do exactly. The points are absolutely correct. If we had dug a hole for ourselves we couldn't have got one better than this. Yes, I think it will just do. Now, will you be good enough to take me to the surface as slowly as you can?"

"No, but yo're not meanin' that, Measter Lennard," laughed the manager. "'Cause if I slowed t' engines down as much as I could you'd be the rest o' t' day getting to t' top."

"Yes, of course, I didn't mean that," said Lennard, "but just slowly – about a tenth of the speed that you dropped me into the bowels of the earth with. You see, I want to have a look at the sides."

"Yo' needna' trouble about that, Mr. Lennard, I can give yo' drawin's of all that in t' office, but still yo' can see for yo'rself by the drawin's afterwards."

The cage ascended very slowly, and Lennard did see for himself. But when later on he studied the drawings that Tom Bowcock had made, he found that there wasn't as much as a stone missing. When he had got into his everyday clothes again, and had drunk a cup of tea brewed for him by Mrs. Bowcock, he said as he shook hands with her husband:

"Well, as far as the pit is concerned, I have seen all that I want to see, and Lord Westerham was just as right about the pit as he was about the man who runs it. Now, I take it over from today. You will stop all mining work at once, close the entrances to the galleries and put down a bed of concrete ten feet thick, level. Then you will go by the drawings that I gave you last night.

"At present, the concreting of the walls in as perfect a circle as you can make them, not less than sixteen feet inner diameter, and building up the concrete core four feet thick from the floor to the top, is your first concern. You will tell your men that they will have double wages for day work and treble for night work, and whether they belong to the Volunteers or Yeomanry or Militia they will not be called to the Colors as long as they keep faith with us; if the experiment turns out all right, every man who sees it through shall have a bonus of a thousand pounds.

"But, remember, that this pit will be watched, and every man who signs on for the job will be watched, and the Lord have mercy on the man who plays us false, for he'll want it. You must make them remember that, Mr. Bowcock. This is no childish game of war among nations; this means the saving or the losing of a world, and the man who plays traitor here is not only betraying his own country, but the whole human race, friends and enemies alike."

"I'll see to that, Mr. Lennard. I know my chaps, and if there's one or two bad 'uns among 'em, they'll get paid and shifted in the ordinary way of business. But they're mostly a gradely lot of chaps. I've been picking 'em out for his lordship for t' last five yeers, and there isn't a Trade Unionist among 'em. We give good money here and we want good work and good faith, and if we don't get it, the man who doesn't give it has got to go and find another job.

"For wages like that they'd go on boring t' shaft right down through t' earth and out at t' other side, and risk finding Owd Nick and his people in t' middle. A' tell yo' for sure. Well, good-mornin', yo've a lot to do, and so have I. A'll get those galleries blocked and bricked up at once, and as soon as you can send t' concrete along, we'll start at t' floor."

Lennard's first visit after breakfast was to the Manchester and County Bank in Deansgate, where he startled the manager, as far as a Lancashire business man can be startled, by opening an account for two hundred and fifty thousand pounds, and depositing the title-deeds of the whole of Lord Westerham's properties in and about Bolton.

When he had finished his business at the Bank, he went to the offices of Dobson & Barlow, the great ironworkers, whose four-hundred-and-ten-foot chimney towers into the murky sky so far above all other structures in Bolton that if you are approaching the town by road you see it and its crest of smoke long before you see Bolton itself.

The firm had, of course, been advised of his coming, and he had written a note overnight to say when he would call. The name of Ratliffe Parmenter was a talisman to conjure with in all the business circles of the world, and so Lennard found Mr. Barlow himself waiting for him in his private office.

He opened the matter in hand very quietly, so quietly indeed that the keen-sighted, hard-headed man who was listening to him found that for once in his life he was getting a little out of his depth.

Never before had he heard such a tremendous scheme so quietly and calmly set forth. Bessemer furnaces were to be erected at once all round the pit mouth, meanwhile the firm was to contract with a Liverpool firm for an unlimited supply of concrete cement of the finest quality procurable. The whole staff of Dobson & Barlow's works were to be engaged at an advance of twenty-five percent on their present wages for three months to carry out the work of converting the shaft of the Great Lever pit into the gigantic cannon which was to hurl into Space the projectile which might or might not save the human race from destruction.

Even granted Lennard's unimpeachable credentials, it was only natural that the great iron-master should exhibit a certain amount of incredulity, and, being one of the best types of the Lancashire business man, he said quite plainly:

"This is a pretty large order you've brought us, Mr. Lennard, and although, of course, we know Mr. Parmenter to be good enough for any amount of money, still, you see, contracts are contracts, and what are we to do with those we've got in hand now if you propose to buy up for three months?"

"Yes," replied Lennard, "I admit that that is an important point. The question is, what would it cost you to throw up or transfer to other firms the contracts that you now have in hand?"

There was a silence of two or three minutes between them, during which Mr. Barlow made a rapid but comprehensive calculation and Lennard took out his checkbook and began to write a check.

"Counting everything," said Mr. Barlow, leaning back in his chair and looking up at the ceiling, "the transfer of our existing contracts to other firms of equal standing, so as to satisfy our customers, and the loss to ourselves for the time that you want – well, honestly, I don't think we could do it under twenty-five thousand pounds. You understand, I am saying nothing about the scientific aspect of the matter, because I don't understand it, but that's the business side of it; and that's what it's going to cost you before we begin."

Lennard filled in the check and signed it. He passed it across the table to Mr. Barlow, and said:

"I think that is a very reasonable figure. This will cover it and leave something over to go on with."

Mr. Barlow took the check and looked at it, and then at the calm face of the quiet young man who was sitting opposite him.

The check was for fifty thousand pounds. While he was looking at it, Lennard took the bank receipt for a quarter of a million deposit from his pocket and gave it to him, saying:

"You will see from this that money is really no object. As you know, Mr. Parmenter has millions, more I suppose than he could calculate himself, and he is ready to spend every penny of them. You will take that just as earnest money."

"That's quite good enough for us, Mr. Lennard," replied Mr. Barlow, handing the bank receipt back. "The contracts shall be transferred as soon as we can make arrangements, and the work shall begin at once. You can leave everything else to us – brickwork, building, cement and all the rest of it – and we'll guarantee that your cannon shall be ready to fire off in three months from now."

"And the projectile, Mr. Barlow, are you prepared to undertake that also?" asked Lennard.

"Yes, we will make the projectile according to your specification, but you will, of course, supply the bursting charge and the charge of this new powder of yours which is to send it into Space. You see, we can't do that; you'll have to get a Government permit to have such an enormous amount of explosives in one place, so I'll have to leave that to you."

"I think I shall be able to arrange that, Mr. Barlow," replied Lennard, as he got up from his seat and held his hand out across the table. "As long as you are willing to take on the engineering part of the business, I'll see to the rest. Now, I know that your time is quite as valuable as mine is, and I've got to get back to London this afternoon. Tomorrow morning I have to go through a sort of cross-examination before the Cabinet – not that they matter much in the sort of crisis that we've got to meet.

"Still, of course, we have to have the official sanction of the Government, even if it is a question of saving the world from destruction, but there won't be much difficulty about that, I think; and at any rate you'll be working on freehold property, and not even the Cabinet can stop that sort of work for the present. As far as everything connected with the mine is concerned, I hope you will be able to work with Mr. Bowcock, who seems a very good sort of fellow."

"If we can't work with Tom Bowcock," replied Mr. Barlow, "we can't work with anyone on earth, and that's all there is about it. He's a big man, but he's good stuff all through. Lord Westerham didn't make any bad choice when he made him manager. And you won't dine with me tonight?"

"I am sorry, but I must be back to London tonight. I have to catch the 12-15 and have an interview in Downing Street at seven, and when I've got through that, I don't think there will be any difficulty about the explosives."

"According to all accounts, you'll be lucky if you find Downing Street as it used to be," said Mr. Barlow. "By the papers this morning it looks as if London was going to have a pretty bad time of it, what with these airships and submarines that sink and destroy everything in sight. Now that they've got away with the fleet, it seems to me that it's only a sort of walk over for them."

"Yes, I'm afraid it will have to be something like that for the next month or so," replied Lennard, thinking of a telegram which he had in his pocket. "But the victory is not all on one side yet. Of course, you will understand that I am not in a position to give secrets away, but as regards our own bargain, I am at liberty to tell you that while you are building this cannon of ours there will probably be some developments in the war which will be, I think, as unexpected as they will be startling.

"In fact, sir," he continued, rising from his seat and holding out his hand across the table, "I am neither a prophet nor the son of a prophet, but when the time comes, I think you will find that those who believe that they are conquering England now will be here in Bolton faced by a foe against which their finest artillery will be as useless as an air-gun against an elephant.

"All I ask you to remember now is that at eleven p.m. on the twelfth of May, the leaders of the nations who are fighting against England now will be standing around me in the quarry on the Belmont Road, waiting for the firing of the shot which I hope will save the world. If it does not save it, they will be welcome to all that is left of the world in an hour after that."

"You are talking like a man who believes what he says, Mr. Lennard," replied Mr. Barlow, "and, strange and all as it seems, I am beginning to believe with you. There never was a business like this given into human hands before, and, for the sake of humanity, I hope that you will be successful. All that we can do shall be done well and honestly. That you can depend on, and for the rest, we shall depend on you and your science. The trust that you have put in our hands today is a great honor to us, and we shall do our best to deserve it. Good-morning, sir."

Chapter XXVI

THE FIRST BOMBARDMENT OF LONDON

When Lennard got out of the train at St. Pancras that evening, he found such a sight as until a day or so ago no Londoner had ever dreamed of. But terrible as the happenings were, they were not quite terrible enough to stop the issue of the evening newspapers.

As the train slowed down along the platform, boys were running along it yelling:

"Bombardment of London from the air – dome of St. Paul's smashed by a shell – Guildhall, Mansion House, and Bank of England in ruins – orful scenes in the streets. Paper, sir?"

He got out of the carriage and grabbed the first newspaper that was thrust into his hand, gave the boy sixpence for it, and hurried away towards the entrance. He found a few cabmen outside the station; he hailed one of the drivers, got in, and said:

"Downing Street – quick. There's a sovereign; there'll be another for you when I get there."

"It's a mighty risky job, guv'nor, these times, driving a keb through London streets. Still, one's got to live, I suppose. 'Old up there – my Gawd, that's another of those bombs! You just got out of there in time, sir."

Even as though it had been timed, as it might well have been, a torpedo dropped from a ghostly shape drifting slowly across the grey November clouds. Then there came a terrific shock. Every pane in the vast roof and in the St. Pancras Hotel shivered to the dust. The engine which had drawn Lennard's train blew up like one huge shell, and the carriages behind it fell into splinters.

If that shell had only dropped three minutes sooner the end of the World war of 1910 would have been very different to what it was; for, as Lennard learned afterwards, of all the porters, officials and passengers, who had the misfortune to be in the great station at that moment, only half a hundred cripples, maimed for life, escaped.

"I wonder whether that was meant for me," said Lennard as the frightened horse sprang away at a half gallop. "If that's the case, John Castellan knows rather more than he ought to do, and, good Lord, if he knows that, he must know where Auriole is, and what's to stop him taking one of those infernal things of his up to Whernside, wrecking the house and the observatory, and taking her off with him to the uttermost ends of the earth if he likes?

"There must be something in it or that shell would not have dropped just after I got outside the station. They watched the train come in, and they knew I was in it – they must have known.

"What a ghastly catastrophe it would be if they got on to that scheme of ours at the pit. Fancy one of those aërial torpedoes of his dropping down the bore of the cannon a few minutes before the right time! It would mean everything lost, and nothing gained, not even for him.

"Ah, good man Erskine," he went on, as he opened the paper, and read that every cruiser, battleship and transport that had forced the entrance to the Thames and Medway had been sunk. "That will be a bit of a check for them, anyhow. Yes, yes, that's very good. Garrison Fort, Chatham and Tilbury, of course, destroyed from the air, but not a ship nor a man left to go and take possession of them."

While he was reading his paper, and muttering thus to himself, the cab was tearing at the horse's best speed down Gray's Inn Road. It took a sudden swing to the right into Holborn, ran along New Oxford Street, and turned down Charing Cross Road, the horse going at a full gallop the whole time.

Happily it was a good horse, or the fate of the world might have been different. There was no rule of the road now, and no rules against furious driving. London was panic-stricken, as it might well be. As far as Lennard could judge the aërial torpedoes were being dropped mostly in the neighborhood of Regent Street and Piccadilly, and about Grosvenor Place and Park Lane. He half expected to find Parliament Street and Westminster in ruins, but for some mysterious reason they had been spared.

The great City was blazing in twenty places, and scarcely a minute passed without the crash of an explosion and the roar of flame that followed it, but a magic circle seemed to have been drawn round Westminster. There nothing was touched, and yet the wharves on the other side of the river, and the great manufactories behind them, were blazing and vomiting clouds of flame and smoke towards the clouds as though the earth had been split open beneath them and the internal fires themselves let loose.

When the cabman pulled up his sweating and panting horse at the door of Number 2 Downing Street, Lennard got out and said to the cabman:

"You did that very well, considering the general state of things. I don't know whether you'll live to enjoy it or not, but there's a five-pound note for you, and if you'll take my advice you will get your wife and family, if you have one, into that cab, and drive right out into the country. It strikes me London's going to be a very good place to stop away from for the next two or three days."

"Thank 'ee, sir," said the cabman, as he gathered up the five-pound note and tucked it down inside his collar. "I don't know who you are, but it's very kind of you; and as you seem to know something, I'll do as you say. What with these devil-ships a-flyin' about the skies, and dropping thunderbolts on us from the clouds, and furreners a-comin' up the Thames as I've heard, London ain't 'ealthy enough for me, nor the missus and the kids, and thanks for your kindness, sir, we're movin' tonight, keb an' all.

"Oh, my Gawd, there's another! 'Otel Cecil and Savoy this time, if I've got my bearin's right. Well, there's one thing, t'ain't on'y the pore what's sufferin' this time; there'll be a lot of rich people dead afore mornin'. A pal of mine told me just now that Park Lane was burnin' from end t' end. Good-evenin', sir, and thenk you."

As the cab drove away Lennard stood for a few moments on the pavement, watching two columns of flame soaring up from the side of the Strand. Perhaps the most dreadful effects produced by the aërial torpedoes were those which resulted from the breaking of the gas mains and the destruction of the electric conduits. Save for the bale-fires of ruin and destruction, half London was in darkness. Miles of streets under which the gas mains were laid blew up with almost volcanic force. The electric mains were severed, and all the contents dislocated, and if ever London deserved the name which James Thompson gave it when he called it "The City of Dreadful Night," it deserved it on that evening of the 17th of November 1909.

Lennard was received in the Prime Minister's room by Mr. Chamberlain, Lord Whittinghame, Sir Henry Campbell-Bannerman, Lord Milner and General Lord Kitchener.

It was perhaps the strangest meeting that had ever taken place in that room, not even saving the historic meeting of 1886. There was very little talking. Even in the House of Commons the flood of talk had ebbed away in such a fashion that it made it possible for the nation's business to be got through at a wonderful speed. The fact of the matter was that the guns were talking – talking within earshot of Palace Yard itself, and so men had come to choose their words and make them few.

After the introductions had been made the man who really held the fate of the world in his hands took a long envelope out of the breast-pocket of his coat, and proceeded to explain, somewhat as a schoolmaster might explain to his class, the doom which would overwhelm humanity on the 12th May 1910.

He was listened to in absolute silence, because his hearers were men who had good reason for believing that silence is often worth a good deal more than speech. When he had finished the rustle of his papers as he handed them to the Prime Minister was distinctly audible in the solemn silence. The Prime Minister folded them up, and said:

"There is no necessity for us to go into the figures again. I think we are prepared to take them on the strength of your reputation, Mr. Lennard.

"We have asked you here tonight as an adviser, as a man who in more ways than one sees farther than we can. Now, what is your advice? You are aware, I presume, that the German Emperor, the Czar of Russia and the French President landed at Dover this morning, and have issued an ultimatum from Canterbury, calling upon us to surrender London, and discuss terms of peace in the interests of humanity. Now, you occupy a unique point of view. You have told us in your letters that unless a miracle happens the human race will not survive midnight of the 12th of May next. We believe that you are right, and now, perhaps, you will be good enough to let us have your opinions as to what should be done in the immediate present."

"My opinion is, sir, that for at least forty days you must fight, no matter how great the odds may appear to be. Every ditch and hedgerow, every road and lane, every hill and copse must be defended. If London falls, England falls, and with it the Empire."

"But how are we to do it?" exclaimed Lord Kitchener. "With these infernal airships flying about above it, and dropping young earthquakes from the clouds? There are no braver men on earth than ours, but it isn't human nature to keep steady under that kind of punishment. Look what they've done already in London! What is there to prevent them, for instance, from dropping a shell through the roof of this house, and blowing the lot of us to eternity in little pieces? It's not the slightest use trying to shoot back at them. You remember what happened to poor

Beresford and the rest of his fleet in Dover Harbor. If you can't hit back, you can't fight."

"That certainly appears to be perfectly reasonable," said Sir Henry Campbell-Bannerman. "Personally, I must confess, although with the greatest reluctance, that considering the enormous advantage possessed by the enemy in this combination of submarine and flying machine, we have no other alternative but to surrender at discretion. It is a pitiful thing to say, I am well aware, but we are fighting forces which would never have been called into being in any other war. I agree with Lord Kitchener that you cannot fight an enemy if you cannot hit him back. I am afraid there is no other alternative."

"No," added Lord Whittinghame, "I am afraid there is not. By tomorrow morning there will be three millions of men on British soil, and we haven't a million to put against them – to say nothing of these horrible airships: but, Mr. Lennard, if the world is only going to live about six months or so, what is the use of conquering the British Empire? Surely there must be another alternative."

"Yes, my lord," replied Lennard, "there is another. I've no doubt your lordship has one of your motors within call. Let us go down to Canterbury, yourself, Lord Kitchener and myself, and I will see if I can't convince the German Emperor that in trying to conquer Britain he is only stabbing the waters. If I only had him at Whernside, I would convince him in five minutes."

"Then we'd better get hold of him and take him there," said Lord Kitchener. "But I'm ready for the Canterbury journey."

"And so am I," said Lord Whittinghame, "and the sooner we're off the better. I've got a new Napier here that's good for seventy-five miles an hour, so we'd better be off."

Chapter XXVII

LENNARD'S ULTIMATUM

Within five minutes they were seated in the big Napier, with ninety horse-power under them, and a possibility of eighty miles an hour before them. A white flag was fastened to a little flagstaff on the left-hand side. They put on their goggles and overcoats, and took Westminster Bridge, as it seemed, in a leap. Rochester was reached in twenty-five minutes, but at the southern side of Rochester Bridge they were held up by German sentries.

"Not a pleasant sort of thing on English soil," growled Lord Kitchener as Lord Whittinghame stopped the motor.

"Is the German Emperor here yet?" asked Lennard in German.

"No, Herr, he is at Canterbury," replied the sentry. "Would you like to see the officer?"

"Yes," said Lennard, "as soon as possible. These gentlemen are Lord Whittinghame and Lord Kitchener, and they wish to meet the Emperor as soon as possible."

The sentry saluted and retired, and presently a captain of Uhlans came clattering across the street, clicked his heels together, touched the side of his helmet, and said:

"At your service, gentlemen. What can I do for you?"

"We wish to get into communication with the German Emperor as soon as possible," replied Lord Whittinghame. "Is the telegraph still working from here to Canterbury?"

"It is," replied the German officer; "if you will come with me to the office you shall be put into communication with His Majesty at once; but it will be necessary for me to hear what you say."

"We're only going to try and make peace," said Lord Kitchener, "so you might as well hear all we've got to say. Those infernal airships of yours have beaten us. Will you get in? We'll run you round to the office."

"I thank you," replied the captain of the Uhlans, "but it will be better if I walk on and have the line cleared. I will meet you at the office. Adieu."

He stiffened up, clicked his heels again, saluted, and the next moment he had thrown his right leg across the horse which the orderly had brought up for him.

"Not bad men, those Uhlans," said Lord Kitchener, as the car moved slowly towards the telegraph station. "Take a lot of beating in the field, I should say, if it once came to cold steel."

They halted at the post office, and the captain of Uhlans, who was in charge of all the telegraph lines of the southeast, was requested to send the following telegram, which was signed by Lord Whittinghame and Lord Kitchener.

> "Acting as deputation from British Government we desire interview with your Majesty at Canterbury, with view to putting end to present bloodshed, if possible, also other important news to communicate."

This telegram was dispatched to the Kaiser at the County Hotel, Canterbury, and while they were waiting for the reply a message came in from Whitstable addressed to "Lennard, oyster merchant, Rochester," which was in the following terms:

> "Oyster catch promises well. Advised large purchase tomorrow.
> "Robinson & Smith"

"That seems rather a frivolous sort of thing to send one nowadays," said Lennard, dropping the paper to the floor after reading the telegram aloud. "I have some interest in the beds at Whitstable, and my agents, who don't seem to know that there's a war going on, want me to invest. I think it's hardly good enough, when you don't know whether you'll be in little pieces within the next ten minutes."

"I don't see why you shouldn't take on a contract for supplying our friends the enemy," laughed Lord Kitchener, as the twinkle of an eye passed between them, while the captain of Uhlans' back was turned for an instant.

"I'm afraid they would be confiscated before I could do that," said Lennard. "I shan't bother about answering it. We have rather more serious things than oysters to think about just now."

The sounder clicked, and the German telegraphist, who had taken the place of the English one, tapped out a message, which he handed to the captain of Uhlans.

"Gentlemen, His Imperial Majesty will be glad to receive you at the County Hotel, Canterbury. I will give you a small flag which shall secure you from all molestation."

He handed the paper to Lord Whittinghame as he spoke. The Imperial message read:

> "Happy to meet deputation. Please carry German flag, which will secure you from molestation *en route.* I am wiring orders for suspension of hostilities till dawn tomorrow. I hope we may make satisfactory arrangements.
>
> "Wilhelm"

"That is quite satisfactory," said Lord Whittinghame to the captain of Uhlans. "We shall be much obliged to you for the flag, and you will perhaps telegraph down the road saying that we are not to be stopped. I can assure you that the matter is one of the utmost urgency."

"Certainly, my lord," replied the captain. "His Majesty's word is given. That is enough for us."

Ten minutes later the big Napier, flying the German flag on the left-hand side, was spinning away through Chatham, and down the straight road to Canterbury. They slowed up going through Sittingbourne and Faversham, which were already in the hands of the Allied forces, thanks to John Castellan's precautions in blocking all railroads to Dover, and the German flag was saluted by the garrisons, much to Lord Kitchener's quietly-expressed displeasure, but he knew they were playing for a big stake, and so he just touched his cap, as they swung through the narrow streets, and said what he had to say under his breath.

Within forty minutes the car pulled up opposite the County Hotel, Canterbury. The ancient city was no longer English, save as regarded its architecture. Everywhere, the clatter of German hoofs sounded on the streets, and the clink and clank of German spurs and swords sounded on the pavements. The French and Austrians were taking the westward routes by Ashford and Tonbridge in the enveloping movement on London. The War Lord of Germany had selected the direct route for himself.

As the motor stopped panting and throbbing in front of the hotel entrance, a big man in the uniform of the Imperial Guard came out, saluted, and said:

"Lord Whittinghame and Lord Kitchener, with Mr. Lennard, I presume?"

"Yes, that's so," said Lord Kitchener, opening the side door and getting out. "Colonel von Folkerström, I believe. I think we've met before. You were His Majesty's *attaché* with us during the Boer War, I think. This is Lord Whittinghame, and this is Mr. Lennard. Is His Majesty within?"

"His Majesty awaits you, gentlemen," replied the Colonel, formally. And then as he shook hands with Lord Kitchener he added, "I am sorry, sir, that we should meet as enemies on English soil."

"Just the fortune of war and those damned airships of yours, Colonel," laughed Lord Kitchener in reply. "If we'd had them this meeting might have been in Berlin or Potsdam. Can't fight against those things, you know. We're only human."

"But you English are just a little more, I think," said the Colonel to himself. "Gottes willen! What would my August Master be thinking now if this was in Berlin instead of Canterbury, and here are these Englishmen taking it as quietly as though an invasion of England happened every day." And when he had said this to himself he continued aloud:

"My lords and Mr. Lennard, if you will follow me I will conduct you into His Majesty's presence."

They followed the Colonel upstairs to the first floor. Two sentries in the uniform of the 1st Regiment of Cuirassiers were guarding the door: their bayoneted rifles came up to the present, the Colonel answered the salute, and they dropped to attention. The Colonel knocked at the door and a harsh voice replied:

"Herein."

The door swung open and Lennard found himself for the first but not the last time in the presence of the War Lord of Germany.

"Good-evening, gentlemen," said the Kaiser. "You will understand me when I say I am both glad and sorry to see you."

"Your Majesty," replied Lord Whittinghame, in a curiously serious tone, "the time for human joy and sorrow is so fast expiring that almost everything has ceased to matter, even the invasion of England."

The Kaiser's brows lifted, and he stared in frank astonishment at the man who could say such apparently ridiculous words so seriously. If he had not known that he was talking to the late Prime Minister, and the present leader of the Unionist party in the House of Lords, he would have thought him mad.

"Those are very strange words, my lord," he replied. "You will pardon me if I confess that I can hardly grasp their meaning."

"If your Majesty has an hour to spare," said Lord Whittinghame, "Mr. Lennard will make everything perfectly plain. But what he has to say, and what he can prove, must be for your Majesty's ears alone."

"Is it so important as that?" laughed the Kaiser.

"It is so important, sire," said Lord Kitchener, "that the fate of the whole world hangs upon what you may say or do within the next hour. So far, you have beaten us, because you have been able to bring into action engines of warfare against which we have been unable to defend ourselves. But now, there is another enemy in the field, against which we possess the only means of defense. That is what we have come to explain to your Majesty."

"Another enemy!" exclaimed the Kaiser, "but how can that be. There are no earthly powers left sufficiently strong that we would be powerless against them."

"This is not an earthly enemy, your Majesty," replied Lennard, speaking for the first time since he had entered the room. "It is an invader from Space. To put it quite plainly, the terms which we have come to offer your Majesty are: Cessation of hostilities for six months, withdrawal of all troops from British soil, universal disarmament, and a pledge to be entered into by all the Powers of Europe and the United States of America that after the 12th of May next there shall be no more war. Your fleets have been destroyed as well as ours, your armies are here, but they cannot get away, and so we are going to ask you to surrender."

"Surrender!" echoed the Kaiser, "surrender, when your country lies open and defenseless before us? No, no. Lord Whittinghame and Lord Kitchener I know, but who are you, sir – a civilian and an unknown man, that you should dictate peace to me and my Allies?"

"Only a man, your Majesty," said Lord Whittinghame, "who has convinced the British Cabinet Council that he holds the fate of the world in the hollow of his hands. Are you prepared to be convinced?"

"Of what?" replied the Kaiser, coldly.

"That there will be no world left to conquer after midnight on the 12th of May next, or to put it otherwise, that unless our terms are accepted, and Mr. Lennard carries out his work, there will be neither victors nor vanquished left on earth."

"Gentlemen," replied the Kaiser, "you will pardon me when I say that I am surprised beyond measure that you should have come to me with a schoolboy's tale like that. The eternal order of things cannot be interrupted in such a ridiculous fashion. Again, I trust you will forgive me when I express my regret that you should have wasted so much of your own time and mine on an errand which should surely have appeared to you fruitless from the first.

"Whoever or whatever this gentleman may be," he continued with a wave of his hand towards Lennard, "I neither know nor care; but that yourself and Lord Kitchener should have been deceived so grossly, I must confess passes the limits of my imagination. Frankly, I do not believe in the possibility of such proofs as you allude to. As regards peace, I propose to discuss terms with King Edward in Windsor – not before, nor with anyone else. Gentlemen, I have other matters to attend to, and I have the honor to bid you good-evening."

"And that is your Majesty's last word?" said Lord Kitchener. "You mean a fight to the finish?"

"Yes, my lord," replied the Kaiser, "whether the world finishes with the fight or not."

"Very well then," said Lennard, taking an envelope from the breast-pocket of his coat, and putting it down on the table before the Emperor. "If your Majesty has not time to look through those papers, you will perhaps send them to Berlin and take your own astronomer's report upon them. Meanwhile, you will remember that our terms are: Unconditional surrender of the forces invading the British Islands or the destruction of the world. Good-night."

Chapter XXVIII

CONCERNING ASTRONOMY AND OYSTERS

In spite of the bold front that he had assumed during the interview, the strain, not exactly of superstition but rather of supernaturalism which runs so strongly in the Kaiser's family, made it impossible for him to treat such a tremendous threat as the destruction of the world as an alternative to universal peace by any means as lightly as he appeared to his visitors to do; and when the audience was over he picked up the envelope which Lennard had left upon the table, beckoned Count von Moltke into his room behind, locked the door, and said:

"Now, Count, what is your opinion of this? At first sight it looks ridiculous; but whoever this Lennard may be, it seems hardly likely that two men like Lord Whittinghame and Lord Kitchener, two of the coolest-headed and best-balanced men on earth, should take the trouble to come down here as a deputation from the British Cabinet only to make themselves ridiculous. Suppose we have a look at these papers? Everything is in train for the advance. I daresay you and I understand enough of mathematics between us to find out if there is anything serious in them, and if so, they shall go to Herr Döllinger at once."

"I think it would be at least worth while to look through them, your Majesty," replied the Count. "Like yourself, I find it rather difficult to believe that this mysterious Mr. Lennard, whoever he is, has been able to impose upon the whole British Cabinet, to say nothing of Lord Kitchener, who is about the best engineer and mathematician in the British Army."

So the Count and the Kaiser sat down, and went through the elaborate and yet beautifully clear calculations and diagrams, page by page, each making notes as he went on. At the end of an hour the Kaiser looked over his own notes, and said to von Moltke:

"Well, what is your opinion, Count?"

"I am not an astronomer, your Majesty, but these calculations certainly appear to me to be correct as far as they go – that is, granted always that the premisses from which Mr. Lennard starts are correct. But certainly I think that your Majesty will be wise in sending them as soon as possible to Herr Döllinger."

"That is exactly the conclusion that I have come to myself," replied the Kaiser. "I will write a note to Herr Döllinger, and one of the airships must take it across to Potsdam. We can't afford to run any risks of that infernal submarine ram or whatever she is. I would almost give an Army corps for that ship. There's no doubt she's lost us three fleets, a score of transports, and twenty thousand men in the last three days, and she's just as much a mystery as ever. It's the most extraordinary position a conquering army was ever put into before."

The Kaiser was perfectly right. There could be no doubt that up to the present the invading forces had been victorious, thanks of course mainly to the irresistible advantage of the airships, but also in no small degree to the hopeless unpreparedness of the British home armies to meet an invasion, which both military and naval experts had simply refused to believe possible.

The seizure of the line from Dover to Chatham had been accomplished in a single night. A dozen airships patrolled the air ahead of the advancing German forces, which of course far outnumbered the weak and hastily-collected British forces which could be brought against them, and which, attacked at once by land and from the air, never really had a chance.

It was the most perfectly conducted invasion ever planned. The construction trains which went in advance on both lines carried sections of metals of English gauge, already fastened to sleepers, and ready to lay down. Every little bridge and culvert had been known and was provided for. Not a bolt nor a fishplate had been forgotten, and moreover John Castellan's operations from the air had reduced the destruction to a minimum, and the consequence was that twelve hours after the Kaiser had landed at Dover he found himself in his headquarters at Canterbury, whence the British garrison had been forced to retire after heavy fighting along the lines of wooded hills behind Maidstone.

It was the old, old story, the story of every war that England had gone into and "muddled through" somehow; but with two differences. Her soldiers had never had to fight an enemy in the skies before, and – there was no time now to straighten out the muddle, even if every able-bodied man in the United Kingdom had been trained soldiers, as the invaders were.

But there was another element in the situation. Incredible as it might seem to those ignorant of the tremendous forces brought into play, the home fleets of Europe had been destroyed, practically to a ship, within three days and nights. The narrow seas were deserted. On the morning of the seventeenth, four transports attempting to cross from Hamburg to Ramsgate, carrying a force of men, horses and light artillery, which was intended to operate as a flying column along the northern shores of Kent, had been rammed and sent to the bottom within fifteen minutes halfway between land and land, and not a man nor an animal had escaped.

There was no news from the expeditions which had been sent against Hull and Newcastle – all the cables had been cut, save the transatlantic lines, the cutting of which the United States had already declared they would consider as an unfriendly act on the part of the Allies, and the British cable from Gibraltar to the Lizard which connected with Palermo and Rome, and so formed the link of communication between Britain and the Mediterranean.

The British Mediterranean Fleet was coming home, so were the West Indian and North American squadrons, while the squadron in the China seas was also ordered home, via the Suez Canal, to form a conjunction with our Italian Allies. Of course, these ships would in due time be dealt with by the aërial submarines, but meanwhile commerce with Europe had become impossible. Imports had stopped at most of the great ports through sheer terror of this demon of the sea, which appeared to be here, there and everywhere at the same time; and with all these powerful squadrons converging upon the shores of Britain the problem of feeding and generally keeping fit for war some three millions of men and over half a million horses would soon begin to look distinctly serious.

Castellan's vessels had hunted in vain for this solitary vessel, which single-handed, marvelous as it seemed, kept the narrow waters clear of invaders. The truth of this matter, however, was very simple. The *Ithuriel* was nearly twice as fast in the water as the *Flying Fishes,* and she carried guns with an effective range of five miles, whereas they only carried torpedoes.

For instance, during the battle of Sheerness, in which the remaining units of the North Sea Squadron had, with the *Ithuriel's* aid, attacked and destroyed every German and Russian battleship and transport, Erskine's craft had done terrible execution without so much as being seen until, when the last of the German Coast Defense ships had gone down with all hands in the Great Nore, off the Nore lighthouse, whence she was shelling Garrison Fort, the *Ithuriel* had risen above the water for a few moments, and Denis Castellan had taken a cockshot with the three forward guns at a couple of *Flying Fishes* that were circling over the town and fort and river mouth.

The shells had time-fuses, and they were timed to the tenth of a second. They burst simultaneously over the airships. Then came a rending of the atmosphere, and descending streams of fire, which burst with a rapid succession of sharp reports as they touched the airships. Then came another blaze of light which seemed to darken the wintry sun for a moment, and then another quaking of the air, after which what was left of the two *Flying Fishes* fell in little fragments into the water, splashing here and there as though they had been shingle ballast thrown out of a balloon.

True, Garrison Fort had been blown up by the aërial torpedoes, and the same fate was befalling the great forts at Tilbury, but their gallant defenders did not die in vain, and, although the remainder of the aërial squadron were able to go on and do their work of destruction on London, whither the *Ithuriel* could not follow them, the wrecks of six battleships, a dozen destroyers and ten transports strewed the approaches to the Thames and the Medway, while nearly thirty thousand soldiers and sailors would never salute the flag of Czar or Kaiser again.

In all the history of war no such loss of men, ships and material had ever taken place within the short space of three days and a few hours. Four great fleets and nearly a hundred thousand men had been wiped out of existence since the assault on Southern England had begun, and even now, despite the airships, had the millions of Britain's able-bodied men, who were grinding their teeth and clenching their fists in impotent fury, been trained just to shoot and march, it would have been possible to take the invaders between overwhelming masses of men – who would hold their lives as nothing in comparison with their country's honor – and the now impassable sea, and drive them back into it. But although men and youths went in their tens of thousands to the recruiting stations and demanded to be enlisted, it was no use. Soldiers are not made in a day or a week, and the invaders of England had been making them for forty years.

While the Kaiser and Count von Moltke were going through Lennard's papers, and coming to the decision to send them to Potsdam, Lord Whittinghame's motor, instead of returning to Chatham, was running up to Whitstable to answer the telegram which Lennard had received at Rochester. The German flag cleared them out of Canterbury. It was already known that they had been received by the Kaiser, and therefore their persons were sacred. In consequence of the loss of the squadron attacking the Thames and Medway, and the destruction of the Ramsgate flotilla, the country was not occupied by the enemy north of the great main road through Canterbury and Faversham, and that was just why the *Ithuriel* was lying snugly in the mouth of the East Swale River, about three miles from the little town, with a shabby-looking lighter beside her, from which she was taking in an extra complement of her own shells and material for making Lennard's explosive, as well as a full load of fuel for her engines. They pulled up at the door of the Bear and Key Hotel, and as the motor came to a standstill a man dressed in the costume of an ordinary worker on the oyster-beds came up, touched his sou'wester, and said:

"Mr. Lennard's car, gentlemen?"

"Yes, I'm here," said Lennard, shortly; "we've just left the Emperor at Canterbury. How about those oysters? I should think you ought to do well with them in Canterbury. Got plenty?"

"Yes, sir," replied the man. "If you will come down to the wharf I will be able to show you a shipment that I can send along tonight if the train comes from Canterbury."

"I think we might as well have a drop of something hot first, it's rather cold riding."

The others nodded, and they went into the hotel without removing their caps or goggles. They asked a waiter to show them into a private room, as they had some business to do, and when four glasses of hot whisky and water had been put on the table, Lennard locked the door and said:

"My lords, allow me to have the pleasure of introducing to you Lieutenant Denis Castellan of His Majesty's cruiser *Ithuriel.*"

Lord Whittinghame's and Lord Kitchener's hands went out together, and the former said:

"Delighted to meet you, Mr. Castellan. You and Captain Erskine have done magnificently for us in spite of all our troubles. In fact, I don't know what we should have done without you and this wonderful craft of yours."

"With all due deference to the Naval Council," said "K. of K," rather bluntly, "it's a pity they didn't put down a dozen of her. But what about these oysters that you telegraphed to Mr. Lennard about?"

"There is only one oyster in question at present, my lord," said Denis, with an entirely Irish smile, "but it's rather a big one. It's the German Emperor's yacht, the *Hohenzollern.* She managed to run across, and get into Ramsgate, while we were up here in the Thames – that's the worst of there being only one of us, as we can only attend to one piece of business at a time. Now, she's lying there waiting the Kaiser's orders, in case he wants to take a trip across, and it seems to me that she'd be worth the watching for a day or two – she'd be a big prize, you know, gentlemen, especially if we could catch her with the War Lord of Germany on board her. I don't think myself that His Majesty would have any great taste for a trip to the bottom of the North Sea, just when he thinks he's beginning the conquest of England so nicely, and, by the Powers, we'd send him there if he got into one of his awkward tempers with us."

Lord Kitchener, who was in England acting as Chief-of-the-Staff to the Duke of Connaught, and general adviser to the Council of National Defense, took Lord Whittinghame to the other end of the room, and said a few words to him in a low tone, and he came back and said:

"It is certainly worth trying, even if you can only catch the ship; but we don't think you'll catch the Kaiser. The fact is, you seem to have established such a holy terror in these waters that I don't think he would trust his Imperial person between here and Germany. If he did go across, he'd probably go in an airship. But if you can bring the *Hohenzollern* up to Tilbury – of course, under the German flag – I think we shall be able to make good use of her. If she won't come, sink her."

"Very good, my lords," said Denis, saluting. "If she's not coming up the Thames tomorrow night with the *Ithuriel* under her stern, ye'll know that she's on the bottom in pieces somewhere. And now," he continued, taking a long envelope from an inner pocket, "here is the full report of our doings since the war began, with return of ships sunk, crippled and escaped; number of men landed, and so on, according to instructions. We will report again tomorrow night, I hope, with the *Hohenzollern.*"

They shook hands and wished him good-night and good luck, and in half an hour the *Ithuriel* was running half-submerged eastward along the coast, and the motor was on its way to Faversham by the northern road, as there were certain reasons why it should not go back through Canterbury.

Chapter XXIX

THE LION WAKES

At daybreak on the nineteenth, to the utter amazement of everyone who was not "in the know," the Imperial yacht, *Hohenzollern,* was found off Tilbury, flying the Imperial German Ensign and the Naval flag, as well as a long string of signals ordering the aërial bombardment of London to cease, and all the *Flying Fishes* to return at once to Canterbury.

The apparent miracle had been accomplished in an absurdly easy fashion. About nine a.m. on the eighteenth a German orderly went into the post office at Dover and handed in an official telegram signed "Von Roon," ordering the *Hohenzollern* to come round at once to Dover, as she was considered too open to attack there.

There was something so beautifully natural and simple in the whole proceeding that, although there were about a dozen German officers and non-commissioned officers in the room at the time that the orderly came and went without suspicion, the telegram was taken by the clerk, read and initialed by the Censor, and passed.

A few minutes later the orderly, marching in perfectly correct German fashion and carrying a large yellow envelope, walked out through the town northwards and climbed the hill to the eastward of the ruined castle. The envelope with its official seal took him past the sentries without question, but, instead of delivering it, he turned down a bypath to Fan Bay, under the South Foreland, gained the beach, took off his uniform in a secluded spot under the cliffs, and went for a swim. The uniform was never reclaimed, for when he reached the submerged *Ithuriel* Denis Castellan had a rub down and put his own on.

The captain of the *Hohenzollern* was only too glad to obey the order, for he also thought that it would be better protected from the dreaded ocean terror in Dover, so he lost no time in obeying the order; with the result that, just as he was entering the deserted Downs, the said terror met him and ordered him to the right-about under pain of instant sinking.

After that the rest was easy. The captain and officers raged and stormed, but not even German discipline would have prevented a mutiny if they had not surrendered. It was known that the *Ithuriel* took no prisoners. In five minutes after the irresistible ram had hit them they would be at the bottom of the sea, and so the Hohenzollern put about and steamed out into the North Sea, with the three wicked forward guns trained upon her, and the ram swirling smoothly through the water fifty yards from her stern.

At nightfall the course was altered for the mouth of the Thames. And so, with all lights out and steered by a thin shifting ray from her captor's conning-tower, the Kaiser's yacht made its strange way to Tilbury.

The instant she dropped her anchor a couple of destroyers ran out from the Gravesend shore and ranged alongside her. The next minute a British captain and three lieutenants followed by a hundred bluejackets had boarded her. The German Commander and his officers gave up their swords, devoutly hoping that they would never meet their War Lord again, and so the incident ended.

It will be easily understood that the Kaiser was about the most infuriated man in the United Kingdom when the *Flying Fishes* arrived at Canterbury and the Commander of the squadron described the arrival of the *Hohenzollern* in the Thames and asked for orders.

In the first place no one knew better than William the Second how priceless was the prize won by the impudent audacity of these two young British sailors. In his private apartments on board there were his own complete plans of the campaign – not only for the conquest of Britain, but afterwards for the dismemberment of the British Empire, and its partition among the Allies – exact accounts of the resources of the chief European nations in men, money and ships, plans of fortifications, and even drafts of treaties. In fact, it was such a haul of Imperial and International secrets as had never been made before; and that evening the British Cabinet held in their possession enough diplomatic explosives to blow the European league of nations to pieces.

Erskine and Castellan were honored by an autograph letter from the King, thanking them heartily for their splendid services up to the present stage of the war, and wishing them all good luck for the future. Then the *Ithuriel* slipped down the Thames, towing half a dozen shabby-looking barges behind her, and for some days she disappeared utterly from human ken.

What she was really doing during these days was this. These barges and several others which she picked up now and then were filled with ammunition for her guns and fuel for her engines, and she dropped them here and there in obscure creeks and rock-bound bays from Newcastle to the Clyde, where they lay looking like abandoned derelicts, until such times as they might be wanted.

Meanwhile, very soon after the loss of the *Hohenzollern,* the Kaiser received two messages which disquieted him very seriously. One of these came by airship from Potsdam. It was an exhaustive report upon the papers which Lennard had left with him on that momentous night as it turned out to be, on which the War Lord had rejected the ultimatum of the Man of Peace. It was signed by Professor Döllinger and endorsed by four of the greatest astronomers of Germany.

Briefly put, its substance amounted to this: Mr. Lennard's calculations were absolutely correct, as far as they went. Granted the existence of such a celestial body as he designated *Alpha* in the document, and its position *x* on the day of its alleged discovery; its direction and speed designated *y* and *z,* then at the time of contact designated *n,* it would infallibly come into contact with the earth's atmosphere, and the consequences deduced would certainly come to pass, viz., either the earth would combine with it, and be transformed into a semi-incandescent body, or the terrestrial atmosphere would become a fire mist which would destroy all animal and vegetable life upon the planet within the space of a few minutes.

The second communication was a joint-note from the Emperor of Austria, the President of the Hague Council, the President of the French Republic, and the Tsar of Russia, protesting against the bombardment of London or any other defenseless town by the airships. The note set forth that these were purely engines of war, and ought not to be used for purposes of mere terrorism and murder. Their war employment on land or water, or against fortified positions, was perfectly legitimate, but against unarmed people and defenseless towns it was held to be contrary to all principles of humanity and civilization, and it was therefore requested by the signatories that, in order to prevent serious differences between the Allies, it should cease forthwith.

The result of this communication was of course a Council of War, which was anything but a harmonious gathering, especially as several of the older officers agreed with the tone of it, and told the Kaiser plainly that they considered that there was quite enough in the actual business of war for the *Flying Fishes* to do; and the Chancellor did not hesitate to express the opinion that the majority of the peoples of Europe, and possibly large numbers of their own soldiers, who, after all, were citizens first and soldiers afterwards, would strongly resent such operations, especially when it became known that the Emperor's own Allies had protested against it; the result of the Council was that William the Second saw that he was clearly in a minority, and had the good sense to issue a General Order there and then that all aërial bombardments, save as part of an organized attack, should cease from that day.

The events of the next twenty days were, as may well be imagined, full of momentous happenings, which it would require hundreds of pages to describe in anything like detail, and therefore only quite a brief sketch of them can be given here. This will, however, be sufficient to throw a clear light upon the still more stupendous events which were to follow.

In consequence of the almost incredible destruction and slaughter during these first four awful days and nights of the war, both sides had lost the command of the sea, and the capture of the *Hohenzollern* in broad daylight less than a dozen miles from the English coast had produced such a panic among the rank and file of the invaders, and the reinforcements of men waiting on the other side of the Channel and the North Sea, that communication save by airship had practically stopped.

The consequence of this was that, geographically, the Allied armies, after the release of the prisoners from Portsmouth and Folkestone, amounted to some three million men of all arms, with half a million horses, and two thousand guns – it will be remembered that a vast number of horses, guns and stores had gone to the bottom in the warships which the *Ithuriel* had sunk – were confined within a district bounded by the coast-line from Ramsgate to the Needles, and thence by a line running north to Southampton; thence, across Hampshire to Petersfield, and via Horsham, Tunbridge Wells, Ashford, and over Canterbury, back to Ramsgate.

In view of the defeat and destruction of the expedition against London, the troops that had been thrown forward to Chatham and Rochester to co-operate with it were recalled, and concentrated between

Ashford and Canterbury. The rest of England, Scotland and Ireland was to the present a closed country to them. The blockade on Swansea and Liverpool had been raised by the *Ithuriel*, and there was nothing to prevent any amount of supplies from the west and south being poured in through half a hundred ports.

Thus the dream of starving the British Islands out had been dissipated at a stroke. True, the dockyards of Devonport and Milford Haven had been destroyed by the airships, but copies of the plans of the *Ithuriel* had been sent to Liverpool, Barrow, Belfast, the Clyde and the Tyne, and hundreds of men were working at them night and day. Scores of battleships, cruisers and destroyers, belonging both to Britain and other countries, which were nearing completion, were being labored at with feverish intensity, so that they might be fitted for sea in something like fighting trim; submarines were being finished off by dozens, and Thorneycroft's and Yarrow's yards were, like the rest, working to their full capacity.

The blind frenzy of rage which had swept like an epidemic over the whole kingdom during the first days of disaster had died away and in its place had come the quiet but desperate resolve that if Britain was to be conquered she should be depopulated as well.

All male employment, save that which was necessary to produce coal and iron, to keep the shipyards and the gun factories going, and the shipping on the west coast running, was stopped. In thousands of cases, especially in the north, the places of the men were taken by the women; and, in addition to these, every woman and girl, from the match-girls of Whitechapel to the noblest and wealthiest in the land, found some work to do in the service of their country.

Every day, thousands and tens of thousands of the sons of England, Scotland, Ireland and Wales were taken in hand by "Mr. Sergeant What's-'is-Name," and drilled into shape with miraculous speed; and every day, as detachment after detachment went to the battle front, which now extended from North Foreland to Portland Bill, the magic of patriotism and the long-inherited habits of order and obedience changed the raw recruit into the steady-nerved, strong-hearted soldier, who learnt his duty in the grim school of battle, and was ready to do it to the end.

In less than a month Britain had become a military nation. It seemed at the time and afterwards a miracle, but it was merely the outcome of perfectly natural causes.

After all, every British man has a strain of fighting blood in him. Even leaving out his ancient ancestry, he remains the descendant of families who have given soldier-sons to their country during five hundred years of almost ceaseless war in one part of the world or the other. He is really born with battle-smoke in his nostrils, and the beat of the battle-drum in his heart – and he knows that, neither on land nor sea has he ever been finally beaten.

Remember, too, that this was to him a holy war, the holiest in which the sword can be drawn. He was fighting for freedom, for the possession of his land, for the protection of wife and child and kindred, and the heritage which his fathers of old time had handed down to him. Was it any wonder, then, that within the space of a few weeks the peaceful citizens of Britain, like the fabled harvest of the dragon's teeth, seemed to spring as men full-armed from the very ground? Moreover, this was no skirmishing with sharpshooters over a vast extent of country, six thousand miles away from home, as it had been in South Africa. This was home itself. There was no right or wrong here, nothing for politicians to wrangle about for party purposes. Here, in a little corner of little England, two mighty hosts were at death-grips day and night, the one fighting for all that is dearest and most sacred to the heart of man; and the other to save itself from what could be nothing less than irretrievable disaster.

Chapter XXX

MR PARMENTER SAYS

Happily for the defenders of Britain the fleet of aërial submarines, from which so much had been expected for offensive purposes during the proposed "triumphal march" on London, soon became of little or no use in the field.

The reason was this: As, day after day and week after week, that awful struggle continued, it became absolutely necessary for the Allies to obtain men and material to make good the fearful losses which the valor and devotion of what was now a whole nation in arms had inflicted upon them, and so all but four were dispatched to guard the route between Dover and Calais – eight under the water and eight in the air – and so make it possible for the transports to cross. Of course, this meant that thousands of fresh men and hundreds of horses and guns could be poured into Kent every day; but it also meant that the greater portion of the defenders' most terrible foes were rendered harmless – and this was not the least of the good work that the *Ithuriel* had done.

Of course, that famous "sea-devil," as the invaders called her, was mostly on the spot or thereabouts, and every now and then a crowded transport would lurch over and go down, or a silent, flameless shot would rise up out of some unknown part of the waters and a shell would burst with a firmament-shaking concussion close to one of the airships – after which the airship would burst with a still more frightful shock and distribute herself in very small fragments through the shuddering atmosphere; but this only happened every other day or so, for Erskine and his lieutenant knew a good deal better than to run too many risks, at least just now.

So, for twelve weeks of bitter, bloody and unsparing strife the grim, unceasing struggle for the possession of the Capital of the World went on, and when the eighteenth of March dawned, the outposts of the Allies were still twelve to fourteen miles from the banks of the Thames. How desperate had been that greatest of all defenses since man had made war on man may be dimly guessed from the fact that it cost the invaders two months of incessant fighting and more than a million men before they planted their guns along the ridges of the North Downs and the Surrey Hills.

Meanwhile Gilbert Lennard passed his peaceful though anxious days between Bolton and Whernside, while Auriole, Margaret Holker, Norah Castellan and Mrs. O'Connor, with hundreds of other heroines, were doing their work of mercy in the hospital camps at the different bases behind the fighting front. Lord Westerham, who had worked miracles in the way of recruiting, was now in his glory as one of General French's Special Service Officers, which, under such a Commander, is about as dangerous a job as a man can find in the whole bloody business of war.

And still, as the pitiless human strife went on with its ceaseless rattle of rifle fire, and the almost continuous roar of artillery, day by day the Invader from Space grew bigger and brighter in the great reflector, and day by day the huge cannon, which, in the decisive moment of the world's fate, was to do battle with it, approached completion.

At midnight on the twelfth of March Tom Bowcock had announced that all was ready for the casting. Lennard gave the order by electric signal. The hundred converters belched their floods of glowing steel into what had once been Great Lever pit; night was turned into day by a vast glow that shot up to the zenith, and the first part of the great work was accomplished.

At breakfast the next morning Lennard received the following cablegram from Pittsburg:

> "All ready. Crossing fourteenth. Give particulars of comet away when you like. Pittsburg Baby doing well. How's yours?
>
> "Parmenter"

In order to understand the full meaning of Mr. Parmenter's curt cablegram it will be necessary to go back for a little space to the day when he made his hurried departure from the Clyde in the *Minnehaha.* It will be remembered that he had that morning received a cablegram from New York. This message had read thus:

> "Complete success at last. Craft built and tried. Action and speed perfect. Dollars out, hurry up.
>
> "Hingeston"

Now the signer of this cablegram, Newson Hingeston, was an old college friend of Mr. Parmenter's, and therefore a man of about his own age. He was a born mathematician and engineer, and, like many another before him, the dream of his life had been the conquest of the air by means of vessels which flew as a bird flew, that is to say by their own inherent strength, and without the aid of gas-bags or buoyancy chambers, which he, like all the disciples of Nadar, Jules Verne, Maxim and Langley, had looked upon as mere devices of quackery, or at the best, playthings of rich people, who usually paid for their amusement with their lives.

His father died soon after he left college, and left him a comfortable little estate on the northwestern slopes of the Alleghenies, and a fortune in cash and securities of a million dollars. The estate gave him plenty to live upon comfortably, so he devoted his million to the realization of his ideal. Ratliffe Parmenter, who only had a few hundred thousand dollars to begin with, laughed at him, but one day, after a long argument, just as a sort of sporting bet, he signed a bond to pay two million dollars for the first airship built by his friend that should fly in any direction, independently of the wind, and carry a dead weight of a ton in addition to a crew of four men.

Newson Hingeston registered the bond with all gravity, and deposited it at his bank, and then their life-ways parted. Parmenter plunged into the vortex of speculation, went under sometimes, but always came to the top again with a few more millions in his insatiable grasp, and these millions, after the manner of their kind, had made more millions, and these still more, until he gave up the task of measuring the gigantic pile and let it grow.

Meanwhile, his friend had spent the best twenty-five years of his life, all his fortune, and every dollar he could raise on his estate, in pursuit of the ideal which he had reached a few minutes later than the eleventh hour. Then he had sent that cable. Of course, he wanted the two millions, but what had so suddenly happened in England had instantly convinced him that he was now the possessor of an invention which many millions would not buy, and which might decide the fate of the world.

Within twelve hours of his arrival at his friend's house, Ratliffe Parmenter was entirely convinced that Newson Hingeston had been perfectly justified in calling him across the Atlantic, for the very good reason that he spent the greater part of the night taking flying leaps over the Alleghenies, nerve-shuddering dives through valleys and gorges, and vast, skimming flights over dim, half-visible plains and forests to the west, soaring and swooping, twisting and turning at incredible speeds, in fact, doing everything that any bird that ever flew could do.

When they got back to the house, just as dawn was breaking, and Mr. Parmenter had shaken hands with Hiram Roker, a long, lean, slab-sided Yankee, who was Hingeston's head engineer and general manager, and had fought the grim fight through failure to success at his side for twenty years, he said to his friend:

"Newson, you've won, and I guess I'll take that bond up, and I'd like to do a bit more than that. You know what's happening over the other side. There's got to be an Aërial Navigation Trust formed right away, consisting of you, myself and Hiram there, and Max Henchell, my partner, and that syndicate has to have twenty of these craft of yours, bigger if possible, afloat inside three months. The syndicate will commence at once with a capital of fifty millions, and there'll be fifty more behind that if wanted."

"It's a great scheme," Hingeston replied slowly, "but I'm afraid the time's too short."

"Time!" exclaimed Mr. Parmenter. "Who in thunder thinks about time when dollars begin to talk? You just let me have all your plans and sections, drawings and the rest of your fixings in time to catch the ten o'clock train to Pittsburg. I'll run up and talk the matter over with Henchell. We'll have fifty workshops turning out the different parts in a week, and you shall have a staff of trustworthy men that we own, body and soul, down here to assemble them, and we'll make the best of those chaps into the crews of the ships when we get them afloat.

"Now, don't talk back, Newson, that's fixed. I'm sleepy, and that trip has jerked my nerves up a bit. Give me a drink, and let's go to bed for two or three hours. You'll have a check for five millions before I start, and we shall then consider the *Columbia* our private yacht. We'll fly her around at night, and just raise Cain in the way of mysteries for the newspapers, but we won't give ourselves away altogether until the fleet's ready."

As they say on the other side of the Atlantic, what Ratliffe Parmenter said, went. He wielded the irresistible power of almost illimitable wealth, and during the twenty-five years that Hingeston had been working at his ideal, he and Maximilian Henchell, who was a descendant of one of the oldest Dutch families in America, and one of its shrewdest business men to boot, had built up an industrial organization that was perhaps the most perfect of its kind even in the United States. It was run on lines of absolute despotism, but the despotism was at once intellectual and benevolent. To be a capable and faithful servant of Parmenter and Henchell, even in the humblest capacity, meant, not only good wages and provision for life, but prospects of advancement to the highest posts in the firm, and means of investing money which no outsider would ever hear of.

Wherefore those who worked for Parmenter and Henchell formed an industrial army, some fifty thousand strong, generalled, officered and disciplined to the highest point of efficiency, and faithful to the death. In fact, to be dismissed from any of their departments or workshops was financial death. It was like having a sort of commercial ticket-of-leave, and if such a man tried for work elsewhere, the answer was "If you can't work for P. and H. you must be a crook of some sort. I guess you're no good to us." And the end of that man was usually worse than his beginning.

This was the vast organization which, when the word went forth from the headquarters at Pittsburg, devoted the best of its brains and skill to the creation of the Aërial Fleet, and, as Mr. Parmenter had said, that Fleet was ready to take the air in the time he had allowed for its construction.

But the new ships had developed in the course of making. They were half as long again as the *Columbia,* and therefore nearly twice as big, with engines four times the power, and they carried three guns ahead and three astern, which were almost exact reproductions of those of the *Ithuriel,* the plans of which had been brought over by the *Minnehaha* on her second trip.

The *Columbia* had a speed of about one hundred miles an hour, but the new models were good for nearly a hundred and fifty. In appearance they were very like broad and shallow torpedo boats, with three airplanes on either side, not unlike those of the *Flying Fishes*, with three lifting fans under each. These could be driven vertically or horizontally, and so when the big twin fans at the stern had got up sufficient way to keep the ship afloat by the pressure under the airplanes the lifting fans could be converted into pulling fans, but this was only necessary when a very high speed was desired.

There was a signal mast and yard forward, and a flagstaff aft. The guns were worked under hoods, which protected the gunners from the rush of the wind, and just forward of the mast was an oval conning-tower, not unlike that of the *Ithuriel*, only, of course, unarmored, from which everything connected with the working of the ship could be controlled by a single man.

Such is a brief description of the Aërial Fleet which rose from the slopes of the Alleghenies at ten o'clock on the night of the fourteenth of March 1910, and winged its way silently and without lights eastward across the invisible waters of the Atlantic.

There is one other point in Mr. Parmenter's cablegram to Lennard which may as well be explained here. He had, of course, confided everything that he knew, not only about the war, but also about the approaching World Peril and the means that were being taken to combat it, to his partner on his first arrival in the States, and had also given him a copy of Lennard's calculations.

Instantly Mr. Max Henchell's patriotic ambition was fired. Mr. Lennard had mentioned that Tom Bowcock, Lennard's general manager, had proposed to christen the great gun the "Bolton Baby." He had spent that night in calculations of differences of latitude and longitude, time, angles of inclination of the axis of the orbit, points and times of orbital intersection worked out from the horizon of Pittsburg, and when he had finished he solemnly asked himself the momentous question: Why should this world-saving business be left to England alone? After all the "Bolton Baby" might miss fire by a second or two. If it was going to be a matter of comet-shooting, what had America done that she could not have a gun? Were there not hundreds of eligible shafts to be bought round Pittsburg? Yes, America should have that gun, if the last dollar he possessed or could raise by fair means or foul was to be thrown down the bore of it.

And so America had the gun, and therefore in after days the rival of the "Bolton Baby" came to be called the "Pittsburg Prattler."

Chapter XXXI

JOHN CASTELLAN'S THREAT

Lennard's first feelings after the receipt of Mr. Parmenter's cablegram, and the casting of the vast mass of metal which was to form the body of the great cannon, were those of doubt and hesitation, mingled, possibly, with that sense of semi-irresponsibility which will for a time overcome the most highly-disciplined mind when some great task has been completed for the time being.

For a full month nothing could be done to the cannon, since it would take quite that time for the metal to cool. Everything else had been done or made ready. The huge projectile which was to wing its way into Space to do battle for the life of humanity was completed. The boring and rifling tools were finished, and all the materials for the driving and the bursting charges were ready at hand for putting into their final form when the work of loading up began. There was literally nothing more to be done. All that human labor, skill and foresight could achieve for the present had been accomplished.

Dearly would he have loved to go south and join the ranks of the fighters; but a higher sense of duty than personal courage forbade that. He was the only man who could perform the task he had undertaken, and a chance bullet fragment of a shell to say nothing of the hundred minor chances of the battlefield, might make the doing of that work impossible.

No, his time would come in the awful moment when the fate of humanity would hang in the balance, and his place alike of honor and of duty was now in the equatorial room of the observatory at Whernside, watching through every waking hour of his life the movements of the Invader, that he might note the slightest deviation from its course, or the most trifling change in its velocity. For on such seemingly small matters as these depended, not only the fate of the world, but of the only woman who could make the world at least worth living in for him

– and so he went to Whernside by the morning train after a long day's talk with Tom Bowcock over things in general.

"Yo' may be sure that everything will be all right, Mr. Lennard," said Tom, as they shook hands on the platform. "I'll take t' temperatures, top, bottom and middle, every night and morning and post them to yo', and if there's any change that we don't expect, I'll wire yo' at once; and now I've a great favor to ask you, Mr. Lennard. I haven't asked it before because there's been too much work to do –"

"You needn't ask it, Tom," laughed Lennard, as he returned his grip, "but I'm not going to invite you to Whernside just yet, for two reasons. In the first place, I can't trust that metal to anyone else but you for at least a week; and in the second place, when I do send you an invitation from Mr. Parmenter I shall not only be able to show you the comet a bit brighter than it is just now, but something else that you may have thought about or read about but never seen yet, and I am going to give you an experience that no man born in England has ever had – but I'm not going to spoil sport by telling you now."

"Yo've thought it all out afore me, Mr. Lennard, as yo' always do everything," replied Tom. "I'm not much given to compliments, as yo' know, but yo're a wonderful man, and if yo've got something to show me, it's bound to be wonderful too, and if it's anything as wonderful as t' lies I've b'n telling those newspaper chaps about t' cannon, I reckon it'll make me open my eyes as wide as they've ever been, for sure. Good-bye."

During the journey to Settle, Lennard began to debate once more with himself a question which had troubled him considerably since he had received Mr. Parmenter's cablegram. Should he publish his calculations to the world at once, give the exact position of the Invader at a given moment in a given part of the sky, and so turn every telescope in the civilized world upon it – or should he wait until some astronomer made the independent discovery which must come within a short time now?

There were reasons both for and against. To do so might perhaps stop the war, and that would, at first sight, be conferring a great blessing upon humanity; but, on the other hand, it might have the very reverse effect upon the millions of men whose blood was now inflamed with the lust of battle. Again it was one thing to convince the rulers of the nations and the scientists of the world that the coming catastrophe was inevitable; but to convince the people who made up those nations would be a very different matter.

The end of the world had been predicted hundreds of times already, mostly by charlatans, who made a good living out of it, but sometimes by the most august authorities. He had read his history, and he had not forgotten the awful conditions in which the people of Europe fell during the last months of the year 1000, when the Infallible Church had solemnly proclaimed that at twelve o'clock on the night of the 31st of December Satan, chained for a thousand years, would be let loose; that on the morning of the 1st of January 1001 the order of Nature would be reversed, the sun would rise in the west and the reign of Anti-Christ begin. Then the remnants of the European nations had gradually awakened to the fact that Holy Church was wrong, since nothing happened save the results of the madness which her prophesies had produced.

But the catastrophe of which he would have to be the prophet would be worse even than this, and, moreover, as far as human science could tell, it was a mathematical certainty. There would be no miracle, nothing of the supernatural about it – it would happen just as certainly as the earth would revolve on its axis; and yet how many millions of the earth's inhabitants would believe it until with their own eyes they saw the approaching Fate?

In time of peace perhaps he might have obtained a hearing, but who would pause amidst the rush of the armed battalions to listen to him? How could the calm voice of Science make itself heard among the clash and clangor of war? The German Emperor had already laughed in his face, and accepted his challenge with contemptuous incredulity. No doubt his staff and all his officers would do the same. What possibility then would there be to convince the millions who were fighting blindly under their orders? No; it was hopeless. The war must go on. He could only hope that the Aërial Fleet which Mr. Parmenter was bringing across the Atlantic would turn the tide of battle in favor of the defenders of Britain.

But there was another matter to be considered. Thanks to the control possessed by the Parmenter Syndicate over the Atlantic cables and the aerograph system of the world, he was kept daily, sometimes hourly, acquainted with everything that was happening. He knew that the Eastern forces of Russia were concentrating upon India in the hope that the disasters in England and the destruction of the Fleet would realize the old Muscovite dream of detaching the natives from their loyalty to the British Crown and so making the work of conquest easy. In the Far East, Japan was recovering from the exhaustion consequent upon her costly victories over Russia, and had formed an ominous alliance with China.

On the other hand Italy, England's sole remaining ally in Europe, had blockaded the French Mediterranean ports, and while the French legions were being drawn northward to the conquest of Britain, the

Italian armies had seized the Alpine passes and were preparing an invasion which should avenge the humiliations which Italy had suffered under the first Napoleon.

In a word, everything pointed to universal war. Only the United States preserved an inscrutable silence, which had been broken only by four words: "Hands off our commerce." And to these the Leagued Nations had listened, if rather by compulsion than respect.

Who was he, then, that he should, as it were, sound the trump of approaching doom in the ears of a world round which from east to west and from west again to east the battledrums might any day be sounding and the roar of artillery thundering its answering echo.

But a somewhat different aspect was given to these reflections by a letter which he found waiting for him in the library at Whernside House. It ran thus:

"Sir, –

"You will not, I suppose, have forgotten a certain incident which happened towards the end of June 1907 in the Bay of Clifden, Connemara. You won that little swimming race by a yard or so, and since then it appears to me that, although you may not be aware of it, you and I have been running a race of a very different sort, although possibly for the same prize.

"You will understand what prize I mean, and by this time you ought to know that I have the power of taking it by force, if I cannot win it in the ordinary way of sport or battle. I am in command of the only really irresistible force in the world. I created that force, and, by doing so, made the invasion of England and the present war possible. I have done so because I hate England, and desire to release my own country from her tyranny and oppression; but I can love as well as I can hate, and whether you understood it or not, I, who had never loved a woman before, loved Auriole Parmenter from the moment that you and I lifted her out of the water, and she smiled on us, and thanked us for saving her life.

"Before we parted that day I could see love in your eyes when you looked at her, if you could not see it in mine. You are her father's private astronomer, and until lately you have lived in almost daily intercourse with her, in which, of course, you have had a great advantage over myself, who have not from that time till now been blessed by even the sight of her.

"But during that time it seems that you have discovered a comet, which is to run into the earth and destroy all human life, unless you prevent it. I know this because I know of the challenge you gave to the German Emperor in Canterbury. I know also of what you have been doing in Bolton. You are turning a coal pit into a cannon, with which you believe that you can blow this comet into thin air or gas before it meets the earth, and you threatened His Majesty that if the war was not stopped the human race should be destroyed.

"That, if you will pardon the expression, was a piece of bluff. You love Miss Parmenter perhaps as much as, though not possibly more than, I do, and therefore you would certainly not destroy the world as long as she was alive in it. You would be more or less than man if you did, and I don't believe you are either, and therefore I think you will understand the proposition I am going to make to you.

"Granted hypothesis that the world will come to an end by means of this comet on a certain day, and granted also that you are able to save it with this cannon of yours, I write now to tell you that, whether the war stops or not in obedience to your threat, I will not allow you to save the world unless Miss Parmenter consents to marry me within two months from now. If she does, the war shall stop, or at any rate I will allow the British forces to conquer the whole of Europe on the sole condition of giving independence to Ireland. They cannot win without my fleet of *Flying Fishes,* and if I turn that fleet against them they will not only be defeated but annihilated. In other words, with the sole exception of my own country, I offer England the conquest of Europe in exchange for the hand of one woman.

"In the other alternative, that is to say, if Miss Parmenter, her father and yourself do not consent to this proposal, I will not allow you to save the world. I can destroy your cannon works at Bolton as easily as I destroyed the forts at Portsmouth and Dover, and as easily as I can and will kill you, and wreck your observatory. When I have done this I will take possession of Miss Parmenter by force, and then your comet can come along and destroy the world as soon as it likes.

"I shall expect a definite answer to this letter, signed by Mr. Parmenter and yourself, within seven days. If you address your letter to Mr. James Summers, 28a Carlos Street, Sheerness, it will reach me; but I must warn you that any attempt to discover why it will reach me from that address will be punished by the bombardment and destruction of the town.

"I hope you will see the reasonableness and moderation of my conditions, and remain, yours faithfully,

"John Castellan"

Chapter XXXII

A VIGIL IN THE NIGHT

Although Lennard had always recognized the possibility of such a catastrophe as that which John Castellan threatened, and had even taken such precautions as he could to prevent it, still this direct menace, coming straight from the man himself, brought the danger home to him in a peculiarly personal way.

The look which had passed between them as they were swimming their race in Clifden Bay had just as much meaning for him as for the man who now not openly professed himself his rival, but who threatened to proceed to the last extremities in order to gain possession of the girl they both loved. It was impossible for him not to believe that the man who had been capable of such cold-blooded atrocities as he had perpetrated at Portsmouth, London and other places, would hesitate for a moment in carrying out such a threat, and if he did – No, the alternative was quite too horrible to think of yet.

One thing, however, was absolutely certain. Although no word of love had passed between Auriole and himself since the night when he had shown her the comet and described the possible doom of the world to her, she had in a hundred ways made it plain to him that she was perfectly well aware that he loved her and that she did not resent it – and he knew quite enough of human nature to be well aware that when a woman allows herself to be loved by a man with whom she is in daily and hourly contact, she is already half won; and from this it followed, according to his exact mathematical reasoning, that, whatever the consequences, her reply to John Castellan's letter would be in the negative, and equally, of course, so would her father's be.

"I wonder what the Kaiser's Admiral of the Air would think if he knew how matters really stand," he said to himself as he read the letter through for a second time. "Quite certain of doing what he threatens, is he? I'm not. Still, after all, I suppose I mustn't blame him too much, for wasn't I in just the same mind myself once – to save the world if she would make it heaven for me, to – well – turn it into the other place if she wouldn't. But she very soon cured me of that madness.

"I wonder if she could cure this scoundrel if she condescended to try, which I am pretty certain she would not. I wonder what she'll look like when she reads this letter. I've never seen her angry yet, but I know she would look magnificent. Well, I shall do nothing till Mr. Parmenter gets back. Still, it's a pity that I've got to gravitate between here and Bolton for the next seven weeks. If I wasn't, I'd ask him for one of those airships and I'd hunt John Castellan through all the oceans of air till I ran him down and smashed him and his ship too!"

At this moment the butler came to him and informed him that his dinner was ready and to ask him what wine he would drink.

"Thank you, Simmons," he replied. "A pint of that excellent Burgundy of yours, please. By the way, have the papers come yet?"

"Just arrived, sir," said Mr. Simmons, making the simple announcement with all the dignity due to the butler to a millionaire.

He went at once into the dining room and opened the second edition of the *Times*, which was sent every day to Settle by train and thence by motorcar to Whernside House.

Of course he turned first to the "Latest Intelligence" column. It was headed, as he half expected it to be, "The Great Turning Movement: The Enemy in Possession of Aldershot and advancing on Reading."

The account itself was one of those admirable combinations of brevity and impartiality for which the leading journal of the world has always been distinguished. What Lennard read ran as follows:

"Four months have now passed since the invading forces of the Allies, after destroying the fortifications of Portsmouth and Dover by means never yet employed in warfare, set foot on English soil. There have been four months of almost incessant fighting, of heroic defense and dearly-bought victory, but, although it is not too much to say in sober language that the defending troops, regulars, militia, yeomanry and volunteers, have accomplished what have seemed to be something like miracles of valor and devotion, the tide of conquest has nevertheless flowed steadily towards London.

"Considering the unanimous devotion with which the citizens of this country, English, Scotch, Irish and Welsh, have taken up arms for the defense of their Motherland, there can be no doubt but that, if the war had been fought under ordinary conditions, the tide of invasion would by this time have been rolled back to our coasts in spite of the admitted superiority of the invaders in the technical operations of warfare, and their enormous advantage in numbers to begin with. But the British forces have had to fight under conditions which have never before been known in warfare. Their enemies have not been only those of the land and sea: they have had to fight foes capable of raining destruction upon them from the air as well, and it may well be believed that the leaders of the invading hosts would be the first to admit that without this enormous advantage not even the progress that they have so far made would have been possible.

"The glories of Albuera and Waterloo, of Inkermann and Balaklava, have over and over again been eclipsed by the whole-souled devotion of the British soldiery, fighting, as no doubt every man of them believes, with their backs to the wall, not for ultimate victory perhaps but for the preservation of those splendid traditions which have been maintained untarnished for over a thousand years. It is no exaggeration to say that of all the wars in the history of mankind this has been the deadliest and the bloodiest. Never, perhaps, has so tremendous an attack been delivered, and never has such an attack been met by so determined a resistance. Still, having due regard to the information at our disposal, it would be vain to deny that, tremendous as the cost must have been, the victory so far lies with the invaders.

"After a battle which has lasted almost continuously for a fortnight; a struggle in which battalion after battalion has fought itself to a standstill and the last limits of human endurance have been reached, the fact remains that the enemy have occupied the whole line of the North Downs, Aldershot has ceased to be a British military camp, and is now occupied by the legions of Germany, France and Austria.

"Russia, in spite of the disastrous defeat of the united German and Russian expedition against Sheerness, Tilbury and Woolwich, is now preparing a force for an attack on Harwich which, if it is not defeated by the same means as that upon the Thames was defeated by, will have what we may frankly call the deplorable effect of diverting a large proportion of the defenders of London from the south to the north, and this, unless some other force, at present unheard of, is brought into play in aid of the defenders, can only result in the closing of the attack round London – and after that must come the deluge.

"That this is part of a general plan of operations appears to be quite clear from the desperate efforts which the French, German and Austrian troops are making to turn the position of General French at Reading, to outflank the British left which is resting on the hills beyond Faversham, and, having thus got astride the Thames, occupy the semicircle of the Chiltern Hills and so place the whole Thames valley east of Reading at their mercy.

"In consequence of the ease with which the enemy's airships have destroyed both telegraphic and railway communication, no definite details are at present to hand. It is only known that since the attack on Aldershot the fighting has not only been on a colossal scale, but also of the most sanguinary description, with the advantage slowly but surely turning in favor of the invaders. Such news as reaches us comes entirely by dispatch rider and aerogram. We greatly regret to learn, through the former source, that yesterday evening Lord Westerham, the last of the six special Service officers attached to General French's staff, was either killed or captured in a gallant attempt to carry dispatches containing an accurate account of the situation up to date from Reading to Windsor, whence it was to be transmitted by the underground telephone cable to His Majesty at Buckingham Palace."

"That reads pretty bad," said Lennard, when Mr. Simmons had left the room, "especially Westerham being killed or taken prisoner; I don't like that at all. I wish we'd been able to collar His Majesty of Germany on that trip to Canterbury as Lord Kitchener suggested, and put him on board the *Ithuriel.* He'd have made a very excellent hostage in a case like this. I must say that, altogether, affairs do not look very promising, and we've still two months all but a day or two. Well, if Mr. Parmenter doesn't get across with his aërial fleet pretty soon, I shall certainly take steps to convince him and his Allies, who are fighting for a few islands when the whole world is in peril, that my ultimatum was anything but the joke he seemed to take it for."

He finished his wine, drank a cup of coffee and smoked a meditative cigar in the library, and then went up to the observatory.

It was a lovely night from his point of view; clear, cool and almost cloudless. The young moon was just rising to the eastward, and as he looked up at that portion of the southwestern sky from which the Celestial Invader was approaching he could almost persuade himself that he saw a dim ghostly shape of the Specter from Space.

But when he got to the telescope the Specter was no longer there. The field of the great reflector was blank, save for the few faraway star-mists, and here and there a dimly-distant star, already familiar to him through many nights of watching.

What had happened? Had some catastrophe occurred in the outer realms of Space in which some other world had been involved in fiery ruin, or had the comet been dragged away from its orbit by the attraction of one of those dead suns, those derelicts of Creation which, dark and silent, drift for age after age through the trackless ocean of Immensity?

There was no cooler-headed man alive than Gilbert Lennard when it came to a matter of his own profession and yet the world did not hold a more frightened man than he was when he went to re-adjust the machinery which regulated the movement of the great telescope, and so began his search for the lost comet all over again. One thing only was certain – that the slightest swerve from its course might make the comet harmless and send it flying through Space millions of miles away from the earth, or bring the threatening catastrophe nearer by an unknown number of days and hours. And that was the problem, here, alone, and in the silence of the night, he had to solve. The great gun at Bolton and the other at Pittsburg might by this time be useless, or, worse still, they might not be ready in time.

It was curious that, even face to face with such a terrific crisis, he had enough human vanity left to shape a half regret that his calculations would almost certainly be falsified.

That, however, was only the sensation of a moment. He ran rapidly over his previous calculations, did about fifteen minutes very hard thinking, and in thirty more he had found the comet. There it was: a few degrees more to the northward, and more inclined to the plane of the earth's orbit; brighter, and therefore nearer; and now the question was, by how much?

Confronted with this problem, the man and the lover disappeared, and only the mathematician and the calculating machine remained. He made his notes and went to his desk. The next three hours passed without any consciousness of existence save the slow ticking of the astronomical clock which governed the mechanism of the telescope. The rest was merely figures and formulæ, which might amount to the death-sentence of the human race or to an indefinite reprieve.

When he got up from his desk he had learnt that the time in which it might be possible to save humanity from a still impending fate had been shortened by twelve days, and that the contact of the comet with the earth's atmosphere would take place precisely at twelve o'clock, midnight, on the thirtieth of April.

Then he went back to the telescope and picked up the comet again. Just as he had got its ominous shape into the center of the field a score of other shapes drifted swiftly across it, infinitely vaster – huge winged forms, apparently heading straight for the end of the telescope, and only two or three yards away.

His nerves were not perhaps as steady as they would have been without the shock which he had already received, and he shrank back from the eye-piece as though to avoid a coming blow. Then he got up from his chair and laughed.

"What an ass I am! That's Mr. Parmenter's fleet; but what monsters they do look through a telescope like this!"

Chapter XXXIII

MR PARMENTER RETURNS

Just at the north of the summit on the top of which the observatory was built there was an oval valley, or perhaps it might be better described as an escarpment, a digging away by the hand of Nature of a portion of the mountain summit by means of some vast landslide or glacier action thousands of years ago.

As he closed the door of the main entrance to the observatory behind him, he saw these strange, winged shapes circling in the air some three miles away, just dimly visible in the moonlight and starlight. They were hovering about in middle air as though they were birds looking for a foothold. He ran back, switched the electric current off the aerograph machines at the base of the observatory, and turned it on to the searchlight which was on the top of the equatorial dome. A great fan of white light flashed out into the sky, he spelt out "Welcome" in the dot-and-dash code, and then the searchlight fell upon the valley.

"Thanks," came the laconic answer from the foremost airship; and then Lennard saw twenty-five winged shapes circle round the observatory and drop to rest one by one in perfect order, just as a flock of swans might have done, and, as the last came to earth, he turned the switch and shut off the searchlight.

He walked down to the hollow, and in the dim light saw something that he had hardly believed possible for human eyes to see. There, in a space of, perhaps, a thousand yards long and five hundred yards wide, lay, in a perfect oval, a fleet of ships. By all appearances they had no right to be on land. There was no visible evidence that they could rise from the solid earth after once touching it, anymore than the albatross can do from a ship's deck.

A light flashed out from a ship lying at the forward end of the ellipse for a moment into the sky and then it swung slowly round until it rested on the path from the observatory to the valley, and Lennard for a moment felt himself blinded by its rays. Then it lifted and a most welcomely familiar voice said:

"Well, Mr. Lennard, here we are, you see, just a bit ahead of time, and how's the comet?"

A ladder, obviously of American design, shot out from the side of the airship as Mr. Parmenter spoke, and as soon as the lower end touched the ground he walked down it with his hand outstretched. Lennard walked to the foot of the ladder and took his hand, and said in a low voice:

"This is all very wonderful, Mr. Parmenter, but I am glad that you are here ahead of time, because the comet is too; and very considerably, I am sorry to say."

"Eh, what's that you say, Mr. Lennard?" replied the millionaire in a hurried whisper. "Nothing serious, I hope. We haven't come too late, have we? I mean too late to stop the war and save the world."

"I don't know about stopping the war," replied Lennard, "but, if no accident happens or is arranged for, we can save the world still, I think."

"Accident arranged for?" echoed Mr. Parmenter. "What do you mean by that? Are you talking about John Castellan and those Flying Fish things of his? I reckon we've got enough here to send him and his *Flying Fishes* into the sea and make them stop there. We've heard all about what they've been doing in the States, and I've got about tired of them. And as for this old invasion of England, it's got to stop right away, or we'll make more trouble for these Germans and Frenchmen and Russians and Austrians than they ever dreamt of.

"Look at that fleet, sir. Twenty-five aërial battleships with a hundred and fifty miles an hour speed in them. Here to London in one hour and twenty-five minutes or less, and guns – you just take a look at those exaggerated peashooters we've got on deck, and believe me, sir, that if we get one of John Castellan's *Flying Fishes* within six thousand yards of the end of one of those things it will do no more flying, except in very small pieces."

"I'm delighted to hear it, Mr. Parmenter," replied Lennard, in a low tone, "for to tell you the truth, we haven't many weeks left now. Something that I can so far neither calculate nor explain has changed the orbit of the comet and it's due here at midnight on the thirtieth of April."

"Great Scott, and this is the nineteenth of March! Not six weeks! I guess we'll have to hurry up with those cannons. I'll send a cable to Pittsburg tomorrow. Anyhow, I reckon the comet can wait for tonight."

While Mr. Parmenter had been speaking two other men had come down the ladder from the deck of the airship and he continued:

"Now, let me introduce you. This is my old friend and college chum, Newson Hingeston, the man who invented the model we built this fleet on. This is Mr. Hiram Roker, chief engineer of the fleet and Lord High Admiral of the air, when Mr. Hingeston is not running his own ships."

Lennard shook hands with Mr. Hingeston and Hiram, and was going to say very complimentary things about the fleet which had literally dropped from the clouds, when Mr. Parmenter interrupted him again and said:

"You'll excuse me, Mr. Lennard, but you'll be better able to talk about these ships when you've had a trip in one of them. We've just crossed the Atlantic in thirty hours, above the clouds, and tomorrow night or morning, if it's cloudy when we've been through things generally, we're going to London in the flagship here – I've called her the *Auriole*, because she is the daisy of the whole fleet – biggest, fastest and prettiest. You just wait till you see her in daylight. Now we'll go down to the house and hear your news. We're thirty hours behind the times."

It need hardly be said that no one went to bed for the remainder of that night at Whernside. In one sense it was as busy a time as had been since the war began. The private telephone and telegraph wires between Whernside House and Settle and the aerograph apparatus at the observatory were working almost incessantly till dawn, sending and receiving messages between this remote moorland district and London and the seat of war, as well as Bolton and Pittsburg.

The minutes and the hours passed swiftly, as all Fate-laden time does pass, and so the grey morning of a momentous day dawned over the western Yorkshire moors. Just as they were beginning to think about breakfast one of Lennard's assistants came down from the observatory with a copy of an aerogram which read:

> "Begins. Parmenter, Whernside. Pleased to hear of your arrival. Proposition laid before His Majesty in Council and accepted. Hope to see you and your friends during the day. – Chamberlain. Ends."

"Well, I guess that's all right, gentlemen," said Mr. Parmenter, as he handed the aerogram across the big table littered with maps, plans and drawings of localities terrestrial and celestial.

The aerogram passed round and Mr. Parmenter continued: "You see, gentlemen, although the United States has the friendliest of feelings towards the British Empire, still, as the President told me the day before yesterday, this invasion of Britain is not our fight, and he does not see his way to making formal declaration of war; so he just gave me a permit for these ships to leave American territory on what the Russians and others call a scientific expedition in order to explore the upper regions of the air and demonstrate the possibility of navigating the air without using gas as lifting power – and that's just how we've got here with our clearance papers and so on all in order; and that means, gentlemen, that we are here, not as citizens of the United States or any other country, but just as a trading company with something to hire out.

"John Castellan, as you will remember from what has been said, sold his *Flying Fishes* to the German Emperor. Mr. Lennard has proved to us by Castellan's own handwriting that he is prepared to sell them back to the British Government at a certain price – and that price is my daughter. Our answer to that is the hiring of our fleet to the British Government, and that offer has been accepted on terms which I think will show a very fair profit when the war is over and we've saved the world."

"I don't think it will take very long to stop the war," said the creator of the aërial battle-fleet, in his quiet voice. "Saving the world is, of course, another matter which no doubt we can leave safely in the hands of Mr. Lennard. And now," he continued more gravely, "when is the news of the actual coming of the comet to be made public? It seems to me that everything more or less hangs upon that. The German Emperor, and, therefore, his Allies and, no doubt, half the astronomers of Europe, have been informed of Mr. Lennard's discovery. They may or may not believe it, and if they don't we can't blame them because it was only given to them without exact detail."

"And a very good thing too," laughed Lennard, "considering the eccentric way in which the comet is behaving. But everything is settled now, unless, of course, some other mysterious influence gets to work; and, another thing, it's quite certain that before many days the comet must be discovered by other observatories."

"Then, Mr. Lennard," said Mr. Parmenter, "we've been first in the field so far and I reckon we'd better stop there. Pike's Peak, Washington and Arequipa are all on to it. Europe and Australia will be getting there pretty soon, so I don't think there's much the matter with you sending a message to Greenwich this morning. The people there will find it all right and we can run across from London when we've had our talk with the Prime Minister and post them up in any other details they want. I'll send a wire to Henchell and tell him to hurry up with his gun at Pittsburg and send on news to all the American observatories. Then we'll have breakfast and, as it's a cloudy morning, I think we might start right away for London in the *Auriole* and get this business fixed up. The enemy doesn't know we're here at all, and so long as we keep above the clouds there's no fear of anyone seeing us. The world has only forty-four more days to live, so we might as well save one of those days while we can."

The result of the somewhat informal council of war, for, in sober truth, it was nothing else, was that the commanders of the airships were invited to breakfast and the whole situation was calmly and plainly discussed by those who from the morning would probably hold the fate of the world in their hands. Not the least important of the aerograms which had been received during the early morning had been one, of course in code, from Captain Erskine of the *Ithuriel* from Harwich, welcoming the aërial fleet and giving details of his movements in conjunction with it for the next ten days. The aerogram also gave the positions of the lighters loaded with ammunition which he had deposited round the English shores in anticipation of its arrival.

Soon after eight o'clock a heavy mist came down over Whernside and its companion heights, and Mr. Parmenter went to one of the windows of the big dining room and said:

"I reckon this will just about fit us, Mr. Lennard, so, if you've got your portmanteau packed, have it sent up to the *Auriole* at once, and we'll make a start."

Within thirty minutes the start was made, and with it began the most marvelous experience of Gilbert Lennard's life, not even excepting his battle-trip in the conning-tower of the *Ithuriel.*

Chapter XXXIV

THE "AURIOLE"

"All aboard, I think, Captain Roker," said Mr. Parmenter, as he walked last to the top of the gangway ladder, and stood square-footed on the white deck of the *Auriole.*

"All aboard, sir," replied Hiram Roker, "and now I reckon you'll have to excuse me, because I've got to go below just to see that everything's in working order."

"That's all right, Mr. Roker. I know where your affections are centered in this ship. You go right along to your engines, and Mr. Hingeston will see about the rest of us. Now then, Mr. Lennard, you come along into the conning-tower, and whatever you may have seen from the conning-tower of the *Ithuriel*, I reckon you'll see something more wonderful still before we get to London. You show the way, Newson. See, here it is, just about the same. We've stolen quite a lot of ideas from your friend Erskine; it's a way we've got on our side, you know. But this is going to be one of the exceptions; if we win we are going to pay."

Lennard followed Mr. Parmenter down the companion-way into the center saloon of the *Auriole*, and through this into a narrow passage which led forward. At the end of this passage was a lift almost identical with that on the *Ithuriel*. He took his place with Mr. Parmenter and Mr. Hingeston on this and it rose with them into a little oval chamber almost exactly like the conning-tower of the *Ithuriel*, with the exception that it was built entirely of hardened papier-mâché and glass.

"You see, Mr. Lennard," said Mr. Parmenter, "we don't want armor here. Anything that hits us smashes us, and that's all there is to it. Our idea is just to keep out of the way and do as much harm as we can from the other side of the clouds. And now, Newson, if you're ready, we might as well get to the other side and have a look at the sun. It's sort of misty and cheerless down here."

"Just as easy as saying so, my dear Ratliffe. I reckon Hiram's got about ten thousand horse-power waiting to be let loose; so we may as well let them go. Hold on, Mr. Lennard, and don't breathe anymore than you can help for a minute or two."

Lennard, remembering his cruise in the *Ithuriel*, held on, and also, after filling his lungs, held his breath. Mr. Hingeston took hold of the steering-wheel, also very much like that of the *Ithuriel*, with his left hand, and touched in quick succession three buttons on a signal-board at his right hand.

At the first touch nothing happened as far as Lennard could see or hear. At the second, a soft, whirring sound filled the air, growing swiftly in intensity. At the third, the mist which enveloped Whernside began, as it seemed to him, to flow downwards from the sky in long wreaths of smoke-mingled steam which in a few moments fell away into nothingness. A blaze of sunlight burst out from above – the earth had vanished – and there was nothing visible save the sun and sky overhead, and an apparently illimitable expanse of cloud underneath.

"There's one good thing about airships," said Mr. Hingeston, as he took a quarter turn at the wheel, "you can generally get the sort of climate and temperature you want in them." He put his finger on a fourth button and continued: "Now, Mr. Lennard, we have so far just pulled her up above the mist. You'll have one of these ships yourself one day, so I may as well tell you that the first signal means 'Stand by'; the second, 'Full power on lifting fans'; the third, 'Stand by after screws'; and the fourth – just this –"

He pushed the button down as he spoke, and Lennard saw the brilliantly white surface of the sunlit mist fall away before and behind them. A few moments later he heard a sort of soft, sighing sound outside the conning-tower. It rose quickly to a scream, and then deepened into a roar. Everything seemed lost save the dome of sky and the sun rising from the eastward. There was nothing else save the silver-grey blur beneath them. As far as he was concerned for the present, the earth had ceased to exist for him five minutes ago.

He didn't say anything, because the circumstances in which he found himself appeared to be more suitable for thinking than talking; he just stood still, holding on to a hand-grip in the wall of the conning-tower, and looked at the man who, with a few touches of his fingers, was hurling this aërial monster through the air at a speed which, as he could see, would have left the *Ithuriel* out of sight in a few minutes.

In front of Hingeston as he sat at the steering-wheel were two dials. One was that of an aneroid which indicated the height. This now registered four thousand feet. The other was a manometer connected with the speed-gauge above the conning-tower, and the indicator on this was hovering between one hundred and fifty and a hundred and sixty.

"Does that really mean we're traveling over a hundred and fifty miles an hour?" he said.

"Getting on for a hundred and sixty," said Mr. Parmenter, taking out his watch. "You see, according to that last wire I sent, we're due in the gardens of Buckingham Palace at ten-thirty sharp, and so we have to hustle a bit."

"Well," replied Lennard, "I must confess that I thought that my little trip in the *Ithuriel* took me to something like the limits of everyday experience; but this beats it. Whatever you do on the land or in the water you seem to have something under you – something you can depend on, as it were – but here, you don't seem to be anywhere. A friend of mine told me that, after he had taken a balloon trip above the clouds and across the Channel, but he was only traveling forty miles an hour. He had somewhat a trouble to describe that, but this, of course, gets rather beyond the capabilities of the English language."

"Or even the American," added Mr. Hingeston, quietly.

"Why, yes," said Mr. Parmenter, rolling a cigarette, "I believe we invented the saying about greased lightning, and here we are something like riding on a streak of it."

"Near enough!" laughed Lennard. "We may as well leave it at that, as you say. Still, it is very, very wonderful."

And so it was. As they sped south the mists that hung about the northern moors fell behind, and broken clouds took their place. Through the gaps between these he could see a blur of green and grey and purple. A few blotches of black showed that they were passing over the Lancashire and Midland manufacturing towns; then the clouds became scarcer and an enormous landscape spread out beneath them, intersected by white roads and black lines of railways, and dotted by big patches of woods, long lines of hedgerows and clumps of trees on hilltops. Here and there the white wall of a chalk quarry flashed into view and vanished; and on either side towns and villages came into sight ahead and vanished astern almost before he could focus his field-glasses upon them.

At about twenty minutes after the hour at which they had left Whernside, Mr. Hingeston turned to Mr. Parmenter and said, pointing downward with the left hand:

"There's London, and the clouds are going. What are we to do? We can't drop down there without being seen, and if we are that will give half the show away. You see, if Castellan once gets on to the idea that we've got airships and are taking them into London, he'll have a dozen of those *Flying Fishes* worrying about us before we know what we're doing. If we only had one of those good old London fogs under us we could do it."

"Then what's the matter with dropping under the smoke and using that for a fog," said Mr. Parmenter, rather shortly. "The enemy is still a dozen miles to southward there; they won't see us, and anyhow, London's a big place. Why, look there now! Talking about clouds, there's the very thing you want. Oceans of it! Can't you run her up a bit and drop through it when the thing's just between us and the enemy?"

As he spoke, Lennard saw what seemed to him like an illimitable sea of huge spumy billows and tumbling masses of foam, which seemed to roll and break over each other without sound. The silent cloud-ocean was flowing up from the sou'west. Mr. Hingeston took his bearings by compass, slowed down to fifty miles an hour, and then Lennard saw the masses of cloud rise up and envelop them.

For a few minutes the earth and the heavens disappeared, and he felt that sense of utter loneliness and isolation which is only known to those who travel through the air. He saw Mr. Hingeston pull a lever with his right hand and turn the steering-wheel with his left. He felt the blood running up to his head, and then came a moment of giddiness. When he opened his eyes the *Auriole* was dropping as gently as a bird on the wing towards the trees of the garden behind Buckingham Palace.

"I reckon you did that quite well, Newson," said Mr. Parmenter, looking at his watch. "One hour and twenty-five minutes as you said. And now I'm going to shake hands with a real king for the first time."

Chapter XXXV

THE "AURIOLE" HOISTS THE WHITE ENSIGN

Rather to Mr. Parmenter's surprise his first interview "with a real king" was rather like other business interviews that he had had; in fact, as he said afterwards, of all the business men he had ever met in his somewhat varied career, this quiet-spoken, grey-haired English gentleman was about the best and 'cutest that it had ever been his good fortune to strike.

The negotiations in hand were, of course, the hiring of the Syndicate's fleet of airships to the British Empire during the course of the war. His Majesty had summoned a Privy Council at the Palace, and again Mr. Parmenter was somewhat surprised at the cold grip and clear sight which these British aristocrats had in dealing with matters which he thought ought to have been quite outside their experience. Like many Americans, he had expected to meet a sort of glorified country squire, fox-hunter, grouse-killer, trout and salmon-catcher, and so on; but, as he admitted to Lennard later on, from His Majesty downwards they were about the hardest crowd to do business with that he had ever struck.

The terms he offered were half a million a week for the services of twenty-five airships till the war was ended. Two were retained as guardians for Whernside House and the observatory, and three for the Great

Lever colliery, and this left twenty, not counting the original *Columbia,* which Mr. Parmenter had bought as his aërial yacht, available for warlike purposes.

The figure was high, as the owners of the aërial battle-fleet admitted, but war was a great deal dearer. They guaranteed to bring the war to a stop within fourteen days, by which time Britain would have a new fleet in being which would be practically the only fleet capable of action in western waters with the exception of the Italian and the American. Given that the Syndicate's airships, acting in conjunction with the *Ithuriel* and the twelve of her sisters which were now almost ready for launching, could catch and wipe out the *Flying Fishes,* either above the waters or under them, the result would be that the Allies, cut off from their base of supplies, and with no retreat open to them, would be compelled to surrender; and Mr. Parmenter did not consider that five hundred thousand pounds a week was too much to pay for this.

At the conclusion of his speech, setting forth the position of the Syndicate, he said, with a curious dignity which somehow always comes from a sense of power:

"Your Majesty, my Lords and gentlemen, I am just a plain American business man, and so is my friend, the inventor of these ships. We have told you what we believe they can do and we are prepared to show you that we have not exaggerated their powers. There is our ship outside in the gardens. If your Majesty would like to take a little trip through the air and see battle, murder and sudden death –"

"That's very kind of you, Mr. Parmenter," laughed His Majesty, "but, much as I personally should like to come with you, I'm afraid I should play a certain amount of havoc with the British Constitution if I did. Kings of England are not permitted to go to war now, but if you would oblige me by taking a note to the Duke of Connaught, who has his headquarters at Reading, and then, if you could manage it under a flag of truce, taking another note to the German Emperor, who, I believe, has pitched his camp at Aldershot, I should be very much obliged."

"Anything your Majesty wishes," replied Mr. Parmenter. "Now we've fixed up the deal the fleet is at your disposal and we sail under the British flag; though, to be quite honest, sir, I don't care about flying the white flag first. We could put up as pretty a fight for you along the front of the Allies as any man could wish to see."

"I am sorry, Mr. Parmenter," laughed His Majesty, "that the British Constitution compels me to disappoint you, but, as some sort of recompense, I am sure that my Lords in Council will grant you permission to fly the White Ensign on all your ships and the Admiral's flag on your flagship, which, I presume, is the one in which you have come this morning. It is unfortunate that I can only confer the honorary rank of admiral upon Mr. Hingeston, as you are not British subjects."

"Then, your Majesty," replied Mr. Parmenter, "if it pleases you, I hope you will give that rank to my friend Newson Hingeston, who, as I have told you, has been more than twenty years making these ships perfect. He has created this navy, so I reckon he has got the best claim to be called admiral."

"Does that meet with your approval, my lords?" said the King.

And the heads of the Privy Council bowed as one in approval.

"I thank your Majesty most sincerely," said Hingeston, rising. "I am an American citizen, but I have nothing but British blood in my veins, and therefore I am all the more glad that I am able to bring help to the Motherland when she wants it."

"And I'm afraid we do want it, Mr. Hingeston," said His Majesty. "Make the conditions of warfare equal in the air, and I think we shall be able to hold our own on land and sea. Your patent of appointment shall be made out at once, and I will have the letters ready for you in half an hour. And now, gentlemen, I think a glass of wine and a biscuit will not do any of us much harm."

The invitation was, of course, in a certain sense, a command, and when the King rose everyone did the same. While they were taking their wine and biscuits in the blue drawing room overlooking St. James's Park, His Majesty, who never lost his grip of business for a moment, took Lennard aside and had a brief but pregnant conversation with him on the subject of the comet, and as a result of this all the Government manufactories of explosives were placed at his disposal, and with his own hand the King wrote a permit entitling him to take such amount of explosives to Bolton as he thought fit. Then there came the letters to the Duke of Connaught and the German Emperor, and one to the Astronomer Royal at Greenwich.

Then His Majesty and the members of the Council inspected the aërial warship lying on the great lawn in the gardens, and with his own hands King Edward ran the White Ensign to the top of the flagstaff aft; at the same moment the Prince of Wales ran the Admiral's pennant up to the masthead. Everyone saluted the flag, and the King said:

"There, gentlemen, the *Auriole* is a duly commissioned warship of the British Navy, and you have our authority to do all lawful acts of war against our enemies. Good-morning! I shall hope to hear from you soon."

"I'm sorry, your Majesty," said Mr. Parmenter, "that we can't fire the usual salute. These guns of ours are made for business, and we don't have any blank charges."

"I perfectly understand you, Mr. Parmenter," replied His Majesty with a laugh. "We shall have to dispense with the ceremony. Still, those are just the sort of guns we want at present. Good-morning, again."

His Majesty went down the gangway and Admiral Hingeston, with Mr. Parmenter and Lennard, entered the conning-tower. The lifting-fans began to whirr, and as the *Auriole* rose from the grass the White Ensign dipped three times in salute to the Royal Standard floating from the flagstaff on the palace roof. Then, as the driving propellers whirled round till they became two intersecting circles of light, the *Auriole* swept up over the tree-tops and vanished through the clouds. And so began the first voyage of the first British aërial battleship.

The Duke of Connaught had his headquarters at Amersham Hall School on the Caversham side of the Thames, which was, of course, closed in consequence of the war, and half an hour after the *Auriole* had left the grounds of Buckingham Palace she was settling to the ground in the great quadrangle of the school. The Duke, with Lord Kitchener and two or three other officers of the Staff, were waiting at the upper end where the headmaster's quarters were. As the ship grounded, the gangway ladder dropped and Mr. Parmenter said to Lennard:

"That's Lord Kitchener, I see. Now, you know him and I don't, so you'd better go and do the talking. We'll come after and get introduced."

"Ah, Mr. Lennard," said Lord Kitchener, holding out his hand. "You're quite a man of surprises. The last time I went with you to see the Kaiser in a motorcar, and now you come to visit His Royal Highness in an airship. Your Royal Highness," he continued, turning to the Duke, "this is Mr. Lennard, the finder of this comet which is going to wipe us all out unless he wipes it out with his big gun, and these will be the other gentlemen, I presume, whom His Majesty has wired about."

"Yes," replied Lennard, after he had shaken hands. "This is Mr. Parmenter whose telescope enabled me to find the comet, and this is Mr. – or I ought now to say Admiral – Hingeston, who had the honor of receiving that rank from His Majesty half an hour ago."

"What!" exclaimed the Duke. "Half an hour! Are you quite serious, gentlemen? The telegram's only just got here."

"Well, your Royal Highness," said Mr. Parmenter, "that may be because we didn't come full speed, but if you would get on board that flagship, sir, we'd take you to Buckingham Palace and back in half an hour, or, if you would like a trip to Aldershot to interview the German Emperor, and then one to Greenwich, we'll engage to have you back here safe by dinner time."

"Nothing would delight me more," replied the Duke, smiling, "but at present my work is here and I cannot leave it. Lord Kitchener, how would you like that sort of trip?"

"If you will give me leave till dinner-time, sir," laughed K. of K., "there's nothing I should like better."

"Oh, that goes without saying, of course," replied the Duke, "and now, gentlemen, I understand from the King's telegram that there are one or two matters you want to talk over with us. Will you come inside?"

"If your Royal Highness will excuse me," said Admiral Hingeston, "I think I'd better remain on board. You see, we may have been sighted, and if there are any of those *Flying Fishes* about you naturally wouldn't want this place blown to ruins; so, while you are having your talk, I reckon I'll get up a few hundred feet, and be back, say, in half an hour."

"Very well," said the Duke. "That's very kind of you. Your ship certainly looks a fairly capable protector. By the way, what is the range of those guns of yours? I must say they have a very businesslike look about them."

"Six thousand yards point blank, your Royal Highness," replied the Admiral, "and, according to elevation, anything up to fifteen miles; suppose, for instance, that we were shooting at a town. In fact, if we were not under orders from His Majesty to fly the flag of truce I would guarantee to have all the Allied positions wrecked by tomorrow morning with this one ship. As you will see from the papers which Mr. Parmenter and Mr. Lennard have brought, nineteen other airships are coming south tonight and, unless the German Emperor and his Allies give in, the war will be over in about six days."

"And when you come back to dinner tonight, Admiral Hingeston, you will have my orders to bring it to an end within that time."

"I sincerely hope so, sir," replied Admiral Hingeston, as he raised his right hand to the peak of his cap. "I can assure you, that nothing would please me better."

As the lifting-fans began to spin round and the *Auriole* rose from the graveled courtyard, Lord Kitchener looked up with a twinkle in his brilliant blue eyes and said:

"I wonder what His Majesty of Germany will think of that thing when he sees it. I suppose that means the end of fighting on land and sea – at least, it looks like it."

"I hope to be able to convince your lordship that it does before tomorrow morning," said Lennard, as they went towards the dining room.

Then came half an hour's hard work, which resulted in the allotment of the aërial fleet to positions from which the vessels could co-operate with the constantly increasing army of British citizen-soldiers who were now passing southward, eastward and westward, as fast as the crowded trains could carry them. Every position was worked out to half a mile. The details of the newly-created fleet in British waters and of those ships which were arriving from the West Indies and the Mediterranean were all settled, and, as the clock in the drawing room chimed half-past eleven, the *Auriole* swung down in a spiral curve round the chimney-pots and came to rest on the gravel.

"There she is; time's up!" said Lord Kitchener, rising from his seat. "I suppose it will only take us half an hour or so to run down to Aldershot. I wonder what His Majesty of Germany will say to us this time. I suppose if he kicks seriously we have your Royal Highness's permission to haul down the flag of truce?"

"Certainly," replied the Duke. "If he does that, of course, you will just use your own discretion."

Chapter XXXVI

A PARLEY AT ALDERSHOT

Lord Kitchener had probably never had so bitter an experience as he had when the *Auriole* began to slow down over the plain of Aldershot. Never could he, or any other British soldier, have dreamt six months ago that the German, Austrian, French and Russian flags would have been seen flying side by side over the headquarters of the great camp, or that the vast rolling plains would be covered, as they were now, by hosts of horse, foot and artillery belonging to hostile nations.

He did not say anything, neither did the others; it was a time for thinking rather than talking; but he looked, and as Lennard watched his almost expressionless face and the angrily-glittering blue eyes, he felt that it would go ill with an enemy whom K. of K. should have at his mercy that day.

But all the bitterness of feeling was by no means on one side. It so happened that the three Imperial leaders of the invaders and General Henriot, the French Commander-in-Chief, were holding a Council of War at the time when the *Auriole* made her appearance. Of course, her arrival was instantly reported, and as a matter of fact the drilling came to a sudden momentary stop at the sight of this amazing apparition. The three monarchs and the great commander immediately went outside, and within a few moments they were four of the angriest men in England. A single glance, even at that distance, was enough to convince them that, at any rate in the air, the *Flying Fishes* would be no match for an equal or even an inferior number of such magnificent craft as this.

"God's thunder!" exclaimed the Kaiser, using his usual expletive. "She's flying the White Ensign and an admiral's pennant, and, yes, a flag of truce."

"Yes," said the Tsar, lowering his glasses, "that is so. What has happened? I certainly don't like the look of her; she's an altogether too magnificent craft from our point of view. In fact it would be decidedly awkward if the English happened to have a fleet of them. They would be terribly effective acting in cooperation with that submarine ram. Let us hope that she has come on a message of peace."

"I understood, your Majesty," said the Kaiser, shortly, "that we had agreed to make peace at Windsor, and nowhere else."

"Of course, I hope we shall do so," said the Tsar, "but considering our numbers, and the help we have had from Mr. Castellan's fleet, I'm afraid we are rather a long time getting there, and we shall be longer still if the British have any considerable number of ships like this one."

"Airships or no airships," replied William the Second, "whatever message this ship is bringing, I will listen to nothing but surrender while I have an Army Corps on English soil. They must be almost beaten by this time; they can't have anymore men to put in the field, while we have millions. To go back now that we have got so far would be worse than defeat – it would be disaster. Of course, your Majesty can have no more delusions than I have on that subject."

A conversation on almost similar terms had been taking place meanwhile between the Emperor of Austria and General Henriot. Then the *Auriole*, after describing a splendid curve round the headquarters, dropped as quietly as a bird on the lawn in front, the gangway ladder fell over along the side, and Lord Kitchener, in the parade uniform of a general, descended and saluted the four commanders.

"Good-morning, your Majesties. Good-morning, General Henriot."

"I see that your lordship has come as bearer of the flag of truce this time," said the Kaiser, when salutes had been exchanged, "and I trust that in the interests of humanity you have come also with proposals which may enable us to put an honorable end to this terrible conflict, and I am sure that my Imperial brothers and the great Republic which General Henriot represents will be only too happy to accede to them."

The others nodded in approval, but said nothing, as it had been more or less reluctantly agreed by them that the War Lord of Germany was to be the actual head and Commander-in-Chief of the Allies. K. of K. looked at him straight in the eyes – not a muscle of his face moved, and from under his heavy moustache there came in the gentlest of voices the astounding words:

"Yes, I have come from His Majesty King Edward with proposals of surrender – that is to say, for your surrender, and that of all the Allied Forces now on British soil."

William the Second literally jumped, and his distinguished colleagues stared at him and each other in blank amazement. By this time Lennard had come down the gangway ladder, and was standing beside Lord Kitchener. Mr. Parmenter and the latest addition to the British Naval List were strolling up and down the deck of the *Auriole* smoking cigars and chatting as though this sort of thing happened every day.

"I see that your Majesty hardly takes me seriously," said Lord Kitchener, still in the same quiet voice, "but if your Majesties will do Mr. Lennard and myself the favor of an interview in one of the rooms here, which used to belong to me, I think we shall be able to convince you that we have the best of reasons for being serious."

"Ah, yes, Mr. Lennard," replied the Kaiser, looking at him with just a suspicion of anxiety in his glance. "Good-morning. Have you come to tell us something more about this wonderful comet of yours? It seems to me some time making itself visible."

"It is visible every night now, your Majesty," said Lennard; "that is, if you know where to look for it."

"Ah, that sounds interesting," said the Tsar, moving towards the door. "Suppose we go back into the Council Room and hear something about it."

As they went in the *Auriole* rose from the ground, and began making a series of slow, graceful curves over the two camps at the height of about a thousand feet. Neither Mr. Parmenter, nor his friend the Admiral, knew exactly how far the flag of truce would be respected, and, moreover, a little display of the *Auriole's* powers of flight might possibly help along negotiations, and, as a matter of fact, they did; for the sight of this huge fabric circling above them, with her long wicked-looking guns pointing in all directions, formed a spectacle which to the officers and men of the various regiments and battalions scattered about the vast plain was a good deal more interesting than it was pleasant. The Staff officers knew, too, that the strange craft possessed two very great advantages over the *Flying Fishes*; she was much faster, and she could rise direct from the ground – whereas the *Fishes*, like their namesakes, could only rise from the water. In short, it did not need a soldier's eye to see that all their stores and magazines, to say nothing of their own persons, were absolutely at the mercy of the British aërial flagship. The *Flying Fishes* were down in the Solent refitting and filling up with motive power and ammunition preparatory to the general advance on London.

As soon as they were seated in the Council Chamber it did not take Lord Kitchener and Lennard very long to convince their Majesties and General Henriot that they were very much in earnest about the matter of surrender. In fact, the only terms offered were immediate retirement behind the line of the North Downs, cessation of hostilities and surrender of the *Flying Fishes*, and all British subjects, including John Castellan, who might be on board them.

"The reason for that condition," said Lord Kitchener, "Mr. Lennard will be able to make plain to your Majesties."

Then Lennard handed Castellan's letter to the Kaiser, and explained the change of calculations necessitated by the diversion of the planet from its orbit.

"That is not the letter of an honest fighting man. I am sure that your Majesties will agree with me in that. I may say that I have talked the matter over with Mr. Parmenter and our answer is in the negative. This is not warfare; it is only abduction, possibly seasoned with murder, and we call those things crimes in England, and if such a crime were permitted by those in whose employment John Castellan presumably is, we should punish them as well as him."

"What!" exclaimed the Kaiser, clenching his fists, "do you, a civilian, an ordinary citizen, dare to say such words to us? Lord Kitchener, can you permit such an outrage as this?"

"The other outrage would be a much greater one, especially if it were committed with the tacit sanction of the three greatest Powers in Europe," replied K. of K., quietly. "That is one of our chief reasons for asking for the surrender of the *Flying Fishes*. There is no telling what harm this wild Irishman of yours might do if he got on the loose, not only here but perhaps in your own territories, if he were allowed to commit a crime like this, and then went, as he would have to do, into the outlaw business."

"I think that there is great justice in what Lord Kitchener says," remarked His Majesty of Austria. "We must not forget that if this man Castellan did run amok with any of those diabolical contrivances of his, he would be just as much above human law as he would be outside human reach. I must confess that that appears to me to be one of the most serious features in the situation. Your Majesties, as well as the French Government, are aware that I have been all along opposed to the use of these horrible engines of destruction, and now you see that their very existence seems to have called others into being which may be even more formidable."

"Mr. Lennard can tell your Majesties more about that than I can," said K. of K., with one of his grimmest smiles.

"As far as the air is concerned," said Lennard, very quietly, "we can both out-fly and out-shoot the *Flying Fishes*; while as regards the water, eleven more *Ithuriels* will be launched during the week. We have twenty-five airships ready for action over land or sea, and, for my own part, I think that if your Majesties knew all the details of the situation you would consider the terms which his lordship has put before you quite generous. But, after all," he continued, in a suddenly changed tone, "it seems, if you will excuse my saying so, rather childish to talk about terms of peace or war when the world itself has less than six weeks to live if John Castellan manages to carry out his threat."

"And you feel absolutely certain of that, Mr. Lennard?" asked the Tsar, in a tone of very serious interest. "It seems rather singular that none of the other astronomers of Europe or America have discovered this terrible comet of yours."

"I have had the advantage of the finest telescope in the world, your Majesty," replied Lennard, with a smile, "and of course I have published no details. There was no point in creating a panic or getting laughed at before it was necessary. But now that the orbit has altered, and the catastrophe will come so much sooner, any further delay would be little short of criminal. In fact, we have today telegraphed to all the principal observatories in the world, giving exact positions for tonight, corrected to differences of time and latitude. We shall hear the verdict in the morning, and during tomorrow. Meanwhile we are going to Greenwich to get the observatory there to work on my calculations, and if your Majesties would care to appoint an officer of sufficient knowledge to come with us, and see the comet for himself, he will, I am sure, be quite welcome."

"A very good suggestion, Mr. Lennard," said Lord Kitchener, "very."

"Then," replied the Tsar, quickly, "as astronomy has always been a great hobby with me, will you allow me to come? Of course, you have my word that I shall see nothing on the journey that you don't want me to see."

"We shall be delighted," said the British envoy, cordially, "and as for seeing things, you will be at perfect liberty to use your eyes as much as you like."

The Tsar's august colleagues entered fully into the sporting spirit in which he had made his proposal, and a verbal agreement to suspend all hostilities till his return was ratified in a glass of His Majesty of Austria's Imperial Tokay.

Chapter XXXVII

THE VERDICT OF SCIENCE

Although the Tsar had made trips with John Castellan in the *Flying Fish,* he had never had quite such an aërial experience as his trip to Greenwich. The *Auriole* rose vertically in the air, soared upward in a splendid spiral curve, and vanished through the thin cloud layer to the northeastward. Twenty minutes of wonder passed like so many seconds, and Admiral Hingeston, beside whom he was standing in the conning-tower, said quietly:

"We're about there, your Majesty."

"Greenwich already," exclaimed the Tsar, pulling out his watch. "It is forty miles, and we have not been quite twenty minutes yet."

"That's about it," said the Admiral, "this craft can do her two miles a minute, and still have a good bit in hand if it came to chasing anything."

He pulled back a couple of levers as he spoke and gave a quarter turn to the wheel. The great airship took a downward slide, swung round to the right, and in a few moments she had dropped quietly to the turf of Greenwich Park alongside the Observatory.

Lennard's calculations had already reached the Astronomer Royal, and he and his chief assistant had had time to make a rapid run through them, and they had found that his figures, and especially the inexplicable change in the orbit, tallied almost exactly with observations of a possibly new comet for the last two months or so.

They were not quite prepared for the coming of an Imperial – and hostile – visitor in an airship, accompanied by the discoverer of the comet, the millionaire who owned the great telescope, and an American gentleman in the uniform of a British admiral; but those were extraordinary times, and so extraordinary happenings might be expected. The astronomer and his staff, being sober men of science, whose business was with other worlds rather than this one, accepted the situation calmly, gave their visitors lunch, talked about everything but the war, and then they all spent a pleasant and instructive afternoon in a journey through Space in search of the still invisible Celestial Invader.

When they had finished, the two sets of calculations balanced exactly – to the millionth of a degree and the thousandth of a second. At ten seconds to twelve, midnight, May the first, the comet, if not prevented by some tremendously powerful agency, would pierce the earth's atmosphere, as Lennard had predicted.

"It is a marvelous piece of work, Mr. Lennard, however good an instrument you had. As an astronomer I congratulate you heartily, but as citizens of the world I hope we shall be able to congratulate you still more heartily on the results which you expect that big gun of yours to bring about."

"I'm sure I hope so," said Lennard, toying rather absently with his pencil.

"And if the cannon is not fired, and the Pittsburg one does not happen to be exactly laid, for there is a very great difference in longitude, what will be the probable results, Mr. Astronomer?" asked the Tsar, upon whom the lesson of the afternoon had by no means been lost.

"If the comet is what Mr. Lennard expects it to be, your Majesty," was the measured reply, "then, if this Invader is not destroyed, his predictions will be fulfilled to the letter. In other words, on the second of May there will not be a living thing left on earth."

At three minutes past ten that evening the Tsar looked into the eye-piece of the Greenwich Equatorial, and saw a double-winged yellow shape floating in the center of the field of vision. He watched it for long minutes, listening to the soft clicking of the clockwork, which was the only sound that broke the silence. During the afternoon he had seen photographs of the comet taken every night that the weather made a clear observation possible. The series tallied exactly with what he now saw. The gradual enlargement and brightening; the ever-increasing exactness of definition, and the separation of the nucleus from the two wings. All that he had seen was as pitilessly inexorable as the figures which contained the prophecy of the world's approaching doom. He rose from his seat and said quietly, yet with a strange impressiveness:

"Gentlemen, I, for one, am satisfied and converted. What the inscrutable decrees of Providence may or may not be, we have no right to inquire; but whether this is a judgment from the Most High brought upon us by our sins, or whether it is merely an ordinary cataclysm of Nature against which we may be able to protect ourselves, does not come into the question which is in dispute amongst us. Humanity has an unquestioned right to preserve its existence as far as it is possible to do so. If it is possible to arrange for another conference at Aldershot tomorrow, I think I may say that there will be a possibility of arriving at a reasonable basis of negotiations. And now, if it is convenient, Lord Kitchener, I should like to get back to camp. Much has been given to me to think about tonight, and you know we Russians have a very sound proverb: 'Take thy thoughts to bed with thee, for the morning is wiser than the evening.'"

"That, your Majesty, has been my favorite saying ever since I knew that men had to think about work before they were able to do it properly." So spoke the man who had worked for fourteen years to win one battle, and crush a whole people at a single stroke – after which he made the best of friends with them, and loyal subjects of his Sovereign.

They took their leave of the astronomer and his staff, and a few minutes later the *Auriole*, still flying the flag of truce, cleared the tree-tops and rose into the serene starlit atmosphere above them.

When the airship had gained a height of a thousand feet, and was heading southwest towards Aldershot at a speed of about a hundred miles an hour, the Admiral noticed a shape not unlike that of his own vessel, on his port quarter, making almost the same direction as he was. The Tsar and Lord Kitchener were sitting one on either side of him, as he stood at the steering-wheel, as the ominous shape came into view.

"I'm afraid that's one of your *Flying Fishes*, your Majesty, taking news from the Continent to Aldershot. Yes, there goes her searchlight. She's found us out by now. She knows we're not one of her crowd, and so I suppose we shall have to fight her. Yes, I thought so, she means fight. She's trying to get above us, which means dropping a few of those torpedoes on us, and sending us across the edge of eternity before we know we've got there."

"You will, of course, do your duty, Admiral," replied the Tsar very quietly, but with a quick tightening of the lips. "It is a most unfortunate occurrence, but we must all take the fortune of war as it comes. I hope you will not consider my presence here for a moment. Remember that I asked myself."

"There won't be any danger to us, your Majesty," replied the Admiral, with a marked emphasis on the "us." "Still, we have too many valuable lives on board to let him get the drop on us."

As he spoke he thrust one lever on the right hand forward, and pulled another back; then he took the telephone receiver down from the wall, and said:

"See that thing? She's trying to get the drop on us. Full speed ahead: I'm going to rise. Hold on, gentlemen."

They held on. The Tsar saw the jumping searchlights, which flashed up from the little grey shape to the southward, suddenly fall away and below them. The Admiral touched the wheel with his left hand, and the *Auriole* sprang forward. The other tried to do the same, but she seemed to droop and fall behind. Admiral Hingeston took down the receiver again and said:

"Ready – starboard guns – now: fire!"

Of course, there was no report; only a brilliant blaze of light to the southward, and an atmospheric shock which made the *Auriole* shudder as she passed on her way. The Tsar looked out to the spot where the blaze of flame had burst out. The other airship had vanished.

"She has gone. That is awful," he said, with a shake in his voice.

"As I said before, I'm sorry, your Majesty," replied the Admiral, "but it had to be done. If he'd got the top side of us we should have been in as little pieces as he is now. I only hope it's John Castellan's craft. If it is it will save a lot of trouble to both sides."

The Tsar did not reply. He was too busy thinking, and so was Lord Kitchener.

That night there were divided counsels in the headquarters of the Allies at Aldershot, and the Kaiser and his colleagues went to bed between two and three in the morning without having come to anything like a definite decision. As a matter of fact, within the last few hours things had become a little too complicated to be decided upon in anything like a hurry.

While the potentates of the Alliance were almost quarreling as to what was to be done, the *Auriole* paid a literally flying visit to the British positions, and then the hospitals. At Caversham, Lennard found Norah Castellan taking her turn of night duty by the bedside of Lord Westerham, who had, after all, got through his desperate ride with a couple of bullets through his right ribs, and a broken left arm; but he had got his dispatches in all the same, though nearly two hours late – for which he apologized before he fainted. In one of the wards at Windsor Camp he found Auriole, also on night duty, nursing with no less anxious care the handsome young Captain of Uhlans who had taken Lord Whittinghame's car in charge in Rochester. Mrs. O'Connor had got a badly-wounded Russian Vice-Admiral all to herself, and, as she modestly put it, was doing very nicely with him.

Meanwhile the news of the truce was proclaimed, and the opposing millions laid themselves down to rest with the thankful certainty that it would not be broken for at least a night and a day by the whistle of the life-hunting bullet or the screaming roar and heart-shaking crash of the big shell which came from some invisible point five or six miles away. In view of this a pleasant little dinner-party was arranged for at the Parmenter Palace at eight the next evening. There would be no carriages. The coming and parting guests would do their coming and going in airships. Mr. Parmenter expressed the opinion that, under the circumstances, this would be at once safer and more convenient.

But before that dinner-party broke up, the world had something very different from feasting and merrymaking, or even invasion and military conquest or defeat, to think of.

The result of Lennard's telegrams and cables had been that every powerful telescope in the civilized world had been turned upon that distant region of the fields of Space out of which the Celestial Invader was rushing at a speed of thousands of miles a minute to that awful trysting-place, at which it and the planet Terra were to meet and embrace in the fiery union of death.

From every observatory, from Greenwich to Arequipa, and from Pike's Peak to Melbourne, came practically identical messages, which, in their combined sense, came to this:

"Lennard's figures absolutely correct. Collision with comet apparently inevitable. Consequences incalculable."

Chapter XXXVIII

WAITING FOR DOOM

This was the all-important news which the inhabitants of every town which possessed a well-informed newspaper read the next morning. It was, in the more important of them, followed by digests of the calculations which had made this terrific result a practical certainty. These, again, were followed by speculations, some deliberately scientific, and some wild beyond the dreams of the most hopeless hysteria.

Men and women who for a generation or so had been making large incomes by prophesying the end of the world as a certainty about every seven years – and had bought up long leaseholds meanwhile – now gambled with absolute certainty on the shortness of the public memory, revised their figures, and proved to demonstration that this was the very thing they had been foretelling all along.

First – outside scientific circles – came blank incredulity. The ordinary man and woman in the street had not room in their brains for such a tremendous idea as this – fact or no fact. They were already filled with a crowd of much smaller and, to them, much more pressing concerns, than a collision with a comet which you couldn't even see except through a big telescope: and then that sort of thing had been talked and written about hundreds of times before and had never come to anything, so why should this?

But when the morning papers dated – somewhat ominously – the twenty-fifth of March, quarter day, informed their readers that, granted fine weather, the comet would be visible to the naked eye from sunset to sunrise according to longitude that night, the views of the man and the woman who had taken the matter so lightly underwent a very considerable change.

While the comet could only be seen, save by astronomers, in the photographs that could be bought in any form from a picture-postcard to a five-guinea reproduction of the actual thing, there was still an air of unconvincing unreality about. Of course it might be coming, but it was still very far away, and it might not arrive after all. Yet when that fateful night had passed and millions of sleepless eyes had seen the southwestern stars shining through a pale luminous mist extended in the shape of two vast filmy wings with a brighter spot of yellow flame between them, the whole matter seemed to take on a very different and a much more serious aspect.

The fighting had come to a sudden stop, as though by a mutually tacit agreement. Not even the German Emperor could now deny that Lennard had made no idle threat at Canterbury when he had given him the destruction of the world as an alternative to the conquest of Britain. Still, he did not quite believe in the possibility of that destruction even yet, in spite of what the Tsar had told him and what he had learned from other sources. He still wanted to fight to a finish, and, as Deputy European Providence, he had a very real objection to the interference of apparently irresponsible celestial bodies with his carefully-thought-out plans for the ordering of mundane civilization on German commercial lines. Whether they liked it or not, it must be the best thing in the end for them: otherwise how could He have come to think it all out?

Meanwhile, to make matters worse from his point of view, John Castellan had refused absolutely to accept any modification of the original terms, and he had replied to an order from headquarters to report himself and the ships still left under his control by loading the said ships with ammunition and motive power and then disappearing from the field of action without leaving a trace as to his present or future whereabouts behind him, and so, as far as matters went, entirely fulfilling the Tsar's almost prophetic fears.

And then, precisely at the hour, minute and second predicted, five hours, thirty minutes and twenty-five seconds, a.m., on the 31st of March, the comet became visible in daylight about two and a half degrees southwestward of the Morning Star. Twenty-four hours later the two wings came into view, and the next evening the Invader looked like some gigantic bird of prey swooping down from its aerie somewhere in the heights of Space upon the trembling and terrified world. The professional prophets said, with an excellent assumption of absolute conviction, that it was nothing less awful than the Destroying Angel himself *in propria persona.*

At length, when excitement had developed into frenzy, and frenzy into an almost universal delirium, two cablegrams crossed each other along the bed of the Atlantic Ocean. One was to say that the Pittsburg gun was ready, and the other that the loading of the Bolton Baby – feeding, some callous humorist of the day called it – was to begin the next morning. This meant that there was just a week – an ordinary working week, between the human race and something very like the Day of Judgment.

The next day Lennard set all the existing wires of the world thrilling with the news that the huge projectile, charged with its thirty hundredweight of explosives, was resting quietly in its place on the top of a potential volcano which, loosened by the touch of a woman's hand, was to hurl it through space and into the heart of the swiftly-advancing Invader from the outmost realms of Space.

Chapter XXXIX

THE LAST FIGHT

It so happened that on the first night the German Emperor saw the comet without the aid of a telescope he was attacked by one of those fits of hysteria which, according to ancient legend, are the hereditary curse of the House of Brandenburg. He had made possible that which had been impossible for over a thousand years – he had invaded England in force, and he had established himself and his Allies in all the greatest fortress-camps of southeastern England. After all, the story of the comet might be a freak of the scientific imagination; there might be some undetected error in the calculations. One great mistake had been made already, either by the comet or its discoverer – why not another?

"No," he said to himself, as he stood in front of the headquarters at Aldershot looking up at the comet, "we've heard about you before, my friend. Astronomers and other people have prophesied a dozen times that you or something like you were going to bring about the end of the world, but somehow it never came off; whereas it is pretty certain that the capture of London will come off if it is only properly managed. At any rate, I am inclined to back my chances of taking London against yours of destroying it."

And so he made his decision. He sent a telegram to Dover ordering an aerogram to be sent to John Castellan, whose address was now, of course, anywhere in the air or sea; the message was to be repeated from all the Continental stations until he was found. It contained the first capitulation that the War Lord of Germany had ever made. He accepted the terms of his Admiral of the Air and asked him to bring his fleet the following day to assist in a general assault on London – London once taken, John Castellan could have the free hand that he had asked for.

In twelve hours a reply came back from the Jotunheim in Norway. Meanwhile, the Kaiser, as Generalissimo of the Allied Forces, telegraphed orders to all the commanders of army corps in England to prepare for a final assault on the positions commanding London within twenty-four hours. At the same time he sent telegraphic orders to all the centers of mobilization in Europe, ordering the advance of all possible reinforcements with the least delay. It was his will that four million men should march on London that week, and, in spite of the protests of the Emperor of Austria and the Tsar, his will was obeyed.

So the truce was broken and the millions advanced, as it were over the brink of Eternity, towards London. But the reinforcements never came. Every transport that steamed out of Bremen, Hamburg, Kiel, Antwerp, Brest or Calais, vanished into the waters; for now the whole squadron of twelve *Ithuriels* had been launched and had got to work, and the British fleets from the Mediterranean, the China Seas and the North Atlantic, had once more asserted Britain's supremacy on the seas. In addition to these, ten first-class battleships, twelve first and fifteen second-class cruisers and fifty destroyers had been turned out by the Home yards, and so the British Islands were once more ringed with an unbreakable wall of steel. One invasion had been accomplished, but now no other was possible. The French Government absolutely refused to send anymore men. The Italian armies had crossed the Alps at three points, and every soldier left in France was wanted to defend her own fortresses and cities from the attack of the invader.

But, despite all this, the War Lord held to his purpose; and that night the last battle ever fought between civilized nations began, and when the sun rose on the sixteenth of April, its rays lit up what was probably the most awful scene of carnage that human eyes had ever looked upon. The battle-line of the invaders had extended from Sheerness to Reading in a sort of irregular semicircle, and it was estimated afterwards that not less than a million and a half of killed and wounded men, fifty thousand horses and hundreds of disabled batteries of light and heavy artillery strewed the long line of defeat and conquest.

The British aërial fleet of twenty ships had made victory for the defenders a practical certainty. As Admiral Hingeston had told the Tsar, they could both out-fly and out-shoot the *Flying Fishes.* This they did and more. The moment that a battery got into position half a dozen searchlights were concentrated on it. Then came a hail of shells, and a series of explosions which smashed the guns to fragments and killed every living thing within a radius of a hundred yards. Infantry and cavalry shared the same fate the moment that any formation was made for an attack on the British positions; the storm of fire was made ten-fold more terrible by the unceasing bombardment from the air; and the brilliant glow of the searchlights thrown down from a height of a thousand feet or so along the lines of the attacking forces made the work of the defenders comparatively easy, for the man in a fight who can see and is not seen is worth several who are seen and yet fight in the dark.

But the assailants were exposed to an even more deadly danger than artillery or rifle fire. The catastrophe which had overwhelmed the British Fleet in Dover Harbor was repeated with ten-fold effect; but this time the tables were turned. The British aërial fleet hunted the *Flying Fishes* as hawks hunt partridges, and whenever one of them was found over a hostile position a shell from the silent, flameless guns hit her, and down she went to explode like a volcano amongst masses of cavalry, infantry and artillery, and of this utter panic was the only natural result.

Eleven out of the twelve *Flying Fishes* were thus accounted for. What had become of the twelfth no one knew. It might have been partially crippled and fallen far away from the great battlefield; or it might have turned tail and escaped, and in this case it was a practical certainty, at least in Lennard's mind, that it was John Castellan's own vessel and that he, seeing that the battle was lost, had taken her away to some unknown spot in order to fulfill the threat contained in his letter, and for this reason five of the British airships were at once dispatched to mount guard over the great cannon at Bolton.

The defeat of the Allies both by land and sea, though accomplished at the eleventh hour of the world's threatened fate, had been so complete and crushing, and the death-total had reached such a ghastly figure, that Austria, Russia and France flatly refused to continue the Alliance. After all the tremendous sacrifice that had been made in men, money and material they had not even reached London. From their outposts on the Surrey hills they could see the vast city, silent and apparently sleeping under its canopy of hazy clouds, but that was all. It was still as distant from them as the poles; and so the Allies looked upon it and then upon their dead, and admitted, by their silence if not by their words, that Britain the Unconquered was unconquerable still.

The German Emperor's fit had passed. Even he was appalled when upon that memorable morning he received the joint note of his three Allies and learnt the awful cost of that one night's fighting.

Just as he was countersigning the Note of Capitulation in the head-quarters at Aldershot, the *Auriole* swung round from the northward and descended on to the turf flying the flag of truce. He saw it through the window, got up, put his right hand on the butt of the revolver in his hip-pocket, thought hard for one fateful moment, then took it away and went out.

At the gate he met Lord Kitchener; they exchanged salutes and shook hands, and the Kaiser said:

"Well, my lord, what are the terms?"

K. of K. laughed, simply because he couldn't help it. The absolute hard business of the question went straight to the heart of the best business man in the British Army.

"I am not here to make or accept terms, your Majesty," he said. "I am only the bearer of a message, and here it is."

Then he handed the Kaiser an envelope bearing the Royal Arms.

"I am instructed to take your reply back as soon as possible," he continued. Then he saluted again and walked away towards the *Auriole.*

The Kaiser opened the envelope and read – an invitation to lunch from his uncle, Edward of England, and a request to bring his august colleagues with him to talk matters over. There was no hint of battle, victory or defeat. It was a quite commonplace letter, but all the same it was one of those triumphs of diplomacy which only the first diplomatist in Europe knew how to achieve. Then he too laughed as he folded up the letter and went to Lord Kitchener and said:

"This is only an invitation to lunch, and you have told me you are not here to propose or take terms. That, of course, was official, but personally –"

K. of K. stiffened up, and a harder glint came into his eyes.

"I can say nothing personally, your Majesty, except to ask you to remember my reply to Cronje."

The Kaiser remembered that reply of three words, "Surrender, or fight," and he knew that he could not fight, save under a penalty of utter destruction. He went back into his room, brought back the joint note which he had just received, and gave it to Lord Kitchener, just as it was, without even putting it into an envelope, saying:

"That is our answer. We are beaten, and those who lose must pay."

Lord Kitchener looked over the note and said, in a somewhat dry tone:

"This, your Majesty, I read as absolute surrender."

"It is," said William the Second, his hand instinctively going to the hilt of his sword. Lord Kitchener shook his head, and said very quietly and pleasantly:

"No, your Majesty, not that. But," he said, looking up at the four flags which were still flying above the headquarters, "I should be obliged if you would give orders to haul those down and hoist the Jack instead."

There was no help for it, and no one knew better than the Kaiser the strength there was behind those quietly-spoken words. The awful lesson of the night before had taught him that this beautiful cruiser of the air which lay within a few yards of him could in a few moments rise into the air and scatter indiscriminate death and destruction around her, and so the flags came down, the old Jack once more went up, and Aldershot was English ground again.

Wherefore, not to enter into unnecessary details, the *Auriole*, instead of making the place a wilderness as Lord Kitchener had quite determined to do, became an aërial pleasure yacht. Orderlies were sent to the Russian, Austrian and French headquarters, and an hour later the chiefs of the Allies were sitting in the deck saloon of the airship, flying at about sixty miles an hour towards London.

The lunch at Buckingham Palace was an entirely friendly affair. King Edward had intended it to be a sort of international shake-hands all round. The King of Italy was present, as the *Columbia* had been dispatched early in the morning to bring him from Rome, and had picked up the French President on the way back at Paris. The King gave the first and only toast, and that was:

"Your Majesties and Monsieur le President, in the name of Humanity, I ask you to drink to Peace."

They drank, and so ended the last war that was ever fought on British soil.

Epilogue

"AND ON EARTH, PEACE!"

On the morning of the thirtieth of April, the interest of the whole world was centered generally upon Bolton, and particularly upon the little spot of black earth enclosed by a ring of Bessemer furnaces in the midst of which lay another ring, a ring of metal, the mouth of the great cannon, whose one and only shot was to save or lose the world. At a height of two thousand feet, twenty airships circled at varying distances round the mouth of the gun, watching for the one *Flying Fish* which had not been accounted for in the final fight.

The good town of Bolton itself was depopulated. For days past the comet had been blazing brighter and brighter, even in the broad daylight, and the reports which came pouring in every day from the observatories of the world made it perfectly clear that Lennard's calculations would be verified at midnight.

Mr. Parmenter and his brother capitalists had guaranteed two millions sterling as compensation for such destruction of property as might be brought about by the discharge of the cannon, and, coupled with this guarantee, was a request that everyone living within five miles of what had been the Great Lever pit should leave, and this was authorized by a Royal Proclamation. There was no confusion, because, when faced with great issues, the Lancashire intellect does not become confused. It just gets down to business and does it. So it came about that the people of Bolton, rich and poor, millionaire and artisan, made during that momentous week a general flitting, taking with them just such of their possessions as would be most precious to them if the Fates permitted them to witness the dawn of the first of May.

The weather, strangely enough, had been warm and sunny for the last fortnight, despite the fact that the ever-brightening Invader from Space gradually outshone the sun itself, and so on all the moors round Bolton there sprang up a vast town of tents and ready-made bungalows from

Chorley round by Darwen to Bury. Thousands of people had come from all parts of the kingdom to see the fate of the world decided. What was left of the armies of the Allies were also brought up by train, and all the British forces were there as well. They were all friends now for there was no more need for fighting, since the events of the next few hours would decide the fate of the human race.

As the sun set over the western moors a vast concourse of men and women, representing almost every nationality on earth, watched the coming of the Invader, brightening now with every second and over-arching the firmament with its wide-spreading wings. There were no skeptics now. No one could look upon that appalling Shape and not believe, and if absolute confirmation of Lennard's prophecy had been wanted it would have been found in the fact that the temperature began to rise *after* sunset. That had never happened before within the memory of man.

The crowning height of the moors which make a semicircle to the northwest of Bolton is Winter Hill, which stands about halfway between Bolton and Chorley, and, roughly speaking, would make the center of a circle including Bolton, Wigan, Chorley and Blackburn. It rises to a height of nearly fifteen hundred feet and dominates the surrounding country for fully fifteen miles, and on the summit of this rugged, heather-clad moor was pitched what might be called without exaggeration the headquarters of the forces which were to do battle for humanity. A huge marquee had been erected in an ancient quarry just below the summit; from the center pole of this flew the Royal Standard of England, and from the other poles the standards of every civilized nation in the world.

The front of the marquee opened to the southeastward, and by the unearthly light of the comet the mill chimneys of Bolton, dominated by the great stack of Dobson & Barlow's, could be seen pointing like black fingers up to the approaching terror. In the center of the opening were two plain deal tables. There was an instrument on each of them, and from these separate wires ran on two series of poles and buried themselves at last in the heart of the charge of the great cannon. Beside the instruments were two chronometers synchronized from Greenwich and beating time together to the thousandth part of a second, counting out what might perhaps be the last seconds of human life on earth.

Grouped about the two tables were the five sovereigns of Europe and the President of the French Republic, and with them stood the greatest soldiers, sailors and scientists, statesmen and diplomatists between east and west.

On a long deck chair beside one of the tables lay Lord Westerham with his left arm bound across his breast and looking little better than the ghost of the man he had been a month ago. Beside him stood Lady Margaret and Norah Castellan, and with them were the two men who had done so much to change defeat into victory; the captain and lieutenant of the ever-famous *Ithuriel.*

Never before had there been such a gathering of all sorts and conditions of men on one spot of earth; but as the hours went on and dwindled into minutes, all differences of rank and position became things of the past. In the presence of that awful Shape which was now flaming across the heavens, all men and women were equal, since by midnight all might be reduced at the same instant to the same dust and ashes. The ghastly orange-green glare shone down alike on the upturned face of monarch and statesman, soldier and peasant, millionaire and pauper, the good and the bad, the noble and the base, and tinged every face with its own ghastly hue.

Five minutes to twelve!

There was a shaking of hands, but no words were spoken. Norah Castellan stooped and kissed her wounded lover's brow, and then stood up and clasped her hands behind her. Lennard went to one of the tables and Auriole to the other.

Lennard had honestly kept the unspoken pact that had been made between them in the observatory at Whernside. Neither word nor look of love had passed his lips or lightened his eyes; and even now, as he stood beside her, looking at her face, beautiful still even in that ghastly light, his glance was as steady as if he had been looking through the eye-piece of his telescope.

Auriole had her right forefinger already resting on a little white button, ready at a touch to send the kindling spark into the mighty mass of explosives which lay buried at the bottom of what had been the Great Lever pit. Lennard also had his right forefinger on another button, but his left hand was in his coat pocket and the other forefinger was on the trigger of a loaded and cocked revolver. There were several other revolvers in men's pockets – men who had sworn that their nearest and dearest should be spared the last tortures of the death-agony of humanity.

The chronometers began to tick off the seconds of the last minute. The wings of the comet spread out vaster and vaster and its now flaming nucleus blazed brighter and brighter. A low, vague wailing sound seemed to be running through the multitudes which thronged the semicircle of moors. It was the first and perhaps the last utterance of the agony of unendurable suspense.

At the thirtieth second Lennard looked up and said in a quiet, passionless tone:

"Ready!"

At the same moment he saw, as millions of others thought they saw, a grey shape skimming through the air from the northeast towards Bolton. It could not be a British airship, for the fleet had already scattered, as the shock of the coming explosion would certainly have caused them to smash up like so many shells. It was John Castellan's *Flying Fish* come to fulfill the letter of his threat, even at this supreme moment of the world's fate.

Again Lennard spoke.

"Twenty seconds."

And then he began to count. "Nine – eight – seven – six – five – four – three – two – Now!"

The two fingers went down at the same instant and completed the circuits. The next, the central fires of the earth seemed to have burst loose. A roar such as had never deafened human ears before thundered from earth to heaven, and a vast column of pale flame leapt up with a concussion which seemed to shake the foundations of the world. Then in the midst of the column of flame there came a brighter flash, a momentary blaze of green-blue flame flashing out for a moment and vanishing.

"That was John's ship," said Norah. "God forgive him!"

"He will," said Westerham, taking her hand. "He was wrong-headed on that particular subject, but he was a brave man, and a genius. I don't think there's any doubt about that."

"It's good of you to say so," said Norah. "Poor John! With all his learning and genius to come to that –"

"We all have to get there some time, Norah, and after all, whether he's right or wrong, a man can't die better than for what he believes to be the truth and the right. We may think him mistaken, he thought he was right, and he has proved it. God rest his soul!"

"Amen!" said Norah, and she leant over again and kissed him on the brow.

Then came ten seconds more of mute and agonized suspense, and men's fingers tightened their grip on the revolvers. Then the upturned straining eyes looked upon such a sight as human eyes will never see again save perchance those which, in the fullness of time, may look upon the awful pageantry of the Last Day.

High up in the air there was a shrill screaming sound which seemed something like an echo of the roar of the great gun. Something like a white flash of light darted upwards straight to the heart of the descending Invader. Then the whole heavens were illumined by a blinding glare. The nucleus of the comet seemed to throw out long rays of many-colored light. A moment later it had burst into myriads of faintly gleaming atoms.

The watching millions on earth instinctively clasped their hands to their ears, expecting such a sound as would deafen them forever; but none came, for the explosion had taken place beyond the limits of the earth's atmosphere. The whole sky was now filled from zenith to horizon with a pale, golden, luminous mist, and through this the moon and stars began to shine dimly.

Then a blast of burning air swept shrieking and howling across the earth, for now the planet Terra was rushing at her headlong speed of nearly seventy thousand miles an hour through the ocean of fire-mist into which the shattered comet had been dissolved. Then this passed. The cool wind of night followed it, and the moon and stars shone down once more undimmed through the pure and cloudless ether.

Until now there had been silence. Men and women looked at each other and clasped hands; and then Tom Bowcock, standing just outside the marquee with his arm round his wife's shoulders, lifted up his mighty baritone voice and sang the lines:

"Praise God from whom all blessings flow!"

Hundreds and then thousands, then millions of voices took up the familiar strain, and so from the tops of the Lancashire moors the chorus rolled on from village to village and town to town, until with one voice, though with many tongues, east and west were giving thanks for the Great Deliverance.

But the man who, under Providence, had wrought it, seemed deaf and blind to all this. He only felt a soft trembling clasp round his right hand, and he only heard Auriole's voice whispering his name.

The next moment a stronger grip pulled his left hand out of his coat pocket, bringing the revolver with it, and Mr. Parmenter's voice, shaken by rare emotion, said, loudly enough for all in the marquee to hear:

"We may thank God and you, Gilbert Lennard, that there's still a world with living men and women on it, and there's one woman here who's going to live for you only till death do you part. She told me all about it last night. You've won her fair and square, and you're going to have her. I did have other views for her, but I've changed my mind, because I have learnt other things since then. But anyhow, with no offence to this distinguished company, I reckon you're the biggest man on earth just now."

Soon after daybreak on the first of May, one of the airships that had been guarding Whernside dropped on the top of Winter Hill, and the captain gave Lennard a cablegram which read thus:

> "Lennard, Bolton, England: Good shot. As you left no pieces for us to shoot at we've let our shot go. No use for it here. Hope it will stop next celestial stranger coming this way. America thanks you. Any terms you like for lecturing tour. – Henchell"

Lennard did not see his way to accept the lecturing offer because he had much more important business on hand: but a week later, after a magnificent and, if the word may be used, multiple marriage ceremony had been performed in Westminster Abbey, five airships, each with a bride and bridegroom on board, rose from the gardens of Buckingham Palace and, followed by the cheers of millions, winged their way westward. Thirty-five hours later there was such a dinner-party at the White House, Washington, as eclipsed all the previous glories even of American hospitality.

Nothing was ever seen of the projectile which "The Pittsburg Prattler" had hurled into space. Not even the great Whernside reflector was able to pick it up. The probability, therefore, is that even now it is still speeding on its lonely way through the Ocean of Immensity, and it is within the bounds of possibility that at some happy moment in the future and somewhere far away beyond the reach of human vision, its huge charge of explosives may do for some other threatened world what the one which the Bolton Baby coughed up into Space just in the nick of time did to save this home of ours from the impending Peril of 1910.

The End

www.ingramcontent.com/pod-product-compliance
Lightning Source LLC
Chambersburg PA
CBHW020926310726
48980CB00005B/404